I Saw You

JULIE PARSONS was born in New Zealand and has lived most of her adult life in Ireland. She has had a varied career – artist's model, typesetter, freelance journalist, radio and television producer – before returning to write fiction.

Mary, Mary, her stunning debut novel, launched Julie onto the literary scene in 1999. She is also the author of *The Courtship Gift*, *Eager to Please*, *The Guilty Heart* and *The Hourglass*. *I Saw You* is a sequel to *Mary, Mary*.

Julie lives outside Dublin, by the sea, with her family.

I Saw You

JULIE PARSONS

PAN BOOKS

First published 2007 by Macmillan

This edition published 2008 by Pan Books
an imprint of Pan Macmillan Ltd
Pan Macmillan, 20 New Wharf Road, London N1 9RR
Basingstoke and Oxford
Associated companies throughout the world
www.panmacmillan.com

ISBN 978-0-330-48887-7

1 3 5 7 9 8 6 4 2

A CIP catalogue record for this book is available from
the British Library.

Typeset by SetSystems Ltd, Saffron Walden, Essex
Printed and bound in the UK by
CPI Mackays, Chatham ME5 8TD

Visit www.panmacmillan.com to read more about all our books
and to buy them. You will also find features, author interviews and
news of any author events, and you can sign up for e-newsletters
so that you're always first to hear about our new releases.

To Harriet, Sarah and John,

as it was in the beginning

MY THANKS TO

Det. Sgt Kevin Morrisey and Det. Sgt Martin Donohue, An Garda Síochána, Garech Onorch a Brun, Paul Bowler, Rory O'Riordan, *Partners at Law*, Dr Edward Rabinowitz and Jessica Johnson for their generous help with aspects of the story.

Alison Dye for her unfailing support and first reading of the manuscript.

Joan O'Neill, Phil MacCarthy, Sheila Barrett, Renate Ahrens Kramer, Cecilia McGovern and Cathy Leonard for their helpful criticism and the tea, biscuits and sympathy.

Julie Crisp for her keen eye for a coincidence and her rigorous editorial sensibility.

And Emily Moriarty for making me laugh.

He lay slumped in the corner of the shed. His hands, cuffed behind his back, were chained to a ring set in the wall. Wide grey tape covered his face. Only his eyes, pale blue, red-rimmed, were visible. He wanted to call out, to beg for help. But he could make no sound. He wanted to bang on the wall to attract attention. But he could not move his hands and arms. He wanted to kick the heavy wooden door, to break through to the outside. But his feet would not reach that far. He needed to drink. But there was no water. He needed to eat. But there was no food. There had been none for days. He had lost count of how many. He had tried to keep track by counting the number of times that the beam of sunlight had drilled through the small crack in the wood that covered the window. One, two, three, four, five, six. He could hold on to six, but after that, pain, confusion, fear blotted everything else out.

And then he was blind.

And then he thought he was somewhere else, and there was a table laden with food, and a running tap, and he could turn his head and open his mouth and the silver dribble of water would drip on to his tongue. His poor swollen tongue.

And then there was nothing more. Just the smell of his body rotting.

And then there wasn't even that.

It was a lovely day to get out of the office, the estate agent thought. A perfect spring day. A cloudless sky, and warm enough to have the car window open as she drove from the city centre along the motorway towards Blessington. According to her information, the property was in Ballyknockan, a village of stone houses up towards the dark green pines that clothed the flanks of the west Wicklow mountains. She slowed to get her bearings and turned the printed email on the passenger seat towards her so she could read it more easily. The cottage had belonged to a German couple, Hans and Renate Becker. They had used it as a holiday home, but now they were both dead and their daughters wanted to sell. The email was from Petra Becker. Her English was just about perfect.

> I do not know the condition of the cottage. We have not been there for many years. My father had a caretaker for it once, but we have had no contact with him for a long time. I will send to you by post the keys. Please put it on to the market as soon as possible. We understand that the value of houses in Ireland has increased by a large amount. Please advise us as to its value now.

Fräulein Becker was right. These houses, even though they were small, were worth a lot of money. A twenty-mile commute was considered nothing these days, the estate agent thought, as she bumped up the lane from the village and stopped at a five-barred gate by a stand of pines.

She got out of the car and fiddled with the gate's rusty

latch. It was stiff and resistant to the touch. She shivered. A breeze stirred the needles on the trees, and a wisp of mist drifted down from the peak of the hill above. She got back into the car and drove slowly up the boreen towards the house. It looked fine from the outside, although the garden was overgrown and neglected. Nothing that a boy with a strimmer wouldn't put right in an afternoon.

She fumbled in her bag for the keys. Inside it was dark. She reached for the light switch, but the electricity must have been turned off. She walked quickly around the ground floor. A simple layout. Large country-style kitchen to the left of the small front hall, and a sitting room with a big open fireplace to the right. Upstairs there was one double bedroom, two singles and a bathroom, complete with free-standing tub. As far as she could see the roof wasn't letting in the rain and the house felt dry. She'd get the electricity turned on and come back with a photographer and by the high selling season in midsummer this would be a very saleable property.

She locked the front door and walked around to the back of the house. The email had said something about outhouses or a garage. Often a selling point with these old properties. Potential for renovation or even development. Behind the house was a yard, cobbles overgrown with grass. And a row of sheds. She tried the doors. Nothing much here. The last was locked. A heavy padlock hung from the bolt. She checked her keys but none fitted. A piece of wood had been hammered over the window. She tugged at it and it began to give. She picked up a stick from the ground and used it as a lever. The wood swung away, revealing a broken pane. She put her face up to it and cupped her hands around her eyes. A beam of light shone from behind her head on to the floor. She could see something. Another coal sack, maybe? Or a bag of rubbish? The kind of stuff that would need to be cleared out.

She pulled at the wood again and this time the whole piece came away. Light flooded the darkness. And now she could see clearly. The thing had a familiar shape. Round and smooth and the colour of ivory. Two dark holes stared up at her. The rest was obscured by what looked like heavy-duty sticky tape. She craned her head to see more. A jacket, with a white shirt inside it, a pair of trousers and shoes, lying as if flung there. And just visible the bones of a hand and fingers and the bright gleam of a chain.

ONE

July 2005. Such a beautiful summer, Michael McLoughlin thought, as he sat on the terrace outside his kitchen. He leaned back into the wooden slats of his old garden bench, and turned his face to the late-afternoon sun. It had been almost too hot out here at midday, but it was almost perfect now. He looked out across Dublin's sprawling suburbs towards the bay and Howth Head beyond. The sea was so beautiful, striped like a piece of agate. Dark navy towards the horizon. Light green, almost turquoise closer to the shore. Every now and then a delicate stippling of white as a breeze ruffled the glittering surface. He got out his binoculars and focused on the boats. A couple of cruisers flying French flags and three from Britain. There was even an American boat out there, a big one, fifty feet or more in length, he reckoned, with that tough, buttoned-down look that deep-water yachts always have. And scattered across the bay, like a handful of children's toys, were the sailing dinghies. On the north side from the club in Clontarf, and closer to home from the clubs in Dun Laoghaire. Where he was headed this evening. For his retirement party.

Retirement, already? He could hardly believe it. After twenty-seven years in the force they had told him he was ready to go. But he'd hung on for another ten years until it became obvious that his time was up. Did he care? Only in as much as he wasn't sure how he would live the rest of his life. That was assuming there would be a rest of his life. So he'd done the sensible thing and gone to all the Preparation for Retirement courses that the welfare office laid on. And he'd tried to pay attention and not be one of the sniggering cynics in the back row. And maybe he'd learned a few things because he'd got himself some class of a job for the rest of the summer. He was going to deliver boats to France and Spain – some for a cruise hire company based in Brittany, returning boats that had been sailed to Ireland on holiday, and others for people who didn't have the time to get their boats to the Med for their few weeks' cruising. The company belonged to a guy he'd crewed for over the years. There wasn't much money in it. Just his keep and a few bob for drinking and a couple of weeks in one of the company's apartments or villas. And who knew where that might lead? There was very little to keep him in Dublin now. His mother was well looked after in the nursing-home. She'd miss him, but she'd understand. She knew he was lonely. That there was little love in his life. She'd wish him well.

He stood up and walked inside. It was dark in comparison with all that light outside. He felt his way into the bathroom, undressed and got under the shower. He'd need to lose a few pounds. Not much room below decks on most of those boats. And he had a sudden image of his ageing, flabby body in shorts. Not a pretty sight. He squatted down and let the water pour on to his neck and shoulders. His thigh muscles quivered and he thought for a moment that he would lose balance and topple forward. He pressed his hands against the tiled walls and pushed himself upright again. His breath was coming in short gasps. Jesus, he hadn't realized how unfit he was. The last couple of years he'd been behind a desk most of the time, out at the airport working in Immigration. Too much administration, not enough action. Well, it would stop now. He'd three weeks until his first cruise. If he exercised for an hour every day, cut back on the alcohol and the fats he'd be in much better shape by then, he hoped.

He turned off the tap, picked up a towel and walked into his bedroom. He rummaged through his wardrobe and pulled out his linen jacket. He hadn't worn it for years and he was sure the dress code for tonight was sober suits. But what the hell? It was his party so he'd wear what he wanted. He'd always been a bit of an outsider. Didn't play golf, wasn't interested in football, soccer or Gaelic, was a better cook than most of the Garda wives he knew. And he was a loner. No wife, not now. No kids, no family to speak of. That was why he'd picked the yacht club for the party. At least there he was known. At least there someone would greet him like a friend. Make him feel he had a place in the world.

He dressed quickly. The jacket still fitted. And it didn't look bad, even if the colour was more ivory than cream. Maybe when he hit the sun he'd get himself a proper linen suit, trousers and a waistcoat to match. He turned away from the mirror and patted his pockets. Wallet, phone, keys, reading-glasses, all the essentials of middle-aged life. And for a special treat tonight, some cigars. Cohibas, the best Cubans. Kept in their own wooden humidor for special occasions. The box had belonged to his father. He had been a lover of cigars too. Not that he could afford them very often. So the function of the box had been subverted. His mother used to keep her favourite recipes in it, and a collection of treasures. A silver locket, a string of pearls.

And some black-and-white snaps of Michael and his sister, Clare, taken with his father's Box Brownie. When she'd gone into the nursing-home the humidor had become McLoughlin's. He had cleaned it out and filled it with as many cigars as he could afford. And sometimes in the bottom section beneath the removable rosewood panel, he put his own treasures.

Now he picked out a dozen cigars. Enough to hand around to the lads and a few for himself. He filled his leather cigar case and slipped it into his pocket. He began to close the lid. Then he stopped. This was such a beautiful summer. Like that other beautiful summer, ten years ago. The year that Mary Mitchell died. That he met her mother, Margaret. That he fell in love with her. That he thought he would die from longing. He lifted out the tray that held the remaining cigars. Underneath was a brown envelope in a plastic bag. He picked it up and weighed it in his hand. He smoothed his fingers over its shiny surface. He didn't need to look inside. He could see all the images as clearly as he had seen them that night in the shed behind the cottage in Bally-knockan. Mary Mitchell in the days before she died, her head shorn of its black curls, her body bruised and beaten. Humiliated and shamed. The moment of her death, her eyes half closed, her pupils fixed and dilated, a smile frozen on her wide, generous mouth. The photographs had been spread out on the floor beside Jimmy Fitzsimons. He was lying there, helpless, chained to a ring on the wall, his face covered with tape. Where Margaret had left him to die. And he had thought that McLoughlin would save him. That the guard would do the right thing. But instead he had wiped the tape, the handcuffs, the chain clean of her fingerprints. He had picked up the photographs and put them into his pocket. He could not bear to think that Mary would be tainted by Jimmy's death. He had brought them home. He had put them into his mother's treasure box. He had kept them and minded them. He had protected Mary's memory as best he could and he had never stopped loving her mother.

He sighed heavily. He put the plastic bag back into the box, carefully replacing the thin wooden panel. He laid the cigars over it, then closed the lid and locked it with its small brass key. Then he turned away. It was time to go. It wouldn't do to be late tonight of all nights. He opened the front door. It was such a beautiful evening. He got into his car and started the engine. The sun dazzled his eyes. He put up his hand to block it out. And thought he saw Mary. As she must have been when she was alive. Dancing through the rays of the evening light.

'Goodnight, Mary. Goodnight,' he whispered.

He put the car in gear. Then he drove slowly down the hill towards the sea.

TWO

So lovely to be back in Monkstown. On a cool clear morning to stand on the doorstep and gaze across the narrow road to the sea wall and the sea beyond. Margaret could smell the salt and the seaweed and the tang of the black mud. It was a fresh smell, washed clean by the twice daily sweep of water in and out of Dublin Bay. She glanced up at the sky. She had forgotten how the light here was always different, how it changed from one minute to the next. How clouds formed, dissolved, re-formed, filtering the sun's rays so the light moved through the spectrum. So different from the hard, unchanging blue of the Queensland sky where she had lived since she left Dublin the last time. When she had driven Jimmy Fitzsimons's car from the cottage in Ballyknockan to the car park in Dun Laoghaire. Waited until it was time to board the ferry for Holyhead, taken the train to London, then the tube to Heathrow. Boarded a plane for Brisbane. Wouldn't go back to New Zealand where Mary had grown up. She'd shed all her ties there. Sold the house, closed down her medical practice. Told anyone who asked that she was going back to Ireland. But didn't say anything else.

She'd rented a car at Brisbane airport and driven north, first to Sunshine Beach, then to Noosa where she stayed in a small hotel on the beach. Just long enough to get her bearings. Then bought a house near the small town of

Eumundi. A low wooden house with a wide veranda on three sides and five acres of land around it so nothing was visible from the road. And there she had stayed. And counted out the days. Until she knew that Jimmy would be dead.

Now she walked back inside. This house, where she had grown up, had been empty for the last year or so. There had been tenants but they had moved out and she had not replaced them. So when she decided to come back it had been simple to get a taxi from the airport and come straight to Monkstown, to Brighton Vale, open the gate, walk up the path, climb the six steps to the front door, put her key into the lock and turn it.

Not much had changed. Her tenants had been happy to get such a lovely house in a beautiful place for a modest rent. They hadn't minded that it was shabby and poorly equipped. Sometimes they talked about their landlady.

'The poor thing . . . Can you imagine losing your only child like that?'

'I know. I couldn't bear it. Bad enough that she would die, but to be murdered. It doesn't bear thinking about.'

'And then that trial. The guards have a lot to answer for. How did the guy get off?'

'Something to do with the length of time they kept him for questioning. I didn't realize the rules were so strict. It doesn't seem right somehow.'

'It's a civil-liberties thing. I suppose you have to have some safeguards. Innocent until proven guilty.'

'Yeah, well, maybe, but it sounded as if he did it. Didn't it?'

And a few years later they'd heard it on the news.

'Wow, incredible. Are they sure it's him?'

'Apparently. It looks like his body's been locked in that shed for years.'

'So how did he die? Was he murdered?'

'Starvation, the pathologist reckons.'

'But who – who would do it? And how?'

Why, how and who? The obvious questions.

The last time Margaret had seen Mary alive it had been here in this house. That hot summer evening ten years ago. It was Saturday. The August bank holiday. She had been sitting in the garden reading the paper. She had been about to go inside and prepare some food for her mother. She had wanted Mary to stay and help her.

'It's not much to ask, for God's sake. You know how hard it is to lift her.' She had been angry and irritated.

'She doesn't want me to help her, Mum, you know that. She doesn't like me to see her in bed. She doesn't even want you to see her. I think you should get a full-time nurse or, better still, why don't you see if you can get her into hospital? Or what about a hospice? They do have them here, don't they?' Mary was already fiddling with her bag, checking her keys, her wallet, her make-up. She was already walking back into the house.

'That's not what I want to do. You know that. That's why we came back. Because she's my mother and she's dying and it's my responsibility to look after her.' Her voice had risen.

'Yeah, yeah, so you keep on saying.' Mary stopped in the doorway and turned to her. 'Why won't you be honest? You don't even like her and it doesn't seem to me as if she likes you very much. So why don't you call it quits? Get her into hospital and then we can go home. Or, better still, to Paris or Rome or even Berlin. I'm bored with Dublin. I need a bit more excitement in my life. Anyway,' she moved out of sight into the darkness of the house, 'I'm off. Don't wait up.'

'Mary,' Margaret had stood up and followed her, 'don't go like that. Wait. Phone me if you're not coming home. Do you hear me? Phone me.' But even as she spoke she heard the front door slam.

She heard it slam now as she opened the back door into the garden and a draught rushed through the house. She'd thought she had closed it, but the lock was loose and sometimes it slipped. Another job to be done, she thought, as she walked out into the sun. Grass to be cut, the beds to be weeded, the hedges to be trimmed. The place was a mess. Her father would have been appalled, if he could have seen it. She would deal with it tomorrow. She would deal with everything tomorrow. Today she was too tired. An old wooden deckchair with a canvas seat was opened out on the flagged terrace. She sat down on it and lay back. Her fingers reached beneath it and found a glass of wine. She lifted it to her mouth and drank. She drained the glass and put it back carefully on the stone. Then she closed her eyes. Her head lolled to one side and her breathing slowed until it was barely audible. There would be plenty of time tomorrow to do what had to be done. Or maybe the next day, or the next or the next. It was only the beginning of July. Nearly a month to go until the anniversary of Mary's death. So much to think about. So many memories. But for now there was the comfort of sleep.

THREE

McLoughlin woke with a jump. He sat up straight, heart pounding, mouth filling with saliva. Christ, he felt bad. He got up slowly and staggered as his weight shifted forward from the bed. He reached out and grabbed hold of the edge of the chest of drawers and saw his face in the crutch mirror on top of it. Not a pretty sight. He stepped over his clothes, which were scattered on the bedroom floor, and pulled his dressing-gown from the back of the door. Light flooded down the corridor, making his eyes smart and his head pound. He stumbled into the kitchen and opened the fridge. He needed orange juice with ice, followed by painkillers and a pint of water. He slid back the glass doors and stepped out on to the terrace, then slumped on the bench and drank deeply. Another beautiful day. Not that he cared much. He wasn't going anywhere except back to bed. The glory of retirement. No one to answer to.

He closed his eyes. It had been a good night. He had drunk far too much, of course, but so had everyone else. He didn't think he'd committed too many indiscretions. He'd been tempted to tell the assistant commissioner who'd come along to do the honours what an arsehole he really was. But he'd bitten his lip and smiled and said nothing. He'd accepted the cheque and the presentation of the Waterford crystal decanter and the half-dozen glasses and stood up and thanked them all for being there. He'd told a few funny stories from way back, and remembered to single out for special mention the lads he'd stayed friends with ever since Templemore. He could sense there was a certain expectation in the air. What would he say about Finney? Finney, who'd fucked up the detention of Jimmy Fitzsimons, Finney, who'd been the reason that Fitzsimons got off. And Finney, who somehow, through some incredible string-pulling, arse-licking and cute hooring, had managed to streak up the ranks, way past McLoughlin, his old boss, and was now poised to make chief superintendent within the year.

McLoughlin had wondered if he'd show up. It would have been just like the fucker. He wasn't the only one who'd been expecting him either. He'd seen the looks on some of the faces and heard the muttered conversations. It would have been something to talk about for years to come. Finney and McLoughlin, the young pretender and the old dog, facing each other for the last time. But in the event Finney didn't appear. It was just as well. It wasn't only that McLoughlin didn't have the energy for the fight. There was also the fact of the body that had been found a few years ago in the cottage in Ballyknockan. Finney had been put in charge of the investigation. He hadn't got far with it. A post-mortem had established that it was a young male approximately six feet in height. Cause of death was dehydration and starvation. A search through the missing persons on file revealed no matches with the dental records. A sample was taken from the remains for DNA testing. But it was such a slow process that Finney got impatient. He found a forensic archaeologist. She took the bones of the face and head and made, first, a model, then from that a computerized image. McLoughlin remembered the consternation in the office when the email arrived.

'Jesus, would you look at this? I don't fucking believe it. Hey, where's McLoughlin? He needs to see this too.'

McLoughlin had been waiting for something like this ever since he'd snapped the padlock shut and walked away from the shed door that cold, dark night. Sooner or later that door would open again and Jimmy would be found.

Now he sat beside Finney and stared at the screen. 'What do you want me to do? Talk to his mother?' He tried to sound helpful.

Finney stood up. 'Nothing. Absolutely nothing. My guys will follow it up. I just wanted you to confirm my identification that the body is that of Jimmy Fitzsimons.'

'OK.' McLoughlin's voice was neutral. 'Yes, from what I can see, from the reconstruction done by Professor Williams, that is Jimmy Fitzsimons. Do you want it in writing?'

McLoughlin drained his glass of orange juice. He stood up and walked back into the kitchen. There was a large bottle of San Pellegrino in the cupboard. He untwisted the metal cap. Bubbles rushed upwards to freedom. He filled his glass, and added a handful of ice with a squeeze of lemon, then put the bottle into the fridge. He walked outside and sat down again. The sea looked so beautiful today. When his hangover lifted, he'd head down the hill to the club and see if he could get some sailing. It was the height of the racing season. There'd be bound to be a berth for him somewhere.

And then he remembered. There was something he'd said he'd do. What was it? Oh, shit, it was all coming back. Why did he let himself get talked into doing favours? It must have been the drink. That wonderful feeling of expansive happiness that overtook him after the third pint. 'Of course, anything you want, I'll do it. Of course I will, don't worry yourself. I'll look after it.' He always meant it at the time. It was only afterwards that he realized what a mess he'd got himself into. He struggled to remember. What kind of a mess was this one? He stood up and stretched. He'd go back to bed now before he began to fret about it.

But as he lay down, the pillow accepting his aching head, his phone beeped. Twice. He picked it up and flicked open his messages. There were two. Both from Tony Heffernan. Of course. Now he remembered.

'You'd be doing her a huge favour.' Heffernan had cornered him. 'She's devastated. She's really in a bad way. Now you're officially retired you could do it for her. Just a few basic enquiries. Nothing too taxing. You know who she is, don't you?' Heffernan had moved closer and was practically whispering in his ear.

'No, I don't know who she is. What did you say her name was?' The noise in the bar was rising. It was the after-dinner crush. They were all loosened up now. Plenty of wine with dinner. A brandy or two, and now a few more pints before the wives dragged them home to bed.

'Sally Spencer. She was married to James de Paor. You remember him, of course. The barrister.'

'De Paor, the senior counsel? Of course I remember him. I came up against him a few times. He was a savage. How do you know her?' McLoughlin was interested now.

'Janet, my wife – my second wife.' Heffernan grinned with pleasure as he said her name and gave her the title. 'She went to school with her. One of those Protestant boarding-schools. All gym slips and hockey. Anyway, Sally had a hard time. Her first husband died of cancer when he was very young leaving her with two small kids and no money. She opened up a little shop selling knick-knacks, ornaments, that sort of thing. Just about keeping the wolf from the door. Then she met de Paor. He'd just got a divorce from his wife. Not a real one, of course. One of those English not-quite-legal ones. But, anyway, they hit it off big-time and the next thing she's gone to London with your man and they're married. Everyone, all her old friends, her family, was very surprised.'

'I'm surprised. She's a Protestant, you say? And she marries de Paor, the friend and protector of every Provo on the run?'

'Yeah, it was a bit of a shock. Anyway, to cut a long story short, you know de Paor died, about twenty years ago? Drowned in the lake where he had that beautiful house. In Wicklow.'

McLoughlin nodded. 'Is that what happened? I kind of remember.'

'Yeah, it was some sort of a boating accident. Anyway, poor Sally, her daughter, Marina, drowned there too, just a couple of weeks ago. From what I know, Johnny Harris did the post-mortem and he reckoned it was suicide. And she left a note. But Sally's convinced it wasn't suicide. So, I was wondering . . .' Heffernan's voice trailed off.

'Wondering?'

'Just go and see her, Michael. She's a lovely woman. You'll like her. She's in bits. Janet had lunch with her the other day. She says Sally can't believe it was suicide. She says her daughter wasn't the type.'

'Tony, come on. That's what they all say.' McLoughlin rocked back on his heels. 'No one thinks their son or daughter is suicidal.'

'You know that. I know that. But Sally doesn't. Please, do it for me. I can't get involved. Not officially. Go and see her, have a chat with her. Show some interest. Maybe that's all it will take. Someone to be nice to her.'

Nice, oh dear. McLoughlin drained his drink and signalled to the barman for another. So it had come to this. He was nice now. A shoulder to cry on, a friendly face, a purveyor of sympathy. Nothing more, nothing less. Then, as he was about to succumb to a deep, alcohol-induced gloom, his old friend Johnny Harris had got to his feet, his pathologist's scrubs swapped for a suit in Prince of Wales check that must have belonged to his father, and delivered a spirited rendition of 'What Shall We Do With The Drunken Sailor', complete with extemporized verses, which raised a few eyebrows and cheered McLoughlin up. After that it was all a bit of a blur.

But now there was the text message to confirm his status as nice guy, do anything for you kind of guy, all round good guy.

THANKS FOR THE GREAT NIGHT.
SALLY WILL CALL YOU LATER TODAY.
SEE YOU SOON.

He switched his phone to silent and let it drop on to the floor. He rolled over on to his side. He'd make an excuse when the woman phoned. The last thing he needed was another grieving mother. They were trouble. That much was for sure.

FOUR

Margaret couldn't sleep. Maybe it was because the nights were so light. The sky never seemed to darken completely. It lost its colour gradually so it ceased to be bright blue and became pale and wan until just before dawn when it turned a soft dove grey. But perhaps it was nothing to do with the brightness of the sky. Perhaps it was because she didn't want to waste any of the time left to her, here in this house, which held so many memories.

She had made up a bed in the small room overlooking the garden where she had slept when she was a child and where Mary had slept for those six weeks before she died. In the hot press under the stairs she found some plastic bags that held sheets and pillowcases, eiderdowns and blankets. They were clean, although the smell of mothballs still lingered in the creases where they had been folded. It was good-quality linen. It would last at least one lifetime, her mother had often said, as she sniffed at the polycottons and synthetics, all the 'non-irons' and 'easy cares', that the shops had begun to offer. Of course, she was right. Margaret had inherited her rigid attitude towards natural fibres. Mary had laughed at her. But she had come back from staying with her friends and confessed that the sheets didn't feel right.

'They're yucky on your skin, Mum, aren't they? And they don't have that nice smell our sheets have.'

She had wanted to wrap Mary in one of her mother's sheets before she was placed in her coffin. She had wanted to swaddle her tightly the way she had seen nurses wrap the dead. It had always seemed humane and dignified, the crisp white cotton, folded over and around, keeping the body intact, its integrity guaranteed. But the undertaker had prevailed and Mary had been clothed in her favourite pink dress. As if it mattered. Nothing could disguise the damage done to her before death. The shearing of her hair. The bruises to her eyes and mouth. The marks on her neck. And beneath the dress, the burns, the scars where he had cut her breasts and stomach with the sharp blade of a Stanley knife. And the internal wounds he had inflicted on her.

She had thought that these images would fade with time. But they hadn't. Sometimes at night when she closed her eyes they were there, as fresh and as raw as they had been the first time she saw them. And they were even more so now as she lay in the narrow bed, her head on her old pillow. Mary had been conceived in this bed too. That weekend all those years ago when Margaret's parents had gone away and Patrick Holland had come to spend the evening with her. She had cooked for him, and after dinner they had sat at either side of the fire, like an old married couple, drinking and talking, and then as the flames died down they had gone upstairs to her room and lain under the eiderdown, still talking until it was time for him to go home to his wife.

She hadn't asked him to stay. He had got out of bed and begun to dress. Then he had stopped, looked down at her and, in a rush, pulled back the quilt and lain beside her, his hands grabbing at her body as if he would never touch her again. Afterwards she had slept so deeply that it was midday before she woke.

She got up now. There was no point in lying staring at the ceiling, all those memories fighting for attention. She walked downstairs into the kitchen. She filled the kettle. Then she sat down at the table. Her laptop was open, its screen dark. She touched the keys and waited for its welcoming purr. Her hands formed themselves into their familiar shape as she logged on, put in her password and waited for her emails to brighten the screen. Here was good news from Australia. The estate agent, Damien Baxter, had received an offer for her house. And another serious buyer was interested too. He'd let her know when they had reached their limit, but for the time being he was keeping an open mind. She'd bought the house from his father, Don, when she'd arrived in Noosa nine years ago. He was a nice man, polite and thoughtful, and his son had inherited his father's quiet, unassuming competence. She hadn't much money to spend. It had been the worst time to sell her New Zealand property. But she had her savings. A sense of thrift inherited from her father. A nest egg put by over the years. And Don had found her the house and got her a good deal. It was run-down and neglected, but he'd recommended his cousin, Jeff, who was a builder and between them they had transformed it. White walls and native-wood floors. A large open-plan kitchen and dining room. Her own small bedroom and bathroom. And four rooms to be rented. Bed and breakfast for passing backpackers, tourists, nature-lovers who wanted to spend some time in the Queensland rainforest. The house was always full. Word of mouth did it. Her name and address, passed from person to person along the trail.

'Lovely place. Very clean. Simple, but nice. Great food. As much as you can eat for breakfast. Scrambled eggs to die for. Good coffee and tea. And she makes her own bread and muffins and scones too. She'll give you a lunch to take on the road that would last you for two days.'

And for a while it had been good. She had been content. But sometimes there would be a face that would remind her. And she would wonder. And then she began to read the Irish newspapers on line. She didn't want to. She wanted to be as remote as possible. Far, far away from everything to do with home. But she was drawn to them. So easy now with the Internet. So instant. And there it was one day. Five years ago. A photograph of the cottage in Ballyknockan. A body found. No idea as to its identity. And then slowly, gradually, inevitably. More and more information. Name and age. And then the rest. The girl's murder. The suspect. Then the trial. The shock of its sudden ending. A smudgy photo of Mary from her student ID card. Her own face, a photograph taken at the funeral, her grief so overwhelming that she barely recognized herself. A Garda investigation set up. Detective Inspector Finney in charge. Finney of all people. Finney, whose incompetence had given her what she wanted. The chance to take her own revenge on the man who had destroyed her life.

She checked the websites daily, but the investigation into the death of Jimmy Fitzsimons soon disappeared. Six months after the finding of his body a couple of paragraphs stated that 'Garda sources' had admitted they had not made any progress towards finding out what had happened to him. The case would, of course, remain open, pending further information.

Then, a few months later:

The death has taken place of the well-known barrister and senior counsel Patrick Holland. Mr Holland died while on

holiday in Marbella. He collapsed while swimming yesterday at approximately 2 p.m. He was rushed to hospital but
was pronounced dead on arrival. A post-mortem will be
held to determine the cause of death, but it appears that he
died from a heart-attack. He is survived by his wife, Crea,
and his three children, Daniel, Alice and Patrick.

Why had she not known that Patrick was dead? Why
had her heart carried on beating after his had stopped? She
checked the date again – what had she been doing that day?
– she worked out the time difference. Patrick had died at
two in the afternoon on 14 June in the swimming-pool of
his villa outside Marbella. There was an eight-hour difference. It would have been ten p.m. in Eumundi. Summer in
Spain. Winter in Australia. Cool but still sunny. She looked
back over her diary for the day in question. All her rooms
were full. An English couple had arrived that evening. She
had cooked dinner for them and sold them a couple of
bottles of wine to go with it. The other guests, a boy from
Sydney, two German girls and an American zoologist, had
gone to Noosa for dinner. They got back around midnight.
She had stayed up with them, drunk some more wine. The
American was curious about her. She had fended off his
questions. He was good-looking in that American-academic
way. It would have been easy. He was leaving the next day.
No strings, just the comfort of a warm body to get her
through another night.

She had finished her drink and stood up. He made as if
to follow, but she shook her head quickly, smiled her
goodnights and left the room. It would have been a mistake.
And what had happened to Patrick after she had gone to her
room? At the time he was in the ambulance, the paramedics

were working on him, his heart was failing, its muscle already dying, his organs shutting down, his brain cells withering from lack of oxygen. She couldn't remember. She would have gone to the bathroom, cleaned her teeth, washed her face, changed into her pyjamas. Picked up a book to read, put it down. Switched off the bedside lamp. Lain first on one side, then on the other, tossed and turned. Dropped off to sleep somewhere between two thirty and three. Slept until the birds woke her at six. The kookaburra's ancient laugh, the whip birds, the male and female calling back and forth to each other. Time to get up, to bake the bread for which she was renowned. Prepare the breakfast. The American had a plane to catch that morning in Brisbane. She'd ordered a taxi to come at eight. She would have called to confirm it. She would have checked the bookings for the day. Made out a shopping list for her weekly super-market run. While Patrick's body lay in a morgue in a hospital in Málaga. Already stiffening with rigor mortis. Already decaying.

She had printed out the death notice from the newspaper. Survived by his three children, it said. Well, that was true. He'd once had four. Now there were three. He had wanted her to have an abortion. He had given her the money. She had gone to England. Then, when Mary was a year old, to New Zealand. As far away as she could go. She had stayed away from him. But he had helped her, later, when she really needed him. He had gone with her to Ballyknockan. He had beaten Jimmy Fitzsimons on the head and knocked him out. He had helped her drag him to the shed and chain him up. Then he had walked away with her, knowing what would happen. All this he had done for her and for Mary.

One day, she had thought, one day he will come to look for me and we will be together. The way we should have been.

But that day would never happen now. And now he was dead she no longer needed to protect him. She closed down her laptop. She poured boiling water into the teapot. She opened the back door and stepped out into the garden. The sky was a clear pale blue. She shivered, suddenly exhausted. She turned back into the kitchen, poured tea into a mug and added milk, then walked upstairs. She would sleep now. Now that it was morning and the time for ghosts was over. She would sleep until the sun was high in the sky. And she could face her past once again.

FIVE

The Lake House was in the Wicklow mountains, barely ten miles or so from the city but another world altogether. Its roof was just about visible from the high road through Sally Gap. Beyond it was Lough Dubh, where Marina Spencer had died. In the summer it was a sliver of silver between the heather-covered hills, in the winter a gleaming slice of polished jet. McLoughlin looked at the row of photographs that hung on the wall. Sally Spencer stood beside him.

'It's such a beautiful place, you've no idea. Just so beautiful.' She reached out and touched the nearest picture with the tip of her finger, then stepped back and sat down on the sofa. She gestured to McLoughlin to take the chair beside the fireplace.

'The estate had been in James's family for years. He was so proud of the place. I remember when I first met him he couldn't wait to bring me out there. We'd go every weekend. Before we got married, even. Winter and summer. Even when Sally Gap was snowed in, he had a Land Rover with special tyres and we'd stock up like we were going to the North Pole. I'd bring Marina and Tom and he'd bring Dominic, his son. And we'd have a ball.' Sally's eyes filled with tears. 'I remember one New Year, it snowed really heavily and even with the special tyres we couldn't get out.

We slept in the one room. Kept the fire going all night. It was such fun.'

McLoughlin said nothing. He sipped the tea she had placed on the table beside him.

'But then, after we got married, it changed. Dominic would have nothing to do with me. Or my kids. Up till then they'd got on quite well apart from the usual teenage tensions, but after the marriage it changed. Especially with Marina. He used to pick on her. Wind her up. Tease her. You know the sort of thing?'

McLoughlin nodded. He knew the sort of thing.

'I did kind of wonder if he was attracted to her. But I don't think it was that. I think he was jealous, resentful. I think he'd always been suspicious that I was to blame for his parents' separation. But that was rubbish. All that had happened before I met James. They'd grown apart. Stopped being . . .' she paused and looked away '. . . stopped being intimate. James wanted a divorce. His wife, Dominic's mother, agreed to it. And they seemed to work things out quite well between them. They had joint custody of Dominic and I knew he was close to both his parents. I thought time would sort everything out between him and me but . . . I don't know. Something went badly wrong and it never got put right.' The tears slipped from her eyes.

'How old was he?' McLoughlin shifted on his chair. He wasn't enjoying this.

'Seventeen. Older than my two. Very adult. Articulate, good-looking, sophisticated. I think, looking back, that I didn't appreciate how close he and his mother were. How much influence she had over him. And he was very possessive about the Lake House and the estate. I think he thought I was a gold-digger.' She smiled and pulled a tissue from her pocket. 'If he only knew. I didn't care about any of it. Looking back, I'm sorry that James and I bothered with the marriage. It caused nothing but trouble. But, well, we can't change it now.'

It was very quiet in Sally's small house. It was tucked into Trafalgar Lane, once a mews behind Trafalgar Terrace, a row of Victorian three-storeys facing Dublin Bay to the north. It was a pretty house, sunny and bright, although there were signs of neglect. The sun shining on the windows showed how long it had been since they were last cleaned, and a pall of dust dulled the shine of the furniture. Sally, too, was worn and neglected. She was small and very thin. Her face was grey with tiredness, and her eyes were red-rimmed. Her fair hair was pulled back in a messy ponytail. She leaned down and stroked the rough coat of the small dog sleeping at her feet.

'Sorry, sorry. I can't stop crying these days. I keep trying to get a grip, but . . .' She shrugged and made a wan attempt at a smile. 'I can't believe this has happened. I thought, when James died, that nothing that bad could ever happen again. I thought in some ridiculous way that I'd had more than my fair share of death and tragedy. That I'd be immune to it for ever. And now this.'

She stood up and walked over to the mantelpiece. She picked up a photograph in a silver frame, turned and held it out to McLoughlin. 'This is my Marina. She was so lovely. Always, from the moment she was born. She was a wonderful little girl, and a gorgeous grown-up. And what's so sad is that for the first time I really felt she'd got her life together. Here.' She kissed the cold glass covering the photograph, then handed it to McLoughlin.

Sally was right. Marina was lovely. Dark hair pulled back

off her face and dark brown eyes to match. A wide smile. High cheekbones. The kind of woman you'd notice.

'How old was she?' McLoughlin handed the picture back.

Sally folded her arms over it protectively and sat down again.

'When that was taken? Or when . . .'

'When she died.'

'She was thirty-two. She didn't look it, though. People always thought she was much younger.'

'You too. You don't look old enough to have a child of that age.'

She smiled, and for a moment his words were not just flattery. 'I was very young when I had her. I was barely eighteen. My husband and I were teenage sweethearts. We got married when I was six months pregnant. Not that either of us cared. We were madly in love. I'd just done the Leaving Cert and Robbie was in college. But he worked part time and somehow we scraped by.'

'And you've another child too?'

'My son, Tom, was born two years later. And then when James and I got married we had Vanessa. She was just a baby when James died.' The tears were flowing again. 'I'd brought two children up without a father. The last thing I wanted was to have to do it again.' She began to sob.

McLoughlin looked away. What on earth was he doing here? All those years of giving people bad news. He'd had enough. He stared out the window. He could see above the high houses on both sides that the sky was a perfect pale blue. A gust of wind stirred the leaves on the old sycamores. Force four to five, he reckoned. Perfect sailing weather. He looked around the room and took in the carriage clock on the bookshelf. It was two thirty. If he could wrap this up soon he'd be in time to meet up with his friend Paul. Get some more info on the next trip to France.

'I'm not sure I can help you with this, Sally. I'm sure the local guards did everything they could to establish the cause of your daughter's death. If they thought it was suicide, well, I know it's hard to accept, but maybe they were right.' Fuck Tony Heffernan for dragging him into this. 'And from what Tony told me there was a note, wasn't there?'

Sally looked at him. Her eyes, he noticed, were a mottled green. Like pond water, he thought.

'It was hardly a note. It was a bit of paper found in her bag. It said something about forgiveness. That's all.' She paused and looked down at her hands. 'Look. I can pay you, if that's a consideration.'

He shook his head. 'Please, it's not about money. It's just that I honestly don't see what I can do for you.' He could feel his cheeks reddening.

She stood up and walked towards a large, handsome desk. As she moved, the little dog stretched and yawned, then rolled over and went back to sleep. Sally pulled open the top drawer. She turned towards him, an album in her hands. 'Please, take this and have a look at it. I collected everything to do with my husband's death, which was an accident, I know that. Since Marina died I've collected everything that's been written about her and what happened. I had a lot of letters from people who knew her. Read them. See what her friends thought. Don't make a decision now. I'll respect whatever you decide.' She held out the album, as if she was presenting him with a precious gift. 'Marina did not commit suicide. Perhaps she died accidentally. Perhaps she was drunk and fell into the lake. But I don't think so. Ever since James drowned Marina has been terrified of water. You know, she was with him in the boat when it happened. I don't think she's ever been in one since. Something happened that night at the house. Something that has not been explained. Please take this. Please.'

The album lay on the passenger seat beside him as he drove down the narrow lane and turned towards the main road. Its shiny black cover seemed to give off its own energy. He reached down and touched it and his fingers slipped to its side. He flipped the pages open.

He stopped at the junction. Ahead, Dublin Bay was blue and beautiful. He looked right and left, then crossed carefully and drove down the narrow slip-road, over the railway bridge, towards the Seapoint Martello tower. Then he turned left again on to the small cul-de-sac facing the sea. He had always loved these houses. They had been built for naval officers in the early nineteenth century. They were unassuming but beautifully proportioned, with the flight of six steps to the front door, double-fronted with bay windows to either side. It was a while since he had been here. In the months after Margaret had left he had sometimes parked here at night, gazing out at the sea and thinking about her. Now he found a space to park just beyond the house. He picked up the album. It was heavy. He rested it on the steering-wheel. There was a Pandora feel to all this, he thought. He didn't want to know what it contained. But, like Pandora's box, he knew for sure that it held nothing good. All of Sally Spencer's tragedy and despair were contained within these pages. And now he would be letting them loose.

He put it back on the passenger seat and got out of the car. He stood in front of the house, then bent down to open the gate. It squeaked and grated noisily on the uneven stone path. He picked his way over the limestone flags. They were cracked and broken, and dandelion and buttercup had seeded freely. Rubbish had blown in from the road. Plastic bags, crisps packets and chocolate wrappers had threaded themselves through the shrubs along the walls. He stopped at the bottom of the steps. The wrought-iron railings were rusting and the paint on the door was faded and peeling.

He walked slowly up the steps. The windows of the front rooms downstairs were shuttered. One, he remembered, was a bedroom. Margaret's mother had lain there for the last few months of her life, keeping an eye on the road as she drifted in and out of her drugged sleep. The room on the other side was a formal drawing room, with a marble fireplace and ornate plasterwork. He had caught a glimpse of it the many times he had visited. But Margaret had never invited him in there. They had always sat in the kitchen downstairs or outside in the garden.

Now McLoughlin bent down and lifted the flap on the letterbox. He let it drop with a loud clang. He lifted it again and this time leaned down to peer through. The hall inside was flooded with sunlight. Blocks of dark reds, greens and yellows from the stained glass on the landing fell across the dusty floorboards. Junkmail was swept into a pile in one corner. He straightened up, then cupped his hands around his face and looked in through the narrow window at the side of the door. And realized how foolish he must seem. What was he doing here? It was time to move forward, not back. He walked slowly down the steps. He closed the gate and got back into his car. He reversed slowly down the road. Bloody awkward place to get out of. Served him right for coming here in the first place. He glanced down at Sally

Spencer's album. Later. He'd look at it later. And then he'd
tell her he could do nothing for her. He was sorry but he
was going away and he didn't know when he'd be back.

Margaret lay curled on her side, her eyes open. It was quiet
inside the house. She could hear the sounds from the world
outside through the heavy wooden shutters. Cars passing,
the hoot of a horn, the loud rumble of the DART train
gathering speed as it moved out of Seapoint station. From
time to time she could hear children's voices, sometimes an
adult shouting. And there was the call of the seagulls as
they floated high above the house. But now there was
another sound. It was the squeak of the gate as it was opened
and pushed back over the uneven stone path. She raised her
head and listened. Now there was silence. She lay down
again and wrapped her arms around her chest. And heard
footsteps outside, the clunk as the letterbox flap was lifted
and dropped, once, then a pause, then again. She lay very
still, waiting for the shrill ring of the doorbell. But all she
heard were the footsteps again, this time retreating back
down the steps, along the path, then the harsh squawk of
the gate as it was opened and closed. She sat up. She stood
and tiptoed to the window. She pressed her face to the gap
in the shutters. The garden was empty. The street outside
was crowded with cars. A group of teenagers were sitting on
the sea wall. They were laughing and shouting at each other,
their movements exaggerated, stylized. She stepped away
from the shutters and got back on to the bed. She was cold
now, and tired. She wrapped the eiderdown around her body
and closed her eyes. And she slept.

Six

'You went to see her yesterday. She was so pleased you took the time. Thanks. You liked her, I'm sure.' Heffernan raised his pint in salute, then took a deep swallow. He sank down on the bar stool and tugged at his tie. 'Jesus, it's hot today. You're a lucky swine. Got your retirement in the middle of the hottest summer on record. It's murder out at the airport, these days. Who'd want to be a guard in Immigration at a time of record effing population change?' He groaned. 'We'd a nasty scene today. Another bloody Nigerian trying to bring in a couple of girls.'

'What is it about Nigerians? They're something else, aren't they?' McLoughlin picked up his glass and swirled it around. 'Prostitution, drugs, what was it?'

Heffernan shrugged. 'Probably both. The girls were headed for a meat market somewhere. The poor little things. The guy went crazy when we challenged him. The kids had no passports, no visas, no nothing. He insisted they were his daughters. And when we told him we were sending them back to Lagos, he head-butted Derek Flynn. You should have seen it. Blood all over everything. His and Derek's. We had to cart both of them off to the Mater.'

'And is Derek OK? I suppose he'll need an AIDS test, poor bugger.'

'Your man was clean, so that's one thing in his favour.

We arrested him for assault but he'll be out on bail before you can spit. He already has refugee status. So we can't do anything with him. Unless we can catch him pimping. He's a nasty piece of work. His wife came to the hospital. Lovely woman, three kids hanging out of her. And you could see she was shit scared of him.' Heffernan drained his glass. 'Same again?'

McLoughlin stared balefully at his drink. Mineral water. Even the thought of it depressed him.

'Ah, come on, Michael, have a proper drink. You're making me feel miserable. Just the sight of your gloomy expression is enough to put me right off.'

'OK, OK, I'll have a bottle of lager, Heineken, Carlsberg, something like that.'

'Thank God for small mercies.' Heffernan made a mock bow. 'Now at least I can relax. Hey, Joe,' he craned over the bar, 'when you're ready.'

He'd wanted to go home after the pub. But Heffernan insisted. He was meeting Janet for a pizza and he wanted McLoughlin to come too. He could see that they were both determined he was going to help Sally Spencer. Or was it more like a bit of middle-aged matchmaking, he wondered. Now that Heffernan and Janet were married and happy they wanted everyone else sorted out. He sat in the restaurant and listened while they laughed and joked and enjoyed each other's company. He was pleased for Tony. He deserved it. He'd suffered for years under the yoke of a dreadful marriage to the vindictive cow who was his first wife. He'd seen his kids go through hell. He'd lost touch with them for long periods, but somehow this marriage had made it better for them all. They'd even been on holidays together. They had the photos to prove it.

'Look at these, Michael.' Janet put the prints on the table. 'We had such a good time.'

'Where in Spain was it?' McLoughlin tried to sound enthusiastic.

'A little village called Jimena, an hour or so from Málaga. Up in the hills. In fact we stayed in a house that belongs to a friend of Sally's daughter.' Janet spread out the photos so he couldn't avoid them. 'Marina was there for some of the time. See, here.' She pushed one of the pictures towards him with the tip of her finger. 'Here's Marina with Tony and the kids. Hard to believe that a couple of weeks later she was dead.'

Even without his glasses McLoughlin recognized her. The same wide smile, high cheekbones, dark eyes and glossy hair. 'Look,' his voice was embarrassed, 'look, really, your friend is very nice and I'm sure she's in a terrible state, but I can do nothing for her. I'm not a guard any longer. I'm a civilian. Even if I wanted to I don't have the access. I don't have the facilities. Best thing she can do is accept that her daughter took her own life. Or if she can't why doesn't she get back on to the Blessington police? Brian Dooley is a good guy. He'll listen to her.' He pushed the picture towards Janet and stood up. 'I'd better go. I'm trying to stay off the drink and all that goes with it. I'm off to France in a week or so. Sorry, Janet, it's not my scene any longer. OK?'

He didn't look to see how she would respond. He picked up his coat and stepped away from the table.

'See you round, Tony.' He headed for the door.

*

Didn't want to get involved. Didn't want to know about another woman's grief for her dead daughter. Had enough of that with Margaret and Mary. Look at the trouble it had got him into. He'd wound up in a nursing-home for six months after that night in the cottage in Ballyknockan. First of all he'd gone on a bender. Then the doctor had prescribed anti-depressants. Eventually he'd gone to the welfare officer. A nice guy. Checked him into a private clinic in Glenageary. Lots of very sweet Filipina nurses. He slept and ate plenty of healthy meals. He watched a lot of daytime TV. And he went for therapy. For the first few sessions he did nothing but cry. The therapist was an American, a woman of about his own age, with pale blonde hair, like a Scandinavian's, pulled into a loose bun on top of her head. She didn't say much. When he began to talk he spoke of his father. Over and over again he told the story of the day he died. It was a Thursday. The first Thursday in the month. Children's allowance day. A big pay-out at the local post office. There should have been an armed escort. Should have been, but wasn't. After the death of Joe McLoughlin there was always an armed escort. He was the blood sacrifice. He was the one who'd had to die. The Provos were waiting for the Securicor van. There were two of them hanging around the bookie's next door. A third was in the car parked outside. When Joe and his partner drove up he flashed his lights to get the guy to move up a space so they could park in the best position. The guy wouldn't move. Joe got out of the car and walked towards him. Just as the two raiders, their balaclavas pulled down, came running from the post office, dragging the money sacks behind them. And the guy in the car aimed his gun right at Joe's face. He blew half of it away.

'I heard about it immediately. I was a rookie working in

the Bridewell. Word came over the radio that a guard had been killed in Dundrum. I knew it was my father. There was this terrible silence. And the look on all their faces. His body was brought to the morgue in Store Street. They asked me to identify him. I didn't want to. I was scared of seeing him. And then my mother arrived. I let her do it. I rationalized it. I said it was her right. She was his next of kin. But it wasn't that. I was a coward. I was too scared. I let him down. I was his son. I should have been brave enough to acknowledge the way he would go into the grave. But I couldn't do it. And I've never been able to forgive myself.'

'And your mother?' The therapist's voice was low. 'What did she say?'

'We never talked about it. She identified him. She sat with him for as long as they would let her. I don't know what she thought.' But he did know. He knew she was disappointed. All through those dreadful few days, when the coffin came home with its lid closed, and the house was filled with relatives and neighbours and guards from every station around the country. And the removal to the church, the night of heavy drinking that followed, and the next day the funeral Mass, the burial, the three-course lunch in the hotel, then the session back at the house where the drink flowed and all the old stories were told time and time again. And he knew what his mother was thinking.

'How could you know? Are you a mind-reader?' The therapist leaned forward in her chair.

'Not a mind-reader, a body-reader. I know my mother. Our eyes didn't meet. Not once. Not during the whole bloody thing.'

'And now? How long is it since your father died?'

'Nearly thirty years.' He looked down at his hands. 'Now, well, now she needs me. She's in a nursing-home. My sister lives in London so there's only me to go and see her, to keep an eye on her. So it's pretty OK between us.'

'And do you talk about your father?'

'Yes, we do. But we don't talk about that. I don't think either of us can bear to bring it up. I don't know why I'm talking about it now.'

But he did know. He wanted to talk about Margaret, but there were things he couldn't say. He doubted that the confidentiality rule would hold if he spilled the beans about what had happened that night. So he'd dug up his father. And then when he could think of nothing further to say about him he prevaricated. Dredged up some other awful cases. A mother who had suffocated her two children, then taken an overdose; a man who had set fire to the family home killing his wife and baby; a son who had starved his invalid mother to death and kept her body hidden in the attic for months. They were all true cases. And they had hurt badly at the time. But he hadn't been directly involved as he had been with the death of Jimmy Fitzsimons.

The death of Jimmy Fitzsimons. The slow, agonizing torture of Jimmy Fitzsimons. He had put it out of his mind. He had put the place out of his mind. He could have got into the car and driven out there any time he wanted. But he hadn't. He went crazy. He went to the clinic. He got better. He put it out of his mind.

Now he sat in the car in the dark. There was music on the radio. Frank Sinatra was singing. That lovely song, 'Bewitched, Bothered and Bewildered'. He remembered. A night in May – was it 1986, '87? Some time around then. Frank Sinatra had come to Dublin. Janey had got tickets to go to the concert in the football ground at Lansdowne Road. He hadn't wanted to go. He had been in the middle of a murder. A girl found in Blackrock Park. Raped and beaten. They'd followed up the obvious leads. Nothing so far. He'd have preferred to go drinking with the lads to talk about it. But Janey had insisted. And she was right. It was a magical evening. Old Frankie's voice was past its best, but he could still weave that spell. And afterwards, as the crowd drifted out through the gates, a woman somewhere up ahead had started to sing. Her voice was thin and reedy but it didn't matter. They had all joined in, a surge of voices. They sang 'Bewitched, Bothered and Bewildered'.

Janey had reached out and taken his hand and he had pulled her to him and kissed her. And for once he'd been genuinely sorry that he had to go back to work and not home to be with her.

He began to sing now, in the car, in the dark, the lights of the city filling the sky with a sickly orange glow. The orchestra came in behind Sinatra's voice, filling and swelling like the sweep of a spring tide. And he felt the tears again as he sang, and his throat tightened and his voice choked and died away, leaving him suddenly bereft.

He checked the handbrake, checked that the car was in gear, switched off the ignition. He opened the door and got out. He walked around to the boot and put the key into the lock. The metal was warm to the touch. He swung it up and open. He'd gone shopping earlier in the day. Vegetables from that nice little greengrocer's in Glasthule and cheese from Caviston's. A soft goat cheese from somewhere in Cork and a big slab of Bandon cheddar. He'd been tempted to buy some squid. Lucky he hadn't. It wouldn't have lasted long in this heat. The goat's cheese gave off a pungent smell that verged on nasty. He gathered together the plastic bags and lifted them up. And saw, underneath, the shiny black cover of Sally Spencer's album. He sighed and reached forward. He picked it up, tucked it under his arm, then slammed the boot. He turned towards the house. And as he moved a piece of paper drifted towards his feet, twirling in the still night air, like a feather. He bent to pick it up. And saw a face he remembered. That he had last seen that night in Ballyknockan. Patrick Holland: Mary's father, Margaret's lover. Who had helped her kill Jimmy Fitzsimons. And who, he knew, was now dead. A heart-attack on holiday in Spain. A huge funeral in Dublin. The great and the good gathered to mourn him. Crowds spilling out of the church, clustering around his black-clad widow to offer sympathy and support. McLoughlin had stood some way off. He had scanned the crowd. He had been sure Margaret would be there. He couldn't believe that she would let Holland go to his grave without saying goodbye. And when he didn't see her at the church he followed the cortège to the cemetery. Stood far enough away not to intrude, but close enough to see who was there. Thought his heart would stop beating, just for a moment, when a tall, slim woman wearing dark glasses, with a black shawl flung around her shoulders, got out of a taxi and walked towards the small knot of mourners by the open grave. Then saw Holland's widow give a little cry of recognition as they embraced. And the woman took off her glasses and, of course, she was nothing like Margaret. He left then. Slunk away, dodging behind headstones, and trying not to trip on the cracked slabs of the old paths. And realized that Mary was buried in this place too. It was fitting, he thought. Father and daughter in the same piece of earth.

He opened the fridge and put away his groceries. And pulled out a bottle of beer. Erdinger, German wheat beer, cloudy to the eye and yeasty to the nose. He flipped off the cap and poured it into a glass. He sat at the table, and laid the newspaper cutting down. He smoothed it out. It was an account of James de Paor's funeral. Patrick Holland was one of the chief mourners. He skipped through the text. Attended the same school, friends at university, called to the Bar in the same year. Some polite read-between-the-lines reference to political differences. And there was a quote: 'James was one of the best. We didn't always see eye to eye, but I never for a minute doubted his integrity and commitment to his beliefs. His death is a tragedy for all.'

There were three photographs. One was of Holland helping to carry the coffin from the church. The second was also of Holland, this time comforting Sally. She looked very young and, despite her obvious grief, very pretty. And the third showed a group of mourners. Marina was immediately recognizable. She had her arm around a younger boy, with the same high cheekbones and a mop of fair hair. Slightly apart from them was an older boy. A young man, really. He was standing stiffly beside a tall, dark woman. McLoughlin read the caption. Dominic de Paor, Helena de Paor, Marina Spencer, Tom Spencer. Dominic de Paor was striking. He was tall and well-built with a jutting nose. His tanned face was without expression but his body said it all. He was tense, withdrawn.

McLoughlin stared at the photographs. Helena de Paor. Must be the first wife. She had the look of one of those Japanese women. Almost like a geisha. Her black hair pulled back from her broad forehead, her face a white mask, her eyebrows dark slashes, like paint. Her son was very like her.

Their bodies seemed to cleave to each other. He opened the album and turned the pages, looking for the empty space from which the cutting had come. He picked up his glass and drank. Then he began to read.

By the time he got up from the table it was dark outside. Three more empty bottles of Erdinger had joined the first under the table. His foot knocked against them as he pushed back his chair and stood up. He leaned down and gathered them together. A four-bottle job, he thought. Like in the old days when they'd go to the pub after their shift was over and sit in the snug for the rest of the evening, going through whatever case it was they were working on. A six-pint night would be the usual. And the next morning he'd take out his notebook. And there would be written, in his small neat hand, everything they had discussed, every conclusion they had come to, every course of action on which they had decided.

And the habit hadn't left him. He picked up the envelope on which he'd made notes, and his glass, then slid back the doors to the terrace. He stepped outside. The lights of the city were a sparkling carpet below. The view at night always made him feel as if he was flying. He looked up at the sky. Even the competition from the lights below couldn't dim the brilliance of the Plough as it arched across the darkness. He lifted his glass and saluted. Its constancy made him feel secure and safe. He drained his glass and walked around the outside of the house. He could smell cut grass from the heap in the far corner and the sweetness of the night-scented stock, which had self-seeded in all the beds. A legacy from Janey. Planted that first year they had moved here. When she had been happy.

He checked that the car was locked, then walked up the

drive, pushed shut the heavy wooden gates and slotted the bolt into place. Towards the south, the bulk of Three Rock Mountain loomed in the distance. Behind it was Kippure, and close by its eastern flank, Djouce Mountain. To the west of Kippure the lake at Blessington and the stone village of Ballyknockan and over the hills, over Moanbane and Mullaghcleevaun and Duff Hill, and down into the valley with Fancy Mountain on one side and Djouce on the other, Lough Dubh where James de Paor had drowned twenty years ago, and where his step-daughter Marina drowned too. One was an accident, the other suicide, so the newspapers said. He leaned against the gate. It was very quiet up here tonight. Hardly a sound, except his feet on the tarmacadam of the drive and his breath. Sometimes the peace was shattered. Like that day on the lake. High summer, the graceful nineteenth-century house. James and Sally, their one-year-old daughter, Vanessa. Dominic and his friends from school. And his step-brother and -sister, Marina and Tom. Swimming in the lake, sailing and fishing. Picnics in the woods that sloped down behind the house to the water. Then one day the roar of a motorboat shattering the quiet. A group of kids, teenagers, had stolen it from its mooring. James and Marina had gone out in the dinghy to remonstrate with them. But something went wrong. The outboard engine stalled. James had stood up to try to start it again as the motorboat careened by. The wash caused the dinghy to swing wildly from side to side. James fell in. Marina tried to rescue him. But he drowned. A tragic accident. And then, twenty years later, another tragic accident. Another party in the house, this time given by Dominic de Paor. The morning after, Marina could not be found. It was thought she had gone back to Dublin with some of the other guests. But her body was found trapped in the rocks where the small stream ran from the upper lake into the lower. Blood tests showed she had drunk three-quarters of a bottle of vodka. There were also traces of cocaine. And one of the tabloids had got hold of details of what was described as a suicide note. It was addressed to her mother. It said she was sorry for what she had done. She could never forgive herself. She hoped that she would be forgiven, if not in this life then in the next.

McLoughlin gave the gate a push. Just to make sure that the bolt was holding. Then he walked back down towards the house. He began to sing the same old Frank Sinatra song. He sang it, slowly, softly, over and over again as he went around to the terrace. He picked up his glass, then gazed out over the lights of the city towards the dark of Dublin Bay and the Irish Sea beyond. The Kish lighthouse flashed twice, then flashed again thirty seconds later. The Baily light to the north flashed once, then flashed again twenty seconds later. The West Pier light gave its three green flashes every seven point five seconds. And the East Pier white light flashed twice every fifteen seconds. And the red Poolbeg light occulted twice every twenty seconds. He stood and watched the lights repeat and repeat and repeat, then turned and went into the kitchen. He ran the glass under the cold tap and left it to dry. He closed the album and walked down the corridor to the bathroom. He splashed water on his face and cleaned his teeth thoroughly. He'd phone Sally Spencer in the morning. He wanted to know more about the suicide note. He undressed and got into bed. The words from the song ran round in his head and he hummed the tune. Then he lay on his side and slept.

*

The Kish light flashes twice, every thirty seconds. The Baily to the north is also white and flashes once every twenty seconds. The West Pier in Dun Laoghaire gives three green flashes every seven point five seconds and the light on the East Pier is white and flashes twice every fifteen seconds. And the Poolbeg? The Poolbeg is occulted, red, twice, every twenty seconds. 'Occulted'. Now that was a word she hadn't thought of or used for years. In the context of lighthouses it meant that it was a constant light, but it darkened or 'occulted' at pre-determined intervals. Is that what I am now? she thought, as she stood at the front window and watched the lights from the lighthouses in the bay. I am occulted, I am darkened by my acts. And how can I bring myself out into the light again?

She turned away. She opened the front door. It was still warm outside, but she shivered as she pulled on her jacket. She checked the pockets. Keys, purse, phone. She pulled the door closed behind her and walked down the steps. She needed to fill her lungs with air. Breathe the saltiness of the sea deep inside her body. She wouldn't be able to do it for much longer. She had to make the most of it while she could. She walked quickly along the road and past the Martello tower. Then she ran down the stone ramp towards the sea.

SEVEN

McLoughlin stood outside the small terraced house just off Ranelagh Road. Marina Spencer had lived here for the last year and a half, so her mother said. He put the Chubb key into the lock and tried to turn it. It resisted, and for a moment he thought it had jammed. He half turned it backwards, then tried again. This time it engaged fully and the barrels of the lock clicked. He pulled out the key and selected the Yale from the bunch in his hand. He slotted it into place. It turned smoothly. He pushed the door and it opened, the hinges squeaking. The sound set his teeth on edge. He stepped over the threshold and closed the door behind him.

'I'll give you her keys.' Sally Spencer had taken the bunch from a large brown leather bag. 'These are for the house. This is the car. I suppose these must be for her office. I don't know about the rest.' She held out the bag to him. 'Maybe you should take this too. It's got nearly all of Marina's life in it.' She shook it for effect. 'Her passport, driving licence, purse, cards, phone. Bills to be paid, bills paid, shopping lists. Make-up bag, hairbrush, toothbrush, toothpaste. Letters, photos, diary, you name it.'

'Did the guards give it to you?' McLoughlin hefted it in his hand.

'Yes, eventually. After they'd finished with their tests.'

'It wasn't in the lake?' He turned it over, noticed its scratches and blemishes.

'No, it was found in the house. It was under a bed, apparently.' Sally's mouth trembled. 'You will go there, won't you? You'll want to see exactly where she was found.'

'Yes, I will, but first things first. I want to see her computer. And tell me about the note. The suicide note. Where was it found?'

'In the bag. But it wasn't a note.' Sally faced him again. 'It was a scrap of paper, a few words.'

'So you saw it? Was it handwritten?'

'They showed it to me. Kind of. They had it in a plastic bag.'

'An evidence bag?'

'Yes, that's right. An evidence bag. It wasn't handwritten, it was typed. Well, computer-written, not typed, strictly speaking. And it didn't ring true. It didn't sound like Marina.'

'What did it sound like? What did it say?' McLoughlin tried to modify his voice so she wouldn't feel he was interrogating her.

She shrugged. 'Something about her begging me for forgiveness. How if I couldn't forgive her now maybe in the next.'

'The next?'

'Just the next. They seemed to think she meant the next life. But it's ridiculous. Marina was the most thorough-going atheist I ever met. She wasn't an agnostic. She had no doubt. She did not believe in an afterlife. We talked about it often. Even when her father died, when she was six, and I tried to soften it by telling her he was with God and the angels. Even then she looked at me as if I was mad. Marina was many things but she wasn't a hypocrite.'

McLoughlin didn't respond. There was no point in hurting her any more. But he remembered the many lectures about suicide he'd sat through. There was a standard form of suicide note. It was common to ask for forgiveness. It was usual to refer to the life to come. The frame of mind, the mental state, whatever you wanted to call it, that allowed the idea of suicide to take hold changed the person in the most fundamental way.

'You know, Sally, I've said I'll look into this. I don't have too much time. I'm supposed to be heading off to France in a week or so. But I have to say to you again, if the guards think Marina killed herself, then you can be sure she did. They don't make decisions like that on a whim.'

'I know, I know, I know all that.' Her anger and impatience were making McLoughlin nervous. 'I know the state pathologist did the post-mortem. I know he said that it was consistent with accidental death or suicide. I know all that. I just don't believe it. Look,' she held up her hands, 'consider this. The week after Marina supposedly killed herself I got a call from one of her neighbours. A deliveryman was at the door. He had a new fridge-freezer that she'd ordered three days before she died. Now, explain that to me. If you were suicidal would you be ordering fridges? Would you?' She was shouting now. Repeating the words over and over again.

He waited for her to finish. Then he picked up the bag. 'I'll be in touch.'

The little dog stood up and wagged its tail expectantly. Its brown, button-shaped eyes looked towards its lead hanging from a hook behind the door. Sally grasped its collar. She nodded dumbly in McLoughlin's direction and sank back down on the sofa. He could see she was exhausted. She'd had enough for one day. He reckoned she'd be asleep before he'd driven down the lane and out on to the main road. Sleep was good. Sleep was healing. And as for the new fridge-freezer, he'd heard variations on that story many times. New sofas ordered. Holidays booked. Tickets to see the Rolling Stones in Rio. They were all part of the terrible mystery of suicide.

The fridge-freezer was jammed into the small entrance hall. It was still in all its polystyrene packing. McLoughlin didn't know much about white goods, but this was an expensive brand. Stainless steel. A classy number. He pushed past and into the sunny, open-plan kitchen. It was all classy. Lots more stainless steel. A rail suspended from the ceiling with pots hanging from it. There were the usual touches of the twenty-first century. Eye-level oven, ceramic hob, island with a round stainless-steel bowl and a tap curved like a tightly held archer's bow. A glass door gave on to a small decked patio. There was a key in the lock. He turned it and stepped outside. It was a real sun-trap. Mica sparkled in the granite garden walls and heat radiated up from the faded wood. There were herbs planted in large terracotta pots. A miniature bay tree, and the feathery fronds of bronze fennel. Oregano and thyme. A large fragrant rosemary bush, and a few smaller pots with the pink tufted flowers of chives, and a couple of mint varieties. He reached down and checked the soil. It felt cool and damp. Someone must be coming in to water, he thought. He glanced around. The patio was overlooked on all sides, but there was no sign of life in any of the windows.

He moved back inside and locked the kitchen door. He walked towards the front of the house and into the sitting room. It was simply furnished with a wooden floor and a black leather sofa. Above the small cast-iron fireplace a large abstract painting glowed in reds, oranges and yellows. The coffee-table had a pile of glossy magazines. McLoughlin sat down. The sofa cushions gave way beneath his bulk with a gentle sigh. He flicked through the magazines. Some had pages marked, notes scribbled in pencil in the margins, and one had scraps of different-coloured fabrics pinned to an article about a new range of paint colours. He replaced the magazines in a neat pile. There were no books, no photographs, nothing personal in this room. It was clean and tidy, like the kitchen, but it could have belonged to anyone.

He stood up and went back out into the hall. He climbed the steep stairs. Ahead was a bathroom, as smart and stylish as the kitchen. Next door was a small bedroom. A large bed took up most of the space and the rest was filled with a mirrored wall of fitted cupboards. McLoughlin slid back the door. Clothes hung from a rail. Beneath them shoes were neatly stacked. A long row of drawers contained underwear, T-shirts, sweaters and a collection of scarves and gloves. Everything was neat and orderly. He searched through the clothes, feeling inside pockets. But there was nothing of any consequence. A couple of scrunched-up tissues. A bus ticket. A few coins. He slid back the mirrored door. He scrutinized himself. He needed a haircut. He didn't like to let his hair get too long on top. It made him look as if he was trying to cover up his gradually increasing baldness.

He walked out of the bedroom and through the other door on the landing. Now, this was more like it, he thought. A workroom or study. A desk covered with papers, books, and a couple of mugs, the dried-out dregs of coffee staining them inside. And, in pride of place, a large Apple screen. He sat at the desk. He reached for the power button and pressed it firmly. He waited for the hum, the familiar clicks and purrs and the machine's gradual return to life. The walls of this room were covered with pictures, some torn from magazines, others photographs. There was a collage of family snaps. He recognized a young Sally, petite and blonde with a turned-up nose and very blue eyes, and a child who was obviously Marina. And a handsome man, with Marina's eyes and cheekbones and her wide smile. What was it Sally had said? That Marina was six when her father died? They looked so happy together. But McLoughlin knew to be sceptical. How many family photos show anything other than the good days? he wondered. In all the houses he'd visited he couldn't remember ever coming across a family photograph that showed anything less than happiness. It was as if the camera acted as a tool of transformation, an alchemy for converting misery to joy, despair to hope.

He leaned closer to the wall and examined the photographs more carefully. They showed different scenes from around the same period. Marina seemed to be three or so. Her brother was a baby. The photos had been taken in different locations – a garden, somewhere by the sea, and others on a boat. She was variously holding the tiller, hauling on a sheet, and there were a couple in which she and her brother were sitting on the bow, their legs trailing over the side. In all of them she was wearing a life-jacket, one of the old-fashioned uncomfortable types with a stiff collar that supported the neck and head.

He turned away from the wall and pulled open the desk drawers. They were crammed with notebooks, sketchbooks, boxes of charcoal and pastels, all kinds of pens and pencils and small bottles of coloured inks. He was rummaging through them as the computer screen brightened and came to life. The blue Apple background was covered with folders. They all seemed to be work-related. He opened them in turn. Drawings and photographs, estimates, records of work completed, copies of invoices. She was doing well. Making money. He closed the files and scanned the folders again. One had the title 'my stuff'. He clicked it open. It contained five emails. He opened them, one after another. The sender names looked like the senders of Spam. Made-up usernames. Each had nothing in the subject line. He read down through them. Each had just one sentence. 'I SAW YOU'. The three words were in huge capital letters. He read them out loud: 'I saw you.' That was all. Three words. Nothing more. He opened the other folders again. Quickly, but systematically, working through the files. But there was nothing else that wasn't work-related. He sat back on the chair, then pressed the 'print' icon. The emails slid on to the floor. He picked them up, folded them in half, then in half again, and put them into his inside pocket. He closed the computer down and switched it off. He was hungry. It must be nearly lunchtime. He walked downstairs and opened the front door. He stepped out into the sunshine and reached into his pocket for the bunch of keys.

He walked away from the house. Somehow his appetite had disappeared. He pulled out his phone and flicked down through the names. He pressed the call button.

'Hi, Johnny. How's the voice? Better than the head, I hope.' He paused. 'Listen, can you do something for me? Marina Spencer – do you remember the name? Can I call in this afternoon? You owe me a favour after your performance the other night and I'm coming to collect. See you later.'

Johnny would sort it out. Separate the dross from the pure gold. Sieve out the speculation and leave the facts for all to see. So there could be no doubt when he faced Marina's mother again. There could be no doubt at all.

EIGHT

Margaret knelt before her daughter's grave. 'Hello, my darling,' she said, her voice low. 'And how are you today?' She set to work clearing the weeds that had taken over the gravel, which marked Mary's resting-place. 'Such a mess. All those years I've been away I should have got someone else to take care of it, shouldn't I?'

The pile of weeds grew. As she cleared away the accumulation of rubbish she found the stones and shells she had brought from New Zealand when she had come back to Dublin for Jimmy Fitzsimons's trial. She had gathered them from the beach below the house in Torbay. Now she took a large bottle of water from her basket and a cloth and cleaned the dirt from them. 'There, now, that's much better, isn't it? Look how the paua shell shines. Such beautiful colours. Do you remember when we used to go snorkelling? You didn't like it at first. But when you learned how to breathe and open your eyes under water it was so beautiful. And do you remember the time we saw the little octopus? And he was so shocked to see you, he shot away. And you got a fright too. And you swallowed all that seawater. Do you remember?'

She sat back on her heels. It was much better now. It was tidy and weed-free, and the shells and stones looked like they belonged there.

'I had to pull you out of the sea and you scraped your leg on the rocks when I was trying to lift you up. And the salt water stung so much you started to cry. And the only way I could stop you crying was to promise that we'd go to the ice-cream shop on the way home.' She smiled at the memory of that day, stood up and stretched. Her thigh muscles were stiff from the unnatural position. She stretched to ease out her back and shoulders. It was another sunny day and warm enough to have left the house without a coat. She pulled a large rubbish bag from the basket, stuffed the weeds into it and tied it tightly in a knot. She looked around for a bin. It was busy here today. From where she was standing she could see the stone walls of the chapel. A large crowd was outside and, as she watched, a group of black-clad pall-bearers slid a coffin from a hearse and shouldered it inside.

She looked down at her daughter's headstone. She read out the inscription:

> 'To see a world in a grain of sand,
> And a heaven in a wild flower,
> Hold infinity in the palm of your hand,
> And eternity in an hour.'

Mary had loved William Blake's work. She had carried a copy of *Songs of Innocence and Experience* everywhere with her. It had never been found. Above the inscription, Mary's name and her dates of birth and death were carved: 1975–1995. She would have turned thirty this year. She could have been a mother. She could have been anything. And I could have been a grandmother, Margaret thought. I could have seen the future spreading out towards infinity. Generations of my descendants. Keeping my memory alive. But there is none of me now. No one to look in the mirror and recognize me in their features. No one to remember her birthday. No one to weep for her or mourn her. No one to put up a headstone and tend her grave. For a moment she thought she would collapse with the weight of her despair.

She bowed her head. 'Bye-bye, sweetheart. I'll see you tomorrow. Sleep well, my darling.'

She walked slowly down the path, past angels and saints and Christs crucified. Then she stopped and put her hand into her trouser pocket. She pulled out a piece of paper and unfolded it. Se turned towards the chapel. The faint sound of music drifted out as she walked past the front entrance and around towards the back. She dumped the plastic bag in an already overflowing bin and went on towards the line of yews she could see in the distance. The security guard in the little hut at the front gate had written down the number of the grave and pointed out the way to her. 'It's over there beside the trees. You see the big tomb with the angel on top? Well, the one you're looking for is beside it. What was the name again?' He looked down at the hard-backed ledger on the desk. 'Holland, was it? Died in 2000. Yeah, here it is, Patrick Charles Holland. You can't miss it.'

The big tomb with the angel on top held Patrick's father and mother and his baby sister, who had died when she was three. Patrick's headstone was more modest. Black marble with the inscription picked out in silver. The grave was covered with marble chips and a large bunch of white lilies filled the still air with their cloying sweetness. Margaret put down her basket. She closed her eyes. The words came to her lips:

> '*Hail Mary, full of grace. The Lord is with thee.*
> *Blessed art thou amongst women,*
> *And blessed is the fruit of thy womb, Jesus.*'

Never forgotten, the old words, the old ways. A decade of the rosary. In times of trouble, at moments of crisis, the words came unbidden. Her father had been a man of strong faith and conviction. A conservative Catholic. Reared in the old way, his belief dominated by fear more than love. She hadn't realized until she became pregnant with Mary. She'd thought his sophistication, his education, his interest in books and music, the theatre and cinema meant something to him. They did, but not as much as his religion. When she'd told him about the baby she'd thought he would forgive her, that he would understand, that after a period of anger and grief he would continue to love and support her. But she had been wrong. He had listened in silence to her words. Then he had exploded with a fury she had never seen before. She wanted him to tell her that everything was all right, that he would look after her, but instead he had hit her across the face, the full force of his body behind his hand. And when she reeled backwards, losing her step and falling to the floor, he had stood and stared at her. And when she reached up to him and called to him for help, he had turned away.

She had prayed that night as she lay in bed. But the merciful God did not answer. And in the morning she left the house without speaking to her father. She never spoke to him again. She went to London, to an abortion clinic, but something happened there. The merciful God intervened. As she was lying on the trolley, the IV already in the back of her hand He gave her the strength to say no. That she would not have the abortion. That she would find another way.

But where had the other way led? She had been lulled into a false sense of security by all those years in New

Zealand when she had been out of reach. She should never have left. She should never have come back to Ireland. The old God was a vengeful God. He had lain in wait for her. And He had pounced and taken the only thing that mattered.

But still the words came. And she began to pray again, over and over, a repetitive drone that dulled the pain, closed down the senses so at first she didn't hear the voice, a girl's voice: 'Hi, sorry, I was wondering, do you know where I could get some water?'

She half turned. The girl had a bunch of bright marigolds in one hand and a glass vase in the other. She was small and slight with glossy brown hair that hung down her back. Her eyes were grey and her skin was sallow with a faint blush of pink across her cheeks. A row of silver rings decorated her ears and a couple of heavy silver chains were looped around her neck. She was wearing a long red skirt and a white blouse with an embroidered yoke and puffed sleeves. She might have stepped from the pages of a picture book.

'Oh, I'm not sure. Perhaps if you ask the guy at the gate. He'd know.' Margaret tried to smile as she spoke.

The girl frowned. 'That's a nuisance. I don't feel like going all the way back over there.' She looked for a moment as if she might cry.

'Here.' Margaret held out her bottle. 'There's a bit left in this. Take it if you like.'

The girl smiled and took it. 'Thanks, that's great.' She opened the bottle and emptied it into the small glass vase. She pointed towards the flowers on Patrick's grave. 'They're lovely, those lilies you brought. Except they make me sneeze. I've an allergy to the pollen.'

'The flowers? Oh, they're not mine.' Margaret shook her head.

The girl looked at her in a puzzled way. 'You didn't put them on Uncle Patrick's grave?'

'Uncle Patrick?' Margaret said. 'He was your uncle, was he?'

'Not my real uncle, not by birth, but he was a really good friend of my father and I always called him Uncle.' The girl stared at her feet. She was wearing red leather clogs. The kind that have a wooden sole. 'My father died when I was little and he's buried over there.' She waved the bunch of flowers in the direction of the trees. 'I thought I'd come and see him today. It's so nice here in the summer. It's quiet and no one bothers you.'

'Yes.' Margaret smiled at her. 'I know what you mean. They're funny places, graveyards, aren't they? Surprisingly beautiful, despite all the grief and sorrow they contain.' She paused. 'Your flowers are very pretty. I love marigolds. Did you grow them yourself?'

A flush spread across the girl's face. 'I didn't, actually. I pinched them from a neighbour's garden. I would have asked her but she was out. Anyway, I'm sure she wouldn't mind. I'll tell her when I go home. I will.'

Margaret wanted to laugh. The girl seemed suddenly awkward, embarrassed and very young.

'Well, I'm sure it's OK. After all, it's in a good cause, isn't it?' She bent her face to the flowers. 'Mm, I like their smell. Marigold flowers are supposed to be really good for blood circulation. Apparently the Arabs feed them to their horses.'

'I didn't know that. My father liked horses. He used to keep them once, so my mother says. When he was alive he had a lovely house and lots of land up in the Wicklow mountains. And he had horses up there. And deer. Anyway, I'd better do this.' She pushed the flowers carefully into the vase. 'Are you related to Uncle Patrick? I've never seen you before. Although,' she cocked her head on one side so the silver rings in her ears jingled, 'you do look a bit like his wife, Auntie Crea. In fact, I thought that was who you were when I saw you first. You're not her sister or something, are you?'

'No,' Margaret said. 'I'm an old friend of Patrick's from years ago. I've been living abroad for a while.'

'Oh, I see. OK, well, I'd better go. It was nice talking to you. But . . .' She looked away towards the group of head-stones under the tall yews.

'Sure, of course.' Margaret smiled. 'Nice to meet you.'

'Yes, you too. Of course, I should have brought more flowers. My sister is here too. Although she's in the new part, down by the road. It's not as nice there. It's noisy – traffic, you know.' The girl seemed suddenly stricken, as if tears would come at any moment.

'Your sister? Oh, I am sorry. Was she older or younger than you?' Margaret wanted to touch the girl. Give her comfort.

'She was older. Quite a lot older. I'm nearly eighteen and she was in her thirties. She was my half-sister, really. My father wasn't her father, you know?' The girl scuffed the ground with the toe of her clog.

'How very sad. For you and your mother too.' Margaret murmured. 'Don't worry about the flowers. I'm sure she'd understand. Why don't you just go and see her anyway? She'd like that.'

'Do you think so?' The girl's expression brightened. She

looked hopeful. 'They like it when you come to visit. The dead, that is. I'm sure they must be bored and lonely. I try to remember as many funny and interesting things to tell them as I can. I read to them too. You don't think that's stupid, do you?'

'No, it's great. My daughter's here too. And because I've been away I haven't visited her for ages. I'm sure she's missed me. But it's lovely that you care so much. What do you read?'

The girl reached into a big patchwork bag and pulled out a paperback. 'I've been doing Shakespeare's sonnets in school. For the Leaving Cert. And I love them. They're difficult to understand but the language is so beautiful. So I read them aloud and, actually, it helps. Listen to this.' She cleared her throat and flicked over the pages.

> *'Full many a glorious morning have I seen*
> *Flatter the mountain-tops with sovereign eye,*
> *Kissing with golden face the meadows green,*
> *Gilding pale streams with heavenly alchemy—'*

She broke off. 'Isn't that lovely? "Kissing with golden face the meadows green. Gilding pale streams with heavenly alchemy." I love it.'

'Yes, I love it too.' Margaret picked up her bag. Tears had suddenly filled her eyes.

'Well, I'd better go.' The girl shoved the book back into her bag. 'Thanks for the water and . . .' she smiled ' . . . well, just thanks.'

Margaret watched the bright figure thread her way through the graves. Then she turned back towards Patrick's headstone. She bent down and fiddled with the flowers. 'I'll come again. I won't leave it so long next time.' She picked up her bag and walked away down the gravel path. A robin hopped ahead of her, jumping on its springy legs from grave to grave, then fixing her with its bright eye. She clicked her tongue at it and it chattered back. Then, with a flurry of its smooth brown wings, it flew up into the dark branches of a spreading evergreen oak. She could see the girl now, her skirt a patch of brightness in the gloom. She was sitting cross-legged on the ground, the book in her hand. She lifted her hand as Margaret passed.

Margaret waved back, then went over to join her. 'I was just curious – I hope you don't mind. I was wondering who your father was.' She leaned down to look at the inscription.

'James de Paor,' the girl said, with pride in her voice. 'He was a barrister, like Uncle Patrick. Are you a barrister too?'

'No, I'm a doctor,' she paused. 'You must have been very young when he died. Only a baby.'

'Not quite a baby. Nearly one. I don't remember him. Although everyone says I look like him.' She uncrossed her legs, then crossed them again. 'It's funny, isn't it? Inherited characteristics. My mother says I sometimes say things that remind her of my father. And I have likes and dislikes, different foods, you know, that she says are the same as his. I sometimes think it's that she wants me to be like him so she's made me like him. You know what I mean?'

'Yes.' Margaret nodded. 'I used to think it was all nurture, and nature didn't matter, but I'm not so sure any longer. Anyway, it's good that you're like him. It must make it easier for your mother. To feel she still has a part of him in you.'

'Well, as long as she doesn't want me to do law. I'm not

going to get the points in the Leaving Cert for that. I'll be lucky if I get in to arts. But I don't care. And she's so miserable since my sister died that she won't care either.'

She opened the book again and flicked through the pages. Margaret watched her. Listened to her voice as she read the poem aloud again. Joined in as she walked along the path towards the main road:

> *'Kissing with golden face the meadows green,*
> *Gilding pale streams with heavenly alchemy . . .'*

She went through the high gates, then walked away towards the canal. She would pick up a taxi and be back in the house by the sea in no time. She was tired. She would sleep when she got home. And perhaps this time it would be a sleep without dreams.

NINE

'Why are you so sure it was suicide? Why not an accident?'
McLoughlin perched on the edge of a high stool at the lab
bench that served as Johnny Harris's desk, lunch counter
and lectern.

Harris picked a black olive from a plastic container. He
popped it into his mouth and sucked hard, rolled it around,
then spat the stone into his cupped hand. 'Mmm. These
are good. Where did you get them?' He helped himself to
another.

'Middle Eastern shop at the end of South Richmond
Street. The guys behind the counter are an unfriendly lot,
but they have lovely stuff. They keep those olives loose. And
lots of others too. Big, small, green, black, stuffed, un-
stuffed. But they also have tins of the small green ones that
are really good and incredibly cheap. Here,' he thrust a hand
into the plastic bag that nestled at his feet, 'have one.'

He put the tin on top of Harris's newspaper, obscuring
the half-finished Sudoku puzzle towards which Harris's gaze
kept straying. Harris picked up the tin and scrutinized it,
then put it down again. 'Got anything else of interest in
that bag?' His cheeks bulged with olives.

'A bunch of coriander, a lump of feta, some hummus.'
McLoughlin dumped them out. 'A large packet of ground
cumin, some paprika – oh, and these are nice.'

'Let's see?' Harris was positively drooling. 'What are they?'

'Pickled green peppers. Very hot, but dee-licious.'

Harris pushed his glasses up on top of his head and looked speculatively at McLoughlin. 'This is all great. And I'm sure we could carry on a long and fascinating conversation about the nature of Middle Eastern food and the rise of Islamic fundamentalism, but tell me, Michael, what do you really want?'

His friend didn't look good, McLoughlin thought. There were dark circles under his eyes and his skin, which usually had the ruddy health of a sailor, was grey and wan. 'And what's up with you? Too many late nights? Is that a healthy social life or are you sleepless for some other reason?' McLoughlin rummaged in the bag again and pulled out a large round of flatbread. He broke off a piece. 'Like some?'

Harris nodded, and for a moment McLoughlin thought tears were making his eyes shine so brightly.

'There's a knife in the drawer.' He reached over and pulled it out.

McLoughlin split the bread in half and filled it with hummus. He handed it to Johnny. 'So, Chicko's gone, has he?'

McLoughlin had never been able to understand Johnny Harris. He was a straight guy in so many ways. Great sailor and tennis-player. A churchgoer to boot. But such terrible taste in men. Chicko, small, dark and handsome, had been the last.

'Chicko? You want to know about the lovely Chicko? He said I was doing his head in. Whatever that means. So I'm on my own again. Footloose and fancy-free.' Harris managed a weak smile. Then he cleared away the remains of the food and wiped the counter-top with his handkerchief. He got up and opened one of the huge filing cabinets that lined the walls and tugged out Marina Spencer's records. 'OK,' he said, 'let's have a look at these.'

They were the photographs taken post-mortem, arranged in chronological order. The first showed Marina's body lying twisted on the rocks of the rapids. Her hair streamed out behind her head, pulled free by the flow of water. She was wearing a long dress with an exotic print. Her feet were bare. There were close-ups of her face, her hands, her torso. Her cheekbones and chin were bruised, but the rest of her body seemed untouched.

'Now, these are the ones that were taken here.' Johnny spread them out.

McLoughlin had seen such photographs tens, possibly hundreds of times before. They didn't shock him in the way they used to. Now he could break the image into its constituent parts. He knew what to notice. And what to ignore. He knew that it was important not to see the person as a person. 'What did you look for?'

'The usual. Signs of violence. Strangulation. Haemorrhage. Abrasions. Bruising etcetera. She has bruises on her face and, see here, on her ribcage, knees and thighs. But they're consistent with being carried down on to the rocks by the force of the water.'

'And nothing else, no sign that she was restrained, tied up in any way?'

'No, absolutely nothing. See here, these close-ups of her wrists and ankles? Not a scratch.'

'And she definitely drowned?'

'Absolutely. Here, I have the content of her lungs. See?

Lake water. And we both know that if she'd been dead when she went under she wouldn't have breathed so there would have been no water.'

'And what about her blood? What did that show?'

'OK. Alcohol, three hundred and sixty mls, traces of cocaine. Oh, and LSD. Lysergic acid diethylamide, the king or queen of the hallucinogens. A synthetic alkaloid related to ergot. She was out of it.'

' "Out of it"? Is that a technical term?' McLoughlin raised his eyebrows.

Harris smiled grimly. 'Very smart. LSD interferes with the natural action of serotonin in the brain. Induces severe hallucinations, what could be called temporary insanity, similar to schizophrenia. Given the combination of drugs she'd ingested, she would also have had bouts of nausea, followed by intermittent unconsciousness, leading to depressed breathing and eventually, possibly, death. So she was definitely out of it.'

'But not so out of it that she wouldn't have been able to get herself into the boat? If she was that bad I can't see how she could have rowed out into the lake. She must have gone quite a distance because otherwise she would have drifted into the shore close to the house. Where was the boat kept?'

'There's a photo somewhere. It was usually tied up at the jetty close to the house. But I doubt she would have been able to row from the house nearly the length of the lake. It must have been somewhere else that night.'

McLoughlin picked up a magnifying-glass and studied the pictures of Marina's head and face. 'And where did the dinghy end up?'

'Umm, let me see . . . Here.' Harris rummaged through

the pile. 'Yeah, here. It got stuck at the top of the rapids, jammed up against the rocks. So they were both caught in the same current.'

'But would she really have been able to manage in the boat? I would have thought she'd have passed out, and the boat would have drifted back into the shore, or even if it had ended up stuck on the rapids, she would have been found under a seat or something. From the amount of alcohol in her system it seems to me, the humble layman, that she might have died anyway from alcohol poisoning, but she wouldn't have drowned. What do you reckon?'

'Well, I reckon that what you say makes sense except for one thing. Have a look at the photo of the dinghy again. See there – what's that?' Harris took the magnifying-glass from him and angled it over the shiny black-and-white print. 'What is it?'

'Yeah, a bottle of Smirnoff. So what you're saying is that she got into the boat, rowed herself out, was probably drinking at the same time, and chucked herself over the side?'

'Well, that's consistent with the blood analysis. The fact that her blood alcohol concentration was so high suggests that she died very soon after drinking it.'

'And what about the others at the party that night?'

'I'm not the person to ask, Michael. You'd better go and talk to Brian Dooley. I'm sure you'll have no problem getting his files.'

'But why suicide, Johnny? I can see accidental, all right.'

'You've read the note, haven't you? I've read it. I've read lots of those notes in my time. It rings true.'

'Not to her mother, it doesn't. And I wasn't convinced either.'

'Well,' Harris began to gather up the photographs, 'it's the coroner's call, not yours or mine. From the physical evidence, she got into that boat on her own, she rowed herself out as far as she could, she got herself into the water and she drowned.'

'OK, you're the expert. I'm sure if there was force involved you'd have found signs of it. So . . .' His voice trailed off.

'Anyway,' Harris rocked back on his stool, 'what are you doing getting involved in all this? I thought you were on your way to Brittany or somewhere.'

'I'm waiting to hear the details. Paul Brady is to call me about it. In the meantime I thought I'd keep myself busy. Old habits die hard, you know.' He slid off the stool and picked up the plastic bag. 'Here,' he held out the bag, 'I'll leave you some of the goodies. Half of everything. The hummus, the olives and the bread. You take them. You look like you could do with feeding up. You're as skinny as hell, Harris, my boy. Take, eat and enjoy.'

The two men walked outside into the sunshine. McLoughlin's car was parked beside Harris's Range Rover, which looked as if it could do with a long session at the car wash. It was mud-spattered from top to bottom. Harris pulled out his gold pocket watch and flipped open the lid. 'Christ, look at the time. I was due at the morgue, like, half an hour ago.' He opened the rear door of the Range Rover and threw the plastic bag inside, next to his sailing gear.

'Anything interesting?'

'Not sure. Did you hear about the woman who was found dead in bed last night?' Harris fumbled with his keys.

'Yeah, it was Rathmines or somewhere, wasn't it?'

'That's right. Heart of suburbia. I had a quick look at her *in situ*. Hard to tell. Could be one of your suicides. Or could be what I've taken to calling "husband-assisted death".'

McLoughlin laughed and put his key into the lock. 'Lot of it about, these days You'd think with the legalization of divorce that guys would take the more conventional route to freedom.'

'Too bloody expensive and too slow.' Harris climbed into the Range Rover. He pressed a button and the window slid down. 'What is it about you straight blokes? Heterosexual relationships have got so dangerous. Don't know what the world's coming to.'

McLoughlin followed Harris out of the car park. He drove behind him as far as Stove Street and eventually saw him swing into his designated parking spot outside the city morgue. He was lucky. It was always a hassle going into the morgue – never anywhere to park. Especially during the week. It was easier on a Sunday. And Sunday was always a big day for bodies. It had been a Sunday, he remembered, the day he and Finney had gone to bring Margaret Mitchell to the morgue to identify her daughter's body. It had been a hot day like this. There hadn't been much traffic on the road into town. He remembered that Finney had been driving. He was driving fast, too fast. McLoughlin wanted to slow him down, give the woman in the back seat more time to prepare herself for what lay ahead. But there was no putting off the horror of the moment when he would pull back the sheet and reveal the child's face to the mother. He had waited for Margaret to respond. He asked the question he had to ask.

'Can you identify her? Can you tell us who this is?'

And Margaret had bowed her head, and said, without taking her eyes off Mary's face for an instant, 'This is the body of my daughter, Mary Mitchell.'

Then she had turned on him and Finney and screamed at them to get out and leave her alone with her child.

The lights turned green. He sat and stared at them until behind him the horns began to blow.

'All right, all fucking right!' McLoughlin shouted, as he inched forward. Ahead was the Matt Talbot bridge over the Liffey, and beyond it, the cranes on the skyline swung like old-fashioned weighing scales high above the new apartment developments. Marina Spencer had been working there, he thought, up to the time she died. He had seen the articles about her that her mother had cut from magazines and newspapers and put in the album.

He swung across the bridge and on to the quays, then turned right. A hoarding advertised the name of the development: Urban Living. He slowed to a crawl, then followed a line of trucks on to the building site. The tall central block of apartments was completed, but the other smaller buildings were still clothed in scaffolding. He bumped over the rough pot-holed ground and parked by the Portakabin that acted as a site office. Outside, the noise was deafening. Pneumatic drills, concrete-mixers and the general cacophony of modern building methods. McLoughlin ducked into the office. A young woman was seated behind a desk covered with piles of paper. She looked up at him and smiled. 'You want?' Her accent was east European.

'Perhaps you can help me. I'm wondering where Marina Spencer's office was?'

'Why you ask? Marina is gone. She is dead, you know.'

'I know.' McLoughlin leaned his two fists on the desk. 'I

know that. I'm a policeman, investigating her death. I wanted to take a look at her office.'

'A policeman, a Garda Síochána.' Her pronunciation was impeccable. 'The police they have been here already, few weeks back.'

'That's right.' McLoughlin felt in his jacket pocket for his wallet. 'I'm doing follow-up work. Tying up loose ends, you understand.' He held out his ID card.

Her eyes flicked across it, then back to his face. 'OK, you go to the apartments. You see sign for Inner Vision design company. They are on tenth floor. You go there, you find Becky Heron. She Marina's assistant. You ask her.'

It was as the woman had said. He followed the signs and took the lift to the tenth floor. As the doors opened he could hear the sound of a radio, the clatter and bang of workmen out of sight down the corridor. He walked towards the sound. And saw an open door and smelt fresh coffee. And heard a voice, saying, 'Come on in, the water's lovely.'

The girl holding the glass pot in her hand swung towards him, an expectant smile on her face. 'Oh.' The smile faded. She put the pot on a long trestle table which was strewn with swatches of fabric, rolls of wallpaper, piles of cushions and a haphazard collection of ceramic tiles. 'I thought you were someone else.' She squared her shoulders, the smile replaced by a look almost of reproach. 'Can I help you?'

'I was told I'd find a Becky here.' He felt like helping himself to a cup, the smell was so good.

'I'm Becky Heron. And you are?' Her tone was cool. She lifted her mug and took a sip. She was small and very pretty with blonde hair in a long plait that flopped over one shoulder. He tried not to stare at her naked stomach, decorated with a tattooed butterfly that disappeared below the waistband of her low-cut jeans.

'My name is Michael McLoughlin. Sally Spencer, Marina Spencer's mother, asked me to look into her daughter's, um, death. I just wanted to talk to you a bit about Marina and her work.'

'And what are you exactly?'

He could feel his self-esteem shrivelling beneath her supercilious gaze. 'Well, let's say that I know my way around the investigation of a suspicious death.' He took a step forward. 'Any chance of a cup of that? It smells fantastic. What kind of coffee is it?'

'Marina's favourite Colombian. She'd been to one of the plantations where it's grown. She has a friend out there still. He sends her packets of his special coffee from time to time.' Becky's lips quivered. She sat down on a high stool. 'I miss her so much. I can't believe she's dead. I keep expecting her to walk in. Every time I hear the lift doors open I think it's her. That's why I said that, about the water being lovely. She always used to say that when we heard people in the corridor.'

'Had you known her for long?' McLoughlin moved aside a pile of brocade cushions and put down his mug.

Becky shrugged. 'A year or so. I came here to do work experience after I left school. And I just kind of stayed. We got on great.'

'So how was she before she died? Did she seem depressed, upset, worried about anything?' He held out his mug for a refill.

'Not depressed. She'd get stressed, all right. This was a very big job and the developers are a right pain. She was a bit frantic, the last while. There was all that trouble over the vandalism in River View just as the apartments were being sold.'

'Vandalism? What was that?' McLoughlin sipped his coffee. He could feel the caffeine vibrating through his system.

'You know River View — just east of the Custom House? They were the first of the really flash apartments. Marina had just finished the show penthouses. They were absolutely gorgeous. And then some gurriers got in and splashed paint over everything. She was really upset. She had to call the painters back and get them to work through the weekend to clean it up. It was a nightmare.' Becky smiled. 'A real nightmare, but we had ways of dealing with it. When she'd finished it was late and she called me and asked if I was on for a stress-buster.'

'What was that?'

'It was Marina's way of getting rid of all the shit. We'd go dancing. Marina was a mad dancer.' Becky's eyes filled with tears. 'We had such a great time that night.'

McLoughlin waited for the sobbing to die down. He took out his handkerchief and passed it across the table.

'Sorry.' She sniffed loudly, then blew her nose. 'Sorry. I just really miss her. I can't believe she's dead. Even though . . .' she hesitated, '. . . even though I saw her, you know, in the coffin. I'd never seen a dead person before.' She closed her eyes as if to take away the sight.

'And how was it?'

'It was weird. She wasn't like herself. And there were all these people there I'd never heard of. And that guy was there, Mark Porter. He was carrying on as if he was her husband or something, but he wasn't. He barely knew her.'

Becky's face was flushed now. Indignation had cut through her sorrow.

'Mark Porter, and he would be who?'

'He was this guy she'd started seeing again. They'd gone to school together or something. He was kind of weird-looking. Very small, but huge muscles. Like a kind of mini Incredible Hulk. I called him the Hulkette. We used to have a giggle about it. Although she was always saying we shouldn't be cruel, that Mark had been through enough in his life. I could never figure out what Marina was doing with him.' And the tears came again.

'I'm sorry,' she whispered. 'I don't know why I'm crying so much. I should be getting over it by now.'

'There's no should about it,' he said. 'Grief is a funny thing. It comes and goes and then one day it doesn't come any more. Which doesn't mean you've forgotten the person, just that you can get on with your own life again. But you can't control grief. It will control you for as long as it wants. Best get used to the idea.'

It was easy to be wise when the grief wasn't your own, McLoughlin thought, as he walked towards his car. Becky's coffee was thrumming through his veins and his head and he felt slightly sick. He got into the driver's seat and pulled out his notebook. He should write it all down while the memories were fresh. Marina was stressed about work. But nothing out of the ordinary. She had told Becky about being invited to the party in the Lake House. She had said, according to Becky, that she was dreading going. That she had nothing but bad memories of the place. That she had never got on with her step-brother. So why go? Becky had said. And Marina had said it was because of Mark Porter. He really wanted her to go. He'd said all kinds of people would be there, people who would be useful for her business with big houses and money, the kind who were always redecorating, looking for new projects.

'I didn't understand it, really,' Becky had continued. 'She didn't need more work. She had as much as she could manage already. She'd just signed a contract with the same developers to do another complex out in Greystones.'

'So was she in love with this guy, this Mark? Was that it?'

'No, I don't think so.' Becky shook her head. 'It wasn't love or even sex or anything like that. I think it was guilt.'

'Over what?'

'She never really said. She started to tell me something about some stuff that went on at school. They all went to the same posh boarding-school. But then we got interrupted, and when I asked her about it later she said it was nothing and changed the subject.'

Not much to be going on with, McLoughlin thought, as he put away his pen and shoved his notebook back into his pocket. Except that he had managed to get hold of Marina's Filofax. It was sitting on the table right by his coffee mug. He hadn't beaten about the bush. He'd asked Becky straight out if he could have a look at it, and she'd said to take it.

McLoughlin smiled as he picked it up. 'Thanks, but are you sure you won't need it for the business?'

'It doesn't matter any longer.' Becky's face clouded. 'Actually, you're lucky you found me here. Today's my last day. I'm clearing things up. The developers have got a new company to take over.' She sniffed and pointed to a pile of cardboard boxes by the door. 'That's Marina's work stuff.

Her reference books, her contact files, her list of who's who and what's what. I'm not sure what to do with it. You take it, if you like.'

McLoughlin lifted his head from his notebook. A man in overalls was wheeling a trolley with the boxes stacked on it towards him. He got out of the car, went around to the back and opened the boot. 'In here, if you can manage,' he called, then stood back and watched as the man stacked the boxes neatly inside. McLoughlin slammed the lid and got back into the car. He'd take them all home with him, and when he was finished he'd deliver them to Sally.

He drove slowly across the rutted surface of the building site and out on to the road. As he stopped at the traffic-lights his phone rang.

'Hey, Paul, how's it going? When are we off?'

The news was not good. The wife of the boat owner had sprained her ankle. The trip was on hold.

'Shit, that's a pity. I was really looking forward to Brittany.' He slowed to take a corner. 'Anything else in the offing? I could do with something to occupy my time.'

But Paul Brady was noncommittal. He'd keep in touch and if anything else came up he'd be sure to let him know. McLoughlin disconnected the call and dropped his phone on the passenger seat. Oh, well, nothing he could do about it. He'd head for home. He'd a night's reading ahead of him. Keep his mind off his own problems, his own regrets, his own sadness. For just a while.

TEN

Flour, warm water, salt, sugar, yeast. Dough between McLoughlin's fingers, around the nails, sticking to his palms. He dumped the dough on to the floured board to be kneaded. Stretched, pulled out, then turned over, pressing down with the heel of the hand. Turn the dough clockwise. Pull, stretch, press, turn. Establish a rhythm. Feel the dough come together. Smooth and elastic. Then put it into a greased tin. Cover it with oiled clingfilm. Leave it. And wait. For the transformation to take place. For the yeast to work its magic. For the separate ingredients – flour, warm water, salt, sugar, yeast – to become one.

The appointments were for Monday mornings at nine a.m. They were written in red capital letters, with a red box drawn around them. The first one was for 10 January 2005 and she had written them down, into the future, right up until 19 December. The pages of her diary were stiff with ink, every scrap of paper covered with names, dates, phone numbers, email addresses, doodles, jottings. Until 21 June, the night she'd died. After that the pages were virtually unmarked, except for the appointments in red. The name written was Simpson. No first name, no title, no phone number or address. McLoughlin flicked through Marina's

Filofax to the address-book section. He opened the page at the S flap. He ran his eye down the list of names. Marina's handwriting was neat, precise and legible. But there was no Simpson.

He got up from the table and walked out into the hall. The large brown-leather bag was where he had left it, in the jumble of umbrellas and boots beneath the coat-stand behind the door. He picked it up and walked back into the kitchen, rummaging among its contents. He pulled out a mobile phone. The screen was blank, the battery dead. It was a Nokia, the same brand as his own. He plugged it into his charger and waited. After a few seconds it beeped and glowed, then darkened again. He opened the fridge and took out a bottle of Erdinger, he flipped off the cap and poured it into his glass. Then he went through into the sitting room. Marina's boxes were waiting. He sat down on the sofa, took a deep swallow of his beer, then untucked the flaps of the nearest one. Plenty to keep him busy until Marina's phone came back to life.

It was late by the time he'd finished. He sat back on his heels and surveyed the scene. There was a large pile of books. Heavy hardbacks. Brightly coloured. Another of the boxes had drawing-books filled with sketches. Birds, cats, dogs, trees, houses. People too. There were drawings of her mother. And a girl with sleek brown hair and almond-shaped eyes. She reminded him of someone, and of course it came to him: she was very like James de Paor. Must be the child, he thought, as he leafed through the rest of the books, the child who was born to Sally and James.

At the bottom of one of the boxes a large padded envelope

was addressed to Marina, and unopened. He ripped the flap. The scent of coffee filled the room. Inside was a brown-paper bag. He took it out, holding it with both hands. He ran his thumbs across the heavy paper. And felt something else inside. He opened it carefully. The coffee smell was over-powering. He took it into the kitchen and emptied it into a bowl. And saw the small plastic bags, the powdery substance they contained white against the coffee's dark brown grains. He got a serving spoon and fished them out. There were five in all. He unsealed one, licked a finger and stuck it in. The white powder coated his skin. He put it up to his mouth and touched it with his tongue. There was a sudden and unmistakable sensation of numbness. He walked into the kitchen and turned on the tap, held his hand underneath the stream of water and washed it thoroughly. A present from her friend at the coffee plantation in the hills above Medellín, no doubt. Some for herself and some for sale. A nice little sideline. No wonder she was such a good dancer on her nights at the club with Becky.

He poured the coffee into a Kilner jar and clicked the top firmly shut. He picked up the rest of the bags and put them into the freezer compartment of his fridge, then looked at the dough. It had risen way above the top of the tin. He could smell the yeast. He dumped it out of the tin on to the floured board. He balled his fist and banged it down hard on the dough. The air pushed out of it with a sigh. He put it back into the tin to wait for its second rising. Then took another bottle of beer out of the fridge. He opened it and walked into the sitting room.

The last box was filled with papers and letters. And underneath them all, another brown envelope: A4 with a stiffened back. 'PHOTOGRAPHS DO NOT BEND' was written across the front beneath a label on which her name and address were printed. The flap was torn open, but tucked back inside. He pulled it free and slid out the contents. And rocked back on his heels with surprise. There were five large black-and-white photographs. He spread them on the floor. They all showed variations of the same scene: a woman at different stages of undress. The first showed her wearing jeans but no blouse or sweater. In the second she was in her bra and pants. Then came a huge close-up of her bare breasts. In the next she was naked. Her face was out of focus, but from her colouring and the general shape of her body it was clear that it was Marina. McLoughlin turned over the photographs. Each bore a small sticker, the kind that would usually give the name of the photographer. But these did not. He read the words out loud. 'I saw you,' he said, then repeated, 'I saw you.'

That was all.

McLoughlin picked up the envelope again. There was no stamp, no postmark, just the label with Marina's name and home address. He looked again at each of the photographs. They were taken from an angle that suggested the camera had been placed above the woman. They were not posed. She had not known what was happening. McLoughlin had seen enough clandestine photography in his time in the Gardaí to grasp that. 'A fucking peeping Tom,' he muttered, as he stood up, stretched and moved back into the kitchen.

He was trying to remember the layout of Marina's bedroom. Had he noticed anything suspicious? Anything that might have alerted him to surveillance equipment? There were no unusual light fittings, as far as he could remember, but these days cameras were so tiny they could be fitted anywhere. He opened the fridge and took out his share of the hummus, the olives and the flatbread. He tore off a piece of bread and spread it generously with hummus, took a large bite and looked at Marina's mobile phone. The screen was blank. He picked it up and pressed the on button. The words 'enter pin number' appeared. He tried a few simple variations but none did the trick. He picked up the Filofax and turned to the address book. He flipped it open at H. He ran his finger down the page. It was late, but Becky would still be up. She's young, he reasoned. But her voice was sleepy and he had a pang of guilt. He explained what he wanted.

She yawned. 'Her pin number? Yeah, I know it. She had a friend who was into numerology and had given her a combination she said was lucky.'

0785. He picked up the mobile phone and tapped it in. Then he sat down at the kitchen table and scrolled through the list of names. And there at last was Simpson. Simpson, Gwen. And a phone number. He helped himself to more hummus, then pressed the call button. The phone rang and a message clicked in. 'This is Gwen Simpson. My office hours are nine a.m. to five thirty p.m., Monday to Friday. Leave a message and I will call you back. Thank you.' He stood up and hunted through the pile of cookery books on the dresser. The phone book was at the bottom. He leafed through it. Here she was. Simpson, Gwen, PhD, Psychotherapist, and an address in Fitzwilliam Square with the same phone number. He sat down again and finished off his flatbread and hummus. It was delicious. He must remember to put some chickpeas on to soak tonight and make some himself tomorrow.

He picked up Marina's phone again and scrolled through the menu. He selected 'messages' and went to the inbox.

There were several unread ones. He began to open them. Some were from Sally, wondering where she was, what she was doing, asking her to phone. The others were from Becky, with the same queries. He moved on to 'archive'. Marina had saved a number of her voicemails. He selected the first and listened. A child's voice whispered, 'I saw you.' His hand jerked with surprise and he dropped the phone. It crashed on to the tiled floor. He bent down, picked it up and selected the next message. This time it was a man's voice. The message was the same. 'I saw you,' he said, his tone neutral. McLoughlin listened to each of the ten saved messages. Each said the same thing, although the voices were different. Men and women, old and young, and there was even a voice with an American accent. He checked the numbers: Dublin land lines. He picked one and pressed call. It rang out. He tried the next and the next and the next. Eventually one was answered. A young man's voice with a strong Galway accent shouted, 'Howya,' and laughed. The background noise was loud. There was music, distorted, and the unmistakable buzz and hum of a bar.

'Who's that?' McLoughlin asked.

'Why d'ya want to know?' the voice responded.

'Is that a pub, a bar?'

'What d'ya fucking think?' the voice shouted back.

'I just want to know, where is this phone?' He tried to keep his voice calm.

'What's it worth?' The voice was high-pitched, almost hysterical.

McLoughlin could imagine the scene. Late-night drinkers, a messy bunch at the best of times. He tried to remove all sound of confrontation from his voice. 'Listen, do me a favour. I missed a call from my wife. She's off on the tear and I want to come and pick her up. Can't work out where she is. She's a terror when she gets going.'

There was silence for a moment. Shit, McLoughlin thought. I've taken the wrong tack. He'll hang up.

But the voice sounded more sober: 'Is she a blonde? There's a gang of girls in here. They're all blondes, all hammered. One of them's just started singing.'

'That'll be her. Tell me where she is and I'll be in to pick her up.'

'It's the Mercantile, in Dame Street. D'ya know it?'

'I do, thanks. You're a star. Tell her I'll see her in half an hour.'

He laughed as he finished the call. That'd be one confused lady. He knew the Mercantile. He could picture the scene. Drinkers crammed into every corner, the noise at headache level. And the phone on the wall at the back by the door to the toilets. He was pretty sure if he'd got through to any of the other numbers they would have come from the same kind of phone. He'd get on to Tony tomorrow, ask him to check them out.

He could smell the dough now. He opened the oven and pushed the tin inside. Then he picked up his beer, slid back the glass doors and stepped outside on to the terrace. It was warm tonight. Heat rose from the stone flags. The city glowed and sparkled in the distance. Poor Marina, he thought. What on earth had been going on in her life? He stepped off the terrace and felt the softness of the lawn beneath his feet. He walked down the slope towards the beech hedge that separated his garden from the fields. He stopped and made a clicking sound with his tongue. A large dark shape moved towards him. There were horses in the field, a couple of mares with whom he was on speaking terms. He held out his hand and waited. The small chestnut with the perfect white star on her forehead got to him first. She poked her head forward and sniffed his fingers. Her nose was soft and wrinkled. She snuffled and blew warm, wet air towards him. He reached out and pushed her forelock back, then dug his fingers into the softness beneath her mane and scratched hard.

' 'Bye, girl.' He stepped away and began to walk back up the slope.

He was tired now. He would leave it until the morning. He went back into the kitchen. The bread was done. He pulled out the tin. The loaf was a beauty, perfect for tomorrow's breakfast. He moved to the store cupboard and took out a packet of chickpeas. He shook half into a saucepan and covered them with water. He looked out again into the darkness and had a sudden image. The lights from his kitchen shining out through the patio doors. Visible for miles around. And the man holding the saucepan. Middle-aged, overweight, unfit, defenceless, his guard down. A target, a sitting duck. The nearest house out of earshot. He put the pan on to the hob, picked up his phone and backed out of the kitchen, switching off the lights. He walked around the house, checking the windows and doors, then turned on the alarm. He had had it fitted at the height of the Provo campaign. Better safe than sorry, everyone had said. You don't want to wake up with the muzzle of an Armalite jammed against your cheekbone, or come home to a ransacked house. Perhaps it was because of his age, or because he could no longer carry a gun, but somehow he felt safer when the electronic beeps signalled that the system had been activated.

He walked into the sitting room and picked up the

photographs of Marina. He slid them back into the envelope and carried them into his bedroom. He opened the top drawer of his bedside table, lifted up the pile of old letters and laid the envelope beneath them. They'd be safe there, he thought, out of sight. He took off his jacket and hung it on the back of a chair. Then picked it up again and slipped his fingers into the inside pocket. He pulled out the folded emails. He opened the drawer and slipped them in with the photographs. Then he undressed and got into bed. Was it blackmail? he wondered, as he switched off the light and buried his face in the pillow. Whatever it was it hadn't been fun. A reason to kill herself? What was it she'd said in her note? She was looking for forgiveness. For what? What could she have done that would have caused her to take her own life? He thrashed around in the bed. He couldn't get the words out of his head. 'I saw you.' What could someone have seen Marina do? What was so bad that it could be used to frighten her, threaten her, upset her? He had been the one who saw. He knew what it was like to be the clandestine watcher.

He spoke the words out loud: 'I saw you, Margaret. I saw what you did.'

Eleven

It was the girl from the graveyard. She was sitting on the sea wall across the road from the house. She was eating a Magnum. Margaret watched her. She was carefully picking off the pieces of chocolate and slipping them into her mouth. Then, when she had removed all traces she began to lick the ice-cream, shaping it into a tall toadstool, then wearing it away with her tongue until nothing was left but the wooden stick.

Margaret moved her position, gazed up and down the road. The girl seemed to be on her own. It was quiet outside today. Too early for the usual crowds, coming from the city to sunbathe, swim and sit in their big family groups.

She picked up her basket and opened the front door. She closed it firmly behind her, pushing back against it to make sure that the lock had caught. Then she walked quickly down the steps and along the path. As she opened the gate the girl turned towards her. She slid off the wall. Her feet in her wooden clogs clicked on the ground. She smiled. 'I know you, don't I?' she said. 'I met you at Uncle Patrick's grave.'

'That's right. You did.'

'Fancy meeting you out here,' the girl said. 'Do you know Aga, the Polish girl who lives there?'

Margaret shook her head. 'She doesn't live there any longer. I do now.'

'Oh,' the girl smiled, 'she was really nice. Very friendly. All the Poles are like that. They seem to specialize in niceness.'

Margaret breathed in the salty smell. 'I have a forwarding address for her, if you want it.'

'No, that's OK. I was just curious. I live up the road in Trafalgar Lane. And we're a nosy lot. We know everyone. And, well, of course, this house,' she waved a hand, 'well, this house is special, really.'

Margaret straightened. 'In what way?'

'Because it's . . . well, you know . . . It's where that girl lived. It was ages ago, I was only little, but there was a girl who lived in that house and she was killed. It was terrible.' The girl stopped. She looked at Margaret. 'Oh, of course, I'm really sorry, I'm a terrible chatterbox, my mother's always warning me to think before I speak. But I never do. I'm awfully sorry.'

Margaret moved away from the wall. She set off along the road towards the Martello tower. The girl kept pace with her. Margaret tried to speak but her throat was tight.

The girl's face had gone bright red. 'I didn't think. I thought you were living in New Zealand or somewhere. When I met you yesterday I was sure I knew you. It's because you look very like the girl, Mary. She was your daughter, wasn't she?'

'Yes,' Margaret said.

'She was so pretty. She was lovely. We gave her a lift into town one day.'

'You did?' Something else she hadn't known. Someone else who could tell her something about Mary.

The girl nodded, and a lock of hair plaited with beads swung from side to side. 'I remember it too. She was waiting for a bus and she stuck out her thumb to hitchhike and my mother said she shouldn't be doing that because it's not safe, so she stopped the car and Mary got in. I remember she was nice. And Mum told her she could get the bus or the DART into town, that she shouldn't hitchhike because it wasn't safe and you never knew who you were getting into a car with.' The girl spoke in a rush without taking a breath.

You never know whose car you're getting into. It's raining, one of those heavy, thundery showers that you get in summer. And you're standing at the bus stop, the rain sluicing down your face, your body, dripping into your little strappy sandals. And you put out your thumb and you're laughing because you're getting so wet. And a young man with hair the colour of a Botticelli angel, driving a big black car, a Merc or a BMW or something like that, a big black car that looks safe and secure and somehow almost official, slows down and pulls over and leans across and says to you out of the open window, 'You want a lift?'

Stop, Mary, just stop and think. But you don't. Maybe you take one look at him, at his smile and his even white teeth and his blue eyes and his fair hair and his smooth skin, and your heart beats faster and you lean into the window and say, 'Thanks, that would be great.'

And that's how it all begins.

'Can I ask you . . .' Margaret turned to her again. 'By the way, my name's Margaret Mitchell.'

The girl held out her hand. 'I'm Vanessa — Vanessa de Paor.'

They shook. Vanessa's grip was cool and firm. 'Tell me,' Margaret said, 'did you ever see my daughter again?'

'Mm.' Vanessa stopped. 'I don't think so. I just remember that one time.'

It was quiet by the sea. A gull floated overhead. It cried out, its harsh voice loud. Margaret followed its progress with her eyes. It glided on an updraught, then banked and swooped low over the ridged sand. It landed, its wings stretched wide, and began to drag a worm into its maw. She watched as the gull gulped and swallowed it whole. 'Your mother, how is she?' Margaret touched Vanessa's arm. 'Didn't you say when we met the other day that your sister had died? Was that recent?'

'It was just a few weeks ago. Midsummer's Night. The shortest night of the year. She'd gone to a party given by my half-brother, Dominic. It was in the house in the Wicklow mountains that had belonged to my father. She went out in a boat and she drowned. The police think it was suicide.'

'And what do you think?' Margaret watched the seagull. It had found a crab and was holding it by the claw in its beak.

Beside her Vanessa played with her hair. 'I don't know. She was a lot older than me and she hadn't really lived here for ages. She'd come back to Dublin about a year ago. It sounds like it might have been an accident, but she left a note.' She paused. 'But my mother doesn't think Marina killed herself. She says she wasn't the type to do it.'

The type to do it. Margaret repeated the words to herself. Who was the type to do it? She had thought she would be. She had tried it. Not long after she left Ireland, after that night in Ballyknockan. When she had gone to Noosa on the Queensland coast and she had walked down the narrow sandy beach in the cool of the evening and immersed herself in the water. It was lukewarm, not much different from the temperature of the water in her shower, and she had lain back, her head parallel to the sand beneath. The sea had covered her ears so she could hear nothing but her heart beating and her breath sucking air in and out of her body. And she had thought that she could float out to sea. No one would see her, no one would notice that she was gone. No one would miss her or come searching for her. But she mustn't have been as ready for death as she had thought because when she swallowed some seawater she felt sick, so she raised her head to clear her throat and then she saw that she wasn't drifting out at all. She was being carried back on to the beach and if she put her feet down she could feel the soft sand between her toes. And she was glad. And she dragged herself out and lay on the sand until the night cold drove her off the beach and into her hotel room to stand under a hot shower, to wrap herself in a bathrobe and to order food and drink from room service. And she remembered how good that steak sandwich and that bottle of wine had tasted. And she had wanted to cry out her apology to Mary that she wasn't ready yet to join her. And so she would go on living. And as time passed it was not only her pain that consumed her, but her guilt as well.

'So she drowned, however it happened. And, of course, what makes it even worse for my mother is that it was in the same place where my father drowned.' Vanessa stooped to pick up a shell. Her hair swung forward across her face but Margaret could see the tears. She said nothing. Vanessa wiped her face with the back of her hand and jumped down from the path on to the beach.

'I'm going to paddle.' She kicked off her clogs and ran towards the sea. 'Are you coming?' she shouted over her shoulder. Margaret slipped her feet from her sandals and followed slowly. The sand was wetter here. Every step created a small pool around her feet. She wriggled her toes and felt the suck of the mud below. And heard the girl calling to her: 'Hey, come and have a look at this. It's a giant, an absolute giant of a jellyfish. Come and look. Quick.'

It was floating in the shallow water, shocking pink and purple, the size of a large dinner plate, its tentacles splayed around it.

'Careful.' Margaret's voice was sharp. 'Mind it doesn't sting you.'

Vanessa's skirt was wet around the hem.

'It's so pretty, isn't it? Why is it so pretty, do you think, when it's dangerous? Is it so everyone will notice it and stay away?' She bent over, one finger poised above its soft, floating back. 'But you'd think, wouldn't you, that it would be the other way round? If it was ugly it would be dangerous, and if it was pretty it would be harmless.'

Margaret didn't answer. Jimmy Fitzsimons had been pretty, so pretty with his bright blond hair and his smooth pale skin. And his smile – what a smile. He had come to Mary's funeral, that terrible day in the church in Monkstown, and he had smiled at her and she had smiled back at him. A reflex action, the way a mother smiles at her baby. The corners of her mouth dragged out to the side and her teeth showing. Of course, she hadn't known who he was then. It wasn't a betrayal of Mary. It was only later that she knew who he was and what he had done. And then she had punished him. And the last time she saw him he wasn't smiling. He was terrified. His face was white with the fear of what lay ahead. He would have done anything to get her to let him go. But it was too late. It was too late for all of them.

Margaret stepped away from the jellyfish. 'I don't know

about you but all this sea air is making me hungry. I'm on my way to Monkstown to do some shopping. Would you like to come with me? We could have a cup of coffee and maybe a scone or something.'

'Yes.' Vanessa nodded. 'That would be very nice. I'd like that. Thank you.'

'You don't need to thank me. It's my pleasure.'

'Well, I want to thank you for being kind to me. And for listening to me. It's kind of difficult at the moment. My mother's in a state all the time. And my friends are away. Gone for the summer.' She tiptoed out of the water, holding up her skirt. 'I was to go too. But then Marina died and everything changed.'

Everything changed. Nothing the same again.

They walked along by the railway line, up and over the metal steps. Vanessa was silent.

'Your father . . .' Margaret began.

'Yes?'

'He had been married before he married your mother, is that right?'

'He was married and he had a son, Dominic, my half-brother.'

'And what happened to his wife?'

Vanessa sighed. 'Well, from what I know, she was, is, a difficult person. Apparently she has all kinds of problems. According to my mother she's been mentally ill for years. I'm not sure exactly what's wrong with her but apparently she was in and out of hospital all the time she was married to my father. Anyway, again, all I know is what my mother has told me, and that is that my father divorced her. Afterwards he met my mother and they got married and I was born.'

'And how did he die?' Margaret glanced at Vanessa. 'That is, if you don't mind me asking. If it's not too . . .'

'No, no.' Vanessa's voice was suddenly loud. 'No, really, it's fine. It's good to be able to talk about it. He drowned in the lake. He and Marina were out in a boat and there was an accident. She tried to save him, but he couldn't swim and he died before she could get help. And then everything was different.'

Margaret said nothing. She waited.

'Because after he died his first wife, Helena, challenged the divorce. She said that he had lied about where he lived. He had said his domicile was in England. So she went to court and the court decided that the divorce was invalid. So my mother wasn't his legal wife. And therefore I wasn't his legitimate child. I was illegitimate. A bastard.' Her small face was very white.

'It's just a word, Vanessa. It means nothing. You were still his daughter, still his flesh and blood.' Margaret put a hand on her shoulder and stopped her.

'But it meant a lot to my mother. And my father hadn't changed his will after he supposedly married her. So my mother inherited nothing. My father had been very wealthy. He had a couple of houses. He had investments, savings, all kinds of stuff. And she got nothing.' The tears were seeping from her eyes, trickling down on either side of her mouth. 'But I was lucky. The law changed not long after I was born and I was recognized as his heir, like Dominic. So my mother was able to get maintenance for me. And in two weeks' time, when I'm eighteen, I'm going to inherit part of his property. There's a little cottage up by the lake, and apparently it's going to be mine. Not that I care. Not that I want it. I don't want anything that came from him. I don't like what he did. If his first wife was ill, he shouldn't have tried to get rid of her. It doesn't seem right to me.'

They had reached the café by the church. There were tables outside. Margaret gestured to the chairs and they sat down.

Margaret spoke slowly. She picked her words carefully. 'Sometimes it can be hard for a child to understand the world their parents inhabit. Sometimes it's not as straightforward, not as cut and dried. There's a lovely book, *The Go-Between* by a man called L. P. Hartley. Do you know it?'

Vanessa shook her head.

'Well, it's about a boy who becomes involved in a secret relationship between two people he loves. He takes messages from one to the other, but he doesn't realize what's going on between them. And when he finds out he's devastated. The opening lines are "The past is another country. They do things differently there." And I'm afraid it's true.'

Vanessa looked at her, then away. She said nothing. Margaret took her hand. 'Don't judge your father and mother too harshly. The one thing you can be sure is that he loved you and she still loves you. Of that there can be no doubt.'

Vanessa didn't answer. They sat in silence. Margaret gazed past her towards the church. She would go there when they had finished. Back to the church where she had first met Jimmy, that day of thunderstorms, when lightning had cut through the sky. And he had slashed her blouse from neck to waist, tried to terrify her, the way he had terrified Mary. But she had stood up to him. And he had seen her for what she was. She would push through the heavy wooden door, and sit, bathed in the light from the stained-glass windows. And she would ask for forgiveness. Perhaps she, too, would not be judged too harshly. Perhaps the Lord would make His face to shine upon her. And remain with her. Always.

TWELVE

She was a busy woman, Gwen Simpson, PhD. McLoughlin had phoned a number of times and got the answering-machine. Each time he'd left a message. She hadn't responded. Now he was standing outside the house in Fitzwilliam Square where she had her office. He scanned the brass plates and pressed the bell beside her name. As he did so, the door opened. A man stood in front of him. He was very small and stocky, dressed in jeans and a leather jacket. He was putting on a motorbike helmet.

'Hold on a minute, if you don't mind.' McLoughlin took a step forward and put out his hand to stop the door from swinging shut.

'You looking for someone?' The man stood in his way, doing up the strap. The helmet gleamed in the bright sunshine.

'Yeah, um Dr Simpson – she's here, isn't she?'

The man pointed to the brass plate. 'That's her. First floor at the front.' He flipped down the visor. McLoughlin's face loomed back at him.

'Thanks.'

The man turned away and McLoughlin pushed past him into the hall. He heard the heavy door slam behind him. There was silence and a sense of cold. He shivered and headed for the stairs.

*

The receptionist said that Dr Simpson wouldn't be able to see him. She was fully booked for the whole day. McLoughlin said he wasn't in a hurry. He would wait. He sat down on the deep, comfortable sofa and sifted through the magazines. They were new and unthumbed. There was even a recent edition of *Classic Boats*. He turned to an article on the restoration of the Roaringwater Bay fishing fleet. Next time he met Johnny Harris he'd surprise him with his expertise. He sat back, crossed his legs and began to read.

It was after five by the time the receptionist came to get him. He'd spent a surprisingly pleasant afternoon. He'd helped himself to coffee from a large Thermos-type jug and biscuits from the selection on offer. He'd watched a succession of Dr Simpson's clients come and go. Most were women. Most were young and obviously affluent. All were clean and shiny. He couldn't imagine how any of them had problems they might need to share with the so far unseen Dr Simpson. The receptionist kept herself busy. There was a little alcove behind her desk. She had a kettle there and every now and then she would boil it and make herself tea. Or open the little fridge on the shelf and take out a bottle of mineral water, place it on a tray with a glass, ice and a slice of lemon and carry them in to Dr Simpson. It was a neat arrangement, McLoughlin thought. A very good use of space. A lesson in ergonomics or whatever it was called.

And then his name was called. He pulled himself up out of the softness of the sofa and stretched.

'She'll see you now, Inspector McLoughlin.' The receptionist glanced pointedly at her watch, then came over to collect his dirty coffee cups and straighten the heap of magazines.

Dr Simpson's office was a beautiful room. It had classic

Georgian proportions. A high ceiling with an elaborate rose
and cornice. Two long sash windows, one of them open a
few inches at the bottom. A crystal chandelier swung gently
in the breeze, making a soft musical sound. The walls were
painted a dull grey-green and there was a deep carpet to
match. Dr Simpson was seated at a desk. It was beautiful
too. Modern, simple, a wide piece of polished wood with
elegant iron legs. Her head was bent over a pile of papers.
She didn't seem to register his presence. She carried on
writing. He swayed uneasily from side to side. He cleared
his throat and looked around. A low couch was pushed
against the far wall. It was covered with smooth red fabric.
He had a sudden desire to surrender himself, to lie back,
close his eyes and talk. Let it all flow out.

'Sit down, why don't you, Inspector McLoughlin?' she
said. She still hadn't raised her head.

He did as he was told, slipping on to one of the upright
chairs facing her. He scrutinized the top of her head. Her
hair was grey, pulled back into a no-nonsense bun. She was
wearing a cream wrap-around blouse, which showed a small
amount of pale cleavage. Neat gold discs shone from her ear-
lobes and her hands were well cared-for, the nails painted
red, and a couple of large gold rings on her third and little
fingers.

He recognized some of the paintings on the walls. There
was a Norah McGuinness abstract and something that might
have been a Mainie Jellett. And was that a Le Brocquy? It
was small but the style was unmistakable. There's money in
the therapy business, he thought.

'So,' she sat up straight, and laid her pen neatly on her
pad, 'Inspector McLoughlin, you're a very persistent man.
I'm surprised you have the time to hang around in my

waiting room all afternoon when a phone call would have done.'

'I tried that,' he smiled at her, 'but I wasn't getting anywhere so I thought a bit of direct action was called for.'

'Right.' She leaned back in her chair and it swung slowly. 'I see.' There was silence in the room, broken only by the tinkle of the chandelier.

'It's nice.' He gestured above his head. 'Very soothing.'

'You think so? Some people find it irritating.' Her long, thin face was without expression. He noticed the dark circles beneath her eyes and the lines around her mouth. Unlike her clients she didn't seem to need the ameliorating effect of make-up.

'Wind chimes are irritating. It's the size of the pieces of metal. But those glass drops are so tiny and delicate. Their sound is much more subtle. I think anyway.'

'Mmm.' Her mouth tightened. 'Perhaps. But you didn't come here to talk to me about sound and its effect on the emotions, did you, Inspector McLoughlin? You told my receptionist you wanted to see me about Marina Spencer. I'm surprised the guards have so much time to spend on her death. I've already spoken at length to Inspector Brian Dooley. I understood he was in charge of the case.'

'Yeah, well, he is.' McLoughlin shifted awkwardly. Suddenly he was very uncomfortable. 'But sometimes someone else is asked to take a look, you know. A fresh pair of eyes and all that.'

'Fresh pair of eyes. Mmm. Jackie phoned Brian Dooley. He was surprised that you were here. He said that not only were you not involved in the case, but that you had retired recently. He said something unrepeatable about you. Funny but unrepeatable.'

There was silence. Even the chandelier was silent.

'OK. OK, I hold up my hands.' He squirmed. For the first time since he had come into the room Dr Simpson smiled. The effect was transforming. The years fell away. She became young and attractive. 'I'm not officially involved in this whole thing. But I'm a friend of Marina's mother. She's very upset.'

'Understandably.' The smile had gone.

'She doesn't believe that Marina's death was suicide. So I said I'd make a few enquiries. See if I could shed any light on what happened. I saw in her diary that she was visiting you regularly. So I thought maybe you might be able to tell me something of what was going on in her life.' He waited. Would the smile come back? It didn't.

'Look, Inspector, Mister, Whatever-you-are, I'm bound by a code of ethics. I gave some information to Inspector Dooley because I felt it would help him. I have no such obligation to you. As far as I'm concerned, you've no more right to know anything about Marina Spencer than any Joe Bloggs outside in the street. Now,' she paused to let the weight of her words make their mark, 'it's getting late. I've had a long day so perhaps you might take yourself off?' She stood up.

'Look,' he stood too, 'I'm sorry I tried to pull the wool over your eyes. I just wanted to ask you, was Marina hiding something? Was she scared of someone? I think she was being threatened. Did she tell you about it?'

She looked down at her desk. 'Threatened? She was threatened by a lot of things. Fear of failure. Loss of love and respect. And, yes, there were things about her past she was hiding. Marina had secrets. But we all have secrets. We all have nasty little things in our past that we wish we hadn't done. Marina had her share of them. That's as much as I'll say to you.' She shuffled some papers.

'So were you surprised when she died? Did you think she was suicidal?'

'If I'd thought that I would have treated her differently. But suicide is a mysterious act. The problem is that after someone takes their life everyone tries very hard to find ways to understand what happened. They start looking for signs, for hints of what was to come. But we can't know what the suicidal state of mind is like. Because, above all, we want to live and we cannot understand someone who does not want that any longer.' She sighed. 'Look, I would help you if I could. The answer to your question is that I didn't know she was going to die by suicide. I was very surprised when I heard what had happened. In one way, that is. But there again, she was at times very self-destructive. She abused alcohol. She abused drugs. But she did have moments of intense happiness. She was a very vivid person. I have to say that I miss her.' She moved away from her desk and across to the window. She was smaller than he had realized, her size emphasized by the wide linen trousers she was wearing. She stretched up towards the catch and slid the window closed. Then she undid the heavy curtain ties on either side of the wooden architrave and pulled the curtains together.

McLoughlin moved towards the other window. The curtains were a heavy grey brocade.

'These are lovely,' he said, as he loosed them from their tasselled keepers.

'Yes, they are. Marina chose them.'

'Oh?'

'I met her when she was doing some work for a friend. I

had just moved my practice here and I asked her advice about decorating. She did a lovely job on this room.' She walked back to the desk and picked up her bag, 'Time to go.'

He followed her down the stairs and into the hall. They went outside into the evening sunshine. She locked the door.

'No alarm?' He looked up at the building.

'No. The guy who owns the house lives and works in the top-floor apartment. He keeps a good eye on the offices. In fact, well, you'll be surprised to hear me say this after my own response to you, but you should talk to him. About Marina.'

'Yeah?'

'Yes. His name is Mark Porter. They were friends. In fact, he—'

'Yeah,' he interrupted. 'He brought her to the party.'

'Well done. I can see you're up to speed.' She smiled and slung her bag over her shoulder. 'Look, I don't really know what to say to you, but to be honest, I think on the balance of probability that Marina either killed herself deliberately or she was so careless of her safety, you know, drinking excessively, taking cocaine, going out in the boat by herself at night, that even if, strictly speaking, it was an accident, it wasn't. Do you see what I mean?'

She began to walk away. He didn't want her to go. She reminded him of someone else. Margaret Mitchell had some of the same combination of intelligence and astringent grace. And she had a smile to match. He wanted Gwen to smile at him again. He wanted to bask a bit longer in its sudden warmth. 'Hey, Dr Simpson, Gwen, hold on a minute.'

She slowed and turned.

'Would you fancy a drink or something? Maybe a bite to eat. Something to repay you for your time and your kindness.'

She stared at him for a moment. 'Sorry, Mr McLoughlin. I think I mentioned that I was tired, had had a long day. Looking forward to a bit of peace and quiet.' She raised a hand. Her keys jingled. ''Bye for now.'

He watched her drive away. Loneliness had him in its steely grip. He couldn't face the thought of his empty house. He took his phone from his pocket and checked the time. It was just six o'clock. If he hurried he might get to the club in time to go sailing. It was Johnny Harris's night. He selected his number and pressed the green button. He heard the familiar welcoming voice: 'Michael, what can I do for you?'

'Johnny, got room for me on board?'

'Sure thing, Michael, sure thing.'

He found his car and unlocked the door. Just what he needed, the wind on his face and the taste of salt on his lips. He started the engine. To hell with women. Nothing but trouble. To hell with the lot of them.

THIRTEEN

'God, I needed that.' Johnny Harris lifted his pint of Heineken and drained half in one long swallow. McLoughlin watched his Adam's apple bob up and down, the skin of his neck, red and wrinkled. He had a sudden unwanted image of Harris in an embrace with the recently departed Chicko.

'What's up, Michael? Pint not agreeing with you?' Harris put his glass on the table and pulled a cigar from the top pocket of his faded denim shirt.

'No, it's fine. I was just reflecting on that broach out there. We nearly ended up in the drink. A bit hairy, wasn't it?' McLoughlin picked up a box of matches from the table, struck one and held it out.

'Nah, not at all. Not with yours truly at the helm.' Harris put the tip of his cigar into the flame and sucked hard. Then he sat back, a stream of smoke pouring from his mouth. 'Isn't that right, Bill? Not a chance of anything going wrong. You have to take a few chances if you want to win.'

Bill Early, one of Harris's regular crew, grunted, then drained his glass. He stood up and gesticulated at the bar.

'Thanks.' McLoughlin raised his pint. 'Same again.'

The terrace outside the yacht club was crowded with sailors, faces flushed, voices raised. The sun was still hot. McLoughlin turned his back on it. He was tired. The sailing had been competitive. Johnny was a demon when he got going. All his polite diffidence vanished as soon as he put on his life-jacket.

McLoughlin regarded him now as he sat back and blew smoke-rings. A steady stream of congratulations came his way. Everyone dropping by to shake his hand or offer him a drink. It must have been hard, McLoughlin thought, when he decided to come out. Hard to ignore the sniggers, the whispers, the cruel asides. But, McLoughlin reckoned, he was protected by his family standing. Hard to ignore the Harris money.

McLoughlin finished his drink and picked up the fresh one Bill Early had left for him. He sat back in his chair and closed his eyes. He could have slept where he was. He should go home, he thought, before he drank too much more. But the thought of the empty house still filled him with dread.

'Hey, Michael, no snoozing allowed.' Harris's voice cut through his gloom. 'What's wrong with you? Isn't this place exciting enough?'

McLoughlin forced one eye open. His friend's face was flushed. He stubbed out his cigar and rocked back in his chair.

'Think it's nearly time to go.' McLoughlin raised his glass. 'It's us retirees, you know. We've no stamina.'

'Yeah.' Harris sounded miserable. 'Yeah, I know what you mean. It starts with such promise, then somehow or other it fizzles out.'

McLoughlin said nothing.

'It's not much to ask, is it?' Harris went on, bitter now.

'What?'

'Happiness, contentment, love.' Harris glared at the crowded terrace. 'All these lucky people, they could have it in spades. Countless opportunities. From the moment they

reach puberty, it's there for them. They just have to reach
out and pluck it. And what do they do? Look.' He jabbed
his finger towards a group standing together at the top of
the steps. 'I know for a fact that he, the guy with the red
hair and the very red face, is shagging his brother's wife and
she, the woman next to him, is a serial adulterer whose
cuckolded husband is in John of Gods drying out.' He
drained his glass and reached for another. 'And, look, you
see that lot at the table next to us?'

'Ssh, Johnny, keep it down.' McLoughlin squirmed. He'd
only been a member for a couple of years and he didn't have
the same kind of casual indifference to convention that
Harris exuded. But Harris ignored him.

'The very good-looking man who's positively drooling
over that young one in the shorts and the halter-neck top,
well, he's married to the rather plain woman. See her, over
there on her own, the one with the big nose and the thick
ankles? A marriage made in the boardroom rather than the
bedroom, if you know what I mean. In fact,' he lowered his
voice, 'you know who they are?'

McLoughlin shook his head.

'The post-mortem I did this afternoon. The woman in
Rathmines?'

'What about her?'

'Well, that's her sister. Poppy Atkinson.'

'Oh?' McLoughlin craned his neck. 'Was it suicide? Or
the other?'

Harris shrugged. 'Looked like suicide to me. Kind of
similar to your one. Your Marina Spencer. Alcohol, cocaine,
although she didn't drown. She died in her own bed. Heart
failure.'

'And the husband? Is there a husband?'

'Very much so. She's married to Charlie Webb. One of the estate agent Webbs. Worth a fortune. Beautiful house in Palmerston Park. I counted four cars in the drive. Poverty wasn't her problem.'

'So what was?'

'Who knows? She left a note. Unsigned, something about asking for forgiveness. I spoke briefly to her husband. He says he can't imagine why she would want forgiveness. As far as he was concerned, they were extremely happy, madly in love, completely faithful, two beautiful kids and everything to live for.'

'Any signs of anything else? Force, violence, anything odd sexually?'

'Nothing. I did find traces of semen on the sheets. But that's hardly surprising. Anyway, Poppy over there is her sister. Although you wouldn't know it to look at them.'

'And where was the dead woman's husband when she was dying?' McLoughlin's glass was empty. He was tempted to have another.

'He was away overnight in London on business.' Harris sat up. The self-pity was gone. 'Went straight to his office in town from the plane the next morning. Phoned home to say he was back and got worried when no one answered. Then the housekeeper called him. Said she'd gone into the house, found the two kids watching TV. They said their mother was asleep, that her bedroom door was locked. The housekeeper couldn't open the door so she phoned Charlie. He phoned the guards and they broke the door down and there she was.'

'Poor thing.' McLoughlin finished off the last mouthful of Guinness. 'Was the husband playing away? Was the London trip a bit more pleasure than business?'

Harris sighed. 'Who knows? He has the means, motive and opportunity. In other words, the money, the looks and the class.'

'Well,' McLoughlin stood up, 'I'd better go. If I have another I'll be here all night.'

'Ah, don't,' Harris pleaded. 'I'll organize you a lift later on. There's plenty of guys who live up your way.'

'No, really, Johnny. I'm trying to keep a lid on the drinking.' He took his jacket from the back of the chair. Harris looked bereft. 'Where's Bill gone? And the rest of the guys? What's happened to crew loyalty?'

Harris grinned broadly. '"Sometimes it's hard to be a skipper,"' he sang loudly.

'Yeah, right.' McLoughlin saluted him. 'I'll see you soon. Thanks for the sail. It was great. And if you want me again, if you want the winning team, I'm all yours. Any time.'

Harris punched his arm lightly. 'Listen, Michael, sorry for the ould maudlin. You know the way it is.' He smiled. 'Thanks again.'

McLoughlin walked back inside and through the bar. It was quiet and almost empty. A group of well-dressed middle-aged women were sitting over their gin and tonic on the heavy leather sofa. They didn't raise their heads as he passed. He stopped in the hall and put on his jacket. This was such a beautiful building, he thought. Early nineteenth century with all the elegance and grace of its period. Above his head was the great domed skylight. He could imagine being here when everyone else had gone home, moonlight and starlight filtering through on to the dark blue carpet. He pulled open the heavy front door and walked out to the granite front step. He stopped and fumbled in his pocket for his keys. And heard a woman crying. She was leaning against one of the pillars that flanked the club's façade, shoulders shaking, her breath coming in great gasps.

'Hey,' McLoughlin moved towards her, 'are you all right? Can I help you?'

She lifted her head and stared at him. Her face was red and tears streamed down her cheeks. She didn't reply. She wiped the back of her hand across her mouth and nose.

'Here.' McLoughlin pulled out a handkerchief. 'It's OK. It's clean.' He held it towards her. She took it without speaking, wiped her eyes and blew her nose. She handed it back.

'No, it's OK. You keep it. Looks like your need is greater than mine.'

She gave him a small smile and, in the light that streamed from the club's windows, he saw who she was.

'Do you need anything? Can I get someone to come out to you?' He jiggled his keys in his hand.

She shook her head.

'Well, if you're sure . . .' He turned to leave.

'Um, just a minute. Where are you going?' Her voice was slightly slurred.

'I'm heading home. Stepaside direction.'

'Could you give me a lift? I don't feel very well. I've had too much to drink. I'd get a taxi but I'm not sure I could handle it.' She swayed a little as she spoke.

'No, that's fine. Come on, I'm parked over here. Where are you going?'

She lived in Terenure. She told him the name of the road, then slumped against the passenger door. He introduced himself. She said her name was Poppy Atkinson. He checked to make sure her door was locked, that her seat-belt was fastened, that she had her handbag. He pushed 'play' on the tape deck. Billie Holiday's voice sang out. He drove slowly and carefully, only too aware that he was over the limit. He hummed along with the songs.

'I like that, it's lovely.'

He glanced at her. Her eyes were still closed but the features of her fleshy white face were calmer and more composed. '"God Bless the Child",' he said. 'Such a great song. Billie Holiday wrote it, you know. She's one of my favourites.'

She shuddered. 'She was my sister's favourite too.' A tear slipped from beneath her closed eyelids.

'Your sister?'

'My sister Rosie. She died yesterday. I can't believe it. We're twins. I can't believe she could have done it without telling me.'

'Done what?' McLoughlin slowed. A Garda car was coming up fast behind him. Its roof light was flashing.

'The doctor said she killed herself. She drank a load of vodka and she took a load of cocaine. I just can't believe it. The kids were in the house. They were in bed asleep, and when they woke up they couldn't get into the bedroom because the door was locked. They're only five and three. Just little ones. She'd never have left them on their own like that.' She was sitting up straight now, her fists clenched in her lap.

'It's hard to know what's going on in someone's head when they're suicidal. They're not thinking straight. They're not thinking like you or me.' McLoughlin's wing mirror showed the guards turning right behind him.

'I know that. But I still don't get it. We'd read all those books about Sylvia Plath. You know – the poet? She put her head into a gas oven when her kids were little. She left glasses of milk and plates of bread and butter in their bedroom and she'd arranged for a new child-minder to come that morning. She tried to protect them. At least she did that. But Rosie – Rosie locked herself into her bedroom. God knows what the kids could have got up to, wandering around in that great big house by themselves.'

'And their father? Where was he?' There was another Garda car behind him now. He reduced his speed, conscious that he was in a fifty k.p.h. zone.

'In London, doing some property deal. If you can believe that.' Her voice was louder, more aggressive.

'And you don't?'

'I don't know. Maybe he was, maybe he wasn't. I was with him earlier this evening. He's in bits. The kids are in shock. I don't know how he's going to explain it to them. I don't know how I would do it, what I would say.' She pushed herself up in the seat and peered through the window. 'I just don't get suicide. It's so cruel. It hurts so many people.' Her voice broke. She held on tight to McLoughlin's handkerchief and raised it to her eyes.

'Yes, you're right. It leaves so many unanswered questions. It's real agony for the families. I was with a woman yesterday whose daughter drowned herself in a lake up in Wicklow. It was six weeks or so ago, but for the girl's mother it's as if it's just this minute happened. You can forget about time and healing.' He pressed the button and his window slid down. He took a lungful of fresh night air.

'Wicklow, you say?' Poppy turned to him. Her voice was loud, the consonants slurred. 'Wicklow. Are you talking about Marina Spencer?'

A cyclist shot off the footpath and wobbled in front of

the car. McLoughlin stamped on the brake pedal. They both jerked forward.

'Sorry, sorry, they're all out tonight.' He hit the horn with the heel of his hand. The cyclist looked back over his shoulder and stuck one finger in the air. 'And fuck you too, mate,' he muttered.

'Are you talking about Marina Spencer?' Poppy repeated the words carefully.

McLoughlin nodded. 'Yeah, that's her name. Did you know her?'

'Yes. Rosie and I went to boarding-school with her.' Poppy sank down in the seat again. 'It was years ago, when we were fourteen, fifteen. You knew her too, did you?'

McLoughlin shrugged. 'No, I didn't. Not when she was alive. I'm a policeman – or at least I was until I retired a couple of weeks ago. Her mother doesn't believe she killed herself so I said I'd see what I could find out about how she died.'

'And?'

'And not much, I'm afraid. She seemed reasonably happy, reasonably successful. She didn't have money worries. And she had friends. A healthy social life.'

'Friends? I doubt that somehow. Marina didn't do friendship.' Her voice was harsh. 'A social life, yes. She'd always have that.'

There was silence. McLoughlin tried to concentrate on his driving.

'Yeah, she'd have a social life,' Poppy repeated. 'Always some poor unfortunate stuck in her greasy web. Even bloody Mark Porter, though what he was doing with her again, God alone knows.' She fiddled with McLoughlin's handkerchief, winding it around her fingers.

'Mark Porter? You know him too, do you?' McLoughlin was sweating, but the road ahead was clear. No crazed cyclists, no predatory Garda cars in sight.

'Oh, yeah, I know Mark. Mark and Marina go way back. That's why it was so odd when she started seeing him again. Rosie told me about it. We couldn't figure it out.' She gave a tight snigger. 'Especially after the way she treated him when we were at school. The bullying and everything that went with it. Did you know about that?'

'No. Tell me.' He was checking the street signs, looking for Poppy's road. He flicked on the indicator and slowed to turn left.

'Well,' she took a deep, shuddering breath, 'you see, Marina didn't like me. Rosie was the one she liked. We're not identical. Rosie got the looks. I got the brains. That's what everyone said. Marina liked pretty people. And Rosie was mad about her. She didn't want me while Marina was around.' Poppy began to sob again. 'I don't know how it started but they had this kind of gang. There was Marina, Rosie, Dom de Paor, or Power as we called him then. Ben Roxby was part of it. And Gilly Kearon, who got married to Dom years later, poor girl. And, of course, Sophie Fitzgerald. Another dumb blonde. Even dumber and blonder than Rosie.'

McLoughlin slowed to a crawl. The street was dark, the lights partly obscured by the luscious growth of chestnut trees. The houses were set back, long front gardens with hedges and brick walls. He waited for Poppy's sobs to quiet. 'What number are you?' he asked.

'Fifty-five, it's just here.' She wiped her eyes again with McLoughlin's handkerchief and blew her nose. 'Thanks, this is really kind of you. I just couldn't stay there any longer, in the club, you know. I couldn't bear to be around all those people.'

'That's OK.' He stopped the car and switched off the ignition. He reached out to give her hand a squeeze, but thought better of it. 'You should be careful, you know. You're probably in shock. You want to get into bed and keep warm.' He pulled up the handbrake and sat back in his seat. 'But tell me about Marina first. What happened with Mark Porter?'

Poppy reached for the release on her seat-belt. 'They bullied him. He was very small, you see. He had some kind of growth problem. He had to take something for it. The stuff is made from pituitary glands. Human pituitary glands. Taken from the dead. Well, Marina found out about this. And every time she saw Mark she'd hold her nose, pretend to vomit, say things about rotting bodies, worms, decay. Make sounds like ghosts. All that sort of thing. It was kind of funny to begin with. Mark wasn't popular. Nothing to do with his disability. He was as pompous as hell. His family were old colonials. They'd been in India, Malaya, wherever. Mark was a terrible snob. Always going on about old money and new money. That didn't go down well in a school where half the pupils came from the new-money brigade.'

McLoughlin knew what she meant. The yacht clubs were sodden with the same kind of stuff.

'Anyway, it got out of hand. Other things happened too. Marina was precocious. She was very pretty. Lovely figure. She and Rosie were runners. They were on the athletics team. Great tennis-players too. I remember that Marina had

the most fabulous long legs. She looked great in shorts.'
Poppy shifted in the seat. 'God, I remember what mine were
like. Fat, white, ugly. Still are, for that matter.'

McLoughlin said nothing. Guiltily he remembered Harris's comments about her ankles.

'Anyway, Marina set her sights on Ben Roxby. He was
Rosie's boyfriend, everyone knew that. Rosie was so upset.
Marina was supposed to be her friend. And there was talk
about other things too.'

She stopped. She felt around with her feet for her bag.

'What kind of talk?' McLoughlin's lower back was aching. He must have pulled something on the boat.

'Oh, that Marina was giving blow-jobs in the basement.'
Poppy let out a shriek of high-pitched laughter. She slapped
her hands on her knees. 'Blow-jobs in the basement. Have
you ever heard the like? Sounds like the title of a soft-porn
movie. I don't think most of us knew what a blow-job was.
Not like teenagers these days. They're all experts.' She
dragged her bag on to her lap. 'Anyway, whatever was going
on, it had a terrible effect on Mark. He got so upset that he
tried to hang himself from the banisters on one of the top
landings. But the rope broke and he fell. It was amazing he
didn't die.' She took out a powder compact. 'The teacher
who found him did CPR until the ambulance came.' She
clicked it open and examined her face in the small round
mirror. 'Marina was expelled. Rosie wasn't. I was so glad
when Marina left. She was a rotten bitch. Bad news.' She
pushed her hair out of her eyes.

'Did you ever see her again?'

'Not for years and years. I heard she'd gone to the States
or somewhere. Her brother, Tom, stayed on in school for
another couple of terms, then he left too. That was for

financial reasons. They'd no money after James de Paor died. But I did see Marina in town not that long ago. It was just before Christmas. I was in Grafton Street and I saw her coming out of Brown Thomas. I got a real shock.'

'Did you speak to her?'

'Speak to her? No, I didn't speak to her.' Her voice was very loud in the car. Loud, bitter, angry. 'She didn't see me. Nothing new in that. She never saw me. She looked great. She was with a girl, a teenager. I think it must have been her half-sister, the child her mother had with Dominic's father. I watched them walking down the street. Christmas lights, carol singers, everyone happy and jolly and I thought, You bitch. One of these days it'll all catch up with you.' She closed her bag. 'And you know what? Finally it did.' She groaned. 'Christ, I don't feel great. My hangover's kicking in already.' She half turned towards him. 'Listen, thank you again. You've been really kind. I'd better go. I should phone my husband. By now he might just have noticed I've left and he'll be wondering what I'm up to.'

She got out of the car. He sat and watched as she pushed open the gate and walked quickly up the front path. He watched her open the door. She turned and waved, then disappeared inside. McLoughlin reached into his pocket and took out his notebook. He flipped it open and wrote. Then he started the car and turned it around.

He was sober now, completely sober, and wide awake. He drove slowly out on to the main road. A bully. So that was what Marina had been. A nasty bully. He could see the photographs. The wide smile, the glossy dark hair, the dark eyes crinkled up against the sun, the high cheekbones and long limbs: that was what she had been like as an adult. But what was she like as a teenager? They bullied the boy until he tried to kill himself. They made his life so miserable that he preferred to end it. He stood on the landing and tied one end of the rope to the banister. He made the other end into a noose and slipped it over his head. Then he jumped. He must have thought his neck would break. He must have thought he would die immediately. But he didn't. He dangled from the rope. Then he fell. A teacher heard him. Breathed life into his body. Shouted and screamed until help came. And the boy was saved.

McLoughlin pushed the tape back into the machine and began to sing again. 'God Bless the Child'. Good for Billie Holiday. She certainly knew how to sum it all up. Rich folks and poor folks and never the twain shall meet. Look at Marina. Out of her depth in more ways than one.

He drove slowly and carefully back towards town, back towards Marina's small, neat house. He was sure he had seen some old school photographs on the wall in her study. He wanted to look at them again. See if they could tell him anything more about her. 'What were you up to?' he asked quietly. Marina's face smiled back at him from the wind-screen. Her mouth was joyful, but her eyes were sad and wary.

He turned into the narrow street and inched forward. Cars were parked bumper to bumper but there was a small spot he reckoned he could just about squeeze into. He stopped and put the car into reverse. He turned the steering-wheel hard. Then he saw. The lights were on in her house. Upstairs and downstairs. He got out of the car and checked the number on the wall. He took out her keys and checked the number on the label: 18 Mount Pleasant Mews. He put his hand on the garden gate. It squeaked loudly as he walked through. Lights and music poured from the front windows, upstairs and downstairs. He moved quickly to the door. He slipped the key into the Yale lock, but the door was already open. At his touch it swung back and he stepped forward into the house.

FOURTEEN

The lights from the kitchen spilled out through the open door into the garden. Margaret lay back in the deckchair, a book open on her lap and a glass of wine in her hand. It was still warm. She could feel the heat coming up from the stone flags beneath her. She supposed it was getting late and she should go inside and to bed. But somehow she couldn't find the energy to move. Another day had passed. Another of the days until the time would come for her to decide what to do. How to live the rest of her life. Whether that might be short or long. She picked up her glass and took a sip. The wine was good. Too good. She would have to learn to live without it. She put the glass back on the ground and closed her eyes. She was tired. It had been a long day. It seemed like an age since the morning.

It had become something of a habit. Every day when Margaret left the house the girl, Vanessa, would be outside on the wall, waiting. She would fall into step beside Margaret and the two of them would walk along the road towards the Martello tower. If the tide was low, they would go down on to the sand, and if it was high, they would take the concrete walkway as far as the railway bridge, then turn inland and go behind the sea wall with the track on their right as far as the West Pier. Sometimes Margaret would turn on to the pier and walk the mile and a half of its length, Dublin Bay wide and bright to her left, the harbour with its bobbing boats and the passage to and fro of the fishing trawlers and the ferries to her right. And Vanessa would walk with her. Other times Margaret would continue on towards the town and the shops. She would do whatever small amount of shopping she needed, then go down to the sea front and sit outside one of the new cafés across from the town hall. She would drink her coffee and eat her muffin or Danish pastry and read the paper, the sun warming her arms and shoulders, the breeze from the sea snatching at the crisp newsprint, and Vanessa would sit beside her, sucking orange juice through a straw, humming snatches of songs and occasionally making comments about people passing or the pigeons that searched for crumbs beside their feet. They didn't speak much. But that seemed to be a state that satisfied both of them. Margaret didn't want to talk. She wanted to absorb as much light and fresh air as she could. Her time was running out. It was already mid-July. The anniversary of Mary's death was 8 August. And that was when she had to act.

Today she was going to the library in Dun Laoghaire. 'Do you want to come with me?' she asked Vanessa, as they walked up the hill from the harbour towards the railway bridge.

Vanessa shrugged. 'Might as well,' she said. 'Nothing else to do.'

'What does your mother think about how you spend your days?' Margaret stopped and turned towards her.

Vanessa shrugged again. Today her face was sad, her mouth downturned, and there were dark smudges like bruises under her eyes. 'She doesn't notice. She's too sad. She doesn't sleep much and at night I hear her walking around the house. She keeps me awake too.'

'It's hard. I know what she's going through. It was a long time before I could sleep and even now I go through periods of insomnia.' Margaret started walking again.

Vanessa sighed, and the sigh turned into a yawn. 'She's worse than she was in the beginning. Then the doctor gave her sleeping pills, but she stopped taking them because she said she couldn't think. Now she still can't think but that's because she's so tired. She's like a political prisoner who's been sleep-deprived. You know, they go mad.' Vanessa's clogs clip-clopped on the footpath like the hoofs of a trotting pony.

Margaret smiled at her. 'I know how she feels. I'd like to be able to suggest a treatment but unless she'll take the pills there's not much she can do.' They stopped at the traffic-lights and waited.

Vanessa jigged up and down. 'And she was so excited when Janet, her old school friend, said she'd get a cop she knows to see if he could find something out about how Marina died. But she hasn't heard anything much from him.'

The lights changed and they went across the road towards the red-brick building on the corner.

'I thought he was sort of nice,' Vanessa continued, 'but Mum had such high hopes. She thought he'd instantly come back to her and say he knew what had happened to Marina. But he didn't inspire her with much confidence. He's retired, you know, so he's a bit ancient and past it, I'd say.'

They walked up the library steps and in through the open

doors. The lobby was cool and dark. Vanessa stopped to look at the noticeboard.

'So has he found out anything?' Margaret asked.

'Not really. He asked her about the suicide note. Of course, Mum doesn't think it is a suicide note. I don't think she was very helpful, really. But that was a couple of days ago and she'd hasn't heard from him since. I told her she should phone him. But she won't. She says she'll wait for him to ring her. She's like a girl waiting for a boy she fancies to call. She's nuts, really.'

Margaret said nothing. She knew how Vanessa's mother was feeling. She moved towards the swing doors. 'I'm going to look at some micro-film. It's kind of slow and boring.'

'That's OK,' Vanessa said, 'I like this library. I've been coming here since I was little. I know all the books really well. I'll sit down and read.'

'Well, if you're sure.' Margaret fanned her face with a hand. 'You don't have to come with me, you know, if there's something else you want to do . . .' Her voice trailed away.

Vanessa shook her head vigorously. 'No, it's better here. If I go home Mum will be going on and on about this policeman, this McLoughlin man, trying to figure out what to do, and I can't bear it any longer.'

'McLoughlin, is that his name?' Margaret looked at her.

'Mm, Michael McLoughlin. Nice name, don't you think? I like the Ms. I just wish he'd phone Mum or do something, but I told her it's probably because he's busy. But she said . . .' she paused '. . . oh, I don't know what she said. I don't care any longer.' She pushed past Margaret. 'I'm going to find something nice to read.'

Detective Inspector Michael McLoughlin. He had sat in

the garden and talked to her. He had told her he would find the man who killed her daughter. He had made her think of a large sad bear. She had treated him with disdain and contempt and he had not taken offence. He had understood the way she felt. There was that day when he and the younger policeman had taken her to identify Mary's body. They had stood on either side of the trolley. The thing between them was covered with dark green. McLoughlin had pulled it away. And Margaret hadn't known what she was looking at. The thing revealed had shorn hair. The whiteness of the scalp was visible. The face was bruised and battered. The eyes were blackened and swollen and the nose was bent to one side. Margaret had reached down to touch her daughter and the younger man had put out his hand to ward her off. But McLoughlin had pushed him away. She had touched what was left of Mary's hair. A tightly sprung coil released itself from the rest and curled around her finger. It reminded her of sweet-pea tendrils, which cling to the trellis supporting the flowering shoots. She had shouted then at the policemen to leave her alone and McLoughlin had pushed the younger man in front of him out of the door. And Margaret had stripped her daughter's body so she could look at it from the top of her head to her toes. So she could see what the man had done. So she could count the knife slashes, the bruises, the bitemarks. So she could see how he had made her suffer before she died.

'Can I help you?' The young man behind the counter leaned towards her. Margaret realized that a queue had built up behind her.

'Oh, sorry, um, yes, I was wondering if I could look at the *Irish Times*.' She swallowed hard. 'The date is April 2000. You have it on micro-film, I think.'

'Yeah, that's right. Take a seat at the micro-film reader and I'll get it for you.' He jerked his head at the row of machines. She moved out of the way and sat down. Detective Inspector Michael McLoughlin, the man with the well-worn face and the kind smile. He had been so upset when Jimmy Fitzsimons got off. She had watched him walk away from the court, his head down, his hands in his pockets. He hadn't known what she would do. He had thought she would be filled with despair. She had been, but it had been a despair that had driven her onwards. Driven her to kill.

'You all right, Margaret?' Vanessa bent down over her. 'You're looking really upset.' Her arms were filled with books. Big picture books.

Margaret smiled up at her. 'I'm fine. I have to wait a while. What have you got there?'

'Oh, lots of lovely things. All my favourites from when I was little. Look.' There was an illustrated *Alice in Wonderland*, *Where the Wild Things Are*, *Orlando, the Marmalade Cat*, and a lovely copy of *Charlotte's Web*. 'I'm going to sit over there,' she indicated the low tables in the children's section, 'and read them all.' Then she asked again, 'Are you all right?'

Margaret nodded, as the young man from behind the counter appeared with two reels of film in his hand.

'These are the ones you want. Do you know how to use the machine?' He put them down beside her.

'Yes, I'm fine, thanks.' She threaded the first reel through the keepers. She switched on the light and spun the wheel. The days of April flashed by. She slowed down and saw the report of the finding of Jimmy's body, the post-mortem, the police investigation. She saw the photograph of Michael McLoughlin and the one of Mary. She saw her own face, the picture taken at the funeral, and the picture of Jimmy. But she wasn't looking for that. She spooled on through the days and found the death notices. She slowed down and read them carefully. And found the one she wanted.

Fitzsimons, James, Killiney, Co. Dublin. Son of the late Brendan and Eileen. Funeral tomorrow after 10 o'clock Mass in the Church of St Matthias, Killiney, to Dean's Grange Cemetery. No flowers please.

There would be no flowers for Jimmy Fitzsimons. No swathes of lilies. No heaped bouquets on the mound of earth below which his coffin rested. Would there be mourners? She remembered his family in the courtroom. His mother with her lips tightly drawn together. His sister, the girl with Down's syndrome, who cried and tried to go to him. And the woman Margaret had met in the ladies' toilet, with her smeared lipstick and her laddered tights who had shouted abuse at her, insisted that her brother was innocent. Where were they now? Margaret wondered, as she spooled on to the next day and the day after. And there was another photograph of the coffin being carried from the hearse into the church. She recognized them all. Jimmy's mother, her face pale, without expression. The young girl, bigger now, overweight, holding a handbag tightly with both hands, and the other woman, with her back to the rest of the group and a cigarette halfway to her lips. She read the report that went with the photograph.

A small group of family members attended the funeral yesterday of Jimmy Fitzsimons whose body was found two weeks ago, five years after he mysteriously disappeared. Parish priest Father Eamonn O'Dwyer spoke of the peace that would now come to the family once the deceased was laid to rest. He spoke of the tragedy of Jimmy's short life, and the healing power of prayer. He hoped that Jimmy's family would find comfort in the sacraments. After the Mass a small group of mourners made their way to Dean's Grange cemetery where Mr Fitzsimons was laid to rest. A representative of the Garda Síochána, Superintendent Finney, confirmed that the investigation into Mr Fitzsimons's death was still active but so far they had not developed any further insights into how he died.

Margaret pressed the print button and waited for the machine to disgorge the photocopy. She folded it and put it into her bag. She spooled the film back, took it out, then stood up and walked back to the counter. 'Thanks very much,' she said.

'Did you get everything you needed?' the young man behind the counter asked.

'Yes, it was great, thank you.'

She turned away and looked for Vanessa. She could see her red scarf, her head above the pile of books. She took a step towards her, then stopped. Vanessa was safe and happy here. Better here than where Margaret was going. She moved back behind the carousel of CDs, then walked quickly towards the heavy swing doors. She pushed them open. Bright sunshine shone into the lobby. She stood for a moment, feeling the warmth on her face. She would walk the couple of miles to Dean's Grange. It would be good to get the exercise. Good to feel the sun on her head and the gentle breeze on her face.

She settled into her stride. Her legs moved smoothly, her arms swung rhythmically. A van passed her, and the men inside leaned out the window, calling and whistling. She smiled, pleased and flattered by the attention. If they only knew, she thought, if they only knew what she had done, what she was capable of doing. If everyone knew what she was really like. What kind of a monster she had become. If Michael McLoughlin knew, what would he think of her? she wondered. He had been interested in her, that much was apparent. She could see it in the way he moved towards her whenever possible, the way he watched her when she spoke, the way he contrived to touch her. Brush against her hand, take her arm, lay his hand on the small of her back. She wondered if he had tried to contact her. She had heard from the letting agency that a man had called to the house, and she had expected to hear that the police had wanted to speak to her. But there had been no more word. No more interest.

Now she could see the graveyard's high grey wall and the tall gates. She stopped at the office. She gave the name of the grave. She followed the directions. She walked up and down the neat concrete paths. There were names here she recognized. Neighbours, women with whom her mother had played bridge and gossiped. Men who had worked in the civil service with her father, who had taken the train every morning from Seapoint station to Pearse Street and walked together through Merrion Square to government buildings. And among them all, among the slabs of marble, the angels and saints, the madonnas and crucifixes, was a small weedy plot, unmarked, unnamed. Just a wooden marker with a number painted crudely on it.

She bent down to get a closer look and to compare it with the number written on the slip of paper in her hand. So this was Jimmy Fitzsimons's final resting-place. The earth had settled unevenly and there was a small hollow at the head of the grave. Dandelions had flowered and now their nimbus of down waved delicately, waiting for the time to let the seeds fly. A tall bunch of thistles swayed from side to side, a butterfly resting on a fearsome leaf, its brightly coloured wings opening and closing slowly. Margaret held her breath as she watched. It was a peacock, the large false eyes on its wings glowing, almost iridescent blue. Its proboscis coiled and uncoiled like the spring of an old Swiss watch. Then, as Margaret watched, holding her breath, it lifted from the leaf and, with a languid flap, drifted away. She had a sudden image of Mary, walking down the front path, turning to say goodbye, a wave of her hand, her black curls lifting and bouncing, tumbling down the back of her dress. Her eyes were so blue, the bright blue of the peacock's eyes. And she moved with such grace and ease. Her feet always seemed ready to leave the ground, so light was her tread. As if she had some kind of a spring in her instep, something that gave her bounce and levity.

Margaret watched the butterfly until she could see it no longer, then gazed at the grave.

'So,' she said, her voice low, 'we meet again. I never thought I'd come back here. I never wanted to see you, to be reminded of what you did to my daughter. I wanted you to suffer as she suffered. To die with the same pain she had. To feel her terror. When you beat her, when you raped her, when you made her feel worthless and dirty. I wanted all that for you and I succeeded. But now I've realized what else I did. I've tied myself to you for ever. My every waking minute, my every minute asleep is filled with thoughts of you and of what I did. And I can no longer bear it. I have not come here to make my peace. I do not forgive you. I am as filled with hatred as ever. But now I must think of myself and of my own future. I must atone for my sin. Do you hear me? Do you hear me down there beneath the earth? Because that's where you are, in the remains of a wooden box, a collection of bones, all that's left. Do you hear me, Jimmy?'

Suddenly she was conscious that she was not alone. A group of mourners were standing near a large well-kept grave. They carried bunches of flowers and they were smartly dressed. A priest stood with them. He walked towards her and smiled in a reassuring way. She picked up her bag.

'Are you all right?' His tone was professionally sympathetic.

Margaret nodded. 'I'm fine.'

'Oh, I'm sorry, you just looked a bit . . . distressed.'

'Well,' she tried to smile, 'this is a place of distress, isn't it?'

'Yes, of course it is. Look,' he said, 'we're here to remember a beloved daughter who died tragically a year ago. Perhaps you would like to join in our prayers. Perhaps it would help you too.'

'No.' Margaret's voice was firm. 'Thank you, but no. I'm going now. I've done all I can here.' She turned away. Behind her she could hear the murmur of voices, random at first then acquiring the pattern, the rhythm, the structure and coherence of the Rosary.

'The Lord be with thee,' she whispered, as she walked through the gates and out on to the road.

Another day had passed. The half-moon was high above her. It had been so strange when Vanessa spoke about Michael McLoughlin. Of course he would be of retiring age now. She couldn't imagine what he would do without his job. It had seemed so much a part of his life. But maybe she was wrong.

After all, what did she know? What did she know about anything or anyone any longer? She closed her eyes. But she saw. Jimmy Fitzsimons. His eyes wide and terrified. His frantic struggles. His body, as it would have been when it was found. And his grave. Neglected. Untended. Unmarked.

FIFTEEN

The door swung open at his touch. McLoughlin stepped tentatively into the narrow hall. He glanced to the left into the sitting room. The coffee-table was strewn with photographs.

'Hallo,' he called. The music was loud, almost deafening. He crossed to the CD-player on the shelf. There were no obvious buttons on the high-tech panel, and no sign of a remote control either. He recognized the music. It was from *Dido* by Purcell, Kathleen Ferrier's voice. ' "When I am laid in earth," ' she sang. It was beautiful, exquisite even, but loud, far too loud.

He walked quickly into the kitchen and peered through the glass doors on to the small patio. There was no one in sight. He moved back towards the stairs and began to climb them.

'Hallo,' he called again. 'Is anyone up there?'

He reached the upper landing and stopped. He turned towards Marina's bedroom and moved to the door. He could see a pair of legs crossed at the ankle. They were shoeless. He took a step closer. The legs were clad in cream-coloured cords. Another step. Now he could see a brown leather belt into which a denim shirt was tucked. Then he was in the room. A man was lying on the bed. His arms were folded behind his head. He swivelled his eyes to look at McLoughlin. Tears were wetting his cheeks. He made no move to brush them away.

'Hallo,' McLoughlin said. The man did not respond. McLoughlin cleared his throat and continued, 'Hi, my name's Michael McLoughlin. I'm a friend of Sally Spencer. She asked me to look in on Marina's house.'

There was still no response from the man on the bed. There was a moment's silence as the music stopped, and then it began again.

'"When I am laid, am laid in earth . . ."' Kathleen Ferrier's voice floated up the stairs.

'And you are?' McLoughlin raised his own voice.

The man looked at him. 'Sally told me about you,' he said in a whisper. 'She thinks you're going to tell her that Marina didn't take her own life. She thinks you're going to find out that something else happened to Marina, that she didn't want to die.' He sat up and wiped his face with the back of his hand. For a moment he reminded McLoughlin of a small child woken in the night by a bad dream. He swung his legs off the bed. They dangled, the tips of his toes resting on the wooden floor. 'But you won't. Marina wanted to die. I tried to talk her out of it. I told her she had plenty to live for. I loved her. I told her how much I loved her. But my love wasn't enough to keep the demons at bay.'

'And you are?' McLoughlin repeated the question.

'You know me. We met earlier today. Don't you remember?' The man's face wore an expression of affront. McLoughlin tried to think. Earlier? What had he done earlier?

'At Gwen Simpson's.'

He was waiting outside on the step, the door opened and a man was putting on a motorbike helmet.

'Oh, of course, I'm sorry.' McLoughlin smiled in what he

hoped was a conciliatory manner. 'It was your helmet. I
didn't see you properly. So, you must be Mark Porter, am
I right?'

'Yes. You'll have heard of me – if you're trying to find
out what happened to Marina, that is. In fact, I was going
to phone you.' He stood up. He was very small. His head
barely skimmed McLoughlin's chest. He slipped his feet
into a pair of white runners and bent over to lace them. His
shiny brown hair flopped forward. McLoughlin could see the
small boy with the new shoes. He straightened up.

'Do you think you could turn the music down a bit?'
McLoughlin moved through the door. 'It's lovely, but a bit
hard on the hearing at that volume.'

'Sure.' Mark Porter squeezed past him and headed for the
stairs. All trace of tears was gone. 'Marina loved it. She used
to listen to it all the time. She always said she wanted it
played at her funeral.'

'That was a bit morbid, wasn't it?'

'No, I don't think so.' He sounded irritated. 'I know lots
of people who like to think ahead. Sensible, it seems to me.
And it was lucky she told me.' He stopped. He was smiling
broadly now. His face, with its freckles and round bright
eyes, reminded McLoughlin of a character from one of the
comics he had read when he was a kid. 'Her mother would
never have had the imagination to do what Marina wanted.'

He ran down the stairs. His head and shiny hair disappeared from view. McLoughlin glanced back into the bedroom. The bed was rumpled and he noticed that the
wardrobe's mirrored door wasn't completely closed. He went
in, pulled it back and looked inside. One of the inner
drawers was half open. Some of Marina's underwear was
poking out. McLoughlin pushed it back inside and closed

the drawer. He slid the door over, then bent down and felt around the edge of the bed. His fingers touched something soft and silky. He pulled it out. It was a pair of black pants. They were trimmed with red lace and a red rose was embroidered across the crotch. He bent down and held them under the bedside lamp. He could see a trace of something white, slightly crusty.

'Ugh.' The sound was involuntary. He straightened up. He held the pants gingerly with his fingertips, turned them inside out and folded them. Then he slipped them into his pocket. He lifted the duvet. The bottom sheet, a bright sea blue, was stained in a number of places with the same silvery sheen. Snail's tracks, he thought, the unmistakable ooze. He flipped the duvet in the air, shook it, then laid it on the bed. The room was neat and tidy now, the way he was sure she would have wanted it.

'Mr McLoughlin, are you coming? There's something I want to show you.' Mark Porter's peremptory tone floated up towards him. McLoughlin wondered about his accent. It was virtually BBC English, barely a trace of the Dublin in which he lived.

'OK, I'm on my way. Just need to use the toilet. Won't be a minute.' He stepped quickly into the bathroom. The room was tiled from floor to ceiling. It had the usual fittings. Bath, with shower. Washbasin, lavatory. Mirrored cabinet. And, above, a circular globe with a pull cord, and beside it a ventilation fan. He put down the toilet seat and climbed on to it. He steadied himself with one hand and with the other reached up to the light. He unscrewed the shade and pulled it away. It looked all right, dusty, but untouched. He put it back, then stretched towards the fan. There should have been four screws holding it in place, but one was missing. He reached up and felt the space with his finger. No problem to take out the screw and replace it with a tiny camera. No problem at all. He could imagine. Marina opened the envelope. She saw the photos. She knew where they had been taken. She stood on the toilet seat. She did what he had. She unscrewed the light. Then she saw the fan. She checked the screws. She found the camera. She stamped on it. Broke it. She smashed it to pieces. The same way her privacy had been smashed, her sense of security. Or perhaps . . . He got down off the toilet seat. He looked in the mirror. He opened the door. She didn't find it. But whoever put it there came back after he had got what he wanted and removed it. But he couldn't be bothered to replace the screw. McLoughlin flushed the toilet vigorously. Then he walked downstairs.

They sat in the sitting room. Porter had gone into the kitchen and opened a bottle of wine. He busied himself with corkscrew and glasses. He had apologized for the lack of something to eat.

'Nibbles,' he said, a number of times. 'So nice to have a few nibbles.'

Marina always had lovely nibbles, he told McLoughlin. It was because she'd lived in so many interesting places around the world. She'd been in Algeria for a while and then she'd moved to Kenya and then she'd gone to Mexico and then to the States. She was such a good cook.

'You knew her well?' McLoughlin sipped his wine cautiously. He tried not to stare at Porter. It wasn't so much that he was small. It was more that his body was completely out of proportion. His head and shoulders were much bigger than his legs. His upper body was well developed, as if he lifted weights. His biceps bulged through his cotton shirt. But his face was round and plump, his hips tiny and his legs hardly big enough to carry him.

'Very well.' Porter gulped from his glass. 'We were very close. She told me everything.' His eyes glistened. 'I miss her very much.' He leaned forward and stirred the pile of photographs with his small hands. 'I thought you'd like to see this.' He handed McLoughlin a large black-and-white picture. 'See?' He stabbed at it with a plump finger. 'We went to the same school. The Lodge, in Ticknock. I'm sure you've heard of it.' He looked at him for confirmation. McLoughlin nodded politely. 'See? There's me, and standing behind me is Marina.'

The pupils were ranged in tiers. Boys and girls wearing identical white shirts with ties with a diagonal stripe and a dark sweater. Seated in the front was a row of adults. Teachers, McLoughlin assumed. He cast his eyes over the group. There must have been about two hundred, maybe two hundred and fifty altogether. They were a good-looking lot. Even though the photograph was faded and creased in places, the teenagers' clear skin, shiny hair and eyes were immediately apparent. Like thoroughbred racehorses, McLoughlin thought. Pampered and nurtured. Bred for strong bones and fine configuration.

'Yes.' He put the photograph back on the table. 'I heard you and she went to school together. A number of people have told me. But I also heard,' he put his glass on the floor, 'in fact just this evening before I came here, that Marina wasn't very nice to you. That she and some of the other pupils caused you a lot of pain. Am I right?'

'Who told you that?' Porter's tone was a mixture of anger and outrage.

'A woman called Poppy Atkinson.'

'Oh, Poppy, for God's sake,' Porter said dismissively. 'The ugly sister, that was what we called her. What would Poppy know about anything?'

McLoughlin shrugged. 'Well, I think she knows quite a lot, Mark. Now, I'll grant you she was upset. You've heard about her sister, I presume.'

'Rosie? Yes, poor Rosie. I wasn't surprised. She was very unhappy with her husband. He's a bad type. Too much money. New money, you know what I mean?'

Not really, McLoughlin wanted to say. But he smiled. 'Be that as it may, the situation as Poppy described it, in relation to the, um, bullying you experienced, sounded horrific. She told me that you . . .'

Mark touched his neck. One finger slipped beneath his shirt collar. He swivelled in his chair. His face took on a rictus that McLoughlin had seen many times before. On the faces of the dead. 'Look I'm sorry. I don't want to upset you,' he began.

'Upset me? You're not upsetting me,' Porter shrilled. 'It was an accident, that was all. A silly accident. I was trying to see if I could do a Tarzan. I'd made some rope out of creepers I found in the woods. And I wanted to see if my plaiting would stand up to my weight. It was an accident, that's all.' He tugged at his shirt collar, twisted awkwardly and McLoughlin saw the rough redness of the scar that encircled his throat.

'It wasn't just Marina, though, was it, Mark? It was Rosie and – who were the others involved? Poppy mentioned a couple of names. Someone called Ben, a Gilly and Sophie?'

Porter leaped to his feet. 'I want you to go now,' he said.

'I don't want to talk about this any longer. It has nothing to do with you or anyone else. They didn't bully me. I don't know why people keep on saying they did. We were just having a bit of fun, that was all. It was a bit of fun.' He walked past McLoughlin and into the hall. 'Get out.'

'Hold on a minute. There's no need to be like that.' McLoughlin stood. He picked up the photograph again. Marina smiled at him. Her wide, generous smile. Mark was directly in front of her. He looked very small in comparison with the others on either side. The expression on his face was one of sadness. He had been a lonely little boy.

'I'll take that, thank you very much.' Mark snatched the picture from him. 'I've told you to get out. Before I have to put you out.'

'Hang on, just hang on.' McLoughlin raised his hands. 'I'm not so sure what your business is here. Sally Spencer asked me to call in and check out the house. I'm doing what she asked. And, for that matter, I'm not so sure she'd want you here.'

Porter's face hardened and he took a step towards McLoughlin. His fists were bunched in tight balls. He dragged open the front door. McLoughlin stepped backwards and stumbled through it. He thought for a moment he would fall. He put one hand down to the path to steady himself, then stood.

'How dare you?' Porter screamed. 'How dare you question me? Marina was my beloved. Get out of here and leave me alone.'

McLoughlin opened his mouth to reply, then thought better of it. He hurried towards the front gate. As he got into the car he looked back at the small figure standing in the doorway. Poor bloke, he thought. A lot of baggage on those shoulders. No wonder he lifts weights. Must be the only way to carry that load.

It was nearly one o'clock by the time he got home. He walked through the dark house, too tired to put on any lights. He cleaned his teeth and stripped off his clothes in the bathroom, felt his way into the bedroom. He pulled back the duvet and sank down on to the cool bottom sheet. It had been a long day. He closed his eyes and turned over on to his stomach, punching the pillow into shape beneath him. Sleep came quickly.

And all too quickly left him again. Something had woken him. He sat up slowly. He had been dreaming. He couldn't remember exactly what about, but Mark Porter had been in it somewhere. He had unbuttoned his shirt and pulled it down. The scar around his neck shone brightly. *Look*, he said, *look what I can do*. He began to unzip the scar, drawing an index finger and thumb slowly from left to right. *Look, look at me*, he said, his voice high-pitched and child-like. He put his hands over his ears and began to lift. His head separated itself from his trunk. The cut was smooth. A small dribble of blood trickled down on to his chest. He placed his severed head on the floor beside him. *Now*, he said, his mouth opening and closing like a ventriloquist's dummy, *now, look at me. Aren't I clever?* And he laughed with a manic, high-pitched shriek.

It was the shriek that must have woken him. McLoughlin sat back against the headboard. He was sweating and his mouth was foul and dry. He got up and walked through the house into the kitchen. He filled a pint glass with water and gulped it down. It tasted metallic. Reminded him of blood. He spat into the basin, rinsed the glass and filled it again. He walked back into the sitting room and sat down on the sofa. And saw the lights of a car track across the wall. Headlights, bright and undipped. They stopped, illuminating the room so McLoughlin was suddenly aware that he was naked and the curtains were open. He swivelled around, reluctant to stand and tried to see who was outside. But the lights were too bright. And as he got up, holding a cushion over his genitals, the lights slid towards the hall, then disappeared so the room was dark.

He went into the bathroom and pulled his robe from the back of the door. He wrapped it around himself and walked back into the sitting room. He sat at the desk and gently touched the computer's keyboard. It purred and sighed like a small friendly mammal. He clicked on the icon for Google and entered the words 'The Lodge, school, Dublin'. He hit the enter button and waited. Seconds later he was scanning the school's official website. He opened the home page. There was a link to the archive. He followed the instructions. He selected the year, 1987. He sat back and waited. And there, on the screen, was the photograph that Mark Porter had shown him. He used the zoom button to scan the individual faces. Marina was easy to find. And so was Porter. And there was Poppy. They had called her the ugly sister. He could see why. She was scowling at the camera. Her face was round and heavy. Her hair was pulled back in two thick plaits and black-rimmed glasses obscured her eyes. The girl standing next to her couldn't have been more different. Her face was round too, but pretty and dimpled. She was laughing, happy and carefree.

McLoughlin clicked on her face and her name appeared.

'Rosie Atkinson', the caption said. Poppy still used the family name, he noticed. It marked her out in a world where women invariably took their husband's name on marriage. He began to click randomly on the faces in the photograph and each was identified. Here was Ben Roxby, and next to him a pretty girl with straight fair hair. 'Gillian Kearon' was the name that appeared. And next to her another girl, her hair as blonde as any Scandinavian pop singer. She was Sophie Fitzgerald and in brackets the title (Hon.). The Honourable Sophie Fitzgerald. McLoughlin sat back in his chair. He'd heard of her. She was a regular in the gossip columns. Come to think of it, he was certain he'd seen a few photos of her this afternoon as he'd been flicking through the magazines in Dr Simpson's waiting room. In the winner's enclosure at the Curragh. Holding the bridle of a horse as beautiful as she was. He scanned across the picture from left to right, reading the names aloud. Not a Murphy or a Lynch or a Kelly anywhere to be seen. And just one name in the Irish language: de Paor, Dominic. He was distinctive-looking. Taller than the other boys. Broad shoulders. A jutting nose and crisp black hair. He wasn't much like his father. He must have got his height and build from his mother, McLoughlin thought. He tried to remember what he knew about her. Mentally ill, unstable, in and out of hospital. He must ask Janet Heffernan more.

He finished examining the photograph. He had recognized a few other names. The son of an oil-rich sheikh with a stud farm in Kildare. The daughters of the French ambassador and the sons of the few remnants of the Irish aristocracy who still had their seats in the House of Lords. He wondered about Mark Porter's background. If he owned that house in Fitzwilliam Square he was doing all right. He wondered about the problem with his growth. He must remember to ask Johnny Harris about it. About the drugs he was taking.

He pressed the print button and waited for the photograph to slide out. The reproduction wasn't that good but it was good enough. He turned back to the screen. He was impressed by the quality of the website. A lot of thought and attention to detail had gone into its design. Each year included a letter from the headmaster. He began to read. It was dull enough. Rugby matches played and won, hockey matches played and won. A cultural trip to London, a skiing trip to Val d'Isère for the senior classes after Christmas. Scholarships awarded by Oxford and Cambridge. And then a more sober note crept into the jolly narrative.

Unfortunately one of our most popular pupils, Mark Porter, had a serious accident when he fell from the top landing in the school Residence. His injuries were extensive, but we are delighted that he has made a full recovery. It has reminded us that the safety and well-being of all our pupils is paramount.

The letter was signed 'Anthony Watson, PhD (Oxon), Headmaster.'

He clicked on the next year. Again the school photograph. He scanned the faces. This time Marina's was missing. What was it Poppy had said? Marina was expelled. Rosie wasn't. Neither was any of the others. They were all in the same places. So there it was. Marina got the boot. The others were disciplined. He moved on to the past pupils' association. There was the usual invitation to join, dialogue box for username, password. Links to Engagements, Marriages and Births and the In Memoriam section.

He clicked on to it and scrolled through the list. And saw someone he recognized. Benjamin Samuel Roxby 1970–2004. He clicked on the name. There was a recent photograph. He looked neat and tidy, with close-cropped hair and dark-rimmed glasses. Young for his age. Still had the schoolboy look. There were several short appreciations. One was written by Dominic de Paor. McLoughlin began to read out loud.

'It was with great sadness that I learned of the death of my old friend Ben Roxby. We shared a dorm at school for five years. Ben was funny, clever and a great spin bowler. He was the kind of person who always downplayed his talents. I never realized when I watched him struggling with his algebra that he would pioneer the development of one of the search engines that has made the Internet such a useful tool. I remember him more for the games of poker we used to play when he and our other close friends came to stay at the Lake House during those wonderful summers of our teenage years. Ben's problem was he could never keep a straight face. Not a great asset in poker, but it made him terrific fun. When I heard that he had fallen from the roof of his beautiful house I was very surprised. Fixing loose slates after a storm wouldn't have seemed his kind of thing. But looking after his family was. I know that the well-being of Annabel, Josh and Sam was uppermost in his mind always. My boundless sympathy goes out to them.'

So, Ben Roxby was dead too. A fall from a roof. A tragic accident. That made three of them. Seemed a high rate of attrition for such a small group. Statistically unlikely, he thought.

He got up from the desk and walked back into the kitchen. He opened the glass doors and stepped out on to

the terrace. The air was fresh, almost cold. Above him the
Plough dug a great furrow across the sky. He sat down on
the bench, leaned back and gazed up at it. Soon, he hoped,
he would be out at sea. Nights spent in the wheelhouse.
Silence all around, apart from the rush of the water beneath
the hull and the thrum of the wind in the sails. And nothing
to see in the darkness but the stars. Paul Brady was a good
skipper. He could sail by the stars if need be. He would
teach McLoughlin how to do it. He remembered Brady
telling him once about sailing in the Hobart–Fremantle
race. And how at night he had realized he didn't know the
names of any of the stars and constellations. All so different
in the southern hemisphere, he had said. Bloody confusing.
And McLoughlin had a sudden image of Margaret Mitchell,
standing in the dark of an Antipodean night, her eyes raised
to the sky. She would be looking for her daughter, he
thought, like a grieving mother from a Greek myth. Trying
to find her child in the heavens. Trying to find where Zeus
had placed her.

Johnny Harris could get hold of Ben Roxby's official
cause of death. There would have been an inquest. A sudden
and unexplained death. He'd have access to the evidence
given. He might even have done the post-mortem.
McLoughlin would call him first thing. Now he stood and
stretched. He was tired. He walked back inside and closed
the doors behind him. And remembered the look on Mark
Porter's face earlier that evening. I should have thrown him
out of Marina's house, he thought. Why didn't I? Was I
frightened by him? Have I become an ever bigger coward
now I'm older? Now I don't have the muscle of the guards
behind me?

He moved through the house to his bedroom. He picked

up his trousers from the floor and felt in his pocket for Marina's black pants. He didn't know what to do with them now. He lifted the lid to the linen basket. He would put them in with his next wash, then return them to her bedroom. Put them back in their place. I should have confronted Mark Porter, he thought. But I didn't. And it wasn't cowardice. That wasn't the reason. It was the savage pain in Porter's face. He looked so helpless, so pathetic. It would have been rubbing his nose in it. Still, he'd better get on to Sally in the morning. Tell her to get the locks changed.

He yawned deeply and got into bed. He closed his eyes. Think of nice things, his mother always used to say. Think of nice things and boredom will bring sleep quickly. He smiled as he remembered her. He must go and see her soon. Bring her flowers. He had seen shafts of delphinium in the local florist. She used to grow them. She'd love to see them again. He rolled over on his stomach. He thought of nice things and, as she had predicted, sleep came quickly.

SIXTEEN

The delphiniums were the colour of the deep sea. He bought five spikes and watched as the florist tied them with raffia. 'For someone special?' she asked, with a smile.

'My mother, actually.' He tapped his credit card against his wallet.

'How lovely. And it's not even Mother's Day.' She ran the back of her scissors along the strip of raffia. He watched it curl up into a mass of ringlets. 'Now, how's that?'

His mother didn't speak as he laid the bouquet on her chest of drawers. She smiled and her face creased into a mass of wrinkles.

'Do you remember, Ma, the way you used to force me out into the garden at night to hunt slugs and snails? You used to chuck them into a bucket and pour salt over them. Do you remember the sound? The hiss? But you didn't care, did you, Ma? You'd do anything to protect your bloody delphiniums.' He sat down beside her and took her hand. The joints and knuckles were swollen and ugly, but the skin was still soft and smooth. He lifted her hand and held it against his cheek, then kissed it.

'Thanks,' she whispered. 'Get a vase quick. They'll die without the water.'

They sat in companionable silence. She lay back against the pillows and stared at the flowers. He flicked through the newspaper and turned to the Sudoku. He worked his way through the easy one. It fell into place. Some days it was like that. The pattern revealed itself without any difficulty. Other times he was beating his head against a brick wall. He put in the final number and sighed with pleasure.

'Today your son is a very clever boy,' he said.

'Hmm,' she scowled, 'makes a change. Don't remember sums being your strong point in school. Although,' she reached out and tapped the paper, 'not exactly applied maths, that stuff, is it?'

Funny the way she could always get to him. He gritted his teeth and reminded himself of her age and infirmity. Time passed slowly. Cups of tea and chocolate biscuits were brought by one of the Filipina nurses. She was a dainty little thing with hair like polished jet. She admired the flowers and giggled when he complimented her on the careful way she handled them as she put them into a tall glass vase.

'She's nice,' he said, as she closed the door quietly. His mother sighed, opened her eyes and blinked a couple of times. She reminded him of one of those ancient tortoises that live on the Galapagos islands.

'Nice, they're all nice. But dull, very dull.' She sipped her tea, holding the cup carefully with both hands. 'Tell me something interesting, Michael. I'm so bored. You must be bored now you've retired. Who'd have thought I'd live to have a son of your age? What are you doing with yourself, these days?'

'Well,' he began, 'I got a phone call from an old friend.'

She listened as he told her Marina's story, a smile brightening her face. Then she sighed with satisfaction and leaned back. 'A bully, you say. How interesting. And she was pretty too. That's an unusual combination. You'd wonder why she did it. Usually pretty girls have to do nothing except exist.' Her voice had taken on an edge of bitterness. She shifted awkwardly in the bed and he reached over to take her cup from her hands.

'Is that right, Ma? You're speaking from first-hand experience? Miss Loreto Convent *circa* 1935?' He shouldn't have said it but her taunt about the maths had left a little scar.

'Shut up, Michael, for God's sake.' For a moment he expected a slap. 'For your information I was very pretty. I could have had any of the local boys. But the only one I wanted was your father and there was a little bitch after him too. And, now I come to think of it, she had something of your Marina about her. A devious creature. Small, like a doll. Big smile, big eyes and a nasty, cruel streak. A boy who lived near us had one of those terrible birthmarks all over his face. A big purply thing. Ugly, very ugly. We used to avoid him. Cross the road if he came near. But she – Annie was her name – she pretended to like him. She had him eating out of her hand. Following her around like a stray dog. Then one day she turned on him. In front of us all. I remember what it was like. It was terrible to see. Taught me a lesson about cruelty, that's for sure.' There was silence in the room. He could hear the clatter of teacups and a trolley with a squeaky wheel moving away from them down the corridor.

'And what did Da think?'

'He never looked at her again. He waited for me after school one day and walked me home.' she smiled. 'Innocent times. A week of walking me home and we were practically engaged.' She pointed to the chest of drawers. 'Open that for me, will you? Get out the photos. I still miss him so much. I want to have a look at him.'

He sat close beside her and turned the stiff pages. She lingered over each small black-and-white photograph. Each was a trigger for her memories. Places, occasions, people. He sat back and listened. He had heard the stories many times before. But he was conscious, as he listened to the breath struggling from her chest, that he might not hear them too often again. After a while she fell silent. Her head lolled to one side, her eyes closed. He took the album from between her hands. He kissed her cheek. ''Bye, Ma,' he whispered. 'Love you.'

His phone rang as he hurried down the steps from the nursing-home.

'Johnny, what do you have for me?'

Roxby had died from internal bleeding. He had also fractured his skull, broken both legs and smashed his pelvis. 'He was most likely dead from the moment he hit the ground.' Johnny's tone was matter-of-fact. 'I have the file here. Time of death was given as between eight p.m. on the twelfth of May 2004 and one a.m. on the thirteenth of May 2004. He wasn't found until the next morning. That's why time of death is a bit vague. But the ambulance was called at ten oh-eight on the thirteenth of May. Arrived at ten forty.'

'Did you do the PM?' McLoughlin stood at the bottom of the steps. He moved aside to allow one of the nurses to pass. She smiled and he smiled back.

'Yeah, I did. I remember it, actually. I vaguely knew the family. Went to the same school as one of his uncles.'

McLoughlin fumbled in his pocket for his keys. 'Was it an accident?'

'Well, the verdict was accidental death. He certainly died from the fall, but there was a bit of talk about the circumstances.'

'Yeah.' He unlocked the car and sat in the driver's seat. It was hot and stuffy inside. He propped the door open with his foot.

'Yeah. Gossip, really. But the facts were that there was a violent thunderstorm that day. Roxby had been in Dublin. Came home to discover a leak in the roof. He had, apparently, some kind of a row with his wife and she insisted he fix it. She then, so the guards on the scene said, took the kids and went off to her mother's house, which was about five miles away. She spent the night there and it was when she came back in the morning that she found Roxby dead on the front drive.'

McLoughlin's shirt was sticking to his back. 'So they had words. He went up on to the roof. It had been raining so it was slippery. And he fell. What were the words about?'

'Well,' Harris's voice took on a confiding tone, 'I did hear unofficially, if you know what I mean.'

'You mean the gay network?' McLoughlin smiled at his reflection in the windscreen.

'Unofficially is the word I'm using. It sounds more official, if you get me.' He laughed. 'Anyway, I did hear that the wife, the very lovely Annabel, suspected he was having an affair with someone in Dublin and that was why she was so angry.'

'But it wasn't suicide? Any suggestion that he took his own life?'

'No evidence of that. But it was reckless behaviour. The Roxbys' house isn't any old country house. It's a bloody Gothic castle, built by a very rich ancestor in the mid-nineteenth century. It has turrets and mansard roofs and all manner of gables. Why he went up there on his own, as it was beginning to get dark, is a bit of a mystery.'

McLoughlin drove along the M50. The traffic was light today. He pulled into the outer lane and the speedometer hit 120 k.p.h. He was tempted. He'd never pushed the car as fast as it could go. He pressed his foot down on the accelerator and watched the needle: 125, 130, 135. The road curved imperceptibly. His hands were slipping on the steering-wheel. He could feel the tarmacadam surface. It vibrated through his feet, his legs, up into his groin. Just one last push. The needle crept towards 140 k.p.h., then he eased back, slowly, slowly, slowly, until he was below 120 again. And just in time. The turn-off that would bring him up into the lower reaches of the Dublin mountains was coming up. He indicated, moved into the inside lane and slowed again. He pressed the button on the control panel and the window slid down. He gulped fresh air. Cold sweat dripped down his back. He peeled himself off the seat uncomfortably. He was getting too old to play the boy-racer.

Ahead was a signpost. The road had narrowed. There were high banks on either side and pine trees pressing close. It was cool and much darker. He took a sharp turn to the right and saw ahead a white-painted gate and a discreet sign among the trees. He clanked across a cattle grid, slowed and stopped. He got out of the car. The drive wound ahead of him. On either side the trees gave way to lush pastures, bounded by white-painted fences. A group of horses were grazing together in one corner and in the other cows and their calves lay in the sunshine. McLoughlin stood still and listened. The silence was broken only by the cooing of wood-pigeons and the faint breeze through the trees. He got back into the car and drove slowly forward towards the large white house that was just visible up ahead.

The school was a large square house, probably early nine-teenth century. From the front it looked untouched, but as he walked around towards the back, he could see that a huge unsightly extension had been tacked on. A typical example of 1980s architecture, he thought. PVC windows, ugly pebbledash and a nasty flat roof. But beyond again was a vista of formal gardens with a fountain, tennis courts and playing-fields. And at the edge of the beech woodland that bounded the view on one side he could see a small cottage-style house with its own front garden. An old Land Rover was pulled into the drive.

He moved away from the car and towards the front door. He lifted the brass knocker. He waited. There was no response. McLoughlin looked around. The garden was well tended, weeded, pretty. A brick path led behind the house, towards a high beech hedge with a wooden gate. He lifted the latch and walked through. A man was squatting between two rows of courgettes. He stood up as McLoughlin approached. He was wearing a pair of baggy shorts and an old vest. Thick, tufts of grey hair sprouted from the top of his chest. It matched in colour and texture the hair on his head. His body was lean and lanky. Thick twisted veins coiled around his arms, and his thighs and calves were well muscled. His skin had the sheen of autumn conkers. And his eyes, under bushy white brows, were a bright, light blue. Anthony Watson PhD (Oxon), McLoughlin guessed. 'I'm looking for Anthony Watson,' he called. 'Would that be you?'

The man looked him up and down. 'Yes, that's me.' He began to walk towards McLoughlin, stepping carefully through the vegetables. 'And you are?' His voice was melodic. His accent was very English.

McLoughlin began to explain. Dr Watson listened, a polite expression on his thin, lined face. 'I see,' he said. 'You want to know about Ben Roxby, what kind of chap he was. Is that it?'

'Among other things. Look . . .' McLoughlin felt awkward. It was very hot behind the high hedge. He took off his jacket, conscious of the sweat patches under his arms. 'Sorry to barge in like this. I was passing so I thought I'd see if you were here.'

'Passing?' Dr Watson's eyes thickened to the view of rolling countryside and wooded hills. 'I see. And you say you're a policeman? Do you have any identification?'

McLoughlin fished in his wallet for his warrant card. It looked official enough. As long as Dr Watson didn't notice the expiry date. He handed it over. The other man held it at arm's length. His eyebrows met in a furry grey line as he tried to focus. Then he smiled and handed it back. 'That's fine. Just had to check. We've been plagued with journalists since one of our former pupils died a few weeks ago. Bloody parasites.'

'Yes,' McLoughlin agreed. 'That would be Marina Spencer, wouldn't it?'

'Marina Spencer,' Dr Watson repeated thoughtfully. 'That's right.' He seemed distracted. 'Fancy a drink?' he said. 'Hang on a tick.' He took a step towards the house. 'Isobel!' he shouted. 'Isobel! Drinks needed – out here if you wouldn't mind. We've got a visitor.'

They sat on low wooden seats in the shade of an apple tree. Dr Watson had offered, in rapid succession, lemonade, Pimm's No. 1 or gin and tonic. Mindful of his drive back along the motorway, McLoughlin settled for lemonade. Isobel Watson carried the heavy tray out to the garden. She was as tall and thin as her husband, greying hair cut short with no concession made to style. Dr Watson introduced her and dismissed her with a kiss on the cheek and a wave.

'Now, Inspector McLoughlin, what can I do for you? You're lucky you caught us. We've going away tomorrow until the middle of August. Tuscany, don't you know. Friends with a villa. Wonderful.' He leaned back in his seat and stretched his legs. He sipped his tall glass of Pimm's with relish.

McLoughlin tried to sound confident as he explained that he'd been asked by the commissioner to re-examine a number of what had been considered accidents. There had been much media speculation recently over a couple of deaths that had appeared to be accidental but had subsequently turned out to be suspicious.

'The commissioner, well, he's new to the job and he's very conscious of PR, if you know what I mean.'

Dr Watson raised his eyes to heaven. 'PR,' he tut-tutted. 'What is the world coming to? Same sort of thing goes on in the army now I notice. My grandfather and two of his brothers were all in the regular army – the British army, I mean, of course. They wouldn't have stood for any of this PR nonsense, but the chappies in charge these days . . . Well, what can I say?' He smiled.

The smile of the conqueror, McLoughlin thought. 'So, looking back over the last year I noticed that Benjamin Roxby had died from a fall. And there was . . . well . . . speculation at the time as to whether it was accidental or—'

'Or what, Inspector McLoughlin?' Dr Watson's face had coloured. 'Ridiculous gossip! Nothing but ridiculous gossip. Ben Roxby was honourable and upright. Came from a very good family. Did wonderful things for us at the school. Gave us a grant to develop our website. Not that I can see much point in it but, then, old fogeys like me can't get to grips with that sort of thing. But everyone else says it's marvellous and it was all because of Roxby's generosity. But the gossip, honestly . . .' Dr Watson crossed his long bony legs and drank some Pimm's.

'And what kind of things were being said, Dr Watson?' His lemonade, he found, was delicious. 'Mm, this is lovely. Is it homemade?'

'Of course. Isobel wouldn't dream of having the other stuff in the house. Full of artificial colouring, preservatives. Carcinogens, the lot of them.' He seemed suddenly confused. McLoughlin waited. Dr Watson shifted awkwardly. 'What were we talking about?'

'Gossip,' McLoughlin prompted, 'about Ben Roxby's death.'

'Oh, yes, that.' Dr Watson straightened up. 'Absolute nonsense. Some silly talk about another woman. I knew him well. His marriage was first class. Annabel's a wonderful girl. From a very good family. And he has two smashing sons. Young Josh starts here next term and Sam will follow the year after.'

'So if Roxby was planning on sending his sons here he wasn't put off by his own experiences as a pupil?'

Dr Watson raised his eyebrows. 'Not sure what you mean by that.'

'Well, the bullying business. Mark Porter. It ended badly, didn't it?' McLoughlin drank some lemonade.

Dr Watson slapped his leg violently. 'Bloody horse-flies. Eat one alive out here in the summer.' His gaze drifted over McLoughlin's head. 'You were saying?'

'Mark Porter, the bullying. Ben Roxby was involved, wasn't he?'

Dr Watson rubbed one leg against the other. McLoughlin was reminded of a rangy old gelding scratching himself against a fence post.

'Not sure what you're getting at, Inspector McLoughlin. Not sure what that has to do with Ben's death.'

It was very quiet in the garden. Very still. The scent from a climbing rose hung in the warm air.

'Well, Roxby's death on its own, perhaps nothing. But there have been two more deaths of your former pupils. And, from what I can gather, they were friends.' McLoughlin waited for Dr Watson to respond, but he said nothing. 'Marina Spencer died a few weeks ago. Suspected suicide. And Rosie Webb, the day before yesterday. All former pupils of this school. And all involved in that same set of incidents. Am I right?'

A pigeon cooed softly. McLoughlin spotted the bird high in the branches of a huge beech tree. Still Dr Watson said nothing.

'Now,' McLoughlin leaned forward, 'it was quite a scandal, wasn't it? Not what you'd expect in a school like this. The bullying was so bad that Mark tried to hang himself. Or, at least, that's what I heard. Fortunately he survived. And his tormentors, well, they were punished. Marina Spencer was expelled. The others, including Roxby, were disciplined. What was it? Detention on Saturdays? Privileges suspended for a while? Was that it? Not allowed to visit the tuck shop? Gated for the rest of the term?'

The pigeon had been joined by another. They were calling from tree to tree. McLoughlin waited.

Dr Watson's hands plucked at the faded linen of his shorts. 'It was all so unfortunate.' His voice had a whining quality, like that of a tired toddler. 'So unfortunate. But sometimes in a school, in a community of individuals, you'll get a bad apple. The person who infects the others with a sense of maliciousness, nastiness, bad manners. And then, well, all hell breaks loose. It doesn't happen often. And, of course, since then we've been much more careful about the type of child we enrol.'

'And you are referring to whom?' McLoughlin was anxious to get the pronoun right.

'Well, I'm reluctant to speak ill of the dead, but Marina Spencer was a very disruptive and destructive influence in the school. She really had to go.' Dr Watson got up. He swayed gently as he moved towards the table. He refilled his glass from the jug, then waved it in McLoughlin's direction. 'Sure I can't tempt you to a dhrop of the hard shtuff?' His attempt at a Dublin accent was grating and foolish.

McLoughlin shook his head. 'Just to get things clear, Dr Watson. Just to clarify the issue. The whole thing happened, as I understand it, after James de Paor died. Am I right?'

Dr Watson sat down again. He nodded and drank.

'That must have been dreadful for the children. Dominic in particular.'

Dr Watson nodded again.

'To die like that, a silly accident. To leave such devastation behind you.' McLoughlin's voice was calm, neutral.

'Yes, poor James. But it was typical of him in a way. He was always reckless.' Dr Watson scratched his leg vigorously again.

'You knew him, did you?'

'Yes, for many years. Long before he had children. I knew him when his name was Power. Before he decided to embrace all things Gaelic. I went to school with his older brothers.'

'I didn't know.'

'Lovely family. That marvellous house in the mountains. They didn't take it seriously when James started learning Irish. Then he changed his name. And when he became a barrister he began to defend those IRA men in the Special Criminal Court. Fortunately his father died before that happened.'

'And did you – do you know his first wife?'

'Helena,' Dr Watson said, with the emphasis on the first syllable. 'Ah, there now, there's a puzzle.' His brow furrowed. 'A beautiful woman. A brilliant woman. A barrister like James. But something happened when she had her children. I believe they call it puerperal psychosis. It's an extreme form of post-natal depression, so my wife tells me. She was pretty bad when she had Dominic, and there was a second child, a little girl. She died. A cot death, they say. After that things went from bad to worse.' Dr Watson gulped his drink.

'So the atmosphere in the school that term. Those bereaved children. It must have been difficult.'

Dr Watson stared hard at McLoughlin. 'Inspector, the people who send their children to this school come from tough stock. They are the descendants of empire builders. They are not easily brought down. They know how to suffer in silence, to move on, to prevail.' His voice was getting louder. 'That was one of the things that was very irksome about Marina Spencer. There was an hysterical quality to her makeup. You know, she reminded me of Diana Spencer. A coincidence that they had the same name, no doubt, but Diana was like Marina. All that pointless emotion, that ridiculous self-examination. Marina didn't know how lucky she was. Through her tenuous relationship with James Power she had been privileged to come here.' He drained his glass. 'No, she had to go. She would have gone anyway. Once Helena had successfully contested the legality of the so-called marriage between James and Marina's mother, the money was going to run out.'

'But to expel her? And only her. Why not the others?'

Dr Watson got up and filled his glass again. He wobbled on his feet, and the hand holding the jug was shaking.

'Isobel!' he shouted. 'A refill – we need a refill. Chop, chop.' His face was now a deep red.

McLoughlin stood too. He picked up his jacket.

Watson faced him. 'I'll tell you why I got rid of Marina. The girl had no hinterland. She was on her own. The others had the institution of the family to protect them. They had wealth and position. Even Mark, with his physical deformities. His family owns half of Georgian Dublin. They came to Ireland with Cromwell. Marina had none of that.'

His wife opened the back door. She hurried across the

lawn. 'Tony, that's enough.' She turned to McLoughlin. 'I think you'd better go.' Her voice was sharp. She took Dr Watson's arm and helped him towards the house. 'It's all right, darling. It's the heat. You know you should be wearing your hat.'

Dr Watson tried to push her away, but her grip was firm. His legs were trembling. He looked old and shaky.

'The girl was a thief. Remember, Isobel, the money that went missing? And we found it under her mattress. She was a slut too!' He was shouting now. 'You know that, Isobel. You caught her in the cellar with Roxby. Disgusting behaviour. Disgusting.'

'Ssh, Tony, inside now. It's time for your nap. We've nothing further to say.' She propelled her husband inside. The door closed. Wasps were circling the jug of Pimm's. One had fallen in and was lying on its back, legs in the air. The buzzing stopped. A happy death, he thought.

He walked out of the garden and towards the school. And saw a window open on the ground floor. He glanced around, then pulled himself up and over the sill. No doubt about it, he needed to lose that bit of weight, he thought, as he landed awkwardly, almost collapsing in a heap on the floor. He stood up. He was in the new building. A long corridor with classrooms opening off it. He began to walk towards the old house. The transition was abrupt. Behind him there were walls painted magnolia, scuffed lino tiles and fluorescent lighting. Ahead was a large square entrance hall, panelled with mahogany, floored with marble diamonds of black and white, lit from a glass dome high above. The staircase curved elegantly away from him, the limestone steps seeming unsupported from below. He climbed them slowly. First floor, formal drawing room and library. Second floor, bedrooms with dark red embossed wallpaper and nineteenth-century furniture. Third floor, and the rooms were smaller with lower ceilings. He looked inside one. It was crammed with narrow beds. Next door was a bathroom, tiled in white with an old-fashioned free-standing bath, a row of washbasins and series of cubicles, each with a toilet, cistern high on the wall and a long chain. There was a smell of Jeyes Fluid.

He stepped back on to the landing and leaned on the banister. The drop to the floor was dramatic. He bent and checked the wooden rods, running his hand down them. One was slightly different from the others. The wood was newer, not original. It had been stained to match the rest, but the job was poor. He slipped his hand around it. Mark Porter had tied the rope to the railing, then put the noose over his head. He had climbed on to the banister. McLoughlin stood up. Above him was the vaulted glass dome. Below, the black and white diamonds shimmered. Mark Porter had balanced on the banister, then launched himself head first, down, down, down. The noose had tightened and jerked him upwards. He was lucky his neck had not been broken. The wood had given way. He fell. He was lucky he hadn't landed on his head and smashed his skull. He hadn't landed on his torso either and suffered internal injuries. He had landed with his legs beneath him. He was winded, he was shocked, he had a broken bone. But he was alive.

McLoughlin walked slowly down the stairs and into the hall. The heavy front door was bolted on the inside. He seized the metal handle and gave it a tug, then clicked open the new Yale lock and went out into the afternoon sunshine. He walked across the dusty gravel to his car, and heard a voice calling his name. Isobel Watson was hurrying from the cottage.

'Mr McLoughlin, a word, please.' Her face was twisted with anxiety. She stopped, chest heaving. She held out her left hand.

'My husband, don't pay too much attention to him. He's not well. He has Parkinson's disease. He doesn't have many of the symptoms yet, but he's been diagnosed. He's going to retire soon and he can't bear it. The school has been his life.' There was a supplicating tone in her voice that made McLoughlin feel like cringing.

He smiled in what he hoped was a sympathetic manner. 'Sure, of course. I can imagine something like that must be very frightening.'

'It is. He's inclined to drink more than is good for a man of his age. He never used to so it has a powerful effect on him. And he says things that maybe he shouldn't.'

McLoughlin nodded. 'Of course. I understand.'

She smiled, a tight mechanical grimace. 'You asked him about Marina and the bullying. I know he sounded cruel. He didn't mean it like that.'

'No?' McLoughlin couldn't keep the scepticism from his voice. 'What was it he said about Marina and Ben Roxby? Disgusting? Was that the term he used?'

Isobel Watson flushed. 'I found them in the cellar. Marina was – well, I won't go into details but it wasn't what we could consider suitable behaviour. We have to be very careful in a school like this. We didn't always take both boys and girls. I was never sure it was a good idea, but Tony . . . Well, the Protestant population of Ireland is very small. He felt it would be a good way to encourage relationships. So many of our boys had married, well . . .'

'Catholics.'

'Well, yes, I suppose so. I know that sounds bigoted, but the Ne Temere decree has had a terrible effect on us. Too many Protestants are diffident about their faith, happy to let their Roman Catholic partner take charge. And once the child is baptized, the rest follows. First communion, confirmation, marriage. That's it, really. Tony thought we should do what we could. So we opened the school to girls. But we have to be careful. Things can get out of hand. Marina was very pretty, very well developed for her age. It had to be stopped.'

'I take it you didn't think she was suitable for a boy like Ben. Am I right?'

She shrugged. 'Personally I didn't care. But Tony takes his role *in loco parentis* very seriously. Look,' she shifted uneasily, 'if you want to know more about what happened I would go and see Dominic Power. Have you met him?'

He shook his head. 'Power? You mean Dominic de Paor, don't you?'

'We called him Power. That's what was on his birth certificate.' Her expression was stern. 'I don't know why I'm saying this, but I always thought there was something going on between Dominic and Marina. I couldn't put my finger on it. But when they came back to school after James had died Marina was different. Her behaviour was different.' She took a small handkerchief from the sleeve of her blouse and touched it to her lips.

McLoughlin waited. Then he said, 'Your husband called her a thief. That's a pretty nasty thing to say about someone.'

'Unfortunately he was right. Money went missing. Small items of jewellery. I suppose we were careless. The boarders were allowed to keep a lot of personal belongings in their rooms. Marina was tempted. She didn't have as much as they had. We should have protected her. But we didn't.' She avoided his gaze. McLoughlin felt sudden sympathy for this woman. She didn't have her husband's carapace of certainty.

'And all this happened after James de Paor died?'

'Yes, I'd always thought Marina was a tough girl. Able to stand up for herself. Not easily intimidated. But, well, I noticed little things. I remember seeing her and Dominic one day. She was playing tennis and he was watching. Marina was good. I used to take the girls for games. Tennis, hockey, lacrosse. I don't any longer. Too old for that now. But I had high hopes for Marina. I thought she had the makings of a first-class player. Plenty of natural talent. Plenty of nerve. That's why I was so struck by what happened.' She dabbed her lips again. The handkerchief had a pretty lace trim.

'What did happen?'

'She was playing Rosie Atkinson. She was winning. Serving beautifully. Returning like a dream. Hitting fabulous passing shots. Lovely stuff. It was all going her way and then Dominic appeared. He stood and watched. And after a few minutes she fell apart. Started serving badly, lots of double faults. She lost her pace, her rhythm. Made stupid mistakes. And when the match was over, well, it's odd but I remember it so clearly, she walked off the court and Dominic followed her. He put his hand on the back of her neck and,' she shrugged, 'I don't know why but it gave me the shivers.'

'And the bullying? What about that?' McLoughlin jingled his keys.

She smiled. 'Dominic was, and I'm sure still is, very clever. Charming, personable, powerful. You know, a school like this goes through phases. It's a bit like human history in miniature. You have your monarchs, your tyrants, your benevolent despots, your democrats. Dominic was a monarch. He had his court and his favourites. And God protect anyone who wasn't a favourite.'

'And who were his favourites?'

'Well,' she said, 'it's funny. So many children pass through this school, I don't remember them all. But there was something about that time. I can still see the group. Dominic, of course, Ben, too, and then the girls. Gilly Kearon, who married Dominic, Sophie Fitzgerald, Rosie Atkinson. Not her sister.'

'That's Poppy?'

'Yes, but Poppy wasn't pretty. She didn't fit the profile, I think you could say.' She smiled fleetingly. For a moment, she looked young, her expression wistful.

'So how did Mark fit the profile? He surely didn't measure up to the other boys?'

'No,' the smile became a downward curve, 'but he was useful in other ways. Every beauty needs a beast. Every hero needs a coward. Every genius needs a fool.'

'And Marina? What was her function?'

'I'm not sure, but maybe she was the catalyst, the accelerant. I don't know.' She took a pace away from him. 'I've said enough. I've really nothing else to add.'

'And did you ever say any of this to your husband?'

'I did, but . . .'

'But Dominic had a hinterland. Even though his father was dead.'

'Yes, he had a hinterland.' She pushed the little handkerchief into her sleeve and clasped her hands at waist level. 'It was a long time ago. The school has entered the phase of liberal democracy. We make sure that nothing like that ever happens now. We're much more careful with our children.' She looked past him towards the gardens and the playing-fields. 'This is a good school. We have an extensive scholarship programme. We take children from disadvantaged backgrounds. We give them a chance.' She turned away. 'I'd better go. It's time for Tony's pills. I have to make sure he takes them.'

He watched her hurry away. He waited until she was out of sight, then walked down the path towards the tennis courts. They looked neglected. The wire netting around them was sagging and holed. The grass needed cutting and the lines were faded and indistinct. He pushed through the gate to the nearest of the three courts, A shabby net drooped from one side to the other. Someone had abandoned a racquet near the base line. He picked it up. It was old and wooden, badly warped, its strings loose and sagging. He lifted it above his shoulder and mimed a serve.

'What happened here, Marina? What happened to you?' His voice was quiet, subdued. A breeze stirred the branches of the tall pines. He dropped the racquet. It was time to go.

SEVENTEEN

Vanessa arrived on the doorstep as Margaret was getting her breakfast. When Margaret opened the door she barged past her into the hall. 'You left me!' she shouted. 'You left me in the library! I didn't know where you were. I went looking for you and you were gone. Why did you do that?' Her face was flushed.

'Well,' Margaret hesitated, 'I'm sorry. There was something I had to do. Somewhere I had to visit. You seemed to be having a really nice time there in the library. I went to look for you, but you were reading. To be honest, I didn't think you'd want to come with me.'

'But you didn't ask me.' Tears ran down Vanessa's cheeks. 'You didn't ask me, you just left me there. You treated me the way everyone always treats me. As if I was a nuisance and a nobody.'

She sank down on her knees, sobbing uncontrollably.

'Vanessa.' Margaret squatted beside her. 'Hey, come on, Vanessa. Don't cry. I'm sorry. I had to see someone. I did look for you. You were reading. You looked happy. I didn't want to disturb you. Please,' she tried to pull the girl's hands away from her face, but Vanessa resisted, 'I'm sorry, I didn't think.' She put her arms around Vanessa's hunched back and stroked it gently. 'There, there, now. There's a good girl.'

Gradually the sobs subsided.

Margaret took her hands. 'Now, stand up. Come down to the kitchen and I'll see if I can find something for you to eat. I'm sure you're hungry, aren't you?'

She made her a mug of cocoa, then toasted some cheese on a thick piece of white bread. Vanessa sat at the kitchen table and ate greedily.

'Better now?' Margaret sat down across from her.

Vanessa lifted her mug and drained it. 'That was lovely. You make good cocoa. It's really nice and creamy.'

Margaret smiled at her. She held out a tissue. 'You've got a bit of cocoa on your chin. You'd better wipe it off.'

Vanessa scrubbed vigorously. 'Is that better?' she asked, her voice a little hoarse.

Margaret took the tissue from her. 'There's a little bit just . . .' she dabbed at her nose '. . . there.' She smiled, leaned over and put her arms around her. 'Now, tell me, what's really wrong.'

It was her mother. She wasn't sleeping. She wasn't eating. All she did was cry. Vanessa couldn't bear it any longer.

'And McLoughlin, the policeman you told me about, has he done anything?' Margaret began to wash their dishes and put them on the draining-rack.

'Mum got a phone call from him yesterday. He said he thought she should get the locks changed on Marina's house. So when I got home we went there. Mum didn't want to go on her own. She wanted me to come too.' Vanessa picked up a mug and began to dry it. Carefully, thoroughly.

'And how was that? Was it difficult?' Margaret watched the expression on Vanessa's face. She had become suddenly very tense.

'It was awful. The house was a terrible mess. There was

stuff all over the floor. Books and photographs, CDs and tapes, and upstairs in Marina's bedroom her clothes were everywhere and the mattress on her bed had been pulled off. It was horrible.' Vanessa's face was white and pinched.

Margaret took the tea-towel from her. 'You don't need to do that. Sit down.'

Vanessa snatched it back. 'No, no, I want to. I want to do something.'

'OK, fine.' Margaret sat down at the table again. She waited for a couple of seconds. 'Do you have any idea who did it? Had the house been broken into?'

Vanessa shook her head. 'No, so it had to be someone who had keys. And as far as we know there was only us, the guard, and Mark Porter. So . . .'

'Mark Porter?'

'He's this guy who went to school with Marina. And recently she'd started seeing him again.'

'A romance?'

'Oh, no, nothing like that.' Vanessa's voice was dismissive. 'No, not at all. She was just being nice to him.'

'So why would he trash her house?'

Now Vanessa was piling the crockery neatly. Mugs, plates, bowls. 'Did your mother call the police?' Margaret asked.

Vanessa picked up a teaspoon. She began to polish it. 'No. I said she should. But she said there was no real harm done and she'd had enough of the police. And anyway, she said, she thought if Mark had done it then it must have been because he was so upset about everything that had happened. And she said she could understand it.' Vanessa put down the tea-towel. 'And then she got really upset because there were some pictures on the floor and one of them was this old school photo. Marina when she was about fourteen and all the other kids. Mark was in it too.'

Margaret remembered how it had been. Finding pictures of Mary. Unexpectedly. Opening an old bag and finding a photograph. Her first day at school. Her curly hair in two pigtails and a big grin on her face. 'And what about the mess in the house?' Her voice was gentle. 'What did you do about that?'

Vanessa was crying now as she polished the knives. Margaret stood up and put her arm around her shoulders. She took the tea-towel from her and pulled her down on to a seat.

'Mum phoned an emergency locksmith and we waited until he came and changed the locks. Then we went home. But I could hear her last night. I kept on waking up and I could hear her walking around the house. All night. And I can't stand it any longer. You have to help her,' Vanessa begged. 'You have to talk to her. Please! I'll phone her, get her to come here. You have to help her.'

The woman whom Vanessa brought to the house was small and frail. Margaret stood at the top of the steps and watched them walk up the path. Vanessa had an arm around her mother's shoulders and guided her carefully over the cracked and uneven surface.

'It's good to meet you.' Margaret held out her hand. 'I'm Margaret Mitchell. Please come inside.'

The woman tried to smile. 'Thank you.' Her voice was quiet, tentative. Her face was pale. There were deep shadows beneath her eyes and lines around her mouth. 'I'm Sally, Vanessa's mother. I hope we're not imposing.'

Margaret drew her into the house. 'Not at all. It's my pleasure.' She looked past Sally to Vanessa, who was hovering uncertainly in the doorway. 'Would you like to go out for a bit? We'll be all right now.'

'Yeah, thanks. I've some things to do.' Vanessa turned to her mother and kissed her cheek. 'I'll see you later, Mum. OK?'

The woman nodded. She lifted her hand and touched her daughter's cheek. 'You go. I'll be OK.'

They sat in the kitchen. The kettle hummed. The clock ticked. Margaret heated the teapot.

'I'm sorry. I hope Vanessa hasn't been making a nuisance of herself. She's had a hard time recently and I haven't been much company for her. I've been neglecting her, I'm afraid,' Sally Spencer fiddled with her watch-strap, her wedding ring, pushed the sleeves of her blouse up her forearms, then pulled them down again.

'No, it's fine, really. She's a sweet girl. I like her.' Margaret poured water into the pot and gestured to the two white mugs on the table.

'Thank you, tea would be lovely.' Sally smiled. 'Mm, it smells good. What kind is it?'

'Darjeeling. My father was very fussy – he would only have the best. And he hated teabags. So I couldn't imagine drinking anything else here, in this kitchen.' She offered milk and pushed a plate of biscuits forward with the tip of her finger.

'The tea is lovely, but I'll pass on the biscuits,' Sally said.

'You're very thin.' Margaret lifted her mug and drank some tea. 'Have you been eating?'

Sally looked at the floor. 'I have no appetite. I feel sick when I eat. I force myself when Vanessa's at home, but I'd be as happy without.'

'It's a phase. You'll get over it. I thought I'd never eat again. I thought I'd never want to taste food. It seemed somehow disloyal to Mary, to think that I could eat and take pleasure from it. That I could eat to sustain my life when she couldn't.' Margaret took a biscuit. She bit into its chocolate coating. And thought of Jimmy Fitzsimons. Her stomach heaved and for a moment she thought she would vomit. She forced herself to swallow.

Sally smiled at her. 'It's good to talk to you. It's so hard to explain to anyone how I feel. People are well-meaning. They want to help. They try to understand. But they don't get it.'

'How can they? They have no experience of such pain. And with pain, you can't feel someone else's, only your own.'

The two women sat in silence as they drank their tea. Margaret's chocolate biscuit remained half eaten on the plate. Sally's eyes closed and her head drooped.

'Sally.' Margaret's voice was low.

'Mm?'

'Come upstairs with me. Let me put you to bed.'

'I can't.'

'Why not?'

'I've things I have to do.'

'No, you don't. You need to sleep. More than anything else. Here.' Margaret stood and took Sally's hand. 'Come with me.' She pulled the other woman to her feet and put an arm around her. She led her up the steps from the kitchen to the hall. She guided her into the bedroom at the front of the house. She sat her down on the bed, then closed the shutters. She laid her flat and lifted up her feet. She took off Sally's sandals. She covered her with the quilt.

'Sleep now,' she said. 'Sleep. I will look after you. Sleep.'

Sally sighed, Margaret closed the door behind her, then walked back down to the kitchen. She picked up the plate of biscuits and dumped them in the bin.

Loose gravel crunched beneath Vanessa's clogs. Their bright red leather was covered with a layer of fine dust. She pulled a crumpled tissue from her pocket, bent down and wiped them clean. Then she straightened up and took a deep breath, filling her lungs with salty air.

She walked on down the pier towards the lighthouse at the end. It was quiet today. A couple of boys cast their fishing lines into the harbour. A jogger passed her, tanned legs moving smoothly. And up ahead she could see a woman with a large dog. Vanessa's heart began to race. The dog was a German shepherd. His coat was the colour of toffee. His ears were pricked. He looked alert, on his guard. Sweat prickled on Vanessa's skin. She cast around for escape. But there was none. The high sea wall was on one side, and on the other a deep drop to the pier's lower level. The dog was getting closer. Vanessa flattened herself against the wall. Panic grabbed her by the throat. She whimpered.

The dog was very close now. He was walking slowly, his long tail waving from side to side. Her legs were shaking and her mouth was full of saliva. The dog stopped. He reached out his large head. His wet nose touched her skirt. He sniffed, his nostrils opening wide. Then he whined.

'Tch-tch.' The woman behind him clicked her tongue against the roof of her mouth. The dog lay down. He rested his nose on his front paws and closed his eyes.

'Are you all right?' The woman put her hand on the dog's head. He blinked, then closed his eyes again.

Vanessa forced herself to nod. She couldn't speak.

'I'm sorry if he frightened you. He wouldn't hurt you, you know. He's an old sweetie, really.'

Vanessa unclenched her fists. 'I'm sure you're right.' She still could not move.

The woman took a heavy leather lead from her pocket. She clipped it to the dog's collar. 'There. Is that better?'

Vanessa nodded again. 'I'm sorry. It's just – when I was little a dog like yours bit me. On my leg.' She reached down and touched the scar through her skirt.

'Oh.' The woman's mouth turned down. 'I'm so sorry. How dreadful. No wonder you were frightened.' She jerked the lead and the dog lumbered obediently to his feet. 'You poor thing. Can I help you at all? Would you like a lift home?'

'No, really, it's fine.' Vanessa smiled tentatively. 'It's OK. I live near here.'

'Oh?' The woman put her hand on the dog's collar again. She stroked his thick ruff. 'I have friends in Monkstown. Where do you live?'

'Trafalgar Lane.' Vanessa's legs had stopped shaking. She felt light-headed with relief. 'Do you know it? It's near Belgrave Square. It's a lovely place to live because it's really close to the sea.'

'Trafalgar Lane,' the woman repeated the name slowly. 'I think I do know where that is. You're right. It is a lovely place to live.' The dog looked up at her. His long pink tongue flopped out of his open mouth. 'Why don't you try patting him? He really won't hurt you.'

'No.' Vanessa's palms were damp at the thought of it. 'No, I couldn't.' She tried to smile. 'Thanks, but really I'm fine now. I know I shouldn't be so frightened. I'm not scared of all dogs. We have a little mongrel called Toby and I love him. It's just, well . . .' She stopped.

The woman held out the dog's lead. 'Why don't you try this? You hold his lead. I'll walk beside you. You'll see, he's really docile. He wouldn't hurt a fly. Honestly.'

Vanessa took the leather strap. The dog stood quietly. He turned to look at her.

'Come on,' the woman gave her a gentle prod, 'we'll walk together. You'll see how easy it is.'

The dog gave a tug at the lead and Vanessa took a step forward.

'That's the way. Come on. Show me how brave you can be.' She smiled and Vanessa realized she must once have been beautiful. When she was young.

And they walked together in step. Woman, girl and dog. Back along the pier.

Margaret stood in the doorway and looked into the bedroom. Sally Spencer had woken up. She had propped herself up on the pillows. She still looked exhausted, but she smiled as Margaret came in. 'Thank you so much for that. I don't know what came over me. I'm not in the habit of falling asleep at other people's kitchen tables.' Her voice sounded stronger.

'That's OK.' Margaret sat down in the rocking-chair by

the window. She pushed with one foot and felt it tilt beneath her.

'What a lovely chair,' Sally said. 'We had one like that when I was a child. I seem to remember I tipped it over backwards once.'

'Me too. I was banned from it for years.' Margaret rocked slowly and smoothly. 'This was my parents' bedroom when I was a child. My mother used to sit here and watch the sea.'

'Has she been dead for long?' Sally shifted her legs under the heavy quilt.

'About ten years.'

Rock, rock, rock, rock. The wooden runners drummed on the wooden floor.

'Oh, of course, I remember now,' Sally said apologetically. 'She died around the same time as your daughter, didn't she?'

'Yes, that's right,' Margaret said. 'We had a funny relationship, my mother and I. I never thought we were close, but I miss her now.' Margaret's eyes closed as she rocked. She could smell her mother's perfume. It had clung to everything she wore, everything she touched.

'They were tough, that generation of women.' Sally rolled over on her side and pillowed her head on her arm. 'I don't know if we match up to them. Loss seems to knock the stuffing out of us. They took it in their stride.'

'I'm not so sure if that's so.' Margaret's eyes opened and her gaze drifted towards the sea. 'I think they just had different ways of expressing it, or not expressing it, if you know what I mean. And, anyway, look at you. I understand from what Vanessa has told me that you've had your fair share of loss, and you've survived.'

'Have I?' Sally murmured. 'Seems like I've been cursed. Or, to paraphrase Oscar Wilde, "To lose one husband was carelessness, but to lose two" . . .' She smiled sadly.

'Vanessa told me something about how her father died. So shocking and unexpected.' The horizon was beautiful. A luminous stripe of green, bright against the darker sea.

'Unexpected, shocking, all those things. And such a beautiful day. I remember it so well.' Her voice dropped. 'It was hot. And when it's hot up there in the hills, it's very hot. The house and the lake are so sheltered. They seem to catch the warmth and cradle it.'

So hot, everyone wearing their swimming togs. The whole family there. James's son and his school friends. Sally's children. Vanessa, the baby, crawling across the fine white sand of the narrow lake beach. They had been swimming in the cold water. It drained from the peat bogs all around. It was a strange dark brown. Like flat Coca-Cola, Sally thought. It made her skin look like pale amber. Now she sat in a deckchair, a glass of wine in her hand. Vanessa was changed and dry, lying in her pram, the little parasol at a jaunty angle, keeping the sun from her pale baby skin. Sally relaxed in her deckchair and closed her eyes. For the first time in years she felt safe and protected.

'I'd looked after myself and the kids ever since Robbie, my first husband, died. I had a little shop and I sold costume jewellery, accessories. Nice but cheap. I made a living, just about. But life with James was very different.'

'What about his first wife?'

Rock, rock, rock, rock. The wooden runners drummed on the wooden floor.

'That was difficult. But James told me that even if she hadn't been ill he would have left her. He didn't love her any more. He had already got his divorce before we met. He wanted to marry me. We went to London for the weekend. We had a ball. Vanessa was conceived there.' Sally rolled on to her back and stared at the ceiling. 'I could never have imagined that it would end the way it did.'

It was so quiet. She would sleep while Vanessa slept. Then she would go and speak to the housekeeper about the party that night. Dinner for ten. It was all planned and organized. James had told her. She didn't need to worry about a thing. She just had to enjoy it.

'And then suddenly there was this terrible noise. An engine revving and revving on the far side of the lake. One of Dominic's friends, a boy called Ben, had brought his motorboat with him when he came to stay. The kids all wanted to try water-skiing. I thought at first it must be them. But it wasn't. The boat came really close to the shore. It sprayed me with water. And there was a group of boys in it. I didn't recognize any of them.'

And James running down from the house. Shouting at Marina. Telling her to start the outboard.

'I stood up. I shouted at him to stop. I said I'd call the guards. But he didn't pay any attention. I saw Marina fiddling with the engine cord. And James pushing her out of the way. And then they began to move out from the beach. James in the stern, holding on to the tiller, Marina sitting in the bow.'

Across the lake. The motorboat now in the distance at the far end where a little stream ran down over the rapids into the bog. Sally got up and waded into the water, shading her eyes against the sun. She could see that the motorboat had turned. It was heading straight for the dinghy. At the last moment it changed direction but she could see the wash, the dinghy rocking violently from side to side. Now it was circling the dinghy, slowing, slowing, then speeding up again and again the wash swamping the small boat. Swamping it, so it rocked from side to side, drifting now. And Sally could see that James was standing up in the dinghy. She could see he was trying to start the engine. He was bent over it, and the motorboat was back. Going so fast she thought they would collide. And she screamed and cried out.

'Dominic, Tom – help! Where are you?' Screaming so loudly that Vanessa woke up, began to shriek. Sally turned away from the lake to pick her up. And when she looked back the motorboat was gone, to the far end of the lake, almost out of sight.

'And the dinghy? What about the dinghy?'

Rock, rock, rock, rock. The wooden runners drummed on the wooden floor.

'Well, the dinghy seemed OK. I couldn't really see. So I put Vanessa back in her pram and started to run to the house. I was calling for the housekeeper. Karen O'Reilly was her name, a very nice woman, and when I told her what had happened, she said that Kevin, her husband, who looked after the grounds and the deer, had seen some boys down in the woods by the lake and told her they must have taken the boat from its mooring. She said she was sure everything was all right. So I gave Vanessa to her and I went back to the water.'

And then she saw the dinghy. It was moving slowly, so slowly. She waved and shouted, but there was no response. Just the slow, stately movement of the boat through the water. And then she realized why there was no response. Because the only occupant of the boat was rowing it. She could see the back of the figure, bending and straightening over the oars. Bending and straightening and the oars dipping, then lifting, the sun glinting off the drops of water that fell from the wooden blades. She waited and watched and then she saw. It was her daughter who was rowing. Her daughter's slight dark-haired figure, sitting in the centre of the boat, her hands grasping the oars, and the sun glistening on the drops as they were thrown back again. And as she got nearer, she turned and shouted: 'Help me! Help me! Help me!'

'But what could I do? I was on my own. And then I heard a shout and the men came running from the house. Kevin, and some of the men who worked for him. There was one called Peadar and another whose name I didn't know. And Kevin stripped off, waded into the water and swam out to the boat. And I saw him pulling himself up over the stern, then leaning down. He seemed to be pulling something up and out of the water. It was heavy because the boat was rocking from side to side. I could see, but I didn't want to see. I didn't want to see that it was James.'

Rock, rock, rock, rock. The wooden runners drummed on the wooden floor.

'And Marina was rowing again. And Kevin was crouching in the boat. I couldn't see what he was doing, but he was bent over, his head bobbing up and down. And afterwards I realized he was giving James mouth-to-mouth. Trying to save him.'

The boat came slowly to the jetty. She could see the body lying on its wooden slats. A rope was looped around James's chest. Tied on to the seat in the stern. The men undid it and dragged James's body out on to the jetty. And Kevin tried again. Tried to blow life back into him. They stood and stared at him. And Sally stared too. She couldn't believe he was dead. He looked fine, just soaking wet. She wanted to shout at him, 'Get up! Stop pretending! You're frightening me.' She wanted to prod him with her toe, take hold of his hands and pull him upright. But she didn't. She knelt beside him and laid her head on his chest. Why wasn't his heart beating? Every night when she went to sleep she put her head on his chest and listened to his heartbeat, slow, strong and steady. But not now. Now there was no deep, resonant vibration. Nothing but his cold wet shirt against her chest.

'And I sat up. I shouted at Marina. She was still in the boat. She was white in the face and shaking. But I shouted at her, "What happened to him? How did this happen to him?" And she started to cry and she said, "I'm sorry, Mummy, I'm so sorry. There was nothing I could do.'

They stood on the small wooden jetty, looking at James's body. And someone went back to the house to phone for an ambulance.

And Kevin said, 'Where are the others? Do they know?'

And Sally couldn't speak. She just shook her head.

And Kevin said, 'I know where they are. They'll be in the woods. Where they always go. I'll get them.'

'And will you tell them?' she asked.

And he nodded and put his arm around her and she smelt the smell of a man's sweat. And she knew it would be a long time before she would smell it again.

The old bed creaked as she sat up. She pushed the quilt away from her small, slight body.

'I should go. I've taken up enough of your time. I should phone Vanessa, tell her we must go home. It's getting late.'

'No.' Margaret stopped rocking. 'Don't go. Stay and have dinner with me. I've spoken to Vanessa. She's been for a walk on the pier and I've asked her to go to the shops. She sounds fine. For the first time in ages I'm going to cook a proper meal.'

'Are you sure? I feel we've imposed on you enough.'

'No, really. It would give me great pleasure.' Margaret stood up, and heard the trill of a ringtone.

'Oh, sorry, that's mine.' Sally reached for her bag. She pulled out the phone and waved it apologetically in Margaret's direction. 'Just a minute.' She held it to her ear. 'Oh, hi, Michael, how are you?' She listened. 'Actually I'm not at home. Is it very important? . . . OK, well, could we make it tomorrow? I haven't been feeling too well and I'm having dinner with a friend tonight . . . Yeah, fine, tomorrow morning then. Say elevenish? . . . Lovely. And thanks, Michael. Thanks very much.'

She put her phone away.

'That's my policeman. Or, rather, my just-retired policeman. I don't know what to make of him, really. And I don't think he knows what to make of me. I think he thinks I'm just an hysterical mother.' She smiled. 'He's probably right.' She straightened the quilt. 'I feel so much better after that. Not just the sleep but being able to talk to you. You know the way it is. People get impatient with tragedy. It's fine when it's fresh and new but when it begins to go stale, well . . . You can't blame them, I suppose.'

'You can't blame them. But you can hate them. Even if it does you no good.' Margaret opened the bedroom door.

'Now, I have a very nice bottle of New Zealand white wine cooling in the fridge. I propose a glass or two. How does that sound?'

It was late by the time Sally and Vanessa left. They had eaten well. Steak and salad, with mashed potato. They had drunk the wine. They had talked, and Sally had even laughed. And when Vanessa had gone upstairs to watch Margaret's old black-and-white television, Sally had talked about the court case that had taken away her marriage.

'It was the first of its kind. An English divorce had never been tested in an Irish court before.' Sally finished her glass of wine and Margaret refilled it.

'I take it his wife challenged its legality,' Margaret said.

Sally nodded. 'Yes, and it wasn't difficult to do. You know that divorce was illegal here until 1996 so the only way to get one was under English law. A lot of people did it. But there was a requirement that the husband be domiciled in England. There were a number of solicitors who would – how should I put it? – facilitate the acquiring of an English address. James was pretty casual about the whole thing. So it wasn't difficult for Helena to prove that he had actually been domiciled in Ireland.'

Margaret got up and opened the kitchen door. She beckoned Sally outside. They settled themselves on the deckchairs.

'But had she agreed to the divorce? She knew what was going on, I presume.' Margaret lay back and looked up at the stars.

'Yes. They had joint custody of Dominic. That was all Helena wanted – so James said. But once he was gone she was determined to punish me. I didn't care about it for myself, but I cared that the legitimacy of James's relationship with Vanessa was challenged.' Sally sipped her wine. 'And, of course, there was the problem of his will.'

'His will?'

'We got married in London. I got pregnant immediately. We discussed James's will. He was going to change it so I would inherit the house in Dublin, Dominic would get the Lake House and the estate in Wicklow. And there would be provision made for Helena. James recognized that she would never be able to work again, never be able to look after herself. She was mentally ill. She'd had very bad post-natal depression and she'd never recovered from it. She was in hospital most of the time.'

'And were you happy with that? The provisions of the will?' It was another beautiful night. Warm, still, the air filled with the scent of honeysuckle.

'It was OK with me. I had no feelings of ill-will towards Helena. Mostly I felt pity for her. She wasn't right.' She tapped her skull. 'They'd had a baby after Dominic, a little girl who died when she was a few months old.'

'A cot death?'

'Well, it seemed as if it was. But James told me that the psychiatrist who looked after Helena thought she might have . . . well, I don't know, really, but she might have . . .'

'Done something to the child?'

'James didn't believe it. He was horrified that anyone would think she was capable of such a thing. He told me that the psychiatrist had some theory that Helena was trying to protect the baby, trying to find a way to let her go to Heaven without having to suffer through her life. A way of bypassing the pain of the world. Something like that. But

James didn't go along with it. He reckoned the doctor was trying to be too clever.' She lifted her glass. Margaret reached over and refilled it. She remembered a case from her days as a psychiatrist in New Zealand. A young woman who stabbed her two small daughters. She had wanted to die, but she couldn't bear the thought that they would be left motherless. Her own mother had died when she was three. She didn't want her daughters to suffer as she had suffered. A neighbour heard the children screaming and tried to intervene. By the time he had broken down the door, the little girls were dead. And their mother had retreated into a catatonic state. Margaret could still see the police photographs of the bedroom. Blood everywhere. And the girls' bodies huddled in a corner. She shook her head to get rid of the images.

'Are you all right?' Sally sat up on her deckchair and half turned towards her.

'Yes.' Margaret smiled. 'Yes, I'm fine.' She sipped some wine. 'So your marriage and the will, what happened about it?'

'Well, as I was saying, Helena went to court. She won the case so my marriage to James was declared bigamous. And because he had never changed his will, Helena inherited virtually everything. But what really hurt was that Vanessa was not considered to be James's legitimate child. However, in 1988 around the time James died, the law was changed so that children born outside marriage were entitled to inherit. So I went to court on her behalf and I managed to extract maintenance from the estate. Enough to keep her clothed and fed and pay her school fees. Enough to send her to university. And as well as that the court decided she should inherit some of James's property. There's a small cottage in Wicklow, a pretty little place, and she'll get that with a parcel of land, twenty acres I think it is, on her eighteenth birthday. In a couple of weeks' time.' Sally took a deep swallow of wine. 'But, of course, it's much more difficult now, since Marina died there. In that place. I'm not sure I want Vanessa to have any part of it. Not now.'

Margaret stretched her arms above her head. 'Does she have any contact with James's son?' she asked.

Sally shook her head. 'He doesn't want to know. We haven't seen him for years. There was a lot of bitterness, anger. Which was why it was so strange when Marina went to the party at his house. She and Dominic, well, their relationship was fraught, to say the least.'

'And you? What did you think of him?'

'Me? Well, if I'm honest I thought he was a spoiled, arrogant brat. He made it very plain that he didn't like me. But that was OK. I could understand that. He was very loyal to his mother, devoted to her. I remember how he'd spend time with her, and when he came back to us again, he'd look like her. He'd have mannerisms, ways of speaking, that were different. Actually,' she looked away, 'I felt sorry for Dominic that time, and it didn't make it any easier for me. As far as he was concerned, I had usurped Helena's place. But I didn't understand why he was so cruel and nasty to Marina and Tom. They were my children, not James's. They didn't want to be his children. They would never have taken Dominic's place or his love. And neither would I. James loved his son.' She drained her glass. 'Now. Time to go home.' She got to her feet and held out her hand.

'I'm sorry, Margaret. I've been very selfish tonight. You must have so much of your own pain to bear and all I've done is go on about myself.' She picked up her bag. Margaret leaned forward and kissed Sally's cheek. She could feel the bone just below the surface of the skin. 'Don't worry,' she said. 'I'll have my turn. I'm sure there'll be a night when you won't be able to shut me up.'

They walked upstairs together. Sally called for Vanessa, stopped her protests and opened the front door.

'Goodnight, and thanks for a lovely evening.' She put her arms around Margaret and hugged her. 'Come on, Vanessa, time to go home.'

Margaret stood on the step and watched them go through the front gate. A full moon hung over the sea casting its blue light across the garden. She closed the door and walked back down the steps to the kitchen. She piled the dishes into the sink and wiped the table clean. Then she went outside. The next-door neighbours had planted jasmine against their wall. It had climbed high and was now trailing its star-shaped white flowers through one of the old apple trees. The air was filled with its heavy, luscious scent.

Margaret sat down on a deckchair. She breathed in deeply. So Michael McLoughlin was coming to see Sally tomorrow. She wondered what he looked like now, if age had been kind to him. It has not been kind to me, she thought, as she ran her hands over her forehead and down her cheeks, feeling the wrinkles, the loose skin. The jasmine was almost too much. It carried with it the odour of decay, rot, putrefaction. She closed her eyes and images crowded in. She blinked and stood up. She went back into the kitchen and up the stairs. She sat down on the rocking-chair. Rock, rock, rock, rock. The wooden runners drummed against the wooden floor. She stared out into the darkness.

EIGHTEEN

Ben Roxby, death from a fall. Marina Spencer, death by drowning. Rosie Webb, née Atkinson, sister of Poppy, death by drug overdose. McLoughlin sat down at his computer and tapped out their names on the keyboard. He highlighted and enlarged the type. Suicide or accident? Or was there some other reason? He swung around on his chair. And he wondered. Roxby's body was found by his wife when she came home after spending the night with her mother. Rosie's body was found by the guards when the housekeeper called them. Who had found Marina's body? He picked up the phone and called Johnny Harris. Voicemail, as always. He left a message.

'Johnny, just one thing I'm wondering. Who found Marina? It'll be in the file somewhere. Could you give me a call? And while you're at it, any more news about Rosie Webb's death? Thanks a mill. Hope you're well. Talk to you soon. 'Bye.'

It was lunchtime when he got to Sally Spencer's house in Monkstown. Her scruffy little dog greeted him with a chorus of yaps and a tail that was wagging so hard it looked like it would fall off. Sally had prepared food for him. Cold meat and salad. She had laid a table in the garden. She poured him a glass of mineral water and topped it with a slice of lemon. She looked better, he thought, as if she'd had a good night's sleep. He said as much. She smiled. 'Yes. I did sleep well last night. For the first time since Marina died.'

'Good. It makes such a difference, doesn't it?' He sipped his fizzy water.

'Yes, but it's not just the sleep. I had a really nice evening. Vanessa and I had dinner with a friend. Funny the way these things work out. I'd never met her before, she's someone Vanessa'd got to know, but I was able to talk to her in a way that I haven't been able to talk to lots of people I've known for years. I suppose it helps that she's lost a daughter too. Very different circumstances, but similarities. So, it was good.' She busied herself with the vinaigrette. She poured it over the lettuce and mixed it carefully. 'Now, how have you been getting on?'

She listened while he talked. She didn't interrupt. He told her about the messages on Marina's phone and about the photographs. He told her about his visit to the school. He told her about the death of Rosie Webb, and what he knew of the death of Ben Roxby.

'Why didn't the police find all this out?' She looked at him with a puzzled expression.

'Well, it seemed very straightforward to them, I suppose. And it probably is. None of this makes Marina's suicide seem less likely. In fact, if anything, it makes it seem more likely.'

She looked away, then back at him. 'I had no idea she was worried about anything.' Her voice was low and uncertain. 'She seemed OK to me.'

'What about this relationship with Mark Porter? Didn't

it strike you as odd, given their history?' McLoughlin speared a small tomato with his fork.

She frowned. 'Who told you about that?'

'Poppy Atkinson, Rosie's sister. And then, well, I'm afraid it's part of Marina's history. It's there.'

'It's there, all right. Don't think badly of her.' Sally seemed close to tears. 'I could never figure out what happened. It wasn't like her. But she was very unhappy at that school. I should have realized sooner. I know I had my own misery to deal with, but I feel responsible for everything that went on there. Marina looked almost like an adult, but inside she was a child.'

McLoughlin helped himself to more salad. 'So why the relationship with Mark? Where did that come from?'

'It wasn't a relationship as such, not romantic anyway. Marina had lost touch with the people from that school a long time ago. Then she'd bumped into Mark, and perhaps she felt it was time to make amends. We never really talked about it, but she seemed to like him. The one thing that was odd though, was that she went to that party. I couldn't understand why.'

'You knew about it before she went?' McLoughlin rummaged through the salad, looking for a lump of feta. It was delicious.

'I found out about it that day. I phoned her to check she was coming for lunch on Sunday, the day after. She often used to come for Sunday lunch. She was always so busy during the week that I didn't see much of her. So I phoned her. It was about eight o'clock on the Saturday evening. When she answered, the reception was bad. I kept losing her. So I asked her where she was and she said she was up at the Lake House.' Sally's face was pale and tense now.

'And you were surprised?'

'Surprised? I was more than surprised. But before I could ask her anything about it, the signal went. I tried again and again, but it went straight to voicemail. So that was the last conversation I had with her.' She got up from the table and went into the kitchen, the dog following closely behind. McLoughlin finished off the salad.

When she came back she was carrying a large glass of white wine. 'Sorry.' She tried to smile, then sat down. 'I can't bear to think that was the last time we spoke.'

'The Lake House. I understand it's very special.' He sat back in his chair and wiped his hands on a white linen napkin.

'It is – or it was when I used to go there – a bit dilapidated, run-down, but the place is absolutely wonderful. It has a magical quality. It's tucked into a deep valley. The lake is a perfect oval. It's an amazing colour. Almost brown. Bog water, you know? And there are the most beautiful trees, the most exquisite beeches. And underneath them the ground is springy with the shells of beech nuts. They call it mast, beech mast. Funny word, isn't it? Old English, I think.' She sipped her wine. 'It's just ... I don't know how to describe it. You'd have to go there to appreciate how beautiful it is.' She was twiddling her wedding ring, 'We were going to live there full time when James retired. I thought he would have been bored, that country life wouldn't suit him, but he said all he wanted was to be with me and Vanessa and that would be enough.' Her eyes filled with tears. She covered her face with her hands. He waited until the sobs abated. The dog whined softly.

'Sorry.' She bent down and scratched behind the little

animal's ears. 'I seem to spend all my time in tears, these days. I'm sick of it. I feel so angry too. Angry with Marina. But that's one of the reasons why I'm sure she didn't kill herself. She would have known the effect it would have on me. And I'm sure she wouldn't have wanted to hurt me like this.'

He stood up.

'Don't go.' She reached out a hand as if to stop him. 'I'm sorry – I just can't seem to cope with anything these days. And listen, there's something else.'

He perched on the edge of his chair. 'Something else?'

'After you phoned me about Marina's house, Vanessa and I went to check it. It had been trashed. It was in a terrible state. Everything all over everywhere. We cleaned it up and I got a locksmith to come, but . . . but it hadn't been broken into, and as far as I know the only people with keys were you, me and Mark Porter. I know Marina had given him a set.' She drank some more of her wine. 'Why would he do something like that?'

McLoughlin cleared his throat. 'Anger? Grief? People do strange things in strange circumstances.' He stood up again. 'I don't know him, but I thought his behaviour was very odd when I met him at the house. He was carrying on as if he was Marina's partner. He told me he'd more or less arranged her funeral. Picked the music, that sort of thing. Is that right?'

'You're kidding?' she exclaimed. 'Vanessa and I chose the music, the readings. We went through all her CDs. Picked out her favourites.'

'Purcell's *Dido*, was that one of them?'

'Yes, it was. It's lovely, and there was a poem, special, for all of us. 'Hinterhof' by James Fenton. Do you know it?'

He shook his head.

She began to speak:

> *'Stay near to me and I'll stay near to you,*
> *As near as you are dear to me will do,*
> *Near as the rainbow to the rain,*
> *The west wind to the window pane,*
> *As fire to the hearth, as dawn to—'*

Her voice choked in her throat.

> *'As fire to the hearth, as dawn to dew.*

'Marina really liked it and Vanessa read it at the funeral. It was fitting.' She stroked the dog's rough head. 'Anyway, what's more to say, really?' She picked up her glass and raised it to him. 'I'm sure you've other things to be doing with your day. Janet was telling me you're off on a sailing trip. Sounds lovely.'

'I hope so.' He took his car keys from his pocket. 'Just one other thing I wanted to ask you. Your son, Tom, where is he these days?'

'In Darfur. He works for an aid agency. He came home for Marina's funeral. I wanted him to stay but he wouldn't. He's dedicated to his job. Why?'

'Nothing in particular, but do you have a contact number?'

'Sure.' She stood and walked back into the kitchen where she scribbled something on a scrap of paper. 'Here, email, the best way to get in touch. They use satellite phones but they're very unreliable.'

'Was he close to his sister?' he asked.

'Close? Once they were, but they drifted apart. The way

siblings do.' She picked up one of the framed photographs on the mantelpiece and held it out to McLoughlin. 'I wish he'd come home.'

McLoughlin took the picture. Tom Spencer was as handsome as his sister had been beautiful. He put it down on the table. 'I'll talk to you tomorrow. Mind yourself.'

The road to Wicklow had been widened and improved recently. The traffic was moving fast. Ahead, the Sugarloaf's crystal summit sparkled in the sunshine. He took the exit at Kilmacanogue and slowed as he turned on to the old Roundwood road. His ears popped as he drove higher into the Wicklow hills. The countryside was beautiful. The grass was an improbable green, speckled with the white dots of grazing sheep. And beyond the dun-coloured slopes of the mountains, lowering against the blue of the summer sky. The road uncoiled in front of him. He slowed to negotiate the sharper bends. There was a surprising amount of traffic today.

Just outside the village of Roundwood there was a right turn, signposted 'Sally Gap'. Picnickers had taken up residence on the narrow verge. Their small table was covered with a bright chequered cloth and an array of sandwiches and drinks. A little girl waved vigorously at the passing cars. He waved back. She jumped up and down, a broad grin on her cheeky little face, stuck out her tongue and waggled her fingers in her ears.

He drove slowly up towards the summit of the hill. Tall pines cast their shadow across the road. And just beyond he saw a high gate set back in the entrance to a driveway. He pulled in and stopped. The gate was locked. A keypad was set into the wall and, above it, a camera. He pressed the key that bore the symbol of a bell. He waited.

He pressed the bell again, leaned against the wall and waited. A truck passed, painted regulation khaki, two young soldiers in the cab and the shadowed shapes of others, gazing out of the open back. There were always soldiers around this part of the mountains. There was a firing range not far away. On still, windless days the boom of the guns was often heard. Now he looked up into the video-camera and smiled. 'Come on, open up,' he said. Still no response. He stepped away, out of the camera's range, and to the opposite side of the gateway. A large sign, painted in dramatic red and black, stated 'Private Property. No Entry except with Owner's Authorization.' But below it the wall was damaged. Some of the stones were loose and had fallen to the ground, leaving foot- and handholds. He looked around, then pulled himself over, dropped to the other side and began to walk quickly down the steep hill.

It was quiet. Silent. The lake, visible now through the trees, shining, like polished metal, a sudden shadow rushing across the surface as the wind pushed up a small shivering wave. He turned off the drive. The trees were tall and beautiful. The ground beneath his feet was springy with decades of leaf mould. And everywhere there were huge boulders, sateened with moss of the most delicate green. He stopped dead. What was that he could see between a huge beech and a Sitka spruce? He held his breath, tried not to move, and watched as the two deer, who had spotted him first, stared at him, their heads turned, their ears pricked, their bodies statue still. Then they began to walk slowly up the hill, over the road and away into the distance. He let his breath out in a rush. He'd never been so close to deer before.

Now he could see their almond-shaped eyes, their mottled backs, their delicate pointed faces.

He moved away, conscious of his clumsiness as a twig snapped beneath his foot. The sound was like a fire-cracker in the absolute stillness of the wood. The slope towards the lake was steep and uneven. He scrambled over rotting logs and tumbled rocks, sat down for a moment to wipe his sweating face on his sleeve. It was surprisingly hot, even with the broad canopy of the crumpled beech leaves and the deep shadows cast by the pines, spruces and larches. Across the lake, the valley wall, bare rock, unwooded, rose steeply. A different landscape, harsh and forbidding. He knew what it would be like here in the middle of winter when the winds would scream down the hill, flailing all before them.

But today the breeze was light, southerly. He stood up and looked down through the trees to the water. Below, there was a clearing, a small flat promontory, surrounded by a group of the tallest pines. And in the middle he could see a circle of stones, blackened by fire, charred branches and beside the stones a couple of large logs pulled up, like sofas at a hearth. He scrambled down towards them, his feet slipping on the mass of needles. Here and there ferns poked their fronds towards the light. They were still fresh and green, not yet tinged with the brown decay of late summer. He reached the clearing. He squatted and stirred the heap of ash with a burned stick. Bottle tops, Heineken's red-star logo, winked up at him, and the charred remains of foil from cigarette packets, with scattered butts and the tell-tale remnants of joints. He picked one up carefully between his fingertips and bent to sniff it. Sure enough, the pungent scent of cannabis. He sighed. And felt the cold hardness of something metallic pressing into his skull, just behind his right ear. The pressure increased. Now there was a hand on his head, forcing him to his knees. He tried to jerk away but he could feel the bite of what seemed like a gun barrel. A long time since he had felt anything like it.

Now he tried to shout: 'Hold on, I'm a guard. I'm here on official business. Let me up.' But his voice was feeble.

'A guard, is that what you are? Official business, is that what you call it? A funny way to go about it. Breaking and entering. Climbing over a wall without so much as a by-your-leave.' And now there was a booted foot, a toe under his buttocks, pushing him so that he toppled forward and landed with his face pressed against the roughness of a fallen branch.

'Now.' The boot was close to his face. It was polished, brown, the leather soft and well worn. 'You were saying?'

The figure above him seemed huge. The boots gave way to long legs with large thighs encased in whipcord jodhpurs. A solid body, big round breasts beneath a checked shirt. The rolled-up sleeves showed arms that were suntanned, with the appearance of strength. The woman seemed somehow familiar. Her hair, unnaturally black, was pushed back from a high forehead. Her face was fleshy, striking, with a jutting nose. Her dark blue eyes were accentuated with liner and her wide mouth was a vivid crimson. He noticed her fingernails. They were long, manicured and painted the same red as her mouth. She held up a walking-stick. Its tip was sheathed in metal. She examined it carefully. 'Give you a fright, did I?' She smiled. 'Thought this was something else?' She leaned down and held out her hand. 'Enjoying yourself down there? The view OK? Or would you fancy a change?'

He allowed himself to be pulled upright. Close to, she wasn't as formidable as she had seemed from the ground. But she was still a big woman. Roughly his height, he reckoned, and with a build to match. Not fat as such, but strong, almost muscled.

'Now,' her voice was amused, 'will we start again?'

She walked him down the road towards the house. He felt foolish, embarrassed, humiliated. She struck the ground with the stick as she walked, her stride long and full of purpose. A dog had joined her. A large, lean German shepherd, with wary amber eyes and a huge mouth. Its teeth shone with a yellow gleam and its long pink tongue flopped wolf-like from side to side as it loped beside her. McLoughlin tried to explain what he wanted. He told her the 'auditing the suicides' version of events. She didn't reply.

'I'm sorry,' he said, 'for not phoning ahead. I was in the area and I thought I'd chance my arm. I was actually looking for Dominic de Paor. I thought he might be here. Do you know him?'

'He's my son. I'm Helena de Paor.' She leaned down and laid a hand on the dog's heavy collar.

'Your son? Oh, of course.' He glanced at her. He could see the resemblance. 'And is he around?'

'No. He lives in the city. He only comes at weekends. Unfortunately. He misses out on so much.' She waved her arm in a semicircle that took in the lake, the woods and now the house.

'Wow.' McLoughlin stopped. 'How beautiful.'

It wasn't very big, or very grand, but it was very lovely. Two storeys, long and low, painted a pale washed pink. A

slate roof, shades of grey and purple. A smooth green lawn
running to the margin of the lake. A cluster of trees, more
beeches, he thought, to one side, and between the road and
the house, a field. And in the field, the herd of deer. Thirty
or forty, at least. They stared at the intruders, so still they
could have been a photograph. He drew in his breath. The
dog was still too.

'Good boy . . . there's a good boy.' Her voice was low and
soothing. The dog whined and licked his pink lips as the
deer stared, motionless, then suddenly, like a knot of star-
lings in an autumn sky, wheeled and scattered, reaching the
trees and disappearing.

'Wow.' McLoughlin whistled. 'I've never seen anything
like that before.'

'Haven't you?' She let go of the dog's collar. He trotted
forward and stood with his nose outstretched, nostrils flar-
ing. 'You'll find lots of surprises here.' Helena started
walking again. 'Now,' she looked over her shoulder, 'I don't
know about you but I could do with a drink.'

She brought him through a cobbled yard with a barn and a
couple of looseboxes, opened a door and led him into a small
room. A row of coats was hanging from hooks on the wall,
boots lined up beneath. There was a rack of fishing rods and
a shelf stacked with reels, hooks and boxes of flies. A long
glass-doored cabinet held guns. McLoughlin peered at them.
Two shotguns and three rifles. A Sauer 243. Perfect for deer.

'They're my son's. He's a very good shot.' Helena prised
off her boots and placed them neatly with the others. 'He
does the cull every couple of years. The deer have no natural

predators so they have to be controlled. The old, lame, sick. Makes you think. The same should happen to people.'

The walls were covered with framed photographs. Men with fishing rods. Men with guns. At least three generations. Moustaches and whiskers in the earlier ones. And in the more recent photographs McLoughlin recognized James de Paor, standing knee deep in a river, a huge fish, a salmon, hanging from a gaff. And beside him a small boy, thick wavy black hair and a broad grin. 'So, hunting's in the family, I see.' He gestured towards the gun cabinet.

'Yes. James taught Dominic to shoot when he was very young. I used to shoot too, but I don't any longer. My hands aren't as steady as they once were. Come on. This way.'

She pushed open the door and ushered him into a large kitchen. It had the air of a traditional farmhouse, but McLoughlin noticed that no expense had been spared on fittings and appliances. They were all new and state-of-the-art. Helena poured a glass of Bushmills for herself and waved the bottle in his direction. He shook his head. 'Driving.' He smiled with what he hoped was a rueful expression.

'Don't you mean "on duty"? Isn't that what they always say in the movies?' She sat back in a large wicker chair, one long leg draped over its arm. The dog slumped at her feet. To the casual observer the animal might have been asleep, but McLoughlin noticed that whenever he moved, its eyelids flicked open and the amber stare instantly locked on to his face. It made him feel intensely uncomfortable. He'd done the regulation dog training course at Templemore, even worked for a while in the drugs squad with a dog team, but this dog was different. There was something about the ridge of muscle under the thick ruff that made his palms sweat.

'You like my dog?' Helena let her fingers trail in front of its nose. The dog's tongue touched them delicately.

'I'm more of a cat person,' McLoughlin said, 'but I'd have to admit that he's a beauty. Although I'd also have to say that I'm glad you were with him when we met out there by the lake. I don't think he'd have been that friendly if I'd been on my own.'

She smiled, and her lips slid back over her teeth. Dog and mistress, the image of each other. 'Now, you were telling me. Suicides, that's your interest. And you came here because of the suicide of Marina Spencer. Am I right?' She sipped her drink.

She was like the actress in that scary movie with Bette Davis, McLoughlin thought. He searched for the name. Joan Crawford, that was who it was, with her curves and her red mouth and her hair that was just too black. One thing was certain. This woman was nothing like Sally Spencer.

'Yes, that's right. Marina Spencer is one of the cases that I've been asked to review. Just a couple of things, if that's OK?' He changed position. He could smell the whiskey. It was making his mouth water. 'Were you here the night she died?'

Helena leaned back into the chair and gazed up at the ceiling. 'Was I here the night she died? Well, yes and no. Dominic wanted to take over the whole house for the party. Most of the guests were going to stay overnight, so the dog and I moved out to the cottage. It's further down the lake, on its own. Away from here. The dog doesn't like noise and strangers, and neither do I.' She fixed her eyes on McLoughlin. 'Do you, Inspector? Do you like noise and strangers and all the fuss that comes with them?'

He shrugged. 'It depends, I suppose. I used to when I

was younger, I loved that kind of party atmosphere. But now – well, a quiet pint and the Sudoku is more my kind of thing.'

'God almighty.' She swung her foot to the floor. 'You make it sound so fascinating.' She stood and refilled her glass. 'Sure I can't tempt you?'

He wavered and she noticed. She handed him a glass and splashed a large measure of whiskey into it. He lifted it to his lips.

'Good. Drinking on my own makes me nervous. Now,' she sat down again, 'I was here the night Marina Spencer died. I stayed in the cottage, just me and the dog. We got up early, as is our habit. We went out to have our early-morning swim and walked around the lake. It was a very beautiful morning. We saw some interesting sights. A number of people asleep in the bracken. Men and women, boys and girls. We kept on walking, the dog and I, close to the water, which is what we like. First of all we saw the dinghy. There's a little harbour at the far end of the lake, the *cuan*, my late husband called it. And that's where I saw the dinghy. I was surprised by that because I had last seen it tied up at the jetty.'

'And the jetty is where?'

She waved an arm. 'Down at the beach. You can see it from the front of the house. Anyway, we stopped and had a look at the dinghy. We thought it must have got free from its mooring and drifted out there. I tied it to one of the rings. And then the dog began to sniff the air.' As she spoke, the animal raised its head, then rested its nose on her leg. 'He looked at me, then he turned away from the boat. The water flows from the lake, over the little rapids and into the bog. It tumbles over the stones. It foams and froths.

Sometimes when it has been raining heavily it rushes and pours. But it had been very dry for the couple of weeks before, so the flow was slower, more sluggish.' Her voice was matter-of-fact. She sounded as if she was reading from a prepared script. 'The dog moved slowly towards the rocks. I followed him. He stopped. I stopped. Then he began to howl. I couldn't see why until I went closer to the water. The woman was lying face down. Her dress was pulled up around her waist and she was wearing a red thong. Her body was very white. Her hair was very dark.' She stopped speaking. It was very quiet. The dog stood, lifted a heavy paw and placed it on her thigh. She lowered her face and it touched her nose. Its nostrils dilated as it sucked in her scent.

'Did you know who the woman was?' McLoughlin sipped his drink cautiously.

'Yes, I did. I had seen her earlier that evening when she arrived with Mark Porter. The dog had seen her too.' It lay down at her feet. Its eyes were wide.

'So you knew who she was?'

'Of course I did.' Her voice rose with indignation. 'I knew she was Marina Spencer. The daughter of that woman who took my husband's love from me.' She stood up and finished her whiskey. 'OK, that's enough now. I want you to go. I've nothing more to say to you.' The dog stood too and leaned against her leg.

McLoughlin got up. He held out a hand towards her. The dog made a sound in its throat. Not quite a growl, but almost. 'I'm sorry if I've upset you. I didn't mean to. Of course it must have been dreadful to see her like that. You never get used to seeing death. I know. In my job it's an occupational hazard, but it's always a shock.' He tried to sound sympathetic.

But she shook her head. 'You misunderstand me.' Her mouth twisted into a distorted smile. 'I wasn't upset. I was delighted. At last she had got what she deserved. Because of her and her family James drowned. Because of her and her family I was humiliated, belittled, treated like scum. My son's future was threatened. Because of her and her mother we were outcasts. So all I could feel was joy. Unconfined.' She laughed. A bray of pure triumph. She laid a hand on his shoulder. Her fingers dug into his bones. She moved closer. He could smell the whiskey on her breath and a faint sweaty scent that rose up from between her breasts. 'Dead. She's dead. And I and mine are alive.' Her voice reached a crescendo. Her eyes gleamed and droplets of saliva gathered in the corners of her mouth as she repeated the words. She put her other hand on his shoulder and pulled him closer. Then there was the sound of a voice shouting in the hall, running footsteps, the kitchen door thrown back. And a man whom McLoughlin recognized. Tall, dark, broad, with her features − her mouth, her eyes, her nose, her stance. Grabbing hold of her, pulling her away, as the dog pranced and yelped, his thick tail wagging, claws scraping on the tiled floor.

'Who the fuck are you and what do you think you're doing here?' Dominic de Paor's voice was angry, aggressive. 'You have no right to be here. You were not given permission to come on to this estate. Now, get out before I call the police. My mother isn't well. Do you hear me? For your own sake, get out of here now.' He turned back to his mother, holding her tightly, as the dog snarled at

McLoughlin, the ruff standing up around its neck and its lips drawn back from his long yellow teeth.

McLoughlin walked quickly from the house. Two men lounged around an old Hiace van, parked beside a new BMW soft-top. One grinned as McLoughlin passed and tipped his forehead with a finger. 'The way out is thataway.' His drawl was more Texan than Wicklow. He cocked his hand into the shape of a gun, 'Bang-bang, you're dead,' he said, and the other man sniggered.

McLoughlin didn't look back as he took the drive at a steady pace. Just as he reached the boundary fence he glanced behind. As far as he could see he was on his own. He paused for a moment, then turned into the wood. He moved with more assurance now, his footing more secure, as he hurried down the slope towards the water. The trees had given way to rough scrubland, punctuated with rocks. He followed the outline of a path, picking his way carefully. And saw a small two-storey house with a garden back and front, a high hedge around it. And, below, the little harbour that Helena had described. Big enough to shelter a dinghy or a couple of canoes. Or, as now, two traditional currachs, tied together, rocking in the little waves.

He could just distinguish the house from where he was, tucked neatly into the grove of trees at the far end of the water. He moved away from the harbour. And saw the tumble of rocks that marked where the stream ran from the lake. The water level was low now, the boulders exposed. He could see Marina Spencer lying face down in the water. He could see her as the Garda photographer had seen her: her skin white against the rocks, her skirt pulled up revealing her underwear, her bare feet, her toenails painted a vivid red, her hands clenched as if she was trying to hold on to something, to save herself, and her face, turned to one side, a large bruise on her forehead. Happened before she died, Johnny Harris had said. Must have banged it on a rock as the water carried her down into the stream.

'Marina . . . Marina,' he whispered. 'Tell me, Marina. What were you doing here? Why did you come to this place? What was going on?'

A cloud passed over the sun and it was suddenly dark. The bare rock wall that faced him was cold and forbidding. And as he turned towards the trees he felt threatened and vulnerable. He began to hurry, his feet catching in the rough grass and tripping over the rocks as he made his way towards the boundary fence. Then he heard barking, looked back and saw the dog, nose down, tail up. He began to run, scrambling up the slope, trying not to panic, as the barking got louder and louder. The breath was burning in his chest now and his calf muscles were screaming at him to stop, but he kept going, forcing himself up the hill until he saw, by the gate, the wall and flung himself at it, dragging his body up, on to the top and over, collapsing, panting, gasping for breath on the ground. He lay for a few moments, the sweat running down his forehead into his eyes and soaking through his shirt. Then he pulled himself up and looked back through the gate. And saw the dog, the growl lifting its lips, saliva dripping on to the ground. And heard the whistle, insistent, repeated, and the dog, stepping back slowly, pace by pace, then breaking into a run as it disappeared down the hill.

NINETEEN

The *penne* swirled in the salted water. It was just short of boiling. McLoughlin opened the fridge and took out a large hunk of Pecorino cheese. He cut off a few thick slices and laid them on a plate. Then he opened a jar of West Cork honey. He dipped a dessert spoon into it and held it high, letting it dribble slowly off the spoon and on to the cheese. Then he sat down at the table and cut the cheese into bite-size pieces. He began to eat.

He'd first eaten cheese like this years ago. He'd gone to a conference on immigration, which had been held in Siena. One of the Italian cops attending had taken pity on him and invited him home to meet his wife. Elizabetta di Luca had patted him on the shoulder as she placed the plate of cheese and honey in front of him.

'*Mangia*,' she had said, and smiled broadly. '*Delizioso*.'

Go ahead.' Her husband cut off a piece. 'She's right. It is delicious.' He remembered that he had wondered if this was some kind of Italian mickey-taking. But one taste was all it took. It was delicious.

He finished his cheese and got up. He checked the pasta. It was perfectly *al dente*. He lifted it from the stove and drained it into a colander in the sink. He tipped it back into the pan and added a large knob of butter, stirring it until it gleamed in a way that made his mouth water. He quickly grated some Parmesan and sprinkled it into the pasta, then seized the peppermill and gave it a few good twists. He mixed it together, then poured it into a bowl. He cut two large slices of bread, then carried the lot outside to the terrace. The garden table was already set with a knife and fork, a small dish of salt and a half-full glass of wine. He sat down. '*Buon appetito*, Elizabetta,' he said, and dug in his fork.

He finished his dinner, poured himself another glass of wine and leaned back. He closed his eyes and slept suddenly, his head drooping sideways. He was dreaming about Marina. She was sitting in the boat. She picked up the oars and began to row. The boat moved quickly over the water. Moonlight brightened the lake. Silver droplets flew from the blades. He could see the light from a fire among the trees. Its reflection rippled in the wake of the boat. And the dog's head broke through the surface of the water. He could see Marina reflected in its eyes. She was lifting a bottle to her mouth. He could see her throat, her larynx moving up and down. The dog turned to look at him. Helena was standing in the water too. Her body was wet and sleek, like that of a large seal. She leaned down towards him and he could see her hands. They were strong and white, the nails red and shiny. She put her lips to his ear. 'Look,' she said. 'Look what I've found.' He could feel her breath on his cheek, his head turning slowly, very slowly, and he knew he was going to have to look. But he didn't want to. He really didn't want to.

He woke, heart pounding, sweat dripping from his forehead. He picked up his glass and drank. He waited for his heart to slow, for the dream to seep away. Then he gathered up his dishes and went into the kitchen.

He turned on the tap and washed them, then dried his hands. He was tired. No wonder he had slept like that. No wonder he had dreamed like that. He put his hand into his pocket and found his wallet. He took out the scrap of paper on which Sally had written her son's email address. He would write to him now. Maybe Tom Spencer could help him. Because McLoughlin could not figure it out. He reached for the wine bottle. And the phone rang. He recognized the voice immediately. It was Finney, or Chief Superintendent Finney, as he knew he should remember to call him.

'Oh, hallo, how are you?' He tried to sound friendly, but Finney's tone did not accord. 'Hey, hold on a minute.' He cut through the hostile barrage. 'You might not have noticed but I'm not a guard any longer. I don't work for you or anyone like you.'

'No, you don't, you fucking arsehole. And if you did, you'd be finished.' Finney's voice was high-pitched. 'I've just had a phone call from the commissioner. Apparently someone has been doing the rounds pretending they're on some kind of secret mission researching suicides and the guards' response to them. And you'll never guess who that someone is.' There was silence. Then Finney started again. 'I always thought you had a few screws loose, but this beats it all. You've pissed off some people with friends in high places. I don't know what you're after but if I hear you've been misrepresenting yourself again you'll be in big trouble. So back off. Do you hear me? Back off.'

There was nothing more to say. McLoughlin put down

the phone. His hands were trembling. He was making a mess of everything. He was retired now. He shouldn't be doing any of this. He should be outside in the sunshine, thinking about his future. He picked up the phone again and found Paul Brady's number. He waited for him to answer. He left a message. 'Hi, Paul, it's Michael McLoughlin. I'm just wondering about the trip. Is there any news? If not, can you let me know as I'd like to sort out something else? Thanks very much. Talk to you soon.'

He walked back into the sitting room and sat down at the computer. He smoothed out the scrap of paper with Tom Spencer's email address. The aid agency he worked for was called Help in Africa. He typed the name into the Google dialogue box and waited for a response. He clicked on the Help in Africa website. It wasn't hard to find Spencer. He featured in a number of the photographs. Tall and graceful, bright blue eyes in a tanned face, faded denims worn with casual elegance. McLoughlin typed in Spencer's email address and began to write. When he had finished he pressed send. Then he went through the kitchen and out on to the terrace. It was still light but the city below was beginning to glow with its reds, oranges and yellows. McLoughlin sat down and watched. The colour in the sky was fading. The moon hung above him, its broad silver face shining. He was overwhelmed with sadness. Sadness for himself, sadness for Sally, sadness for Marina. Why could he not work out what had happened to her? The messages on her phone said, 'I saw you.' The photographs had 'I saw you' written on them. So, someone had spied on her, taken pictures of her. So what? She could have gone to the police. She could have put up curtains or blinds. She could have taken all kinds of security measures to make sure it didn't happen again. She had bullied Mark Porter so badly that he had tried to kill himself. She had paid a heavy price for that. And then, recently, she had become friendly with him. She had gone out with him. She had brought him home. She had gone to the party at the Lake House, a place of sadness. She had witnessed her step-father's death on that same lake. She had sat in the dinghy and seen him drown. Was it the same dinghy, McLoughlin wondered, as the one she had rowed out on to the lake that night last month? And what had happened at that party? She had drunk the equivalent of three-quarters of a bottle of vodka. She had taken cocaine and LSD. No one in their right mind would have done that, then got into a boat. What had made her do it? He shivered. It was dark now, dark in his garden, dark around his house.

He got up and went inside. He walked through to the sitting room. He pulled open the cardboard flaps of one of Marina's boxes and scrabbled around until his fingers felt the cold hard plastic of her phone. He switched it on and tapped in her PIN. He scrolled through the menu looking for call register. He clicked on received calls. One number was repeated five times. He clicked to dialled numbers. The same number was repeated six times. He took a deep breath and pressed the green button. The number rang and rang, then clicked to voicemail. He recognized the voice on the recorded message. He had heard it a few hours ago in the kitchen at the Lake House.

'This is Dominic de Paor. Leave a message and I'll call you back.'

McLoughlin dropped the phone as if it had suddenly become red hot. It lay on the floor, silent. He leaned down and picked it up again. He rechecked the call register and made a note of the dates and times of the calls. The day before the party de Paor had phoned her five times and she had phoned him six times. McLoughlin pulled some of the files out of the box. He flicked through them until he found her phone bills. He scanned the itemized list. And found the same number. In the month before Marina died, she and de Paor had been in constant contact. He thought back over what he knew about their relationship. Sally had told him they had got on reasonably well until she married James. But then it had all got very difficult. Dominic had teased and bullied Marina. Isobel Watson had said that Marina had been able to stand up to him. But when they came back to school after James had died their relationship had changed. She was cowed by him, scared of him. So why was she phoning him now?

He picked up his own phone and called Tony Heffernan.

'Hi, Michael, what's up?' Heffernan sounded happy, light-hearted.

'Tony, listen, I need you to do something for me. It's about Marina Spencer.' He told Tony he needed a list of the people who were at the party that night. Brian Dooley would have it. He also wanted whatever statements had been taken.

'One of the guests was called Mark Porter. You've probably heard Sally talk about him. And I know the names of some of the others. Rosie Webb, Sophie Fitzgerald, Dominic de Paor and his wife, Gilly. If you could get me the other names I think it would be helpful, and particularly their whereabouts when Marina's body was found.'

'You don't want much, do you?' Heffernan sounded incredulous. 'I can't get all that.'

'Tony, you got me into this. I don't have the time and energy to do all the legwork. At the very least I need to know who was there. You know Dooley. You'll come up with some plausible excuse.' McLoughlin could imagine the look on the other man's face.

'Does this mean you think there was something funny about Marina's death?' Heffernan sounded excited.

'I don't know. But they're an odd lot, those people. And another thing. Does Janet know anything about James de Paor's first wife? Is she nuts or what? And the court case over the divorce, what was that about?'

'Don't you remember, Michael? It was a big deal. It was in all the papers. A huge scandal. I'd been thinking I might go the English-divorce route myself, but after that I thought again.' Heffernan sounded rueful now. 'Do you have access to the *Irish Times* archive? You'll read about it there, I'm pretty sure. If not, I'll check tomorrow at work and email you whatever I can find.'

'And the other stuff? Will you get me that?' McLoughlin wasn't letting him off that lightly.

'I'll see what I can do. I'll get back to you tomorrow, Michael. And thanks. Janet was talking to Sally yesterday and she says she's much more cheerful.'

Nothing to do with me, McLoughlin thought, as he sat down at the computer again. He touched the keyboard, then logged on to the *Irish Times* website. He put in his username and password. He typed 'Helena de Paor' and 'High Court' in the search dialogue box and waited.

An hour later he got up from the desk. He picked up the stack of paper that had shunted from the printer and carried it into the kitchen where he laid it on the table. He was hungry again. He cut a couple of slices of bread and opened the fridge. He wanted olives, salami and goat's cheese. He spread his booty on a plate and sat down, cutting off chunks of the cheese and the sausage and eating them quickly. It all tasted so good. He spread out the pages. He was beginning to understand. The anger, the hatred, the desire for revenge. The black-and-white newspaper photographs were grainy and smudged, but Helena de Paor's beauty was unmistakable. She stood out from everyone else. She looked triumphant, magnificent. Sally, on the other hand, was small and insignificant. Pale and wan. And it wasn't just the photographs that held his interest. The details of the case were extraordinary. James de Paor had done what many people in his situation did in the days before divorce was legal in Ireland. He had applied for divorce in England. He had faked his domicile. He had persuaded Helena to agree to a settlement. They had agreed to joint custody of Dominic. She had received a more than generous allowance and a house in Foxrock. He had then married Sally in London. But after his death Helena had challenged the legality of the divorce and, of course, the subsequent marriage. And she had won.

She had issued a statement that she had read standing on the steps of the Four Courts. She was dressed in black. She had long hair in those days. It was tied back from her face. He could hear her voice in the printed words on the page.

'I have been vindicated. My husband tried to deny me, deny my rightful place in the world, take my son from me, take away my rights to his property. When we got married we made a promise, a vow, an oath before God. We said that nothing would ever part us, nothing but death. My husband tried to break his vow, to despoil our marriage.

We are parted now. But only by death. I hope that no other woman will ever have to suffer what I have suffered. Will ever have to struggle in the way that I have struggled. But now I want to give thanks. To the Irish state and its constitution, which has upheld and vindicated my rights, and to God, who has stood by me and my family in our hour of need.'

'Wow.' McLoughlin whistled and sat back in his chair, a hunk of bread and a piece of salami poised in mid-air. 'Well, fair play to you, that's all I can say.' He filled his glass with wine. 'Here's to you, Mrs de Paor. You're a class act.'

He drank it and stood up. He picked up his dishes and dumped them in the sink. It was late. Just after half past one, according to the clock on the wall. As he turned towards the door his phone rang. He pulled it from his pocket.

'Hey Tony,' his tone was admiring, 'that was quick. I knew you were good, but not that good.'

'Michael, something else has happened. One of the people you mentioned. It was Mark Porter, wasn't it?'

'Yeah, that's right. What about him?'

'Well,' McLoughlin heard the sharp intake of breath, 'I'm in the office, catching up on a bit of paperwork, and a call's just come in. Someone of the same name has been found dead in a house in Fitzwilliam Square. Thought you'd like to know.'

McLoughlin leaned against the wall, then stood straight. 'How long ago?'

'Just now, fifteen minutes or so. And the person who made the call, let's see, it was a woman. A Dr Gwen Simpson.'

'Who's on the job?' Now McLoughlin was hurrying down

the corridor, dragging on his jacket, checking his pockets for his keys.

'Pat Hickey. Remember him? He's a good guy.'

McLoughlin switched on the alarm and locked the front door behind him. 'Yeah, he sure is. Listen, Tony, I'll give you a call tomorrow. Thanks.'

'Don't mention it. Mind yourself now, OK?'

McLoughlin got into his car and reversed out of the drive. He drove carefully through the outer suburbs towards the city centre. He was conscious that he had drunk at least three-quarters of a bottle of wine, but it was quiet now and there was no sign of the traffic police. As he turned into Fitzwilliam Square he could see the white shape of an ambulance and a cluster of Garda cars. The front door to the building stood open and a knot of men was standing together in the glow of light from the hall. He parked his car as close as possible, and walked briskly towards them. He recognized a few faces. 'Hi, Pat, what's the story?' He held out his hand.

Sergeant Pat Hickey mimed a double-take. 'Hey, Michael McLoughlin? What brings you here?' His round face broke into a smile.

'I'm a friend of Gwen, Dr Simpson. She phoned me in a right state, so I told her to get on to you, but I said I'd come down and make sure she was all right. Where is she? Can I see her?' He tried to sound confident, at ease.

'She's upstairs in her office. She's pretty upset.' Pat peered at him in the half-light. 'Are you well in there, McLoughlin? You're a sneaky bugger, aren't you?' He laughed. 'Go on up and do your bit of hand-holding.'

McLoughlin stepped over the threshold. Mark Porter lay

face down on the limestone flags. Blood had spread from his head and was now a neatly congealed dark red puddle. McLoughlin moved a little closer. And saw the frayed rope end and the loop around his neck.

'What happened? Was it suicide?'

Hickey shrugged. 'Looks like it. Barry,' he indicated the uniformed guard standing by the door, 'checked in the guy's flat upstairs. There seems to be a note. But we won't know for sure what happened until Harris gets himself out of bed and gets his arse down here. But . . .' He pointed upwards. McLoughlin's gaze followed his. A length of rope, six feet or so, swung gently in the updraught from the open door. It seemed to be tied to the banisters on the upper landing.

Hickey's phone rang. He snapped it open. McLoughlin moved past him and mimed going upstairs. Hickey gave him a thumb's up.

McLoughlin took the stairs two at a time. When he reached Gwen Simpson's door he looked down. No one was paying any attention to him. He moved against the wall and kept going. Up the next flight of stairs, the next and the next. The door to the top flat was half open and a length of crime-scene tape was draped loosely from the handle to the banisters. He ducked beneath it and took a handkerchief from his pocket. He used it to take hold of the handle and close the door behind him. Up here, at the top of the house, the rooms were low-ceilinged. The walls were painted a rich dark red. The furniture was antique. The only concession to the twenty-first century was the Apple laptop on the large mahogany desk. McLoughlin stood in front of it. The screen was black. The desk was covered with papers. He leaned over to have a closer look. The top sheet was covered with writing, scrawled in thick black strokes across the page.

I've had enough. I can't take any more. I've tried to forget. I've tried to pretend that it never happened. But it happened then and now it's happened again. Enough is enough.

Beside the note was a brown padded envelope, and a small plastic CD case. Porter's name and address were printed in black marker. There was something familiar about the writing. McLoughlin used his handkerchief again to pick it up. He pulled out a piece of paper. The words 'We saw you' were written on it. McLoughlin leaned towards the computer. He touched the keyboard. It did not respond. He looked for the down button and touched it. The laptop clicked, purred and came to life. A video image was frozen on the screen. A group of people around a bright fire. He clicked on the arrow and it began to play. He held his breath as he watched. Then, using his handkerchief again, he stroked the touchpad, clicking on the eject-disk symbol. With a mechanical whirr the disk slid from the slot at the side of the computer. He picked it up and slipped it into the envelope. Then he hurried back to the door. He opened it slowly, tiptoed down the stairs and heard a familiar voice. He peered over the banisters and saw Johnny Harris bending over the body. McLoughlin slipped quietly into Gwen Simpson's office. He moved through the waiting room.

'Hi, Dr Simpson, are you there?' he called. He knocked on the door and pushed it open. She was sitting at her desk, her face milk white. She looked shocked. And worn out.

'Mr McLoughlin, what are you doing here?' Her voice was shaky.

'I heard what happened to Mark. I got a call from a friend.' He waved towards the stairs. 'I thought you might need a hand. I thought I'd see if there was anything I could do.'

Her mouth trembled into a smile. 'Thanks. It's pretty awful, really. I don't know what to do.'

'Did you see what happened?'

She nodded. 'Yes, I was here.' She put her hands over her face. Her shoulders were shaking.

He moved towards her. He laid a hand on the small of her back. He could feel the bones of her spine through her blouse. 'It's OK,' he said.

'It's not OK.' Her voice was muffled. 'I feel terrible. I should be doing something. But I can't think what.' She raised her face. Tears were spilling from her eyes.

'There's nothing you can do. That's the hardest thing to bear. There's nothing you can do.' He took her hands. They were chilled. They made him feel cold too. 'You stay there, I'll make some tea.' He set off towards the waiting room. 'I'll be back in a minute.' He closed the door behind him.

TWENTY

The images wouldn't leave him. Even when he closed his eyes he could still see them. The group of people around the fire. The light flickering over their faces. And the couple on the ground. Their skin turned to gold. Bright and shiny and beautiful. But the cry that came from the open mouth. 'No, no, no.' The repeated cry. Until he could bear it no more.

It had been after dawn when he got home. He had gone to make tea for Gwen Simpson and had been about to play the disk on the receptionist's computer when Pat Hickey had walked into the waiting room. Hickey jerked his head in the direction of Gwen Simpson's office. 'She's in there, is she?' He pulled his notebook from his pocket.

'Yeah.' McLoughlin stepped back from the desk. He walked ahead of Hickey and opened the door. 'Gwen,' his voice was soft, 'this is Sergeant Pat Hickey. He wants to ask you a few questions. Would you like me to stay?'

She was lying on the couch. She had kicked off her shoes. She looked small and defenceless. She sat up slowly. Her eyes were red and puffy. 'Yes, that would be good – if that's OK with you?' she asked Hickey.

He nodded. 'Sure no problem. Now.' He pulled one of the upright chairs towards her and sat down heavily.

McLoughlin closed the door and leaned against it. 'Tell me what happened tonight.'

Her voice assumed its usual calm clarity. She had gone home at six, but had come back at about nine thirty. She was writing a paper for an international conference on the long-term effects of child abuse. It was easier to work in her office, she said. It was always very quiet here at night. And she had her notes to hand. She didn't think there was anyone else in the building, certainly none of the other tenants. At about midnight she heard the front door slam. She went out on to the landing and saw Mark Porter in the hall. He came up the stairs towards her and they had a bit of chat as he took off his motorbike helmet.

'How did he seem?' Hickey lifted his head from his notebook.

She made a little face. 'The way he always seemed. He was a funny mixture of shyness and arrogance. He was always very conscious of his height. Especially, I think, around women.'

'And tonight when you saw him, how was he in particular?'

'In particular he seemed fine. He said he'd been visiting his friends in Kildare. The people with the stud farm.'

'And who are they? Do you know?'

Sophie Fitzgerald, McLoughlin thought. The gorgeous blonde.

Gwen shook her head. 'Not the name, but he's quite close to them, often goes out there at the weekend.' She paused. 'He said if I felt like having a drink he'd be up for a while. But I told him I still had a lot to do on my paper. He asked me what it was about, and when I told him he got agitated, almost angry.'

'Oh?' Hickey raised his eyebrows.

'Yes. He said he thought all that stuff was hugely exaggerated.'

'Oh?' Again the raised eyebrows.

'Anyway, that was it. I went back to my desk. He went upstairs. I didn't hear anything else until . . .' her face was stricken '. . . until I heard . . .' She stopped.

'Nothing else? You didn't hear anyone come into the building? No doors opening or closing? Phones ringing? Anything?' Hickey's voice was gentle but his questions were direct.

She shook her head. 'Nothing.'

McLoughlin thought of the disk he had taken from Porter's flat. It was in the computer in the waiting room. The envelope was pushing through his jacket pocket. He knew he had committed a crime. Removing evidence. He should make an excuse, go back upstairs and return it. But he didn't. He wanted to know what was on it.

Hickey stood up. 'If you wouldn't mind staying for a bit longer? The pathologist is examining the body and we don't want too many people tramping up and down. We'll let you go home as soon as we can. I'm sure Michael will keep you company.' He winked at McLoughlin. 'Won't you, Michael?'

'Sure thing.' McLoughlin smiled. 'If that's OK with you, Gwen. I'll get that tea for you now. Hot and sweet, just what the doctor ordered. Why don't you lie back there again? Take it easy.' He opened the door and Hickey left. 'I'll be back in a minute,' McLoughlin said.

'Thanks. You're being very kind.'

He followed Hickey out of Gwen's office and waited, listening to the other man's footsteps on the stone stairs. Then he shut the door firmly and went into the receptionist's little alcove. He found the kettle, a box of teabags and a couple of mugs. He plugged in the kettle, then sat behind the desk. He touched the computer keyboard, clicked on the DVD icon. And waited.

It was dark. It was night. There was a fire. The flames were shooting up, flickering, showers of sparks. People were standing in a semicircle. Their faces were glowing. Their mouths were open. Then the camera moved. Towards the ground by the fire. Two people were lying there. He could see the man's back. It was broad and muscular. He was on top of a woman. Her face was very white. McLoughlin recognized her from the photographs. It was Marina. Her arms were up behind her head. The man had his hands on her breasts. His head was bent to her neck. Her eyes were open, staring up. The camera jerked away. Towards Dominic de Paor. He was staring fixedly at the couple. And now the man was standing. It was Mark Porter. The camera zoomed in on his penis. It was soft, flaccid, small, hanging like a fat worm in his pubic hair. The camera moved to his face. He pointed to the woman. She was sitting up now. She looked dazed, only half awake. She turned her head and vomited. No one helped her. No one did anything. The camera moved back to Porter. His hands were over his eyes and his shoulders were shaking as he sobbed and sobbed. The screen went black.

The kettle was whistling. McLoughlin switched it off. He pulled open the drawers in the desk one by one. He found a box of CDs. He slid one into the computer and pressed the icon for burn. He stood up and poured boiling water into the mugs. He stirred the teabags around, then fished them out with a teaspoon and dropped them into the bin. There was a pint carton of milk in the little fridge, and on the shelf above, a half-bottle of brandy. He put them all on the desk and sat down at the computer again. He clicked on the disk icon and both slid out. He put the original back into its box in the envelope and the copy into another envelope in his pocket. Then he went to the door. He looked on to the landing. He could hear the murmur of voices below. He tiptoed out and moved quickly and quietly towards Porter's flat. He ducked beneath the crime-scene tape and opened the door. The room was as he had left it. He wiped the disk with his handkerchief and carefully slotted it into Porter's laptop and put the envelope back on the desk. Then he hurried out. He slunk down against the curving wall and slipped back into Gwen Simpson's waiting room. He picked up the mugs of tea, the carton of milk and the bottle of brandy. His chest was heaving and he could feel sweat on his forehead.

'Gwen, here, have this now.' He pushed open the door. She was sitting at her desk, a pen in her hand. She looked at him and for a moment it was as if she didn't know who he was. 'Hey, what are you doing?' he asked. 'You should be lying down.'

'What?' She seemed puzzled. 'Oh, tea, of course. How kind of you. Don't put the hot mugs on the wood. Here.' She pushed a pile of papers towards him.

'What are you doing?' he repeated. He held up the milk and the bottle and gestured to them. He noticed that his hands were shaking. She pointed at the brandy. He unscrewed the cap and poured a good measure into both mugs, then passed one across the desk. She sipped it slowly. 'Thanks. That tastes good.' She sipped again. 'I'm making a few notes about Mark.'

Mark Porter, naked, vulnerable, exposed, humiliated.

'Oh?' He tried to look noncommittal.

'Yes, I don't know how much you know about him but he tried to kill himself when he was a teenager.'

McLoughlin nodded. 'I did hear that.'

'And the circumstances were very similar. Again he used the banister on the top landing. At his boarding-school.'

His tea was bitter. Not improved by the brandy. He could feel it burning as it slipped down his oesophagus. 'Yes, I know. The consequence of bullying, the poor guy.'

'No,' she said. 'I don't think that was the reason. I know that's what everyone said, but Mark had other demons to fight. He had been damaged long before then.'

'Oh?' McLoughlin didn't feel good. He wanted to get out into the fresh air. 'His disability must have made his life hard. It's never easy being different.'

'It was more than that. And a lot worse, although he tried to play it down. He would never accept any form of weakness.' She fiddled with her pen. 'Mark wasn't just bullied. He was also abused at school.'

'At the Lodge? By a teacher?' He couldn't keep the surprise from his voice.

'Yes, at the Lodge, but it wasn't one of the school staff. It was a Scout-master. It seems like a cliché now, but unfortunately it's true. Poor Mark. I don't think he was physically able for all the hiking and camping out, but he told me it was what was expected of him so he did it. And some bastard took advantage of his helplessness. Just goes to show that paedophiles are no respecters of class.' She looked down at her papers. 'Although as far as Mark was concerned being abused was part and parcel of that kind of school life. He told me once,' and she mimicked him, ' "Every chap gets buggered. It's as common as morning prayers and cold showers after games."'

'So he didn't make a complaint? There was no police involvement?'

'No, that wasn't the way. Least said, soonest mended.'

'I see.' He looked over her head at the vivid colours of the painting on the wall. And saw Mark Porter's head lying smashed open in the crimson of his blood.

'Do you, Michael, do you really see? I'm not sure that you do. I'm not sure that any of us who hasn't experienced it first hand understands how it damages your sense of self, your self-esteem. Mark was a client of mine for a while. He told me about it, and then, not long afterwards, he stopped coming to see me. He never referred to it again. He was, I'm afraid, a very damaged person. And I was unable to help him.'

'Like Marina? She was damaged too.'

Before she could reply the door opened and Hickey came in. 'You can go home now, Dr Simpson. We've finished downstairs. However, this is still a crime scene for the time being. The building will be closed tomorrow. You might want to make alternative arrangements.' He sounded apologetic.

'For how long?' She tidied her papers and stood up.

'We're not sure at the moment. When the pathologist has issued his report on Mr Porter's death we'll have a better idea.' Hickey moved back into the outer office. 'We're closing up now so if you could make a move too, Michael?'

McLoughlin followed Gwen Simpson down the stairs. She was carrying a laptop in a bag over her shoulder and a box of books and papers. Mark Porter was no longer a misshapen heap on the floor. A puddle of congealed blood was all that was left of him. Johnny Harris had propped himself against the wall beside a huge gilt-framed mirror. He looked tired. McLoughlin patted his shoulder. 'Hey, Johnny, long night?' he said.

'Michael. What has you here?' Harris turned to watch Gwen Simpson as she brushed past.

'He's a friend of the lady,' Hickey hissed.

'Mm?' Harris cocked his head to one side.

'Ssh,' McLoughlin put a finger to his lips. He hurried outside after Gwen. The square was busy. There were two police cars, and a police motorbike parked up on the footpath. An ambulance stood with its doors open. A couple of paramedics were pushing a body-bag from a trolley inside it. A small crowd of onlookers was hanging around, and among them McLoughlin noticed a couple of journalists he knew.

'Let me help you. This lot can be a hell of a nuisance.' He took the box from Gwen. 'Where's your car?'

She jerked her head, then walked towards a red Mercedes soft-top parked under a street-light. 'Thanks.' She opened the door. 'I can manage now.'

'Would you like me to see you home? You've had a hard time.'

'No, I'm fine, really. Thanks for the tea and for, well . . .' She smiled up at him, then reached into the car to put the laptop and books on the passenger seat.

He stood back. The images kept crowding in.

She straightened up. 'You don't look so good either. I hope you'll be able to sleep after all this. Don't drink too much tonight. OK?'

He grinned at her wryly, then turned away. Johnny Harris was waiting for him.

'Pretty woman,' Harris remarked.

'Yeah, but not my type. She has the world all figured out. And someone like me isn't part of her figuring. Now,' he put an arm around Harris's shoulders. 'Tell me what you've been figuring. How did Mark Porter die? Was it suicide or what?'

The images wouldn't leave him. Even when he closed his eyes he could still see them. The group of people around the fire.

'Marina,' he whispered, 'how could you let this happen? *Why* did you let this happen? And why was de Paor phoning you? Why were you phoning him? Tell me, Marina, please tell me.'

He picked up the school photograph. He thought about the faces around the fire. He tried to match them up. He could definitely recognize Rosie and Dominic de Paor. And he was almost sure he could identify a couple of the other women. One was Gilly Kearon and there was the Honourable Sophie Fitzgerald. From the stud farm in Kildare. And who, he wondered, had been behind the camera? Who was the witness to it all? Who wanted a record of what had happened? Who wanted to be able to say, 'I saw you. We saw you.'

TWENTY-ONE

The two women walked along the West Pier in the morning sunshine. Sally's little dog rushed ahead, then stopped to wait, his springy tail wagging, his mouth open as he panted with the effort.

'He tries hard, doesn't he?' Margaret tugged at his ears gently.

'Yeah, he sure does.' Sally held up a worn tennis ball. 'Come on, Toby – look!' She threw the ball as far as she could and the dog yapped, jumped into the air then took off after it.

'Would it be fun to be a dog, do you think?' Margaret held up a hand to shade her eyes as she watched him run.

'Fun? I'm not sure,' Sally pushed her hair off her forehead. 'It's hot today. It's not usually out here.'

'No, it's usually bloody freezing. My father was what you could call a daily communicant when it came to walking the pier. Winter and summer, wet and dry, freezing or not. I spent my teenage years trying to avoid the summons to join him.'

'Well, that's one of the pluses about having a dog. The pier walk has to be done, whether you like it or not, so you stop considering it a choice.' Sally put two fingers into her mouth and gave a surprisingly loud whistle. The dog stopped and turned back.

Margaret's expression was admiring. 'That's fantastic. I thought only teenage boys could whistle like that.'

Sally smiled. 'Yeah, it's one of the things I'm most proud of. My first husband, Robbie, showed me how to do it. When we were teenagers, when he was coming to see me and my parents didn't approve, he'd whistle as he walked up the road and I'd sneak out through the back garden.'

They walked, in silence then, as far as the lighthouse at the end of the pier. They sat on the granite wall and looked across the bay to Howth. The dog found a patch of shade, lay down and panted, his sides heaving and drops of spittle forming on his shiny black lips.

'Where's Vanessa?' Margaret asked. 'I haven't seen her for a couple of days. Has she gone off me?'

'I doubt it. She likes you very much. Which is good. She's not usually that impressed with people.' She shaded her eyes against the sun. 'I'm not sure what's going on with her at the moment. She's getting up early, which she never used to do, and going out, then not coming home until late.'

'Is it a boy?'

Sally shook her head. 'I don't think so. If it was I'd be pleased for her. She doesn't have much confidence, you know. Her hippie look, the clogs, the headscarf, the beads, it's a disguise, really.'

'Kids are good at disguises, aren't they?' Margaret followed the progress of a long, elegant yacht as it sailed into view between the two pier walls. 'Mary was much better at it than I'd thought.'

'In what way?'

'Well, it was very strange. After she died I discovered all kinds of things about her that I hadn't known. I discovered she'd had an abortion. I discovered she'd had a number of boyfriends in New Zealand whom I'd never met. And, of course, there was her relationship with . . .' She stopped and stared at the ground. She swallowed hard, the lump heavy in her throat. '. . . the man who killed her.'

'A relationship? Could you call it that?' Sally turned to look at her.

'Yes, it was a relationship. Not one that I would have wanted. Not one that was healthy or worthwhile or any of the good things. But it was a relationship. He knew a version of Mary that I didn't. And that was one of the things that really hurt.' She clenched her fists and drummed them on her thighs. 'He knew her in a way that I didn't. He told me things about her that I didn't know.'

'He told you? You met him?' Sally's voice was shocked.

Margaret nodded. She stared out across the sea at the yacht. It was on a run. Its spinnaker was flying, a bright design of reds and blues, the wind pushing it into a great, swelling billow.

'I met him. I spoke to him.' It was on the tip of her tongue to say, 'I killed him.'

'How? Under what circumstances? After he was freed?'

'Before and after, but I don't want to go into it now. It's difficult to talk about. But it made me realize how little I knew Mary.' She pushed herself up to standing.

'But was he telling you the truth?' Sally got up too. 'Are you sure he wasn't lying? To justify what he did to her.'

'He was lying about some things, but not about others. I had to accept it. There were just some parts of Mary that I didn't know. You must have found that about Marina since she died, haven't you? Haven't you discovered that she was a different person?'

'Not really. I think I know all about Marina. She wasn't

perfect, but that doesn't matter.' Sally stooped to catch the dog's collar.

'It didn't matter to me either. That's not what I'm saying. My love for Mary was as deep and powerful as ever. I was just sorry that I wasn't able to talk to her any more. That we weren't able to continue our friendship. I always thought we would be friends as she got older. That we would share our lives. Even if she got married, had her own children, that we would always be close. But . . .'

They began to walk back along the pier. The gravel was dusty underfoot. Again there was silence. It was even hotter. Margaret was tired. Sally threw the ball for the little dog. He scampered backwards and forwards, tail wagging, high-pitched yelps of pleasure coming from his mouth.

'You know, don't you,' Sally said, 'that we were all very interested in what happened to your daughter? Not just because it was sad and awful, but because Patrick Holland was the defence barrister. We knew him very well. And when he took on the case I phoned him and asked him how he could do it.'

'And what did he say?' Margaret turned to her.

'He said that everyone was entitled to a defence. That was the law. Innocent until proven guilty, no matter what the crime. I said to him – I remember because I was really angry – "You don't honestly believe that, do you?"' She threw the ball again. 'And he said he was surprised I was challenging his argument, given that I, too, had needed an advocate after James's first wife had had our marriage declared illegal and I had gone to court to get maintenance for Vanessa. And he had been my barrister.'

'Was he? Did Patrick help you?' Margaret stopped.

'Yes, he was very kind. And he did it for nothing. I

wanted to pay him, but he wouldn't take any money. It was a terrible time. I hadn't realized what the process of going to court would be like. And Helena, James's first wife, she turned up every day. Watched it all. Watched me. It was horrible.' Sally turned towards the sea. 'I'm so lucky to live here, you know. The case went on for ages. It kept on being adjourned, put off, put back, I don't know what. When I came home I'd change, get the dog, put Vanessa in her buggy and we'd come down here. There's something very cleansing about sea air. I don't know what it is, but it gets rid of a lot of shit.'

She held up the old tennis ball. The dog barked and sprang high. She threw it as hard as she could. They watched the little animal scrabble after it.

'Anyway, we got through it. And I told you, didn't I, how I got something for Vanessa?'

'Yes, you did. The cottage in Wicklow she'll inherit when she's eighteen. And that's soon, isn't it?' The dog had found the ball and was running back to them.

'Next week. But Marina died almost within sight of it, and now I don't want Vanessa to have anything to do with the place. I'd like her to sell it.' The dog dropped the ball at her feet. He was panting loudly. Sally patted his head, then picked up the ball again. 'In fact, we had a bit of a row about it last night. I said that to her and she got indignant. Said it was nothing to do with me. That I wasn't a de Paor, so what did I know about anything?' She smiled. 'Funny, isn't it, when your kids start telling you what's what? So that's the way it stands. She's a de Paor. I'm not. I suppose she's entitled to her membership of the family. That's what Patrick would have said anyway. If he was here.'

'You knew him well?'

'Pretty well. I remember, when I first met him I didn't like him. I thought he didn't approve of me. He was always abrupt and brusque. But when I got to know him better I realized that was just his way. Underneath it all he was lovely. Of course, you probably wouldn't agree.'

Margaret stopped. She felt light-headed. The sun was very hot on the nape of her neck. 'No, I liked him too. I knew him, as it happens, from a long time ago.'

'Did you?' Sally turned to look at her. 'How?'

'Oh, you know. We had friends in common.' Friends who had invited her to a Christmas party. Somewhere out in County Meath. They had arranged a lift for her. Patrick arrived. He was on his own. He made it plain he wasn't pleased to have a passenger imposed on him. He didn't speak much as they drove out of the city and through the winter countryside. He didn't speak much to her at the party either. She was relieved when she found some of her own friends. But somehow, later on, they danced. And when he held her it was as if no other man had ever touched her. And later on when he drove her home, he stopped the car and kissed her. And it was as if no other man had ever kissed her. And when he asked if he could see her again, she said yes without thinking that he was married, that he had a child. None of that mattered. And when she got pregnant with Mary all that mattered was that she had a part of him. And she would hold on to that part for ever.

'So what did you think when you saw he was defending that man?' Sally's face was a mixture of curiosity and anguish.

What did I think? I thought he would help me get justice my way. That's what I thought. Margaret chewed her lip. 'I thought he was doing his job, that's all. I thought that justice is a legal concept. It has nothing to do with what you or I might consider to be justice. What the court considers to be justice is the evidence that can be brought and proven. That's all it is, plain and simple. And anyone who expects anything else from the court is a fool.' Her voice was bitter.

'Is that really what you think?'

'Yes, it is. You have to get your own justice in whatever way you can. You can't expect the state to do it for you. The way the courts function, it's a game that clever men play with other people's lives. You must know that, Sally. You lived with a barrister. You must have seen what he did. How many of the men he defended had killed? And how many walked away from the court as free men?'

Sally didn't reply immediately. She stared at the water. Flotsam had piled up against the rocks. Plastic bottles and chunks of white polyboard. A doll's head, the size and shape of a baby's, floated beside a rotten orange. It gave her a start. She caught her breath. Then she spoke: 'James was an honourable man,' she said slowly. 'He had beliefs and principles. I respected them. He made me think about this country in a different way. He made me understand the nature of the repression of Catholics in Northern Ireland. He cared deeply about those men who had been driven to violence. He didn't judge or blame them. He considered that their actions were political. They were motivated by the desire for political change, by greed or selfishness or the pursuit of pleasure. And he, like Patrick, was determined that they should have the best defence possible.'

Margaret didn't reply. There was no reply she could make. She who had killed too. She who had not paid for her crime. She who was still alive, here in the sunshine, with the wind on her face and the smell of the sea in her nostrils. Jimmy Fitzsimons had suffered in agony, on his own, in the dark shed at Ballyknockan. She reached for Sally's hand and squeezed it. Sally smiled at her and squeezed back. They walked on towards the railway line and the path home, the little dog running happily ahead.

They lay in the garden on deckchairs. A bottle of white wine, beaded with condensation, rested in a cooler. The dog drowsed in a pool of shade beneath the apple tree. His eyes were closed. His small paws twitched and he whined softly in his sleep. The smell of honeysuckle wafted down from the wall that bounded the garden. Margaret's father had shown her how to suck nectar from the stamens when they had gone on holiday to West Cork. Wandering along country lanes, pulling honeysuckle from the hedgerows, bending his face to the roses as she twisted ripe blackberries from the briars, her fingers stained purple. It was years since she had eaten a blackberry. They were rooted out in Australia, poisoned, burned as a noxious weed. And she would not eat another, she thought. By the time they were ripe she would have made her choice and she would not be able to wander the fields and pick them.

Sally stirred in her chair and refilled her glass. 'Tell me,' she said, 'it was you, wasn't it?'

'Me? What do you mean?' Margaret looked at her.

'It was you Patrick had the affair with. James told me about it. Everyone, all his friends, knew there was someone, but no one was sure who it was.' She smiled. 'I can see it in your face when you mention his name. You must have loved him a lot.'

Margaret picked up the bottle and topped up her own glass. 'It was a long time ago. I was young. I didn't know what I was getting into. I didn't think about the consequences. For me or for anyone else.' She drank some wine. It was very dry and very cold.

'And what were the consequences?'

Margaret didn't reply immediately. 'It was a long time ago,' she repeated quietly. Consequences unimagined. And what was to come next? She felt a clutch of fear in her stomach. It had seemed so straightforward when she was in her house in Eumundi. Mary was dead. Jimmy Fitzsimons was dead. Patrick was dead. There was no one left who could be hurt. She had to face what she had done. She had to atone for her sin. She had to come back and face the consequences. But now? She pushed the fear back down into the darkness. She closed her eyes and turned her face to the sun. She felt its soothing warmth on her face. She lifted her glass. She drank.

The afternoon passed slowly. They ate bread and cheese, small, juicy tomatoes and fat black olives. The dog woke and scratched, snapped at flies, then lapsed back into his dream-filled sleep.

'Thanks for this,' Sally said.

'For what?'

'For letting me sit here with you. For not expecting anything from me. For allowing me to grieve without making any demands.'

It was almost midnight by the time Sally left. Margaret walked with her past the Martello tower and up the steep hill to the main road. The dog snuffled in the ditches.

'Thank you again,' Sally said.

'It's my pleasure. It's been a long time since I had some friendship in my life.' Margaret smiled.

Sally looked across the road towards the tall terrace of houses. 'I hope Vanessa's home. Of course, I feel neglectful of her now.'

'Don't. I think it's about time Vanessa got back to teenage pursuits, don't you?' Margaret crossed her arms. She shivered. Tonight there was a chill in the air.

'You're probably right.' Sally began to cross the road. Then she turned back. 'Just one thing I wanted to ask you. You know the man who killed your daughter?'

Margaret nodded, her throat suddenly tight.

'Well, I was wondering, what happened to him? They found his body, didn't they, out near Blessington? But they never said how he died. Not really.'

Margaret swallowed. Her mouth was dry. 'He died of hunger and thirst. The most basic and simple way to die.'

'But how?' Sally's expression was full of curiosity. 'How did that happen?'

'Someone locked him up. Someone made it impossible for him to eat or drink ever again.'

'But who did it? Who would do such a thing? Who would want him to die like that?'

Their eyes met. Then Margaret looked away. 'Goodnight, Sally.' She turned to walk home.

'Wait. Wait a minute,' Sally moved towards her. She kissed her on both cheeks, then took her head in her hands and kissed her forehead. 'Goodnight, Margaret, goodnight.' Her voice was gentle.

Margaret nodded. No words would come.

TWENTY-TWO

The phone was ringing, shrill and insistent. McLoughlin buried his face in the pillow. He put his hands over his ears. Silence. He drifted back into sleep. Then the phone rang again. He turned on to his front and reached down beside the bed. His fingers scrabbled for the hard plastic. He dragged it up and peered blearily at the screen. But there was no vibration, no lights, nothing. He lifted his head from the pillow. He peered at the clock on the bedside table. It was bright outside, the sun edging around the curtains. It was late, nearly one o'clock. He yawned loudly, and heard the phone again. The sound was coming from the sitting room. He got up quickly, stumbling as he hurried from the bedroom along the corridor. Just as he went through the door the ringing stopped.

'Shit, fuck it,' he muttered, as he bumped into the coffee-table and cracked his knee on the corner. And then the phone beeped. Twice, loudly. And he saw it, on the desk beside the computer, its lights shining, then dimming. Marina's phone. Where he had left it after he had rung the number and heard Dominic de Paor's voice. He limped across the room and picked it up. There were three missed calls registered and the symbol for a message, the tiny closed envelope in the top left-hand corner of the screen. He carried it with him into the kitchen and put it down on the table as he filled the kettle with water. He plugged it in and switched it on, then picked up the phone, slid back the glass doors and stepped out on to the terrace. He slumped on to the bench. His mouth was dry and foul and he felt disoriented and weak. He pressed the numbers to get the message. He held the phone to his ear. He heard the voice.

'I know it wasn't Marina who phoned me. So who are you? And what do you want? Whoever you are, back off. Leave me alone.'

He got up, went into the kitchen and made himself tea. He replayed the message. De Paor's tone was angry and hostile. 'Back off. Leave me alone,' he said. But he had been wondering. Who had Marina's phone? And why had they called him? He probably figured it was a random thing, McLoughlin thought. Some kid had got hold of the phone and was flicking through the numbers. Well, he was wrong. And perhaps it was about time McLoughlin went to see him. And told him. And told him a few other things too. Told him that he knew what had happened that night at the party. Told him how he had seen what had been done to Mark Porter and Marina. Asked him what he knew about Marina's death. Asked him about his school days.

He headed for the bathroom. He turned on the shower and stepped under the jet of water. He hadn't got far with the weight loss. His body still made him cringe. And when he touched his skin it was as if it was covered with a thick unresponsive cuticle. He tried to remember what it was like to be touched by someone who loved him. And when was the last time he had touched someone he loved? Or thought he loved, perhaps. A long time ago. Shaking Margaret Mitchell's hand when he said goodbye to her after the Jimmy Fitzsimons trial collapsed. Maybe that was it. That was the last time he'd had physical contact with her. Of course he had seen her after then. Saw her that night out in Ballyknockan. Watched her as she got out of the car that Jimmy was driving. Wanted to rush to help her. But stopped when he saw Patrick Holland. Realized he had no place in her life. And since then? She had come into his dreams at night, and filled his idle thoughts during the day. He remembered the shine of her dark hair, the grace of her stance, the timbre of her voice. Remembered how she lay in the deckchair in the garden in Brighton Vale. Made up stories about how they would meet again, what he would say, what she would say, what they would do.

He stepped out on to the bathmat and pulled a towel from the rail. He flailed at his body. There had been a couple of others, brief encounters, one-night stands. The sex had been all right, but it had left him with a sense of guilt. Silly, really. He sat down on the toilet seat and dried between his toes. Margaret was gone. He would never see her again. And anyway, anyway, there could never be anything between them. Not since that night in Bally-knockan.

'I saw you,' he said the words out loud. 'I saw you and what you did.'

'I saw you.' The same words that had been sent to Marina. What had she done? What had she been seen to do? Who had seen her? And what was the secret that those words threatened to reveal?

He hung the towel on the rail to dry. And heard the phone ring again. This time it was his own ringtone. He hurried back into the bedroom and reached for it. And saw the name 'Harris' on the screen. 'Hey, Johnny, how goes it? How's my man?' His tone was distinctly transatlantic.

'Thought you'd like to know. Mark Porter . . .' Harris said.

'Yes, go on?' McLoughlin cradled the phone between his ear and his shoulder.

'Doesn't seem to be much doubt. It was suicide. By hanging.' His tone was matter-of-fact.

'Anything strange about it? Anything about the rope?' He pulled open the chest of drawers and rummaged one-handed for a clean T-shirt and underpants.

'Well, it's good-quality natural fibre. And he made a proper hangman's noose. The right kind of knot and every-thing. Would he have been a sailor, do you think?'

'Probably not. More likely a Scout.' McLoughlin remem-bered what Gwen had told him. About the abuse.

'Ah, that explains it.' Harris sighed. 'A knot for every occasion. Anyway, it's a sad business. Suicide leaves a nasty aftermath. I kind of know the family, the Porters. Very stiff-upper-lip. Very private. They won't like this one bit. Such a public death.' He paused. 'Do you fancy sailing tonight? I'm a bit short, crew-wise.'

'I'm not sure. Johnny, I've a few things to do.' He sat down on the bed, slipping his feet one at a time into his pants. 'But listen, anything else about Rosie Webb?'

'Not really. Doesn't seem as if her death is suspicious. No signs of violence or force or anything like that. Anyway,' his tone was brisk, business-like, 'got to go. Things to do, people to see. Maybe we'll catch up later.'

'Sure thing, pal, sure thing.' McLoughlin put the phone down and concentrated on dressing. Then he walked into the sitting room and sat at his computer. He checked his emails. There was the usual rubbish, but among the sugges-tions for stock investments, online drugs, special offers from the local supermarket, he saw the name 'Tom Spencer'. He opened the email.

Dear Michael McLoughlin,

My mother said you might get in touch. It's hard to find a bit of quiet here but you asked me a few questions so I'll try to answer them, even though I don't really see the point. Number one, you asked me if I was surprised that Marina took her own life. The simple answer is no. My sister was always deeply unhappy. Looking back, it seems to me that she never got over the death of our father. Marina was six when he died. I was four. They were very close. As the first-born, she was special to both my parents. I can remember, even though I was very young, that she always seemed to be sitting on my father's knee. Maybe it was because I was a boy but I don't think he was ever as close to me. Anyway, whatever, I think that was her first and greatest loss. And her first meeting with death. Marina was always fascinated by death. I remember we talked about it a lot. She wanted to imagine what it would be like. And to imagine what dying would be like. She asked me once, when she was about twelve, if I would put a pillow over her head. Stupidly I did and I sat on it too. But then I got scared and I got up and took away the pillow. She was mad with me and said I should have carried on.

Her second experience of loss was when my mother married James. Marina was very upset by that. She felt it was a betrayal. Of my father and of us. I tried to explain to her that our mother needed someone but Marina didn't buy it. She didn't like James at all. He was very different from anyone else we knew. We had always been close. We were a neat and tidy unit. But James broke our little family wide open. He was noisy and gregarious. He had lots of friends. He loved entertaining and the houses – the Lake House and his house in Leeson Park where we lived for a couple of years – were always full of people. And, of course, there was our step-brother, Dominic. He and Marina were always fighting. He used to tease her. But she gave as good as she got. I sometimes thought it was a kind of a game going on between them. But to give him his due, James was pretty OK about it. He was good to Marina. He bought her that sailing dinghy. She took it from him and sneered behind his back. After his death she went to pieces. I remember she kept on saying it was her fault. She should have made him wear a life-jacket.

And then there was all that stuff at school. I couldn't understand what was going on. I tried to stay out of it. To be honest, I was embarrassed by Marina. The other kids were always sniggering about her. I don't think I was very loyal. I suppose I couldn't understand what was happening. Marina was never like that before. She came across all confident and in control but she wasn't really. She badly wanted to be loved and, for whatever reason, she didn't feel she was. I thought she was like one of those black holes in deep space. Gravity was always threatening to swallow her.

The other thing you asked me was what happened the day James died. Well, it was a long time ago so I'm not sure how many of the details I remember. But Dominic had a bunch of his friends staying. One of them, a kid called Ben, had brought his motorboat with him. It was fantastic. They launched it on the lake. The weather was amazing that summer. They all went water-skiing, sunbathing. There was a lot of drinking going on. Anyway, that day, the first I knew there was trouble was when I heard the boat revving. I wasn't with the other kids. Dominic didn't want me around. They'd all gone off into the woods. My mother had taken Vanessa, the baby, down to the lake shore to paddle. Marina was messing around in the dinghy and I was up a tree in the woods, watching the deer through my binoculars. Then I heard the boat. It startled the deer and they took off in a group. I climbed down from the tree and I started following them. When I got to the top it was incredible. I could see the house and the woods. I could see the lake and the rock face rising up from it. I could see my mother lying in a deckchair and the baby in her pram. And I could see a little plume of smoke coming from the pine trees by the lake shore where Dominic and his snooty friends hung out. And then I saw a motorboat down the far end of the lake. It was doing circles. It was swirling around, these big white circles on the surface of the water. And I could see the dinghy, and this tiny figure, Marina, standing up and she was leaning over the side. I went on tracking the deer, but when I looked down at the lake and the shore I could see there was something going on. Dominic and all of them were running towards the house. My mother was standing on the beach. She looked so tiny, just like a little doll. And every now and then, when the wind was in the right direction, I could hear someone shouting. Eventually I went back down the hill. I came in behind the house but there was no one there. I walked down to the lake and everyone was standing around. looking at James. He was lying on the jetty. My mother was screaming, completely hysterical. And so was Marina. She was crying and shouting. She kept on saying that it was her fault, that she should have made James wear a life-jacket. That he wouldn't have drowned if he'd worn a life-jacket. And for a long time afterwards, even after the funeral, even when we went back to school, she kept on about it. How it was all her fault, the whole thing.

Finally, you asked me if there was anyone who would want to harm Marina. I don't know. She was expelled from the Lodge. She pretty much dropped out after that. She wouldn't go back to school. She moved out of the house. We didn't see much of her. Then she went to the States. We didn't hear from her for months at a time. And by the time she came home I had left. My mother used to pass on bits of news. I was glad she seemed to be getting on well. Although, to be honest, I wasn't convinced. So when my mother called me and said she was dead it wasn't that much of a surprise. And I can see it suddenly clearly. The view from the top of the hill that day. The lake, the dinghy and Marina. 'My fault,' she kept on saying. 'My fault.'

Have to go now. It's very busy here. Too many hungry mouths. Not enough food. All donations gratefully received.

All the best,

Tom Spencer

'I can see it now,' Tom Spencer had written. And McLoughlin could see it too. He could see Spencer's vantage-point from the top of the hill. And all that Spencer could see from it. He began to doodle with a pen. The oval shape of the lake. The long rectangle of the house. The square of the big field that went down to the water's edge. He filled in with cross-hatching the area of woodland by the house and along the lake shore. He defined the narrow, sandy beach. And he drew the snake of the drive from the gate, putting in the small square shape of the lodge. And at the far end he marked, with a series of small circles, the rapids where Helena had found Marina's body and the little stream that flowed over the stones and down into the next valley. He picked up a red pen and uncapped it. He scanned his map and marked with an X where everyone had been. Marina and James in the boat. Sally and Vanessa on the beach. Dominic de Paor and his friends on the little promontory. Tom Spencer at the top of the hill. And who else might have been there? he wondered. Where was Helena on that hot summer day in 1985? Was she in the clinic in the city? Or was she somewhere else? In the cottage, perhaps? Or in the woods too? Watching, waiting, hating.

He got up and walked into the kitchen. He opened the fridge. He was hungry but he couldn't decide what he wanted to eat. He slid back the glass doors and stepped outside. His phone rang. He sat on the bench and scanned the screen. The number wasn't familiar, but he recognized the voice immediately.

'Michael McLoughlin?' Poppy Atkinson's tone was more measured than it had been the last time they had spoken. 'I've just heard about Mark Porter. I'd like to meet you. Are you free at lunchtime today?'

She suggested they meet in the bar of the Shelbourne Hotel. She worked, it turned out, at the Anglo-Irish Investment Bank, just around the corner in Kildare Street. She was a partner and fund manager. He hadn't realized she had such a prestigious job. But, as she had said, she'd got the brains and Rosie the looks.

She was waiting for him at a table in the corner. The bar was dark and empty. Her wine glass was empty too. He asked the barman for a refill, and a mineral water for himself.

'Very sensible.' Poppy lifted her glass and saluted him.

'Now,' he leaned back into the deep leather chair, 'what did you want to talk about?'

It was mid-afternoon by the time they left the bar. He walked with her to the bank's revolving door. She wasn't completely steady on her feet. He suggested a taxi home, but she brushed aside his suggestion.

'I'm fine.' She gave him a little push with both hands. 'If the guys can have their long lunches, so can I.' Then the door swallowed her. He moved away and crossed the road. He walked past the uniformed guards on duty outside the dáil and in through the wrought-iron gate to the National Library. He went quickly up the marble stairs and into the Reading Room. It was quiet and calm. He sat down at one of the desks and switched on the green glass lamp. He took out his notebook. He began to write.

Ben Roxby and Rosie Webb had been having an affair. It had ended when he had fallen off the roof. Rosie blamed herself for his death. Annabel had found out about them and she had challenged Ben that evening when he came home. His guilt had made him go up on to the roof. His guilt had killed him.

'Did Rosie's husband know?'

'Everyone knew.'

'Everyone?'

She explained. The group from school had continued to be close. But Ben's father was ambitious for him and sent him to America to study at MIT. By the time he had come back to Ireland, Rosie had met and married Nick Webb. Ben then married Annabel Palmer, whom he'd known all his life, but it wasn't long before he and Rosie became lovers again. Their old friends colluded. Provided alibis, places to meet. Dominic gave them the use of the Lake House. Mark Porter would keep one of his flats in Fitzwilliam Square specifically for them.

'And what happened after Ben died?'

The group supported Rosie through it. They gave her succour and comfort. And Dominic gave her more.

'Such as?'

He supplied her with cocaine. He had his sources. Her addiction grew. She would do anything for the drug. And then . . .

'He wanted something from her, did he?'

'Yes.' Poppy nodded. 'No such thing as a free lunch. Or a free line of coke.'

'And her husband, he must have known something was going on?' He drummed his fingers on the table.

'You know,' she drained her glass and beckoned the waiter over, 'I could never figure Nick out. He's a smart guy, sophisticated, all that. But either he knew and he didn't care, or he genuinely didn't know. And I actually think it's the latter. I was always waiting for the shit to hit the fan, but it never did.'

'And what about Mark? What did he have to do with it all?' He fished the piece of lemon from the bottom of his glass and sucked it.

'Mark was their gofer. Their delivery-boy. Their messenger. He was party to all their sordid secrets, all their messy relationships. Rosie wasn't Dominic's only conquest.' She sniggered. She picked up her fresh glass. 'I've known a few in my time. And they always told me how Mark would show up with flowers and presents. It was almost as if they became Mark's lovers by association.' She took a gulp of wine. 'I used to think that the group were like the Famous Five. You know, the Enid Blyton stories?'

McLoughlin nodded. 'I was a Secret Seven kid, actually.'

'Yeah, well, no accounting for taste. But you'll remember that the Famous Five included a dog. Well, Mark was the dog.' She crossed her legs, bumping one knee against the table. Their glasses shuddered. 'He got the leftovers. When Dominic was done with someone, Mark would show up.'

McLoughlin lifted his eyes from his notebook. The Reading Room was almost empty. A few grey heads bent over books. A girl who might have been a student reading a newspaper. A couple, Americans probably, scanning a dusty ledger that the librarian had brought out from the stacks. He wrote the word 'party' in his notebook. Now, what had Poppy said about it?

'The party? Well, I wasn't invited, of course. I'd volunteered to babysit for Rosie's kids.'

'So Nick was there?' McLoughlin didn't remember seeing him in the group by the fire.

'No, he was away on business. So I said I'd look after the kids. I love them, love spending time with them.'

'You don't have any of your own?' McLoughlin shifted in the leather chair. It creaked loudly.

'No. As I said, Rosie got the looks. She also got the perfect Fallopian tubes. I got the brains and the ectopic pregnancies. I can't have children so I make do with my sister's.' She drank some more wine. 'It must have been one hell of a night. Rosie was in a bad state when she came home. I put her straight to bed with a Valium.'

'Well, I presume she was upset about Marina's death.'

Poppy shook her head. 'No, it wasn't that. It was something else. I assumed it was to do with Dominic. After all, his wife, the ever so cute Gilly, was there too. And Sophie Fitzgerald. All Dominic's lovely ladies. And, of course, his mother was in residence. Anything could happen if she was around.'

'Do you know her?'

Poppy made a face. 'Not really. I doubt if anyone knows her now, except Dominic. And Rosie used to say that the only person who understood Dominic was his mother. So what does that say about him? If the only person who has a clue what's going on in his head is a nutcase. A certified paranoid schizophrenic. Not very healthy, is it? Actually, I think Rosie was quite jealous. Apparently, whenever they went to the Lake House, Dominic would disappear for hours up to the little cottage where his mother stayed when he had guests. And I remember her telling me that when he came back he always smelt of her. Ugh, what a thought.' She gave an exaggerated shiver.

'Smelt of her in what way?' McLoughlin remembered her perfume. Saliva filled his mouth and his stomach heaved.

'What way do you think? Scent, body odour, whatever. Rosie was very put off.' Poppy's long nose twitched. 'But as far as the party was concerned, Rosie didn't mention Helena. Anyway, who knows what happened that night? One thing I do know, however. There was a lot of cocaine involved.'

'What about LSD? Acid?'

'Doubt it somehow. It's not a cool drug, these days. It's

for teenagers, the ecstasy generation. Not for Dublin's sophis-
ticates.' She smiled.

McLoughlin wrote 'cocaine' and underlined it. Hard to
believe that five years ago cocaine was a rarity. Only the very
rich and the very famous had had access to it. Now every
suburban party, every family get-together, every wedding,
every night on the town got lift-off from those little plastic
sachets of white powder.

'So, tell me, what do you think about Mark now? About his
suicide? What caused it, do you think?'

'I don't know. I was hoping you might be able to tell
me. You were there last night, after all.' She touched the
back of his hand briefly.

'How do you know that?' McLoughlin slid his hand to
his lap.

'Your photo's in one of the tabloids. You're leaving
Mark's house with a woman.' She finished her drink. 'Did
you see him?'

'Yeah. I did. It wasn't nice.'

'No.' She played with the heavy gold bracelet on her
right wrist. 'It never is. So, what I wondered . . . it said in
the paper there was a note. What was in it?'

'Why do you want to know?'

'Well,' she wriggled in her chair, 'it occurred to me that,
with all that's happened recently, Mark might have said
something about people we know. And to be honest, we
could do without the publicity.' She leaned towards him.
He could smell the alcohol on her breath. 'You're a good

guy, Michael McLoughlin, aren't you? One of us. If there was anything you thought I should know, you'd tell me, wouldn't you?'

He was glad now he'd resisted the temptation to drink. 'I think it's time we were going.' He stood up and held out his hand.

'Oh, come on, you're not cross with me, are you?' She pushed back the table. It scraped noisily across the tiled floor. She got to her feet. She was slightly unsteady.

'Not cross with you, Poppy. And, anyway, I didn't see the note. I haven't a clue what was in it. And I wouldn't worry. The guards will keep it quiet.' Like hell, he thought. These days, any guard worth his salt was a favourite of the fourth estate. 'Come on,' he took her arm, 'it's time we were going.'

They walked through the lobby. McLoughlin was conscious of Poppy's unsteadiness. He held her arm tightly as they went through the swing doors and on to the crowded pavement.

'You know,' he said, as he steered her towards Kildare Street, 'you were pretty hard on Marina when we spoke about her before. But she doesn't sound that different from the others now. As far as Mark goes, anyway.'

'No? You don't think so?' Poppy's voice got louder. 'Well, I think she was the corrupter. I think she started it all. If it hadn't been for Marina, none of this would have happened.' She swayed out of his grip and faced him. 'She taught them what to do. She showed them how to hurt. My sister would still be alive if it wasn't for her. And so would Mark.' She stepped backwards and almost toppled off the pavement, the spike heels of her boots giving way beneath her weight. He grabbed her and held her upright.

'I'm fine,' she protested. 'I don't need an escort.'

'Yeah, right. Come on, it's this way to your office.' They walked together at a brisk pace. 'Anyway, it's a pleasure, it's not often I get to ramble around the city centre on such a nice day. I like this part of town. The seat of government and all that.'

'Yes, it's cosy, isn't it?' She stopped and leaned against the hotel railings. 'My husband and I work within five minutes of each other. Rosie's husband's office is two minutes from here. And do you know who else is just down the road?' Her face broke into an exaggerated smile. She didn't wait for him to answer. 'Why it's Dominic de Paor, senior counsel. In a fine old Georgian building that just happens to belong to the Porter family. Now, is that cosy, or is that cosy?'

McLoughlin peered at his notebook. She was right. It was all very cosy. All those years since they'd left the Lodge and they were still gnawing away at each other. It made him feel claustrophobic and sick. He closed it and put it back into his pocket. Then he switched off the lamp and left the Reading Room, went down the wide stairs and out into the sunshine. He had asked Poppy why she was at work. After all, it was only days since her sister had died. She hadn't been buried yet. Didn't she need time to grieve?

'Grieve? We don't grieve. Not publicly. We observe the formalities and in Rosie's case that will be a private crema-tion. Family only. And until then we will carry on.' Her face was fixed in a rigour of pain. He could feel sorry for Poppy Atkinson, he thought, as he crossed the road. Not that she wanted his pity. She had made that very clear.

He walked slowly along Kildare Street, scanning the

discreet brass name plates beside the Georgian doors. And found the one he was looking for. He pressed the buzzer on the intercom and noticed a tiny camera pointing at his face.

'Hello?' a woman's voice answered. 'Can I help you?'

'I'm looking for Dominic de Paor. I was wondering if I could see him.' He smiled up at the camera.

'Do you have an appointment?' The tone was efficient and bored.

'No, but my name is Michael McLoughlin. I'm a friend of Mrs Sally Spencer. I'm sure Mr de Paor will see me.' He smiled again, encouragingly.

He waited. Time passed. Then the voice again: 'I'm sorry. Mr de Paor isn't available.' There was a loud click.

'Hey.' McLoughlin jammed his finger on the buzzer. 'Hey, can I make an appointment to see him?'

But there was no reply. He crossed the road again. Dominic de Paor's office was opposite the National Museum. McLoughlin lounged against the tall black railings by the entrance. The footpath was crowded, as always in summer, with busloads of tourists. He moved back and out of their way as his phone rang. It was Paul Brady.

'Hey, Paul, how's it going?' His voice was resigned.

'Michael, are you set for the off on the tide tomorrow evening?' Brady sounded excited.

'What? You're kidding? I thought it was going to be weeks.' McLoughlin felt suddenly disappointed.

'Don't ask me to explain the vagaries of some people's lives.' Brady laughed. 'I got a call yesterday from the owner. They've changed their holiday plans. The wife's ankle's on the mend. Now they're going to drive through France and Switzerland, ending up in Venice. And they want us to bring the boat to the marina and meet them there. We've ten days to do it, so we have to leave as soon as possible. I'm in the middle of provisioning. I just wanted to know if you've any what they call special dietary requirements.'

McLoughlin didn't reply immediately. His eye had been caught by movement at the second-floor windows in the building across the road. Dominic de Paor was standing there, looking out at him. 'Paul, listen, I've a problem.' He began to walk slowly away from the crowded gate. De Paor moved to keep him in sight. 'I've a job on at the moment. I'm really sorry, but I didn't think this trip was ever going to happen.'

'Shit, Michael.' Brady's voice held a pleading note. 'You're giving me real trouble here. I don't know how I'm going to replace you at such short notice. I thought you were retired. I thought you were your own man.'

'Yeah, well, I am. But I'm doing some work for a friend and it's important that I see it through.' He kept his eyes fixed on the window. De Paor was out of sight now. 'Look, I'm really sorry, Paul. You couldn't hang on for another few days, could you?' He walked back towards the crowd as the door to de Paor's office opened and he saw him standing on the step, anger on his narrow face.

'Can't do it, Michael, doesn't give us enough time.' Brady sounded annoyed. 'I thought I made it clear this would be a last-minute number.'

McLoughlin pushed himself in among the tourists. They closed around him. 'Yeah, well, I was ready to go weeks ago, and I'm sorry, but I can't do anything about it now. Good luck with the trip.' He pushed himself up on tiptoe and peered over the heads. De Paor had stepped out on to the pavement and was searching the scene before him. McLoughlin shrank down into the group.

'Your loss, then. We're going to have a great time. I'll send you a postcard from St Mark's Square, OK?'

Someone stood on McLoughlin's foot and he stifled a cry, '*Bon voyage*, Paul. Have fun.' The light on the screen dimmed. Shit. Another lost opportunity. So much for suiting himself.

He pushed his way out of the crowd, squinting back. De Paor was still on the pavement, looking up and down. Then he pulled his phone from his pocket. He began to make a call. As he finished McLoughlin felt a vibration and heard a subdued ringtone. It was Marina's phone. The name was on the screen. 'Dominic,' it said. He could see that de Paor had spotted he had it. He felt suddenly exposed, threatened. De Paor made a move in his direction as a tour bus rolled up to the stop. There was bedlam now as the tourists crushed towards it. McLoughlin saw his chance. He ducked out into the street behind the bus and headed across, not looking back in case he drew De Paor's gaze. He could see the glass porch of Buswell's Hotel. He took the front steps two at a time and pushed through the swing doors into the lobby. It was quiet, cool and dark in comparison with outside. He stuck his head into the bar. It was virtually empty, just a couple of sober-suited men with pints in their hands and their heads together over the *Independent*'s racing pages. 'A pint, please,' he said to the barman.

'A pint?' The accent was Polish. 'A pint of what, sir?'

'Guinness.' Time was when a pint meant one thing and one thing only.

'Sure thing, comin' right up.' The accent segued into mid-Atlantic.

He carried his drink to a small table in the corner and sat down. He took a long swallow. It was delicious. He leaned back into his chair. This used to be one of his favourite places for lunch. A toasted ham sandwich and a pint. Sometimes two, depending on the company. Those were the days, he thought, as he hefted the glass. Lunchtime drinking was positively compulsory. Not like now, all sparkling mineral water and cups of coffee.

He shifted uncomfortably in his seat. Another reason for cutting back on the pints, he thought, as he stood up and headed out into the lobby again, towards the stairs that led down to the toilets in the basement. It was cool and dark after the brightness of the sunshine outside. He stood at the urinal, then ran his hands under the cold tap. A filthy roller towel lay on the floor. He pulled his handkerchief from his pocket and wiped his hands as he pushed open the door. Two men were standing on the stairs in front of him. The tallest of the two put out his hand and gave McLoughlin a push so he lost his balance and fell back.

'Hey,' McLoughlin said, 'what's your problem?'

The other man came towards him. McLoughlin could smell cigarette smoke and sweat. He put his left hand on McLoughlin's shoulder and gripped it tightly. Then he went through his pockets with his right hand

'Hey, what the fuck do you think you're doing?' McLoughlin tried to free himself, but the man's grip was strong. He felt him pull out his wallet, his phone and then Marina's. He handed it over to the other guy. McLoughlin heard the phone beeping, then his voice. 'Yeah, we got it. OK. No problem.' He saw Marina's phone disappear into his pocket. He dropped McLoughlin's, with his wallet, on to the floor. Then he grasped McLoughlin's throat and squeezed.

'OK, got it? Let the fucker go now,' the man behind said quietly.

'Let him go? Will I let him go?' The guy smiled, and McLoughlin stamped hard on his foot. He shouted, his face reddening, then lifted his arm. McLoughlin saw a tattoo below his wrist. A snake coiled, its jaws open, ready to strike. A fist smashed into his face – a searing pain in his nose and cheekbone, the taste of blood on his tongue and a second, harder blow, which made black spots appear before his eyes. The sound of his blood loud in his ears, then a sudden sickening dizziness and nothing.

TWENTY-THREE

The snake coiled around the wrist. The jaws wide open. The fangs extended. The pain in his head, the blood pouring from his nose, its metallic taste on his tongue. He sat on a hard plastic seat in the A and E department of St Vincent's hospital. It was bedlam. There had been a traffic pile-up on the M50 and the ambulances were still arriving, bringing the walking wounded. He hadn't wanted to come to hospital, but the barman who'd found him, who'd dragged him up to sitting, had already made the phone call before he could protest. And when he'd called Johnny Harris, hoping that he would come and get him, he'd said he should stay, get his face and head X-rayed. Make sure there was no more damage than a broken nose, a couple of black eyes and a large dose of wounded pride.

But it was the snake that was bothering him. He'd seen it before. Poking out from underneath a white shirt, an arm raised in triumph, a fist clenched in defiance. Posing for photographs outside the Special Criminal Court. A hot day in summer, some time last year. The man had been charged with conspiracy to murder, to import drugs for sale. Charged on the testimony of a supergrass. Found guilty, and sentenced to thirty years in prison. Until he'd got out on appeal. The defence barrister had made mincemeat of the evidence. And the defence barrister had been Dominic de Paor.

McLoughlin shifted from buttock to buttock. The seat was getting harder as afternoon turned into evening. His eyes were so swollen now that he could hardly see. He knew he looked a sight from the way in which everyone who walked past recoiled. He hadn't told the barman or the paramedics what had really happened. He'd said he had tripped on the top step and tumbled all the way to the bottom. The last thing he wanted was some rookie asking him tedious questions. But now he had questions of his own that needed answering, so he had to get out of there and quick.

He stood up. His head ached and he felt sick. He swayed, then steadied himself and headed for the exit. He checked his wallet and pulled his phone from his pocket. There were two calls he had to make. He punched in Tony Heffernan's number and waited. Fucking voicemail.

'Tony, listen. Gerry Leonard, remember him? I've just had a close encounter. It wasn't fun. Can you do some digging? I want his background, his history, his seed, breed and generation. Can you do that for me? Thanks, Tony.'

He stepped through the door and into the sunshine. He leaned against the wall and punched in another number.

'Hi, Johnny . . . Yeah . . . No. Look, I can't stay here any longer. It's complete chaos. I don't know when they'll get around to seeing me. I'm sure there's nothing broken. I just need someone to clean me up. Can I come to your place? You can check me out. Please, Johnny, a favour for a friend. OK?'

He listened for a few moments, then walked slowly and carefully, holding his ribs with one hand, towards the main road, already searching the traffic for a taxi.

*

The traffic was heavy as Margaret waited at the lights outside Connolly station. She had taken the train from Monkstown into the city centre. It was crowded, packed with tourists. Guidebooks open, maps spread across knees. The tide was out and the dull brown of Sandymount Strand seemed to stretch to the horizon. Just the distant band of dark blue to mark the retreat of the sea.

Connolly station was crowded too. She elbowed her way down the escalator to street level. She hadn't remembered Dublin like this. An endless stream of vehicles. She had remembered a quieter city, easier to manage. A casual indifference to traffic-lights. Always possible to dodge from one pavement to the other, the cars slowing to make allowance. But this was different. There was a dangerous edge to this traffic. She was conscious of her flesh and bones, her skin beneath her calf-length cotton skirt.

The lights changed and the pedestrian signal gave out its high-pitched bleat. She hurried over the crossing and turned towards the North Circular Road. She began to walk quickly, holding her bag tucked under her arm. So many changes in the city. Small local shops with signs in Cyrillic script. Veiled women with dark children clustered together outside a greengrocer's where huge bunches of coriander, smooth, glossy aubergines and pointed spears of okra were piled high. She waited at Drumcondra Road for more lights to change. It wasn't far now to Mountjoy gaol. Already she was in the prison's slipstream, carried along with the others whose lives were bound up with those who lived behind its high grey walls. She could see them everywhere. Slouching along the pavement, their eyes dulled, their voices loud and complaining. Their children slouching beside them. She slowed down and stopped. The prison was on her right at the top of a small slip-road. A grey Portakabin was parked by the metal barrier. A uniformed prison officer lounged in the doorway. He greeted the passers-by with a mixture of familiarity and casual contempt. They didn't seem to notice. They streamed up the narrow road towards the prison's high wooden gate. Margaret followed them. As she passed the Portakabin she noticed that the officer was looking at her. He smiled and stepped out of the door.

'Can I help you?' His tone was friendly.

'Um.' She stopped. 'The women's prison, can you tell me where it is?'

He moved closer. She could smell his aftershave. It was rich and cloying. He lifted one arm and pointed to the red-brick building on the other side of the road. 'The gate's up at the top. If you ring the bell someone will open up for you.'

She nodded, making a stiff grimace. 'Up there, you say?' She pointed towards the tall building with slit-like windows.

'That's it.' He stepped back into the doorway. 'Have fun.'

She crossed to the other path, which ran beside the women's prison. There were windows at ground level, but their thick Perspex panes were frosted. Ahead she could see the entrance, a crowd of girls in a noisy cluster. She stopped to watch. The gate was made of heavy metal. Every few minutes it slid back slowly, with a rumbling, grating sound. The girls pressed forward, pushing and shoving. The gate slid to, swallowing them up. She moved closer. From here she could see through. Behind the gate there was a scruffy entrance hall, the paintwork scuffed and dirty. A hatch led into an office. And beyond, a frosted-glass door heavily reinforced with metal bars. She could see nothing more. As she stood and watched, the gate rumbled back again and a uniformed officer, this time a woman, came out. 'Can I help you?' she asked, her voice cool and business-like. Margaret didn't reply. She began to walk quickly down the slope towards the main road. She wanted to run. To feel the hardness of the pavement through the soles of her sandals, the sun on her face, to fill her lungs with air. To hear the noise of the traffic and see the people in the streets. She wanted to know that she was free. That she could go anywhere she wanted. Catch a bus, take a train, hail a taxi to the airport. Get on a plane. Disappear. Back to the life she had created for herself. Anything but the sudden reality of the future that faced her. That she had tried to imagine as she lay awake, night after night, in the house at Eumundi. Trying to decide how to redeem herself. How to make amends for what she had done.

McLoughlin sat with Johnny Harris on the balcony of Harris's brand-new riverside apartment. They watched the city around them. The lights along the river winked back from the water's iridescent surface. People were sitting at tables along the Liffey boardwalk. Harris opened a bottle of Prosecco and they sipped its biscuity bubbles. He had washed McLoughlin's wounds with warm water and disinfectant, put some butterfly plasters over the cuts on his eyebrows and upper lids. He'd peered up his nose and manipulated it with both hands, then declared himself satisfied that nothing was broken.

'Your skin tones will leave a lot to be desired for the next week or so, and your face will be sore for a while but it seems to me that you got off lightly. If the guy who hit you is the guy you think, then the surprise is that they're not scraping your brains off the walls and floor as we speak.'

McLoughlin sipped gingerly. The alcohol stung the cuts in and around his mouth. It was hard to speak so he nodded and tried to smile. They sat in friendly silence drinking and nibbling olives until the warm air chilled. Then they moved inside, into the huge open-plan sitting room/dining room/ kitchen area, which constituted the whole of the top floor of Harris's duplex. Even McLoughlin, with his scepticism about modern apartments, had to admit he was impressed.

'You've been busy. I thought you'd only just moved in. You've done all this in what? Three weeks? I didn't realize you had such good taste,' he muttered, through pursed lips. He gestured towards the hardwood floors, the stainless-steel gas fire, the sofas and chairs covered with glowing oranges and yellows.

Harris closed the huge American-style fridge. The door made a satisfyingly solid sound and McLoughlin was reminded that his friend was something of an expert on fridges. They were, after all, part and parcel of his working day.

He put another bottle on the low glass table and sat down.

'Show apartment. I bought it fully furnished, decorated, the lot.' He uncorked the bottle and sniffed appreciatively. 'Thank God it doesn't smell like formaldehyde. A day at the office can be a smelly old day.' He poured it, and motioned to McLoughlin to help himself. 'In fact, now I come to think of it, your suicide lady was the designer here. She did a great job.'

McLoughlin picked up his glass and stood. He walked around the huge room, inspecting the paintings on the walls, the vases on the sideboard, the pot plants on the balcony. Then he moved to the stairs.

'Be my guest, Michael.' Harris smiled up at him. 'You'd better stay the night anyway, so pick your room. There's three down there. Mine's the messy one. And there's two bathrooms, so feel free.'

Downstairs was as attractive as upstairs. The bedrooms were spacious. Two of them opened out on to balconies. The bathrooms were luxurious. One had an exquisite modern free-standing bath and basin. Taps as beautiful as pieces of modern sculpture gleamed. His bathroom at home, with its pale green fittings and pitted lino, seemed very third world. He walked into the larger of the spare bedrooms and sat down on the bed. Suddenly he was exhausted. He lay back against the pillows and closed his eyes. And for a few moments he slept. Then woke, heart pounding, sweat dripping from his forehead, stinging as it seeped into the cuts around his eyes. He opened them, closed them, then opened them again. He stared up at the ceiling. And noticed it had been badly painted. They'd skimped on the coats, he thought. Bloody typical. There was a dark shape under the white. A swirl of some other colour. Red or black, maybe. He stared up at it, trying to figure out what it could be, and twisted the wall light to get a better view. Just as Harris walked in.

'So this is where you've got to. I was getting worried. Thought maybe concussion had hit, after all.' He moved to the window and closed the curtains. 'How's the bed?'

'Very comfortable, thanks.' McLoughlin shifted slightly. 'Here, come and lie down and look at this.'

'What? An invitation? I thought you'd never ask.' Harris smirked and made as if to leap up beside him.

'Get off, Johnny,' McLoughlin said. 'Now, look up at the ceiling. Can you see something there?'

'Oh, that.' Harris leaned back, 'They didn't do a good job, did they, covering it up?'

'Covering what up?'

'There was some kind of break-in around the time I was signing up for the apartment. Vandalism. Despite the new building and the trendification that's going on, this area's still a bit rough. They reckoned it was probably local kids from the old flats down the road who did it.'

'Did what exactly?' McLoughlin propped himself up on his elbows.

'Wrote all over the walls. In here and upstairs in the sitting room too. The agent said they'd fix it immediately and they did it pretty quick. But whoever it was, used red paint so I suppose it was pretty hard to cover it up.'

'And you don't know what they wrote?'

'No, I didn't see it. I got a very apologetic phone call. They even knocked off a few hundred because of what they called the inconvenience.' Harris sat up. 'I didn't care. They said they'd increase the security on the site, and they've done that so it's grand. Now, what I came to tell you was that Tony Heffernan phoned. He has some news for you about the guy who hit you. He's coming around in half an hour so on your feet. Pronto.' He swung his legs off the bed. 'You're a bit of a dark horse, Michael. I never knew you were such a popular guy. Your phone's been beeping nonstop. Don't worry,' he wagged his finger in front of McLoughlin's face, 'I haven't read them. I wouldn't want to intrude. Now, you'd better get up. Tony will be here soon.'

*

Tony Heffernan arrived with a plastic bag filled with files. He tipped them out on the glass table. 'Don't ask me how I got this stuff,' he said, face red and sweaty. 'Give me a drink, Johnny, quick.' Favours from years back had been called in, he explained. And it all had to be returned before the night was over. 'Otherwise I'll be in deep shit. Anyway, have a look. You were right about the snake man. And you'll probably identify the guy with him too.'

McLoughlin leafed through the pages. Gerry Leonard, born 19 July 1968. Brought up in Fatima Mansions in Rialto. Youngest of six children. His convictions went way back – petty theft, joy-riding, minor assault – to the late 1980s. Then his name started appearing with some of the really well-known criminals. Guys who were importing heroin by the containerload. Flooding the streets and the working-class estates with the drug. Leonard was arrested and questioned on a number of occasions, but the guards could never hold him. There was never enough evidence. So the police found themselves an informant. They set up a witness-protection programme and a man called Martin Kennedy was their first lure. The haul was impressive. They got Gerry Leonard and all his mates. McLoughlin looked at the photos. 'Yeah, that's him. And that's the other fucker, Peter Feeney. He was the backup.' He stabbed the picture with his finger.

Peter Feeney, Gerry Leonard and Shane Ward had stood trial for drug importation. The DPP had thrown in a few more charges just to be on the safe side. But the problem was that Martin Kennedy was an idiot. McLoughlin remembered the way they had winced as they listened to him stumbling through his evidence. The guy was so drugged with tranquillizers he could hardly stand, barely remember his own name. He was so frightened that the banging of a door drained the colour from his face and made his legs shake. Still, his evidence was convincing. Leonard and Ward were convicted, sentenced to thirty years in prison. Feeney, who was obviously a minor player, got off. But a year ago Leonard had appealed. His barrister, Dominic de Paor, cut through the prosecution case like a knife through butter. And Leonard had been released.

'What's he been up to since he got out?' McLoughlin asked Heffernan. 'Anything interesting?'

'Actually, nothing, so far as anyone knows. He went to Spain for a few months. But he's been keeping his nose clean. Although you can be sure that he's still controlling his piece of the drug action in the inner city.'

McLoughlin sifted through the pile of paper in front of him. Leonard's career was a microcosm of the way that Dublin's crime and criminals had changed over the last twenty years. He checked back to see what was his first offence.

'Hey.' McLoughlin's voice rose with excitement. '"Interviewed on the twenty-ninth of June 1988 Bray Garda station. Suspect was questioned in connection with the taking without permission of a motorboat on Lough Dubh. Suspect was with three other men, Shane Ward, Peter Feeney and Lawrence O'Toole. All were questioned but no charges were put forward."' He took a sip from his glass. 'How extraordinary. You know what that means, don't you?'

Harris and Heffernan looked blankly at him.

'It means that Gerry Leonard was one of the boys who were indirectly responsible for the death of James de Paor. They stole the boat from its mooring. It was because of them that James and Marina went out in that dinghy. And as a result James drowned.' He dropped the file on top of the rest and leaned back. 'And nearly twenty years later James's son gets him out of prison.'

'Do you think he knew?' Heffernan wiped his hands on a clean white handkerchief.

'Maybe, maybe not. Like father, like son. It was the kind of case that James used to specialize in. Controversial, very high profile, very well paid.' McLoughlin gestured to Harris for a refill.

'Yes.' He lifted the bottle. 'How much per day? Couple of grand?'

'And then some. At least.' McLoughlin nodded his thanks. 'At least.'

For a while they contemplated.

'Incredible, isn't it?' Heffernan sat back and stretched his legs. 'Free legal aid. Set up to help the deserving poor. And made millionaires of all those clever boys. Doesn't seem fair.' He sighed, then sat up. 'Oh, Michael, I knew I wanted to tell you something. You asked me about Helena de Paor, what Janet knew about her.'

'Yeah.' McLoughlin watched the bubbles in his glass rise to the top.

'She's some cookie. She and James had a baby girl who died. It was assumed it was a cot death but, according to Janet, the doctors suspected it might not have been death by natural causes. James wasn't convinced. He couldn't believe it of her. Anyway, the end result was that she was committed. She was having delusions, hallucinations. Hearing voices, that sort of thing. James was very protective. And even though they were separated he carried on looking after her.' Heffernan spread his arms wide. 'But Helena de Paor, it has to be said, was as clever as she was mad.' He crossed his legs.

'Yeah,' McLoughlin interrupted, 'I know about the court case. But tell me, is she still sick?'

Heffernan shrugged. 'Well, as far as everyone knows she's out of hospital. But that's because her son is looking after her.'

'Dominic?'

'Yeah, the one and only. Janet reckons there's a bit of a Mr-Rochester-and-the-mad-wife-in-the-attic going on there. Apparently he has her put away on the estate in Wicklow. He's devoted to her. Without him, by all accounts, she'd still be in Grangegorman and there'd be no way she'd ever leave.'

McLoughlin lay in bed and stared up at the ceiling. And he thought about the email that Tom Spencer had sent. He had placed the motorboat at the far end of the lake. He had said nothing about its occupants. He had given the positions of everyone else. McLoughlin pictured his little sketch map. Sally and Vanessa on the beach. Dominic de Paor and his friends in the woods. Marina and James in the dinghy. And Gerry Leonard, Shane Ward, Peter Feeney and Lawrence O'Toole in the motorboat. He rolled over on to his side. Then on to his back again. He sat up and switched on the bedside lamp. He angled it towards the ceiling. He could see the shapes beneath the white paint. Loops and swirls of letters, maybe. He got up and went to the window. He opened it and gazed down into the apartment block's central courtyard. The grounds were landscaped, paved with limestone flags with a large round pond in the middle. A fountain tinkled sweetly. He could hear the clang of the high metal gates as they swung back to admit residents. It was very secure here, he thought. Guards on duty twenty-four hours a day. No chance of any incursions from the outside world.

He moved away from the window and began to dress. Then he stepped quietly into the corridor, walked past Harris's bedroom and up the stairs into the sitting room. He took the keys from the hook by the door and let himself out. The lift was swift and silent. He stepped into the lobby. The floor was tiled with marble and the walls were painted a dull ochre. The only light came from behind the long desk where a security guard was seated. As McLoughlin approached he said, 'Can I help you, sir?'

His accent was thick. Russian, McLoughlin thought. He took out his ID card. 'I'm looking for some information about an incident that took place here a few months ago. Someone went into the show apartment and painted all over the walls. I'm wondering if you know anything about it.' The guard looked bored. He didn't reply.

'I'm investigating a death by suicide that happened a couple of months ago. You may have known the dead woman. Marina Spencer? She was the designer here. We have reason to believe that her death was not quite as it seemed.' He rested his elbows on the desk.

'Sure, Marina, I know her well. She very nice lady. Very sad when she die.' The guard pointed at McLoughlin's bruises. 'You have a bit of trouble?'

'I walked into a plate-glass door. Didn't realize it wasn't open. You know how it is,' McLoughlin told him. 'As I was saying, I'm interested to know exactly what was painted on the walls in the apartment.'

The guard reached down and pulled open a drawer. He fumbled around, then spread a number of computer print-outs on the desk. 'These. You want these?'

McLoughlin picked them up. The words 'I saw you' were scrawled in huge red letters across the walls and ceiling.

'Who did it? Did you ever find out?' He tapped the pictures with a finger.

The guard shrugged. 'The developer, he not want any trouble, any fuss. He not call the police or anything like that.'

'But,' McLoughlin glanced up at the ceiling, at the camera that was trained on him, 'you have CCTV. I'm sure you have it on all the entrances and exits, don't you? Did you not check it?'

'Sure,' the guard said. 'Sure we did. We not see the painting being done. We see some men who come into building. Here, if you interested.' He stood up and took out a large bunch of keys. He opened a cupboard concealed behind him in a decorated wall panel. Inside, McLoughlin saw a row of monitors and a bank of DVD machines. The guard rummaged in another drawer.

'My boss he mad. He say we need to stop this kind of thing. He check the disks. He see the man he think is doing painting. He tell the developer. The developer say he not interested. You want come in? I show you.'

McLoughlin squeezed around the back of the desk and into the narrow space. The guard slipped a disk from its cover and slotted it into one of the machines. He picked up a remote control and pressed a button.

McLoughlin saw the picture come up on the monitor.

The guard fast forwarded, then stopped and pressed play. Gerry Leonard and Peter Feeney walked in through the front door. They headed purposefully for the lift. 'No one stopped them?'

'They say they work for agency who sell apartments. They say they have things to do in show apartment. They go on up.' The guard pressed eject. He took another disk from the pile and began to play it. 'Look, here, camera on penthouse landing. See?'

McLoughlin saw, all right. He saw Leonard roll up his sleeves. He saw the snake tattoo. He saw the can of paint and the brush. He saw the door to the show apartment open, then close behind them.

'That's great, thanks.' He put his hand into his pocket and found his wallet. He pulled out a fifty-euro note. 'Thanks,' he said again, as he pressed the money into the guard's top pocket. He took the disks from him. 'I'll look after these. Don't worry about that.'

The guard smiled. His teeth were shiny, metallic. 'No problem. I like Marina. She very nice lady. I very sad when she die. You think this painting thing have to do with her?'

'I think maybe. *Spasiba bolshoi.*' McLoughlin held out his hand.

'Thank you very much too. You're welcome. *Perzhalsta.*' The guard shook it vigorously. '*Spackoyny noitch.*'

'And goodnight to you.'

McLoughlin got into the lift and pressed the button for the penthouse. He leaned against the cool marble wall and closed his eyes as it moved quickly upwards. 'I saw you' painted on the walls. 'I saw you' whispered into her phone. 'I saw you' written on the back of the photographs. The lift hissed to a stop and the doors slid open. He stepped out on to the landing and felt in his pocket for the keys. He opened the door and walked into the sitting room. He sat down at Harris's computer and touched the keyboard. He slipped the DVD from the camera in the lobby into the slot and clicked it open. He found Gerry Leonard. He watched him talk to the guard on the desk, then wait for the lift. He clicked forward. And a woman came into the lobby. She was slim, dark. She was wearing a summer dress. She waved to the guard as she passed his desk, then spoke to him. She reached into a big wicker basket. She pulled out a watermelon. She threw it towards him and he caught it. She was laughing. He was laughing. McLoughlin took out the DVD and inserted the one from the camera on the upper landing. He found Leonard as he went into the apartment. Then he found Marina. She stepped from the lift. She pushed open the door. She went in. He watched, he waited. Five minutes later she came out. Her phone was to her ear. She looked stricken, frightened. She pressed the button for the lift. She put away her phone. Then she turned from the lift and pushed open the door to the stairs. She disappeared.

He moved back through the DVD. He wanted to see her again. Bring her to life on the computer screen. The lift doors opened. Workmen stepped out. Painters, decorators, men in suits with brochures and briefcases. The lift doors opened. Marina stepped out. But this time she was not alone. The camera showed a tall man with dark hair. His shoulders were broad, his features distinctive. He turned towards the camera. He put his hand on her shoulder. She smiled at him. That wide, welcoming, smile. Dominic de Paor opened the door to the apartment. He stood back and she walked through. He followed her. The door closed behind them.

McLoughlin stared at the computer screen. He replayed the scene. He watched them come out of the lift. He watched them on the landing. He checked the date. It was two days before the paint incident. He switched the DVDs. He saw her come into the lobby. She waved to the guard as she passed the desk. She was alone. She stopped to look at a large plant in a huge terracotta pot. De Paor came through the automatic doors. He didn't look at her. She joined him at the lift. They didn't speak. They didn't look at each other. They got into the lift. The doors closed. He switched the DVDs again. The lift doors opened. Marina stepped out. De Paor put his hand on her shoulder. She smiled at him. She opened the door. He stood back and she walked through. He followed her. The door closed behind them.

'What were you doing, Marina?' he whispered.

And he heard her voice: 'Help me, please, help me.'

And he remembered what Poppy had said. About Mark Porter and Dominic de Paor. How Porter would show up with flowers and presents. And when de Paor was finished with a woman, Porter got the leftovers.

His phone rang. He pulled it from his jacket. He looked down at the screen. It was the local Garda station.

'Inspector McLoughlin,' the voice was young, female, 'this is Stepaside station. Just wanted to let you know that your house alarm has been activated. We rang your land line, according to procedure, but there was no answer. Where are you?'

'I'm in the city centre. I'll go home immediately.' He pressed eject and the DVD slid out of the computer.

'We have the number of your local key-holder. Will I call him?' The voice sounded calm.

'No, it's fine. I'll be home in half an hour.' He put both DVDs into his pocket. 'It's probably a false alarm. Thanks.'

He'd have to wake Johnny. Borrow his car. His own was still in the city centre where he'd left it that afternoon.

'Fine, but in the meantime a car from Stepaside is on its way. I'll let you know if there's a problem. Is that all right?'

'Yeah, that's great. I'll be there as soon as I can. Thanks.'

He looked around the room. It was as before. Bright, cheerful, welcoming. He hurried down the stairs and into Harris's bedroom. He was lying face down, spreadeagled across the bed.

'Johnny.' He shook his shoulder. 'Johnny, wake up. There's a problem. I need a hand.'

TWENTY-FOUR

The bus let the girl off at the turn for Sally Gap. The driver watched her as she crossed the road and began to walk away up the hill. It was the third time this week she had travelled with him. A pretty little thing, he thought, with her shiny brown hair tied back under a red scarf, her long patterned skirt and sandals. She reminded him of girls he had known when he was young, way back in the sixties. Hippy girls who smelt like this young one, of that Indian perfume – patchouli, it was called – wearing clogs or sandals, with a leather thong tied around the ankle. He had warned her to be careful up that mountain road. 'You never know,' he said, as he slowed to a stop. 'Don't take any lifts up there.'

But she just smiled and shook her head, so her silvery earrings tinkled, then lifted her hand and waved to him as she crossed to the other side of the road. He waited until she had disappeared around the first bend, then drove slowly away towards Roundwood. He wouldn't let any of his daughters go up there by themselves, he thought.

Vanessa heard the bus move off. She didn't look back. Silly man, she thought, with all his warnings of the dire consequences of walking up the road to Sally Gap. He didn't know how lucky she was. He didn't know that she wasn't going off on some stupid quest for adventure. He didn't know that she was going home, back to the Lake House, that she was part of the family who owned it, and in three days' time, when she became eighteen, part of it would be hers. For ever.

She fumbled in her bag for her iPod and slipped on the earphones. Helena had played her some opera. A singer called Maria Callas. She had told her all about 'La Callas', as she called her. How she came from a poor family in Athens. How she had had a voice that moved men to tears. How she had been in love with a man called Onassis, a small, ugly man, but a man of power and influence who filled her with passion and desire. But he had left her, abandoned her for Jackie Kennedy, a pale and bloodless woman, Helena said, whom he married for show and respectability. Callas's voice filled her head as she walked quickly along the narrow road. Helena had shown her the old records she had collected. A huge pile of them. The covers were beautiful. And so was Callas. Helena had held her photograph up to her face and kissed it. 'Look,' she said. 'Don't you think there is a resemblance between us?'

And Vanessa had agreed that there was. The jet black hair that framed the white face with the high cheekbones, the strong nose, and the eyes rimmed with dark liner.

She stopped to catch her breath, then jumped into the shade as a convoy of army trucks lumbered past. There were always soldiers up here. She had never seen so many before. They waved and smiled from the back of the truck and she waved and smiled too, then stepped out into the sunshine so she could see the view ahead. The road, like a narrow dark ribbon, curling up the side of the mountain on one side, and on the other, the deep valley and the lake just visible like an antique mirror, the kind she had seen in the Lake House, the silvered glass uneven and patchy so it reflected imperfectly. She was too far away to see the house. It was hidden deep at the end of the valley, but she could see the tops of the trees that surrounded it. And she could picture it in her mind's eye. The front door standing open to welcome her. And Helena in the kitchen making scones, the dog asleep in the corner by the Aga. The dog that now did not fill her so full of dread, that did not bark, but stood up and wagged his long tail, smiled, opening his pink and black lips, then ambled over, sniffing her skirt and resting his head on her thigh, his large yellow eyes liquid and glossy like clover honey. As she stood still as a statue, heart thumping in her chest, then reached down to pat him.

She began to walk again, impatient to get there, not to waste a second of the time she would have with Helena. She was so interesting. She knew so much. About art and books, about music and antiques, about history and archaeology. It was amazing to be with her. She had a way of making all her knowledge come to life. She could describe how the landscape around the lake had been created and make it far more vivid and real than any of the CGI effects in TV programmes about dinosaurs. She was awesome. In the dictionary sense of the word.

Now Vanessa could see the gate ahead. She stopped and reached into her bag for a bottle of water. She unscrewed the top and took a long drink, then walked down the slight incline towards the keypad on the gatepost. She tapped in the code, the gate swung open and she walked through. She crossed the pressure panel on the other side and waited for it to swing shut. She still couldn't get over it. Helena had told her the code.

That day, not long ago, the first day they had met, Vanessa had been walking down the pier, daydreaming, trying not to think about her mother and Marina and the grief that hung around the house like a giant black shawl. And she had seen the tall dark woman with the huge dog. The dog, padding along by her side, so calm, so quiet, so completely at ease. And the woman had shown her that the dog wouldn't hurt her. Had made her feel secure, powerful, even. They had walked together down the pier. And when the time had come to go their separate ways, the woman had told her she knew her name, she knew who she was. And she wanted to be her friend.

'I don't know what you've heard about me.' The woman had taken her hand. 'All kinds of terrible things, I'm sure. But life's too short to carry a grudge. Soon we will be neighbours. Won't we? Soon you will inherit Dove Cottage. So, please, come and see me. It's not far. There's a bus you can get most of the way.' She had squeezed her hand tightly. 'You've never been to the Lake House, have you, since you were a baby? Well, it's time to remedy that. You are James's daughter. I can see that just by looking at you. You remind me so much of my son Dominic when he was your age. And if my daughter had lived, I'm sure she would have been like you too. So, please, make an old woman happy. Come and see me.'

'Your daughter? I didn't know you had a daughter?' Vanessa said. 'What happened to her?'

The woman didn't reply.

'Sorry.' Vanessa winced. 'I shouldn't have asked. My mother's always telling me to think before I speak. Sorry, it's none of my business.'

'No, it is your business,' the woman told her. 'After all,

my daughter was your half-sister, wasn't she?' She paused. 'It was what they call a cot death. She was six months old. She was healthy, strong, beautiful. I went in to her one morning and I thought she was still asleep. Then I noticed she was very pale. I touched her cheek and it was cold. I picked her up and her body was white and stiff. Like a hard plastic doll. The doctor said she had died not long after I put her to bed.'

The dog leaned close to the woman's leg. It whined.

'So you're Helena – is that right?' Vanessa tried to sound calm.

Helena smiled. 'Yes. And you're Vanessa. Such a pretty name. Your father's godmother was called Vanessa. Did you know that?'

Vanessa shook her head.

Helena patted the dog's head. He looked up at her, his forehead wrinkled. 'Yes. James loved her very much. I remember him saying to me that he was closer to her than he was to his own mother. You know how that can be, I'm sure. Sometimes one's mother isn't the easiest person in the world to talk to,'

Vanessa nodded. 'That's true. They say it's because you're so alike. Although I don't think I'm like my mother. I don't look like her.'

'No,' Helena said slowly. 'No. You obviously take after the de Paor side of the family. So,' she smiled, 'you will come and see me, won't you? Sometimes I get lonely by myself, even though Dominic comes every week, sometimes more often, and he phones me all the time. He's such a wonderful son. I'm so lucky to have him. Although,' she frowned, 'you may not want to come after what happened to your other half-sister. How sad and how strange that she should die in the lake too. How awful for your mother. How is she?' Her eyes were sympathetic and concerned.

And Vanessa couldn't help but reply: 'She's very sad. She misses Marina very much and can't believe that she took her own life. She says it wasn't like her.'

'And what do you think?' Helena reached down and dug her fingers into the thick ruff around the dog's neck.

Vanessa felt awkward at the question. 'I don't know. She didn't seem like the kind of person who would do it.'

'That must have been hard for you. Were you close?' Helena's voice was soft and kind.

'I don't know, really. She was a lot older than me. She took me out shopping and things and she had lunch with us most Sundays, but I often felt she did it more for my mother than for me.'

They stood then in silence. Vanessa knew she should go. But somehow she didn't want to leave the woman. And Helena began to tell her about the Lake House and the grounds, the lake and the deer, the woods and the mountains, and Dove Cottage. 'It's such a lovely little house. Perfect for a couple. Years ago, when your grandfather was still alive and living in the big house, your father used to take me to stay there. It was like a doll's house. Everything was very small. The rooms were little, with low ceilings. But it was lovely. It's neglected now, so it will be good that you can give it some attention, won't it?' And Helena had pulled a pen from her bag. Taken Vanessa's arm, turned it over and written a number on her fine white skin. 'You need a code to get into the grounds. You know how to get there, don't you?' And Vanessa had listened as Helena explained. 'Now, that will get you in through the gate. You can come any time. I'll always be happy to see you.' And she walked away, the dog by her side. Up the steps and across the footbridge over the railway.

Now Vanessa began to walk down the hill. She could see the lake ahead and to her left. Its surface gleamed like burnished metal. It looked solid, hard, as if it could bear weight. And then a breeze stirred the trees and a wave like a feather dipped in ink dribbled its pattern across the water. She turned off the main drive, down a narrow path that led towards the water. And there was the cottage, with its own little garden front and back, surrounded by a high hedge with a pretty wrought-iron gate. Vanessa felt in her pocket for the key Helena had given her the first time she came to the Lake House. She opened the pink front door and stepped inside. It was cool and dark. She walked through the rooms, the sitting room, dining room, old-fashioned scullery and kitchen. Then up the narrow stairs and into the two bedrooms and bathroom. She was so excited. She couldn't believe how lucky she was. She peered out of the windows to the woods and the lake, then moved to the windows at the back. The garden had a small greenhouse and shed. She had pulled open the door. Inside was a lawnmower and all kinds of old garden tools. Shears and clippers and bottles of weed-killer with 'POISON' written on them in faded black capitals. She would watch all the gardening programmes on TV. She was going to make it beautiful. Grow vegetables and fruit, and invite her mother to stay and cook her lovely meals. And maybe Sally and Helena would be friends, and out of all that sadness and anger something good would come.

Now she heard the sound of horse's hoofs outside and ran back to the front windows. Helena was riding up the drive. Her horse was huge and as black as her hair. He made

Vanessa nervous, even though Helena had said he was a pet, really, and very quiet. Helena had said she could ride him if she wanted, but Vanessa had said she didn't know how. And Helena had shown her photographs of James when he was young, seated on a horse like this, jumping over huge fences, winning prizes.

'Did your mother not tell you all the things he could do?' Helena's voice held a hint of disapproval. 'He had so many talents. When I first met him, when we were teenagers, we used to go riding together all the time. We used to come out here and stay for weeks in the summer and take the horses and go all over the mountains. And I used to pretend we were pioneers, discovering this wonderful world that was just for us.'

Now she watched as Helena stopped at the gate and leaned down to open it, then walked the horse through, the dog behind. And she called, 'Vanessa, are you there? So glad you could make it today. We're going to have such a good time. Come out and see what I have planned for you.'

Vanessa waved to her, then hurried down the stairs, out through the low front door and into the sunshine.

TWENTY-FIVE

The house was a mess. The patio doors had been forced open and the locks broken. Someone had rampaged through the kitchen, smashing glasses and plates and pulling food from the cupboards. McLoughlin stepped over the remains of the glass decanter that had been his retirement present. He hadn't had the chance to use it and now he never would. There was worse to come in the sitting room. Everything had been ruined. The TV had been lifted from its table and smashed on the floor. The sofa cushions had been ripped with a knife and every painting and print had been pulled from its hook on the wall and stamped on. Glass crunched underfoot as he picked his way across the room towards the table where he had left Marina's laptop. It was no longer there. Neither were the cardboard boxes that had contained her files, her books, her bills and letters. And his own computer was wrecked.

He walked down the corridor into his bedroom. It was a similar scene here. The drawers in the bedside locker were pulled out. Someone had been through his letters. They had ripped the pages from their envelopes and scattered them everywhere. And they must have found the photographs of Marina because they were no longer there. And neither was the piece of paper he had taken from Marina's computer with the words 'I SAW YOU' in capital letters. He knelt down and sorted through everything, gathering it together in an effort at a neat pile.

He felt nauseous. He thought of all the burglary scenes he had attended through the years. He had taken notes, offered words of advice about future security, even made the odd cup of tea. But he had never really understood. He had walked away from houses with smashed front doors, broken windows — even, he remembered, one case where a burglar had removed some roof slates to gain entry. Walked away, closed his notebook, got into the car, and thought nothing more about it. But now bile filled his mouth and he got up quickly, half ran into the bathroom and knelt over the toilet to vomit.

The young uniformed guard who stood behind him in the doorway filled a glass with water and handed it to him.

'Thanks.' McLoughlin sat on the side of the bath and sipped it.

'They made a hell of a mess, didn't they?' she said. 'Do you have any idea who might have done it?'

McLoughlin wasn't going to tell her about Gerry Leonard and his friend so he said nothing.

'Apart from all the damage, is there much missing, do you think?' She moved out into the corridor and he followed, checking the spare bedrooms as he passed them.

'Actually, there isn't. The only thing I can't place is a laptop that belonged to the daughter of a friend of mine. An Apple iBook G4. Quite new, I'd say, but not worth much.' He couldn't believe he had been so stupid as to leave those photographs lying around. But at least he had the disk with the scene at the party. He patted his jacket pocket and felt the hardness of its plastic case.

'We'll ask the neighbours, but I don't think we'll get

very far with this.' She smiled apologetically. 'You know the way it is with burglaries.'

'Yeah.' He opened the fridge and took out a bottle of Erdinger. 'You don't happen to see the bottle-opener, do you?'

She bent down and fumbled under the table. 'Here you go.' She handed it to him.

He prised off the cap, picked an unbroken mug from the counter top and poured the frothy liquid.

'You look like you could do with some sleep – and what happened to your face?' Her expression was concerned.

'I fell down some stairs. Think I need new glasses. Anyway,' he raised the cup to her, 'you get off. I suppose the fingerprint guy will be here in the morning.' Her expression was now sceptical. 'Oh, I see, cut-backs, is that it?'

'I'll do what I can, but given the level of loss, well, it won't be top of the list.' She stepped out of the broken patio door. 'Nice to meet you at last. You've quite a reputation. I've heard a lot about you from your old friends.' She held out her hand. 'You should get some rest if you can.' She looked down at her watch. 'It's late, after two. Sleep would be good for you.' He felt tears prick and turned away, embarrassed. Couldn't figure it out. Why was he crying? He wiped his eyes surreptitiously with the back of his hand.

It was mid-morning when he woke. He had cleared up the worst of the damage, and phoned for an emergency lock-smith. He had sat up and waited for him, drinking beer until the guy arrived, fixed the patio door and changed the locks, 'just to be on the safe side', on the front door and the windows. It seemed too much of a coincidence that the break-in had happened on the same day that he had been beaten up by Gerry Leonard. And when he thought about what had been taken, the boxes of Marina's books and papers, her laptop, it seemed even more obvious who was the culprit.

He was ready for bed now, but he couldn't bring himself to sleep in his own. Instead he got into the narrow single in the boxroom, and pulled the blankets up around his head. It was, inevitably, his phone that woke him. He peered sleepily at the screen. He had three new text messages. He sat up and began wearily to scroll through them. They were all from Gwen Simpson. The first and second had been sent last night, the latest a few minutes ago. She wanted to meet him. There was something she needed to tell him. He got out of bed and walked slowly into the kitchen. He hunted in the fridge and found a carton of orange juice. He slid back the glass doors and stepped out on to the terrace. He lifted the juice to his mouth and took a long swallow, then picked up his phone. 'Hi, Gwen, Michael McLoughlin here. What can I do for you?'

They met in the large ugly pub across the road from Mount Jerome cemetery. Gwen, in black, was sitting by herself at a table in the corner. The pub was crowded and very hot. Most of the customers were dressed similarly in black. The noise level was high. The tables were crowded with drinks and plates of food. McLoughlin recognized a few other faces. Anthony and Isobel Watson were sitting, looking awkward and out of place, on a bench seat, and standing at the bar, he saw Dominic de Paor with his wife and Sophie Fitzgerald.

McLoughlin pushed his way through the crowd. It was customary for mourners to come to this pub, but he wouldn't have thought it matched the social standing of those at Mark Porter's cremation. They must need a drink badly, he thought, as he saw Gwen.

'I didn't realize Mark's funeral was today,' he said, as he sat down beside her.

'Your face, what happened?' she asked.

'Oh, nothing much. Wasn't watching where I was going.' McLoughlin signalled to a passing waitress. 'How was the service?'

Gwen grimaced.

'Same again for the lady,' he told the girl – Gwen's glass was half-empty. 'And a pint of Guinness, please.'

McLoughlin waited for her to speak. He was conscious that he was being watched. De Paor couldn't keep his eyes from straying towards him. And there were others, too. Poppy Atkinson and her husband were at a table near by. She was not completely sober.

Eventually Gwen said, 'I haven't smoked for years but I'd give anything for a cigarette now.' She gave a brief laugh. 'I wanted to see you because, as I said, I need to tell you something. But this isn't the place to do it. I was going to wait until later but I couldn't bear it any longer. I'm sorry I didn't tell you when you first came to see me. I was preoccupied with issues of confidentiality. But now—' She finished her wine with a gulp.

'Now?'

'Those considerations don't seem to matter. What matters is that this dreadful business is brought to an end.' She stood up. 'Come with me. My car is parked down the road. We'll go there.' She picked up her bag, and before

McLoughlin could finish his drink she was heading for the door. He stood up quickly and followed. He could feel the eyes watching him. He glanced around the bar. There was no sign of Gerry Leonard.

Gwen had walked on ahead and was unlocking her car door. She sat into it and reached across to open the passenger door for McLoughlin. He settled himself beside her. 'Now,' he turned to her, 'what's this all about?'

It was a hot Saturday at the end of July. Marina wasn't happy. She hated being at the Lake House. She hated being cooped up with him and his son. She hated him so much she couldn't even bring herself to call him by his name. But she had to be nice because her mother got so upset if she made a fuss. And she loved her mother. And she was terrified of losing her. Terrified of being like one of those girls at school whose mothers didn't care about them, who hardly ever wrote to them. Who, even in the holidays, contrived to spend as little time as they could with them. And, besides, there was one compensation. He was so keen to make her like him that he was always giving her presents. And the most recent and the best was the dinghy. It was an Enterprise, bigger and faster than anything else she had ever sailed. Painted blue with sails to match. And a 10cc Seagull outboard engine. She had named the boat *Bluebird* even though Dominic sneered and said it was a cliché. But she didn't care. She was happy when she was out in *Bluebird*, far away from the rest of them.

A hot afternoon. There was to be a party that night. Mummy was nervous about it. Lots of people were coming. Lots of his friends. Mummy was having a rest before she had to go and get ready. She and the baby, Vanessa, were asleep on the beach. Marina couldn't help but like the baby. She hadn't wanted to, but Vanessa had such a big smile and she was so funny, crawling everywhere and waving and clapping her hands. And Marina liked her soft round body. Liked to cuddle her and hold her close. Dominic didn't like her. But he didn't like anyone except his snotty friends. There were four of them staying. Ben Roxby, who'd brought his ugly, noisy boat. Poor Mark Porter, who everyone teased because of his height. And the two girls: Gilly Kearon, who did nothing but giggle and pout, and Sophie Fitzgerald, who was tall and elegant and very clever. They went off by themselves most of the time. Dominic had places in the woods that were secret. He wouldn't show them to Marina or Tom. Tom didn't care. All he wanted was to follow the deer, climb the mountains, make fires and pretend he was an Indian. Marina wished she was like Tom. He was always happy, always carefree. She couldn't understand him.

Everything peaceful and quiet. The sky blue, no clouds, no wind. Then, suddenly, the roar of an engine. Someone was in the motorboat. It had been moored at the far end of the lake, tied up in the little stone harbour. But it was speeding fast across the lake, far too fast. It looked as if it would flip over, it was so fast. So out of control. Marina watched it. She couldn't work out who was at the wheel. It didn't look like anyone she knew.

She stood and watched as the boat seemed to charge at the shore, then, at the last moment, wheel away like a horse refusing a fence. The wake from its charge washed up and over her feet and made her little boat shake. And then she heard him shouting and turned. He was running down from the house. Calling, 'Marina, in the boat now. Get in and we'll go out and see what on earth is going on.' And before she could stop him he had pushed out the dinghy and jumped in.

And she said to him, 'You've no life-jacket. You need a life-jacket.'

But he ignored her and bent over the outboard, jerking the cord so it spluttered into life, a little puff of blue smoke colouring the air around it. 'Push us off, Marina, then get in,' he shouted.

She struggled to pull herself over the gunwales, her shorts getting wet, her life-jacket bulky, making her clumsy, as he jerked the handle of the engine, spinning the dinghy in a tight circle. 'Be careful!' she shouted, her voice angry. 'Be careful what you're doing.'

But he was in charge now, and he was aiming the dinghy out towards the middle of the lake where the motorboat was idling, the boys on board sitting on the bow, feet trailing over the side. He stood in the stern, shouting at them, while Marina tried to keep the dinghy balanced, dismayed at his recklessness, his lack of sense. Remembering how her father had drilled into her, even when she was young, four, five, six: Never stand up in a boat. Always wear a life-jacket. Remember the danger. Be careful.

And as they got closer to the motorboat, its engine began to roar again, and again it leaped into life, its bow rising up, a wave with a white crest foaming in front of it as it ploughed through the water. And it seemed to Marina, as she crouched low in *Bluebird*, that they were doomed to be overwhelmed by it. But at the last minute it turned away so it was the wash that rushed towards them, that caused them to rock from side to side, the propeller of the outboard to lift from the water so it screeched and ripped at the air. But then the boat was back again, and this time Marina thought it really would smash into them – it was so fast, so direct. And she turned and screamed to James to see what was happening and he swung the tiller so they almost capsized and the engine stalled, coughed, spluttered, then died.

'Shit.' His voice sounded wild with rage and he bent over the stern, while the dinghy rocked and water sloshed in the bilges. And as he bent over, fiddling with the fuel line, the boys turned the motorboat towards them again, and again it came so close that Marina put her hands over her eyes, heard the sound of the engine, then the sudden lurch from side to side as the bow wave hit them again. And heard James shouting, 'Marina, help me!' and saw him topple over, try to hold on to the stern, then fall, head first, into the water. Screaming, sudden fear in his voice, 'Help me, Marina, help me!' as she sat frozen, and looked at him, thinking, *You stupid man, I told you to put on your life-jacket. You wouldn't listen to me. You thought you knew best.* And remembered. When he had gone into the water from the beach, holding the baby against his chest, her mother had called, 'Be careful, James, remember you can't swim.' And he had laughed and lolled around in the warm shallow water, holding up the baby so she giggled with pleasure and waved her chubby little arms.

But now there was panic on his face as he sank beneath the surface. Then kicked himself up gasping for breath, calling to her, 'For God's sake, Marina, help me! Throw me something – a rope, an oar, anything!' as he sank again, and this time it was longer before he came to the surface and his movements were weaker and his voice was feeble. And Marina looked at him. She sat and looked at him, just looked at him. And did nothing.

A hot afternoon. A hot Saturday afternoon. The lake, the blue sky, the woods, the mountains, the motorboat with its engine idling and the man drowning in front of her eyes.

And, suddenly, it was as if she woke from a dream. She jumped into the cold, dark water, her life-jacket keeping her head up so she could breathe, and she called out to him. She screamed his name over and over again. Then she tried to dive to find him, and she caught hold of his arm and began to pull him to the boat. But he was heavy, so very heavy. And she pulled and pulled, dragging the painter from the bow and tying it around his waist, then hauling herself back into the boat. Unable to pull him in with her. And she began to cry out, 'Help me, please, someone help me! Help me!'

And saw the boys in the motorboat, turn it away, take it back into the shore. Scramble from it and run up the hill towards the road. Leaving her behind. Leaving her with the body of the man she hated.

'Leaving her with the body of the man she hated,' Gwen repeated.

'I saw you.' McLoughlin's voice was quiet.

'You know about that, do you?' Gwen drummed her fingers on the steering-wheel.

'And you do too.'

'She told me when she got the first text message. She thought it was just a child or a joke or something. She didn't get anything else for quite a while, a couple of months, really. Then she had phone messages. All different voices but all saying the same thing. Then silence again. And then someone sent her photographs that were taken of her at home.

And the last straw was what happened with the apartments. Did you hear about that too?'

'Yes, I did.' It was very warm in the car. McLoughlin tapped the window. 'Can I open this?'

Gwen turned the key and pressed the button. The window slid down. And McLoughlin saw, in the wing mirror, Dominic de Paor staring at them as they talked. 'So who did she think it was?'

De Paor took his phone from his pocket.

'Well, she knew it had to be someone who was there that day. But she couldn't figure out who. She thought first of all that there might have been someone in the woods, with binoculars maybe. And one morning she phoned me early, very early, before I was up. She was hysterical. She said it must have been one of the boys in the motorboat, that was who it was. They were closer to her than she had thought. But then she changed her mind. Said it couldn't have been them, because how would they have known who she was? She was all over the place about it.' Gwen rubbed her eyes with the heels of her palms. 'She was so upset. And, of course, her big fear was that whoever it had been would tell her mother.'

'Tell her mother what exactly? That she saw James drown?'

De Paor had turned away now. He was pacing to and fro.

'Tell her mother that she let him drown. Not that she saw him drown, that she let him drown.'

'And did she?'

'She said she did. She said she hated him. She wanted him dead. She saw the opportunity. She acted upon it.'

'But she was fifteen.'

De Paor had ended his phone call. But he was still staring at the car.

'Old enough, strong enough, a good enough swimmer. She certainly could have tried to do something. She was wearing a life-jacket. He wasn't. The outcome might have been the same. He might still have drowned. But at least she would have done the right thing. And she knew she hadn't. And that knowledge consumed her. Even before she began to get the messages and the rest, she had never been able to forgive herself for what she had done,' Gwen said. 'Or, rather, what she had not done.'

She began to chant: 'We have left undone those things that we ought to have done; and we have done those things which we ought not to have done; and there is no health in us.'

They sat in silence for a moment. Then McLoughlin said, 'She hated him that much? Why? What was going on between them? He wasn't – you know?'

She shook her head. 'No. I did wonder when she spoke of him with such vehemence. But I think it was something much more obvious. She was jealous of James. She, her mother and her brother were a tight-knit family unit.' She tucked a wisp of hair behind her ear. 'But when Sally got together with James he blew it apart. And Marina was truly bereft.'

She leaned across McLoughlin and opened the glove compartment. He was conscious of her pressing against his thigh.

'This is something else you should know about.' She sat up again. She was holding a cassette tape in her hand. She fed it into the slot on the dashboard. 'She got this just before she died. She brought it into the office.'

She pressed play. There was a moment's silence. Then a voice began to sing. McLoughlin recognized the song. He had heard it on an old album of American folk singers, one that Janey had loved and played over and over again.

> '*I'm gonna tell,*
> *I'm gonna tell,*
> *I'm gonna holler and I'm gonna yell,*
> *I'll get you in trouble for everything you do,*
> *I'm gonna tell on you.*'

The chorus repeated again. McLoughlin reached out and ejected it from the machine. 'Is there anything else on it?' He turned the tape over in his hand.

'Just the one song. You know it?' She seemed surprised.

'Yeah, I know it all right.' He whistled a couple of notes. 'Funny little thing, isn't it? I always thought it sounded sinister, sort of creepy.'

'Marina was terrified when she got it. I wanted her to go to the police about all of it. Especially the photographs. But she wouldn't. She said that when the job on the apartments was finished she would leave Dublin. She still had friends in New York. She said she would go there. Her mother could come and see her in America. She thought she could leave it all behind.'

McLoughlin glanced in the wing mirror again. De Paor had gone.

'You know, there's a couple of things about Marina that I don't understand,' he said. He put the tape into his pocket. 'I don't understand her friendship with Porter, or why she went to the party. It doesn't make sense.'

'She didn't tell me she was going. She told me Mark had asked her. I advised against it. Not something I would usually do. Nothing good could come of it, I said.'

McLoughlin took his keys from his pocket.

'And the second thing?' Gwen asked. 'The other thing you don't understand?'

'I spoke to her mother and I emailed her brother.' McLoughlin scratched his chin. 'They both told me that she and Dominic de Paor did not get on. The word "hate" was used. Sally said that Dominic was jealous of Marina and Tom, and felt threatened by them. Tom said he thought there was a bit of a game going on between Dominic and Marina. That to begin with she was well able for him. That it was only after James died that he intimidated her. And yet I have reason to believe that she was having a relationship with him – recently that is. Did you know about that?'

'Dominic?' Gwen's voice rose. 'No, I didn't. Although, to be honest, it doesn't surprise me. There was always a self-destructive element in Marina's personality. The abuse of drugs and alcohol, the way she depersonalized her sexual relationships. She knew Dominic was bad news. She talked about him. She admired him in some ways. She told me he was very good-looking, very clever, successful. Everything I suspect she thought she wasn't.' She sighed. 'But if she was involved with him, in any way, it was the one thing she never told me. She always spoke of him in the past tense. Why do you think there was something going on between them?'

McLoughlin described the images from the CCTV.

'So, they were in the apartment block at the same time. Maybe Dominic was involved with the developer. Maybe it was that?'

'I'm no expert on body language, but you wouldn't need to be one to figure out what was happening. They went into that apartment for one thing, and one thing only. And it wasn't to look at a colour card or to pick a few cushion covers.' He smiled at her. 'Anyway, I'd better go. My house was burgled last night. It's still a terrible mess.'

'Was much taken?'

'No, but there was a lot of damage, and I'm afraid it won't clear itself up.'

She put her hand on his arm, then kissed his cheek. 'In that case I owe you even more for coming to meet me. It's not like me, you know. I'm not usually in confession mode. But I had to tell you about Marina. I feel so bad about her. If I'd been able to make her feel that her step-father's death wasn't her fault then maybe none of this would have happened.'

'And you're really sure she didn't contribute to it?'

'Yes, I am. Absolutely sure.' Her voice was calm.

He patted his pocket and opened the car door. 'I'll hold on to the tape, if you don't mind, for the time being.' He got out of the car. 'Look, I'll give you a ring tonight. And if you need anything, well, you have my number.'

He watched her drive away, then went to find his own car. The traffic was heavy and progress was slow. He was tired. It was hot. His eyes closed as he sat and waited for the traffic-lights to change. He forced them open. Pressed the button and the window slid down. Tried to fan some air into his face. It was stuffy, dusty. Like the air in a prison cell. And as he sat in his car, the engine idling, he could imagine Portlaoise high-security prison. Its population a potent mix of paramilitaries, drug-dealers, murderers and what the newspapers called crime bosses. A man called Gerry Leonard sits in a small, windowless, inner room and waits. His barrister is due to visit. He is going to discuss his appeal against his sentence. He's been lucky to get this particular guy. His reputation is first class. He's the best.

He's never met him before. But he knows what he looks like.

The door opens. He doesn't stand. He doesn't speak. Dominic de Paor takes a seat. He opens his briefcase and pulls out his files. He goes through the case. He explains his defence. Leonard nods and smiles. It sounds good.

'OK, Mr Leonard, is there anything else you want to say? Any questions?' De Paor gets ready to leave.

Leonard looks at him and smiles again. 'It was terrible what happened to your da. Terrible to die like that.'

De Paor doesn't answer. He puts on his coat.

'It was that girl's fault. She just sat there, the fucking bitch. Sat there and watched him drown.'

De Paor looks at him. 'What did you say?'

Leonard waves towards the chair. 'You didn't see it, did you, Mr de Paor? Well, why don't you sit down?' He twists himself sideways and crosses his legs. 'I've a story to tell you. If you're sitting comfortably I'll begin. Once upon a time there was a gang of lads and they went off one day out into Wicklow. It was a grand hot day. And they fancied a bit of a swim or, even better, a spin in a big, fast boat.'

The lights had turned to green. The car behind was hooting its horn. The sound was all around him. 'OK, keep your fucking hair on.' McLoughlin jerked forward. The car behind was on his tail. He looked in the mirror. 'Arsehole,' he shouted.

The driver smiled. He put his hand out the window. He held up his index finger. His shirt was rolled up. The snake coiled around his wrist, the jaws wide open. And the fangs extended.

Twenty-Six

The water was cold, but not unbearable. Vanessa lay on her back and floated. It had been such a lovely day. Helena had brought a picnic and they had walked down the hill towards the little clearing by the edge of the lake. The horse had followed and so had the dog. Helena had lit a fire, in the circle of stones, and she had boiled water for tea, then heated a frying-pan when the stones were hot and fried eggs. She had cut thick slices of bread and buttered them, and Vanessa had eaten her egg, the yolk dripping on to her skirt. She had thought it the most delicious meal she had ever had.

'When's your birthday?' Helena had asked. And Vanessa had told her it was the day after tomorrow.

'What are you doing to celebrate? It's a big day, your eighteenth.' Helena stirred the embers with a stick and a flame shot out, glowing orange with a hint of green.

'I don't know. Mum isn't very happy at the moment. And all my friends are away. That's one of the problems with having a birthday at the beginning of August.' Vanessa held out her mug for more tea. 'I'd have been going too if my sister hadn't died. I was going to Italy for the summer, to stay with a family.'

'Lovely.' Helena broke up some twigs and fed them to the embers. 'But maybe not as lovely as here. And, anyway, if you were so far away you wouldn't be able to take possession of your new house, would you?' A twig snapped loudly in her hands. The dog looked up. 'Are you going to the solicitor in the morning to sign the papers?'

'I don't know. We haven't talked about it. Anyway, I don't need to do anything like that. I can just come out here. You gave me the key already.'

Helena didn't reply. She got up and walked over to the horse who was grazing the rich grass that grew in the crevices between the rocks. She fumbled in one of the saddle-bags and pulled out a small video-camera. 'Here,' she held it up, 'I love making little movies. I like recording the truly important things that happen. When Dominic was little I had a cine-camera. I have all the old films. I must show them to you. Then I was sick for a long time and I couldn't do anything like that. But when I got better and I came to live here Dominic got me this and it's so easy and so much fun. Now,' she held up the camera, 'let's find out what kind of person young Vanessa is. What do you have in your big bag? Show me the contents.'

Vanessa rummaged through it. 'Well, I've got my phone and my purse and an apple and a make-up bag. And my iPod. And a couple of books.'

'What are the books? Show me.' Helena changed the focus of the camera and zoomed in.

'There's this by Sylvia Plath, the poet. It's her novel, *The Bell Jar*. Well, of course it's hardly a novel, really, more of an autobiography.' She held it up towards the camera. 'It belonged to my sister. She loved Sylvia Plath's poetry.'

'And you do too?'

'I never really bothered with it before. We did her in the Leaving Cert. But when Marina died I started to read her. It's very sad stuff. Sad when you think what happened.'

Helena put down the camera. 'Well, that's enough for now. Such a lovely day. I fancy a swim. Do you?'

'I don't have my togs.' Vanessa closed her bag.

'That doesn't matter. There's no one around for miles and miles. No one but me. And I won't mind.' She began to unbutton her shirt. 'Go on, it's fine.'

Vanessa lay in the water. She floated on her back. She moved her arms and propelled herself slowly from the shore. She stared up at the sky. She kicked her feet up and down and the frothy wash floated past. The dog's big head broke the surface. He moved quickly, his coat gleaming and shiny. And behind them both Helena stood, her large body white in the sunshine. Her breasts hung down, pendulous, heavy. She took a step deeper into the lake and her thighs quivered. She crouched down and let the water coat her body. Then she straightened and lifted her arms high. Drops of water streamed down her white skin. She waded further into the water.

The girl floated on her back just out of reach. Her skin was sallow, pallid on her breasts and at her groin. Her hair streamed out behind her like the long tangles of lake weed. More lake weed curled over her pubic bone. Her nipples were tight and dark against the pallor of her small breasts. Helena wanted to take hold of her helpless white body. Wanted to suck the life out of her. Spit out the remains. In the same place that she had left the other interloper. The woman she had watched through the lens of her camera. On the ground with Mark Porter. Dominic had told her that she was the one who had let James drown. She had sat in the boat and watched him. She had done nothing.

'You must make her suffer,' Helena said to him, said to her son. 'Imagine how your father felt as the water pulled him down. Imagine how time slowed for him. Every second like a year. I know that feeling,' she said, 'when time slows down. You feel as if you're drowning in slime and mud. So you have to make her pay for that. You have to make her suffer too.'

Helena felt the cold creep up her legs, over her knees, her thighs. The dog swam around the girl. He was a strong swimmer. He had swum with Helena that morning. That morning when they had come down here and they had found the dinghy, floating gently, bumping up against the walls of the little harbour. And inside it the woman was lying on her face, a pool of vomit on the slatted floor. And the dog scrambled up into the boat and began to sniff the vomit, then the woman's face. She opened her eyes and stared into his. And said, 'I'm thirsty, so thirsty. Help me.'

Then fell back. Back into a deep, deep sleep. The dog jumped from the boat, and it rocked and rocked and water splashed into it. And Helena leaned on the boat and pushed it down and watched how the woman fell on to her side, her head banging against the rowlocks. Her eyes opened a little. They looked as a baby's eyes look when it falls deeply asleep. Helena pulled herself up on the gunwales and the water poured in and the woman half fell into the lake. And Helena grabbed hold of her dress, pulled her out of the boat, gave her a push. And the woman floated, buoyed up by air filling her skirt, towards the little rapids. Then she went under as the weight of her clothes dragged her down. Down, down, down. And she struggled, coughing, choking. But not for long. Less than a minute. And a trail of big bubbles floated on the surface showing where she had gone.

TWENTY-SEVEN

4 August 2005. The day after tomorrow would be the tenth anniversary of Mary's disappearance. Ten years since Margaret had seen her daughter alive. Now she stood outside the front door of Jimmy Fitzsimons's family home, high on the hillside above Killiney Bay. She rang the doorbell and waited. There was no reply. She rang again, then walked around to the back of the house and peered in through the kitchen window. The girl, his younger sister, was at the sink. She had a tea-towel in one hand and a plate in the other. She gesticulated, waved at her, then disappeared and reappeared a few minutes later, with a woman in tow.

Mrs Fitzsimons recognized her immediately. She opened the back door a crack. 'What do you want?' Her voice was defensive.

'I want to talk to you, that's all. I just want to talk to you.' Margaret put her hand on the doorknob. 'Can I come in?' She moved closer. The girl, no longer a girl, a woman now with a round body and a face that showed her age, even though the Down's syndrome almost made her seem like a child, pulled her mother back.

'Come in, then.' Mrs Fitzsimons disappeared into the house.

They sat at either side of the fireplace. The grate was stuffed with rubbish. Newspapers, milk cartons, egg boxes.

The girl crouched on a footstool beside her mother. No one spoke.

'It's been a long time,' Margaret said.

'What do you want?' Mrs Fitzsimons's voice was plaintive now.

The girl touched Margaret's face. 'I'm Molly,' she said.

'And I'm Margaret.' Margaret took Molly's hand and shook it. 'How do you do, Molly?

Molly giggled. 'I'm very well.' Her voice assumed a tone of politeness. 'And how are you? Are you a good girl?'

Margaret smiled. 'I certainly hope so.'

They sat in silence. Then Margaret spoke again. 'I wanted to see you, Mrs Fitzsimons, to say how sorry I am for all that has happened over the last ten years. We have both suffered, you and I. We have both lost people we loved—'

'Don't,' Mrs Fitzsimons cut across her. 'Don't say that. I didn't love Jimmy. I'm not sorry he's dead. He killed your daughter. I know he did. And when he disappeared I was glad. I thought maybe he'd gone to America or Australia. I didn't care where it was. I just didn't want to have to look at him, be reminded of what he was and what he had done.' She put her face in her hands. Her shoulders shook. There was no sound. She took away her hands and her face was set with bitterness. 'And when they found him and he was dead I was relieved. He was gone from this world to the next where God will be his judge. And He will judge him harshly.'

'Judge him harshly,' Molly repeated. 'Judge him harshly.'

They sat in silence again. Until Mrs Fitzsimons stirred and turned to her daughter. 'The book,' she said. 'Get the book.'

Molly left the room.

'I want you to have this,' Mrs Fitzsimons said quietly. 'I found it in Molly's room.'

Molly stood before her. She held out a battered paperback.

'You have it. Mammy says you have it.' She put it on Margaret's knee. Margaret opened it. The title page said *Songs of Innocence and Experience*. The author was William Blake. And scribbled in black biro, in Mary's hand, 'This book belongs to Mary Mitchell, Torbay, Auckland, New Zealand, Southern Hemisphere, World, Universe.'

She walked from Killiney down the hill towards Dun Laoghaire. She walked fast, sweat dripping between her breasts and shoulder-blades. She wanted to get home. To lie in the garden, to close her eyes, to sleep. To try to banish the pictures that came again. Mary's body in the morgue. Jimmy Fitzsimons's face as she wrapped the tape around it.

She walked through the town, then down to the path by the railway line. The beach at Seapoint was crowded today. She took off her sandals, stepped on to the sand and ran towards the sea. She stood ankle deep in the lukewarm water. Small, benevolent waves rolled in from Dublin Bay and broke with ruffles of white along the beach. A little girl with tight curls stood beside her and kicked at the water.

'Why it wet?' she enquired, and glanced up at Margaret.

'Because it is,' Margaret replied. 'Because it's water and water's wet.'

'Why is it coming on the beach?' she persisted, and put out her hand to steady herself, her plump feet planting themselves firmly in the sand.

'Because the wind pushes it towards the land and when it meets the beach it waves its little hands, see?' Margaret bent down to the child's height. 'See the way the water is waving at you? And that's why it's called a wave because when it sees a nice little girl like you with curly hair, it waves at you.' She twined a curl around a finger. 'You've got lovely curls. Where do they come from?'

The child looked up at her with a stern expression. Her blue eyes were uncompromising. She's heard that one before, Margaret thought.

'I growed dem myself,' she replied, and shook off Margaret's hand, then turned away and stomped back across the wet sand, breaking into a trot as she approached a small woman, dark hair streaked with grey, who had begun to walk towards her. Margaret watched the greeting, the way the woman scooped her into her arms, nuzzling the child's neck and holding her tightly against her body. The child pulled away from the embrace and turned back towards the breaking waves, the shallow water, the bay, the sea beyond, and the horizon.

And Margaret felt again the pain of her loss. Of her continuing loss. Of her loss that would last for ever. She began to walk away. She sat down on a rock. It was encrusted with baby mussels, sharp ridges of black. She ran her fingertips over them. And thought of the pipis that grew on the rocks near the house in New Zealand where she and Mary had lived through the years of Mary's childhood. She would never go back there. It would stay for ever locked into her memory. A perfect place to bring up a child. The long garden that sloped to the top of the cliff. The wooden gate and the steps cut into the rock. The huge Pohutakawas that hung out over the sea. The deep pool in the bend of the creek that flowed below the cliff into the sea. And the branch that hung out over it, the thick rope from which Mary and her friends would swing, backwards and forwards, then let go and drop like stones into the water. She had stood on the far bank, watched them and wanted to stop her daughter. Couldn't quite believe that the small girl with the skinny arms and legs could survive the swing and the drop, that seconds later her head would push up from the frothy water and she would wave her arms and shout, 'Mum! Did you see me, Mum? Did you see me do it?'

All those tiny triumphs. All those accomplishments. All those achievements. Photographs of school sports days, reports decorated with As and Bs, splodgy paintings and lumpy pieces of pottery, lovingly kept. So much love, so much attention lavished. For what? she thought, as she eased herself off the rock to go home. For a cruel death and a lifetime of longing. A cloud crossed the sun and it was suddenly dark. She shivered, and moved towards the steps up to the concrete walkway. And saw a familiar figure hurrying towards her.

'Margaret! Margaret, I've been looking for you.' Sally's face was white.

'What's wrong? What is it?'

'It's Vanessa. She didn't come home last night. It's not like her. And she always phones me. Here,' Sally held out her mobile, 'I've been ringing her and ringing her but her phone's switched off. Listen.'

'I'm sure she's all right.' Margaret put her arm around Sally's shoulders. She took a deep breath. 'Don't worry, you know what kids are like at her age.'

'But it's her birthday tomorrow. We always spend the day before planning it. Always.'

'It's her eighteenth, Sally.' Margaret's tone was calm. 'It's a big one. She probably wants to spend it with her friends. Don't worry. Look, it's early yet, it's only just after three. She'll be home by dinnertime I'm sure.' And felt the chill creep through her body.

'No, it's more than that – I don't know what to do.' Sally's voice was breaking.

Margaret tried to calm herself. 'We'll go home. We'll have a glass of wine. We'll sit in the garden. And if she hasn't come back in two hours we'll make a decision. Together.'

'To do what? What will we decide?' Sally's voice was trembling.

'We'll call the police. We'll report Vanessa missing. They'll know what to do.' And Margaret was back, that hot summer evening nearly ten years ago. Standing in the hall in the house in Brighton Vale. Trying to be polite. *Listen to me, listen to me. My daughter's been gone for more than twenty-four hours. I wouldn't be on the phone to you if I didn't have a reason. There's something wrong, I know there is.* And the sound of bored resignation in the policeman's tone. *How old did you say she was?* And now she shouts, all politeness, all restraint gone, *For the third time, she's twenty.* And he sighs and says, *At her age she can, if she wants, leave home. She isn't a minor. I'm sorry but people disappear all the time.* And she wants to grab him and shake him. *Listen to me, listen to me, take her description. Do something. Find her.*

'Don't worry, Sally.' She spoke slowly, carefully. 'We'll phone Michael McLoughlin.'

'Will you speak to him? Will you explain? I can't think straight. I don't know.' Tears spilled from her eyes. Margaret pulled her head down on to her shoulder. She guided her through the crowd. It will be all right, Margaret said to herself. It will be all right. But she put her hand into her bag and her fingers felt the cover of the book. She stroked it. And it was as if the years had dropped away. Dropped away and left a dark pit in front of her eyes.

TWENTY-EIGHT

Mail2Web.com. McLoughlin tapped the domain name into the Google subject line. He pressed return. He waited. The dialogue box asked him for his username and password. The username was easy. He wasn't so sure about the password. He had so many, these days, and he could never remember which one belonged to which bank account, website, whatever. He typed in the letters MPJM, his initials, Michael Patrick John McLoughlin, and pressed return. The screen filled with his emails. A relief. It was bad enough that his own computer was banjaxed. Bad enough that he had nagged Johnny Harris to let him use his home PC. But if he'd had to fiddle around with passwords, well, that would have been the last straw.

He began to scroll though his messages. They were all here, the emails Tony Heffernan had sent him when he had first asked him to look into Marina's death. He had emailed him the statements that Dominic de Paor, Mark Porter, Gilly, Sophie and the others at the party had given. Helena's was also there, with the forensics reports, Johnny Harris's post-mortem report. And the photographs taken of the scene. He clicked on them to open them, drinking his coffee as they unfolded down the screen. He still wasn't convinced that there was much mystery about how Marina died. So she had contributed somehow or other to the death of her step-father. So someone was threatening her. So she had been humiliated at the party, drunk far too much, snorted too many lines of coke and drowned. It still looked like suicide or an accident. Not much more than that.

One thing surprised him, though. The boat was riding low in the lake. It was barely floating. It was more than half full of water — it reached almost to the middle seat. He hadn't thought much of it before. He printed the picture and put it on the desk. Then he hunted through the other emails for a description of the boat's condition. The forensics people had taken it out of the water for a detailed examination.

The boat is an Enterprise sailing dinghy, probably twenty-five years old. It is constructed of marine ply, with a trim of varnished teak. Although it is old it has been well maintained and is seaworthy. Rubber bungs are fitted securely in the stern. Its rigging has been removed and it appears to have been used as a rowing-boat. The oars were still in the rowlocks, but they had been shipped. The name *Bluebird* is still visible, although considerably faded, on its stern.

Bluebird, the dinghy James de Paor had given Marina that summer. She had sailed it. She and James had gone out in it to challenge the boys in the motorboat. She had left it at the Lake House after James's death. But someone had taken care of it. Someone had painted it, varnished it, made sure that the wood did not rot, that it did not develop any leaks. So if it was, he checked the statement, 'well maintained and seaworthy', why had it taken so much water on board? How had the water got there? He ticked off the possible reasons. Number one; rain? He'd have to check the weather reports but he was certain there had been no rain for the couple of weeks before midsummer. Choppy water, wind? Again, as far as he could remember, high pressure had dominated. Virtually no wind, and the lake as smooth as glass. He tried to imagine it. Marina, drunk, stoned, sitting in the boat, rowing herself out into the middle of the lake. Shipping the oars in the way she had been taught, the kind of thing that would have been automatic to her. Sliding her legs over the gunwales, then slipping or falling into the water. The boat would have lurched as her weight shifted. But he didn't think it would have dipped below the surface. There might have been splashes, maybe. But not much. What if she'd changed her mind? Turned back, grabbed the sides, tried to haul herself into the boat. It would have been hard. He tried to visualize it. But he still couldn't see, even if she had succeeded in getting back into the boat, how so much water would have poured into it.

He got up and paced the room again. He tried to remember. Had he seen the dinghy that day when he was at the lake? He didn't think so. But he had noticed a small boathouse at the far end of the beach, near the field where the deer were grazing. He drained his coffee, rinsed and dried the mug and put it away. Then he picked up his keys, his phone, his wallet. The boat had had water in it. Why? He closed the apartment door behind him and got into the lift. He pressed the button for the ground floor. Only one way to find out.

The dog's collar was tight around her neck. It cut into her chin when she moved her head. And every now and then

Helena jerked the lead, just to let her know she hadn't forgotten about her.

Vanessa lay on a rough blanket in the small back bedroom at Dove Cottage. Tremors ran through her body from her head to her white feet. She was trying to keep calm. Trying to work out what to do. She couldn't understand how this had happened. One minute she was splashing around in the lake, feeling so happy she thought she would burst, the next she was lying on a rock with Helena's hands around her neck, strapping on the collar. Vanessa had seen Helena take the collar off the dog. But she had thought nothing of it. Thought, if at all, that it was because he was swimming, and that maybe weed might catch in it and drag him down. But nothing could have dragged that dog down. Vanessa had tried to struggle, to flail with her hands, but the dog growled. His lips had pulled back from his teeth and the sound, a rumble that turned into a sharp snarl, filled her ears.

'I wouldn't do that.' Helena smiled down at her. 'He doesn't like it. And he can get very upset if he's not happy.'

'My clothes,' Vanessa reached in vain for her skirt and blouse. But Helena jerked her away, so that she thought her neck would break or she would choke.

'You don't need clothes where you're going. The only thing you'll ever need now is a winding sheet. You know what that is, don't you?'

Vanessa lay now curled into a ball on the blanket. Helena was on the bed. The dog was by the door. She wanted to move, to stretch her legs, uncurl her body, but she was scared to draw attention to herself. She was so thirsty. She hadn't had anything to eat or drink since the picnic in the woods. The thought of food made her feel sick, but she was longing for water. Her mouth was dry and dusty and her lips were cracked. She stirred and raised her head from the floor.

'What?' Helena lifted her head too and took in the slack of the lead, twining it around her hand. 'What now?'

'I'm thirsty. Could I have a drink?'

Helena cackled. 'You know your problem, little girl? You shouldn't have cried so much. If you hadn't, you wouldn't be nearly so thirsty. So, it's your fault. Your fault. Now be quiet. Enjoy your time here. Lie on the floor on your nice soft blanket and thank your lucky stars that I'm not as young as I used to be. That my energy is on the wane. Lie there until it gets dark. Then, I think, it will be time for another swim. Or,' she pushed herself up on the pillow, 'how would it be to go out in the boat? Your sister's boat. The boat your sister and your father went out in that day, seventeen years ago when he drowned. You don't remember it, do you? But I do.' She lay down again. 'They told me that night that he was dead. They told me my son was fatherless. They didn't want to let me out of hospital for the funeral. They said it would be bad for me, that it would upset me, that it would slow down my recovery. But I insisted. I demanded. I got my solicitor to force them to let me go.'

She turned on to her side and jerked the lead. Vanessa's head jerked too. 'And I stood beside my son. And I watched your mother. Such a pathetic little creature. Like a house sparrow. And I knew one day I would deal with her. So,' she jerked the lead again, 'come here to me, my little swallow. Come here to me, my little blue-tit. My little blackbird. My little starling.' She began to drag the girl across the floor.

'And let me crush your whimpering body beneath mine. Let me feel your heart flutter in your breast. Let me feel your pulse dance in your wrists.'

Vanessa tried to resist. She grabbed the leg of the bed and held on to it, but the pressure around her throat forced the air from her windpipe and she choked. She began to pray, as the tears slid silently down her grubby face.

McLoughlin drove up the narrow hill road. He passed the gate with the keypad and the CCTV. He drove on upwards, winding towards the summit. He could see the lake below. It was dark, shiny, glossy, like a Roman warrior's polished metal shield. He pulled off the road and parked. Then he crossed the road and began to walk. It was hot, very hot. He'd be down in the trees soon and it would be cooler there. He walked on and came to a stone wall, waist high, topped with a few strands of barbed wire. He pulled himself up and managed to climb over, just avoiding snagging his trousers. He jumped down awkwardly, catching his hand as he landed. He swore loudly. The jagged tear in his left palm was oozing blood. He pulled a handkerchief from his pocket, wrapped it around and tied it with a clumsy knot. It would have to do for the time being. He straightened up and tried to get his bearings. He could see the lake and, below to the right, the grey slate roof of the house, and the stables behind. He must be close to where Tom Spencer had been that day. The view was spectacular. He could see across the lake to the little rapids and the stream, a silver snake as it wriggled down into the next valley. To his left was the gate lodge and the drive, and as he watched, the sun glinted off the roof of a car moving slowly down through the trees towards the house. He wished he had his binoculars. He couldn't, from up there, identify the make or model. But he'd have to be careful where he went. He didn't want to encounter Gerry Leonard or any other of Dominic de Paor's friends. He scrambled down from the rock. Better get going. No point in hanging around.

'You didn't know that, did you?' Helena uncapped a bottle of mineral water.

Vanessa heard the hiss as the bubbles escaped. Her lips were cracked. Her tongue felt huge in her mouth. 'Know what?' It was hard to speak. She had to struggle to control her voice.

'Know that about your name. That my baby was called Vanessa. James loved that name. He loved the baby too. I sometimes thought he loved her more than he loved me. Of course, it was inevitable that he would give you the same name. It wasn't you he wanted or loved. It was my baby, my little Vanessa.' She lifted the bottle to her lips and water ran down her chin as she drank. 'She's buried here. Did you know?'

Vanessa could think of nothing but the water. If she could have a drink, nothing else would matter.

'Yes, she's in the deer pasture. There's a large slab of granite over her grave. It has her name carved on it. Just her name. That's enough.' Helena rested the bottle on her stomach.

Vanessa could almost smell the water. 'Please,' she whispered. 'Please.'

'I wanted James to be buried here. If I'd had my way he would be in the deer pasture too. Under another slab of granite. But it wasn't to be. Your mother took care of that. But I took care of her. I made sure she would never be able to claim his name, or his property. And after all,' she lifted the bottle and swirled the water, 'why should she? It was her daughter, after all, who killed him. There,' she sat up and pressed the cold bottle hard against Vanessa's cheek, 'something else you didn't know, my little bird.' She swung her legs off the bed and stood up.

'Please.' Vanessa held out her hand for the bottle. 'Please.'

'Water? You want water? I should take you out to the lake again. I should tip you out of the boat. And I should sit and watch you drown. Just the way your sister Marina sat and watched your father drown.' She lifted the bottle high and turned it at an angle. 'It's true, you know. My son found out what she did. And we decided she should be punished. Humiliation, torment, terror – she should feel them all.' The water dribbled from the bottle. Vanessa watched the sparkling drops.

'And all Dominic's friends would watch. Those girls who loved him. They would do anything for him. And that pathetic creature, Mark. His shadow we called him. Born on the same day. In the same hospital. His mother was my best friend. My son was strong and handsome. Hers was weak and helpless. Stunted. But Dominic was good to him. And he said that night, he said, "It's your turn now to have some fun. Your turn to have Marina." Helena sat down on the bed beside her. 'It's a pity she's gone. She was pleasure. And now, in gratitude to your sister, I will let you drink. Here.' And she thrust the bottle into Vanessa's mouth, banging it against her teeth, trapping her tongue so that Vanessa gagged, choked and spat.

'So much for gratitude.' Helena stood up. She dropped

the bottle on the floor. It rolled under the bed. Vanessa's eyes pricked again.

'More bloody tears.' Helena walked to the door. She opened it. The dog lifted his head. Helena bent down and stroked his ears. 'There's a good boy,' she crooned. She stepped over him. Vanessa heard her footsteps on the stairs. The dog got up. He walked to the bed. He lay down and put his head between his paws. His eyes, the colour of toffee, stared at her.

McLoughlin reached the trees. Sweat was dripping down his forehead. His knees were aching from the stress of the downhill slope and he wanted badly to sit down. He was beginning to regret coming here on his own. Too old, he thought, for this kind of caper. He moved carefully, keeping his eyes on the rough ground underfoot. The last thing he needed was a sprain or a twisted ankle. And felt his phone vibrate in his pocket. He pulled it out. It was Sally. 'Hi, Sally. Listen, I've been meaning to ring you. I think I may be getting somewhere. I didn't want to worry you, but I think maybe you're right. Maybe there is more to Marina's death than I thought.'

'Michael,' Sally said. 'Michael, I need to talk to you. Vanessa's missing.'

'Missing? How long?' He stopped.

'Tomorrow is her eighteenth birthday. We had agreed we'd spend the day together. We always spend her birthday together. We have a routine. The evening before we always have a special dinner. That's tonight, Michael, but she's not here. And her phone is switched off. Something's wrong.'

He could hear the hysteria in her voice. It made the hairs rise up on his arms.

'Look, Sally, I know this is a bad time for you. But, please, don't worry.' He was conscious of how loud his voice sounded in the quiet of the wood, but as far as he could see he was on his own. He tried to speak softly. He held the phone close to his lips. 'Vanessa is probably out with her friends. After all, she's been through a lot recently. Maybe she needs some time on her own, away from you.'

Margaret watched Sally. Her face was white, her lips quivered. Margaret held out her hand and Sally gave her the phone. She grasped it. It felt heavy. Her palms were damp. Butterflies danced in her stomach.

'Michael, hallo. Do you remember me?' She waited for an answer. There was silence. 'Michael, it's Margaret Mitchell. Remember? I'm sorry to surprise you like this, but I need to talk to you. About Sally and her daughter.'

McLoughlin couldn't speak. His throat seemed to have closed. He felt the warmth of the sun fade. It was a cold night in winter. And he was standing in the dark, looking at the man who was lying trussed up on the floor.

'Michael, are you there?'

He cleared his throat. 'Yes, I am. Where are you?' It was suddenly very important that he could visualize her.

'I'm in my house in Brighton Vale. And Sally is with me. And you have to listen to her. The way you listened to me.' Her voice was urgent.

'Why are you there? Why have you come back? I don't think you should be there.'

There was silence for a moment. Then she spoke again. 'That's not important now, Michael. You have to listen to Sally. Her daughter is missing. Remember Mary? My Mary?'

'OK, Margaret. This is what you must do. Tell Sally to get in touch with Tony Heffernan. I can't do anything at the moment. Tony is the person to contact. He'll help.' McLoughlin began to walk again. He felt exposed and vulnerable.

Margaret looked at Sally. 'She's done that, Michael, she did that first thing. He gave her all the usual stuff about waiting, being sure. The kind of things that were said to me when I reported Mary missing. Michael, Sally can't wait any longer. She knows there's something wrong. You have to help her. Please, Michael, the way you helped me.'

He remembered. Sitting in the garden in Monkstown. Trying to explain to her what they were doing. What they were going to do. Where they were going to search. How confident they were that they would find her.

'Listen, Margaret, I'm out in Wicklow. I have to check on something to do with Marina, Sally's daughter. I'm sure she's told you about her. Give me a couple of hours and I'll be back. In the meantime, go to Dun Laoghaire Garda station. Take a photograph. Tell them she's been gone for two or even three days. Cry, do whatever you can to get them moving on it.' He paused. 'Look, I'm sure it'll be OK. Not every missing girl ends up the way your daughter did.' He added, 'I'm sorry. That sounded harsh. I didn't mean it like that.'

'That's OK, Michael, I understand. We'll do that. We'll do as you suggest.' Margaret smiled at Sally again.

'Margaret, wait! Margaret, listen to me!' McLoughlin was shouting now.

'Yes?'

'I have to see you. I can't believe you're here. I can't believe you've come back.'

Margaret turned away from Sally. She moved towards the garden. 'Yes,' her voice was low, 'but I won't be here for long. There's something I have to do. Something that will take me away again.' He could hear Sally's voice in the background. 'Look, we have to go. I'll see you later. 'Bye for now.'

McLoughlin leaned against a huge beech. The light filtered through the canopy of branches. His heart was pounding, he felt sick. He was back in his car, driving towards Blessington. It was dark and cold. There was a bottle of vodka on the passenger seat and he was drinking it as he drove. He was following the black Mercedes, the taxi Jimmy drove. He watched it turn up the lane towards the cottage beneath the pines. He stopped his car, got out and followed on foot. Saw the woman emerge from the back seat. Then saw the other man come around from behind the house. The tall, good-looking man he recognized from the Four Courts. Saw him hit Jimmy across the head so he dropped to the ground. Saw them drag him to the yard behind. Saw what happened next. And now she was back. He had dreamed about this moment for years. Gone over and over it countless times. All he would say. All he would do. And now here he was out on a hillside in Wicklow, following up on some half-arsed notion about water in a dinghy. It would be so easy. He could climb back up the hill, scramble over the wall, get into his car and drive back to the coast. So easy.

'You've come this far, Michael,' he said. 'You might as well see it through.'

He moved away from the tree. Not far now to the lake. The sooner he got a look at the boat, the sooner he'd be out of there.

Vanessa lay on the bed. She was half asleep. Helena had come back. Had at last given her something to drink. It looked like wine, but it tasted different. It made her drift off. Drift away. It was a good sensation. Comforting, like resting on a big, soft pillow. She could hear a sound. Someone was singing. She tried to hear the words. A children's song or a nursery rhyme.

Gonna tell, gonna tell, gonna tell on you.

The words repeated over and over again. She drifted back to sleep. Then woke with a start. She could see out of the window from here. See below, the small front garden and the path from the road. Could see someone coming. A man was wheeling a trolley along the path. It was stacked with cardboard boxes. On the top was a white laptop. It was an Apple iBook. Vanessa knew the type. Marina had one. She'd said she'd give Vanessa one for her birthday. The man came through the gate. Helena went out to meet him. They moved closer to the front door. Vanessa couldn't see them, but she could hear them. She strained to listen to their conversation.

'Your son . . . He said you'd know what to do with this stuff.' The man's voice was gruff and low.

'Of course. He told me you were coming. You can bring it all in. This way. Follow me.'

She heard the tramp of the man's feet as he came up the

stairs. He was moving slowly. His tread was heavy. She heard a loud thump. The boxes. maybe, hitting the floor, she thought. And the bang as the door to the other bedroom was closed. She tried to sit up.

'Help me. Please help me.' Her voice was weak.

The door creaked open.

'Please,' she whispered.

The man didn't speak. He backed away. He closed the door. She heard his steps on the stairs again. She was so tired. Her legs were heavy. She could barely move them. She sighed again. And at last she slept.

TWENTY-NINE

The butterfly perched on a clump of nettles. Its wings opened, showing orange and white markings. McLoughlin held his breath. He held out his hand and extended a finger. The butterfly rose slowly, hovered in front of him, then opened its wings wide and glided away. McLoughlin turned to follow its progress. He watched it until it was no longer visible, as it disappeared among the branches of the huge beech trees. Then he continued down the hill towards the house.

He could see it clearly now below him. A Land Rover was parked in the yard. There was no sign of its passengers. The door to the kitchen was open. He tried to figure out how he was going to get past the house and around to the boathouse at the far end of the beach. He sat down to catch his breath. He was thirsty and his calves were aching after the steep descent from the top of the hill. He wondered where Helena de Paor might be and, more to the point, her dog. He had asked Tony Heffernan, 'Is she still bonkers?' He had said it as if she was some kind of harmless old lady who muttered to herself in the supermarket. But she wasn't like that. She was frightening – dangerous.

It was cooler now and the sweat on his back had chilled. He pulled out his phone. It was eight fifteen. He hadn't realized how much time had passed since he had driven out here.

He got to his feet. The only way to get past the house

without being in full view of its windows was to go behind the stables. The trees came down right behind them and he could make his way through them and come out at the far side in the deer pasture. From there it wasn't too far to the boathouse. He hoped. He pulled the handkerchief from his hand. The ripped skin had stopped bleeding. He wiped his forehead and took a deep breath. Time to go.

Vanessa woke with a start. For a moment she thought she was at home in Monkstown. The shape of this room was like that of her bedroom in the mews. Its ceiling sloped down to the floor and the windows were low and small. She could hear the sound of the radio coming from downstairs. A chatter of voices. Perhaps one was her mother's. She would be cooking dinner, listening to the evening news programme. Talking to one of her friends on the phone. Maybe Janet whom she had known from school. Or Margaret – so sad always, but she had helped her mother, there was no doubt about that. It was such a relief to be able to leave her. To go out without worrying about her all the time. But now, she was sure, her mother would be worried about her. It was the day before her birthday. They had planned her birthday dinner. Her mother had told her she could have all her favourite things.

'I'll make you an Indian feast,' her mother had said. There would be *dal* and spinach and potato. Okra, cooked with sugar and lemon. And chickpeas done in the sweet-and-sour fashion. There would be cucumber with mint and yoghurt, and carrot salad with mustard seeds and lemon juice. 'And one meat dish. You must have one meat dish,' her mother had said.

So she had picked *rogan josh*, made with lamb and yoghurt. There would be a bowl of rice with peas and a pile of *naan* bread, hot and puffy from the grill.

'And to drink – what will we have to drink?' she had asked.

'Well,' her mother lifted her pencil and tapped the shopping list, 'I remember your father saying there was only one thing to drink with Indian food and that was champagne. So that's what we'll have tonight. Champagne. How does that sound?'

Imagine that, she had thought. Imagine having a father who knew that champagne was the right thing to drink with Indian food. And it made this man whom she had never known, who had always been a face in a photograph with hair the same colour as hers, seem real and alive for once.

She rolled on to her back. She was alone. The dog lead trailed across the floor. She sat up slowly. She began to crawl towards the door. It was half open. She peered around it, then moved out on to the landing. And saw. The dog was lying across the end of the stairs. He lifted his head and looked at her.

'Ah, you've decided to join us.' Helena stood beside him. She had a bundle of clothes in her hands. 'Here, put these on. We're going for a walk.' She flung the skirt and blouse up to her. 'Hurry up, now, it's getting late. And there's something else I want you to do before we go out. Quickly now. Don't keep me waiting.'

'My shoes. Where are my shoes?' Vanessa held out her hand.

'Christ almighty, you want everything, don't you? Count

yourself lucky that you've anything to wear. And don't start getting any ideas about going home. Home is the last place you're going.' Helena's face split into a grin. 'Of course, you could say that you're being called home. But that phrase will be lost on you, I'd say. You're too young to have heard it regularly. Now,' she put a hand on the dog's head and he rose to his feet, 'put that stuff on. Quickly, before I feel the need to come and do it for you.'

McLoughlin could see the boat through the stand of beeches at the lake end of the deer pasture. It was tied up at the little jetty. There was still no sign of life in the house. He hurried through the trees, his feet crunching on the beech mast that lay inches deep on the mossy ground. He reached the boat. He stopped and flopped down beside it to catch his breath. The wood of the jetty was warm. He leaned over and scooped up a handful of lake water. He splashed his face, then wetted his handkerchief and mopped his neck, letting the warm liquid dribble down his back. It felt lovely. He'd have given anything to strip off and lower himself into its smooth, silky darkness. But this wasn't the time or place, he reminded himself. He got up on to his knees and peered into the boat. It was in pretty good condition. The paint was faded but there were no signs of rot or decay. He leaned down on the gunwales and the boat tipped beneath his weight. Tipped, but did not sink beneath the surface. He stood up, then untied it from its mooring ring and began to pull it around the end of the jetty, then back towards the shore and the entrance to the boathouse. He pushed at the wooden door, which swung back on its hinges. He moved quickly inside, the dinghy following like an obedient pony on a leading-rein.

It was dark and cool. He stood on the wooden walkway and tied the boat loosely to a ring on the wall. Then he stepped down into it. The boat dipped and swayed beneath his weight. Imagine, he thought. Imagine you're drunk and stoned and lying here in the dark. He sat on the rear seat and let himself slip to the side so his head was resting on the gunwales.

'You have decided that you're going to end it all. You're going to jump overboard,' he said aloud, as he swung his legs over the side. As his weight shifted, the bow reared up. He took off his shoes and rolled his trousers as far above his knees as they would go. Then he sat on the edge and pushed down. The boat gave way beneath him. Water slopped up and dribbled over the side. He swung his legs in and bent down to look at what had accumulated in the bilges. There was hardly enough to fill the bailing bucket. Certainly not nearly as much as there had been in the boat after Marina's body had been found. The only way water could have got into the boat was if someone had poured it in. Or? Or? Or?

He got out of the boat and slipped down beside it. The water sneaked up his legs. Shit, he thought. He should have taken off his trousers. Too late now. He stood beside the boat. Then he leaned down on the gunwales, half pulling himself up but keeping his feet firmly anchored on the lake's sandy bottom. As the boat tilted at a steep angle, water poured in. He stood back, let it go and watched as the boat righted itself. The lake water slopped from one side to the other, then settled. He leaned over and looked in. At least six inches. Not as much as there had been the morning

Marina was found. But he could see now how it might have got there. Someone leaning on the gunwales, maybe holding the boat down, that would do it. Someone leaning on the gunwales while the woman was asleep so she fell out into the water. Someone leaning on the gunwales, pushing and pulling the woman out of the boat. Someone strong, heavy, pushing their weight down, so the woman in the boat toppled out, and as she disappeared into the lake, water rushed in to displace her.

He pulled himself back on to the walkway. He thought back over the statements he had read. He remembered sitting in the kitchen here, listening to Helena as she described how she and her dog had got up early to go for their morning swim. She had described it vividly. They had seen the boat drifting. She had waded out to catch it, to make it fast to the mooring ring on the rock wall. She had seen the woman's body lying in the rapids. She had gone to look at her. She had realized that she was dead. She had raised the alarm. He bent to roll down his trousers, put on his shoes. But what if she had found the boat, as she said, and Marina was still in it? Unconscious, perhaps, but alive. And she had leaned on the side of the boat, and tipped her into the lake so that she drowned? Johnny Harris had said she drowned. Her lungs were filled with water. So she was alive when she went into the water. Alive, but unable to save herself. Alive, until Helena found her.

He pulled his laces tight and tied them in neat bows. He stood up. It was about time he brought Brian Dooley in on this. Of course, he'd probably dismiss it as the fevered imaginings of a retired guard with too much time on his hands. But maybe he wouldn't. Dooley wasn't the worst. He bent down and untied the dinghy. He'd better put it back where he had found it. Try not to alert anyone that someone had been here. But as he put out his hand to push open the door he heard a voice. He drew back, but there was no escape. The door swung open.

'Well, looky, looky, what do we have here?' Helena's voice was loud, triumphant. She clicked her tongue against the roof of her mouth and the dog sprang forward. It stopped just short of McLoughlin, its front feet planted wide, the hackles on its shoulders rising with its growl. But McLoughlin's attention was on the girl standing in the doorway, her head slumped forward and a band of leather around her thin white neck. 'What have you done to her?' he asked quietly.

Helena turned to Vanessa. She jerked the dog lead and Vanessa's head jerked in response. 'Not much. We've just had a bit of fun, haven't we?' She tightened her grip on the leather strap and forced Vanessa's head up. Tears slid from the girl's eyes. She did not speak.

'Let her go.' McLoughlin made as if to move. The dog barked once, a short, sharp sound, which stopped him.

The girl sobbed, shoulders shaking. McLoughlin could feel his own legs trembling. 'Let her go,' he whispered. 'Please, take me instead.' Remember Mary, Margaret had said. He remembered. Her body wrapped in black plastic as she was pulled from the canal, beaten and abused. Her black curls shorn. He remembered Margaret's face as she looked down at her daughter. He had seen other mothers' faces too. Before that day and after it. He couldn't bear to think of Sally Spencer. And the look on hers.

'You? What would I want with you? You're nothing to me. Nothing to anyone. I know you, Michael McLoughlin.

You're a nothing man.' Helena turned to Vanessa. 'This is who I want. This little one, who twitters like a bird.' She reached out and touched Vanessa's hair. The dog whined. 'You know what day it is tomorrow, don't you, Mr McLoughlin? It's her eighteenth birthday. And you know what that means? Tomorrow Dove Cottage and the land around it become hers. Isn't she a lucky little girl?' She jerked the lead again. 'Look at me, girl, when I speak to you. Pay attention.' Vanessa's head snapped up. Her eyes were closed. Her face was the colour of skimmed milk. 'Dove Cottage, pretty name. But it's not called after the bird, with its smooth feathers and neat little beak. It's the Irish word, *dubh*, the same as the lake, Lough Dubh. Black, black, black.' She shook her head so her hair fanned out around her head. 'Black, black, black is the colour of my true love's hair.' Her voice was strong and melodic. 'Black because of the water from the bog. Black because of the lake's depth. It's bottomless, you know. No one knows how deep it is. Will I put rocks in your pockets, Vanessa? Will I let you sink? Or will you float, as your sister floated? Such a pretty sight in her red dress, floating with her face in the water.' She stopped, smoothed her hair back, tucked it behind her ears. 'Now, to the business at hand. I have a plan.' She clicked her fingers in Vanessa's direction. 'The note. Give me the note. Such a nice note. Just like the note I wrote for her sister. Now, where to leave it? That was the question.' She tilted her head to one side. 'And then a brainwave. She had left her bag up in one of the top bedrooms. So I popped the note in it, and kicked it under the bed. Such a good idea to put it there.'

Vanessa pulled a folded piece of paper from her pocket. 'Now, read it for the nice man.' Helena put out her hand

and twined a lock of Vanessa's hair around her fingers. 'Smarten up, girl, off you go. Loud and clear.'

McLoughlin listened. The words were familiar. She asked for forgiveness, if not in this world then in the next. Her voice faltered as she reached the end. 'I love you, Mum. I'm sorry for all the pain I've caused you.' She began to sob.

'When?' He stared at Helena, at the smile on her face.

'Soon. We'll go out for a row on the lake. The dog, the girl and me. Out to the deepest part. And then the girl will say goodbye. She will leave her clothes in the boat. The note will be in her pocket. The dog and I will swim to the shore. We're strong swimmers.' She clicked her tongue. The dog moved forward. McLoughlin could feel the sweat prickle in his armpits. His mouth was dry. The dog lifted his nose. His nostrils opened wide. The inner skin was pink and shiny. McLoughlin tried to think.

'Just tell me one thing.' He shifted carefully from foot to foot. The dog followed his movements with its shiny brown eyes. 'Marina. You did kill her, didn't you?' He looked at Vanessa. She was shocked, disoriented. Her pupils were huge.

'Kill her? Well, did I kill her? That's a debatable proposition. I leaned on the boat and she fell overboard.'

Leans on the boat. The girl opens her eyes. Help me, she says, please help me. The water pours into the boat. The girl falls to one side. The water pours into the boat. The girl slides out.

'She deserved it. She let my husband die. She sat here,' she pointed to the boat, 'she sat here and she watched him drown. That man told Dominic. He saw her. He saw what she did.'

'She was fifteen, Helena, not much more than a child.'

He slipped his hand into his pocket. He could feel the hard plastic of his phone.

'Fifteen? Not much more than a child? She was strong, she was healthy, she could swim. She was wearing a life-jacket.'

She sits and watches him. She'd told him to put on his life-jacket. He ignored her. I hate you, she thinks, you never listen to me. She sits and watches him. He sinks beneath the water. He kicks himself up into the air. Help me, help me, he cries. She sits in the boat and watches him drown.

Helena was shouting now. 'He was helpless! She let him die!'

Vanessa whimpered. 'It's not true, is it? She didn't do that, did she?'

'Shut up! Shut the creature up!' Helena hit her across the face and Vanessa fell back.

McLoughlin's fingers slipped across the keypad. 'And why did she do that, Helena? What was James doing to her that made her hate him so much?'

Helena hit him then, her fist balled, a blow to the nose that made him stagger.

'You think he was interested in her? You haven't a clue. You know nothing. You're out of your depth. You're drowning. The water's creeping up over your chin, over your mouth, over your nose. Soon you'll disappear completely. You'll be gone and no one will even miss you.' She screamed. A scream of triumph. 'And we'll be on our own again. My son Dominic and me. We need no one else. No one. We're all that matters.'

McLoughlin could taste blood. He could feel it on his lips, his chin.

'Poor Marina. She wanted Dominic to like her.' Helena's face was lit up. A bright shining light that came from within. 'She was so frightened that he would find out what happened in the boat. She would do anything to please him. When they went back to school after James died, Dominic told me, he was having the best time. Marina was at his beck and call. He got her to torment that boy, Mark Porter. They were all at it. It was his game. And they played it for him.'

She walks towards the tennis courts. She has to do it. Dominic has told her. And she is so scared that Dominic knows. Knows what happened in the boat. And he will tell her mother. And her mother will never forgive her. She will do whatever Dominic asks. He has a list of tasks. Ben Roxby is top of the list. Give him what he wants. And then there's little Mark. We'll have some fun with little Mark, won't we, Marina? Poor little Mark. He doesn't realize what we're doing. He just wants us to like him. He wants you to love him. Go on, Marina, and I'll watch you and tell you if you're doing well.

Blood was dripping down his shirt and on to the wooden floor. The dog sniffed. Vanessa whimpered again.

'So what is it about the men in your family and Marina?' He had to concentrate. He had to keep calm. He had to think. He tried to visualize the buttons on the phone. 'You know that Dominic was fucking Marina, don't you?'

'Of course he was. Of course I knew!' Helena screeched. 'He was playing her. Like a trout on the end of a line. Letting her out, then reeling her in. Until she was exhausted. And he could grab her, pierce her with his gaff, net her, drag her on to the ground. Watch her gasping for breath. Then smash her head with a rock.' She raised her arms high in the air, then let them drop. 'He found out what happened in the boat. And he was punishing her.'

'Punishing her with the messages and the photographs?'

She smiled again. It struck him that her lipstick was smudged. She clapped her hands. 'I wish I'd been there to see her face when she got those photos. But I saw plenty of her that night at the party. I saw her and I made a nice little film with my camera. Plenty of details. Pity you haven't seen it, as you seem to be so interested in her.'

A beautiful night. A full moon. The house filled with people. Loud music playing. Tables laden with food, with bottles of wine, vodka, whiskey, gin. Mark drives Marina down the track by the lake. She is scared. She doesn't speak. She should never have come. Dominic will be here. She is frightened of him. Does he know what she did? She has tried to find out. She has been getting the messages, the photographs. The words written on the walls of the apartment. Dominic must know. But she can't bring herself to ask him. The lake is so beautiful. The moon hangs above. Its blue light ripples across the water. Dominic will be here with his wife. Marina hadn't wanted to come. But Mark begged her. She felt so sad for him. So sad for what she had done, how she had made him suffer. But she knew it would be a mistake to come here.

She stands and looks out at the lake. She sees the little boat tied up at the jetty. Dominic catches her arm. Here, he says, come here. He takes her into the house. Up to a bedroom at the top. He lays out a line of coke on the dressing-table. She bends down and puts the rolled-up note to her nose. And now how about this? he says. He gives her the small white pill. Acid, he says, you've had it before. Haven't you? She nods. She swallows it.

They walk through the throng. She takes a bottle of vodka from the table. He leads her into the wood. He brings her to the little clearing. A huge fire is burning. She sees the familiar faces. She feels warm, content. For a moment she feels loved. Dominic kisses her. Over his shoulder she sees his wife. Gilly smiles at her. Maybe everything will be all right. Then Mark takes her by the hand. He pushes her to the ground. She looks at Dominic. He nods and smiles. Mark lies on top of her. The fire is warm on her bare legs. Mark pulls down her dress. He kisses her breasts. But something is wrong. He stands up. He is crying. She rolls over. She vomits. She stands. She shouldn't be here. This place is cursed. She picks up the bottle of vodka. She staggers away. She is dirty. She smells. Her mouth tastes foul. She staggers towards the lake. And sees the little boat. Bluebird, her little Bluebird. She stumbles to the jetty. Fly away, little Bluebird, we'll fly away together. She unties the rope and steps in. The boat rises and falls beneath her weight. She pushes it from the jetty. It is so beautiful on the lake. Quiet. Peaceful. She raises the bottle to her lips and drinks. She lays her head on the seat. She sleeps.

'But I have seen it.' McLoughlin's mouth was dry. He tried to lick his lips but he had no saliva. 'And I saw what it did to Mark Porter. I saw him after he died. I saw what humiliation can do. Why hurt Mark so much, Helena? Why punish him?'

'Oh,' she shook her head, 'collateral damage – isn't that what they call it? How were we to know that he wouldn't be able to perform? He'd always been able to do it before. And what was important was that Marina would know Mark's interest in her meant that Dominic was done with

her. That was the way it worked. Mark got the leftovers.'
Helena giggled. The dog lifted its head and watched her.

'But what was it all for, Helena? What was Dominic
going to do next?' Keep her talking, keep her attention
focused. Anything to stop her leaving and taking the girl
with her.

'Oh that was going to be the best bit. He had decided he
was going to see Sally Spencer the day after the party. He
was going to tell her what her daughter had done. It was
going to be the greatest fun. But then,' she looked away,
'when he discovered what I had done he decided – well, he
decided—' She stopped. She stroked Vanessa's cheek. The
girl shook convulsively. 'He decided . . .'

*'Tell me,' Dominic says, 'that when you found Marina, she was
already dead. Tell me you didn't touch her. You didn't hurt her in
any way. Tell me, Mother.'*

*'Well,' Helena shrugs, 'she was nearly dead. Her head was
trailing in the water. I tried to pull her to the shore but she
was too heavy for me. She fell into the lake. There was nothing I
could do. Nothing, honestly, nothing I could do.' She begins to
panic. 'Please don't tell anyone. Don't tell the police. They'll send
me back to the hospital. Please, Dominic, I'm begging you. I'll die
if that happens. I'll die.'*

*And he puts his arms around her and holds her to him. He
kisses her hair. He smells her perfume. 'Don't worry, Mother, don't
worry.' And he closes his eyes and holds her body close to his. And
she rocks from side to side. Together they rock from side to side.*

*

And McLoughlin had unlocked his phone. He began to press the buttons. Randomly, frantically. Suddenly the phone rang.

Helena leaned forward. She grabbed his hand from his pocket. 'Give that to me!' she shouted.

He tried to push her away but the phone spun from his grasp. Helena kicked it out of his reach. And the dog was on him. Snapping at his wrist, catching his hand between his jaws. Pain shooting up his arm. He screamed, a high-pitched, pathetic sound. And Helena kicked the phone again. Into the water. She turned quickly and pulled a mooring rope from a coil on the floor. The dog's grip tightened on his hand. He couldn't move. Helena shoved a loop of rope over his head and around his neck. She pulled his hand from the dog's mouth. She twisted his arms behind his back and tied the rope through one of the iron rings on the wall. She pulled it tight. His throat closed. He coughed. He choked. He gasped for breath. Helena moved away. She grabbed Vanessa's hair – the girl shrieked in agony. She dragged Vanessa to her feet and pushed her sideways so she fell into the boat. The dog barked. Helena beckoned and it jumped in beside the girl. Helena spread her legs wide. One on the boat, one on the walkway. The boat shuddered beneath her weight, then moved. Vanessa screamed. 'Please!' Her voice was frantic. 'Please, help me!'

Helena jumped into the boat. Then she picked up the oars, slotted them into the rowlocks and began to row.

McLoughlin slumped against the wall. The rope was tight. He tried to swallow. His hand was badly torn. The rope dragged at the wound. He tried to shout, but his voice was caught in his throat. He kicked out with his legs and banged his feet on the decking. 'Remember Mary,' Margaret had said. 'Remember Mary.' He bowed his head. Then heard. Quick footsteps outside. He shouted again and the door to the boathouse opened.

A man stood in the entrance. He was holding a gun. 'Where is she? Where are they?' Dominic de Paor lifted the gun to shoulder height.

'Your mother and half-sister are in the boat. Out on the lake.' McLoughlin tried to pull himself up. 'Help me. Get me out of here. Quick. Your mother's going to drown her. The way she drowned Marina.'

De Paor stared at him. He lowered the gun. 'She didn't drown Marina. It was an accident. She tried to help her. She tried to get her on to the beach. She didn't mean to do it.' He wiped his hand across his face.

McLoughlin twisted his head frantically from side to side. 'That's not what she told me. And I believe her. You would believe her, too, if you'd seen her here with Vanessa. If you love your mother, you must stop her. You did this. You made this happen. It's your fault. Do something.'

'She doesn't mean it. She's not well.' De Paor's face was white.

'Not well? Is that what you call it? She's out of control. She's dangerous. She needs proper help.'

'I have helped her. I love her. I've looked after her – I've kept her from harm!' De Paor was shouting now.

'Kept her from harm? Are you as mad as she is? You haven't kept her from harm. You've let her harm others. Let me go. Let me help you – let me help *her*.'

But de Paor wasn't listening. He picked up the gun. 'I am her help. Her help and her salvation. No one else can do anything for her. She can't go back to that prison they call a hospital. I remember what it was like. The madness there. The smell. The indignity. The drugs. The ECT. They strapped her down. And afterwards – afterwards she was like a zombie. All sensation dead. And I promised her. Never again. I would never let anyone touch her again.'

Together they rock from side to side. He remembers when he was little and his head reached barely to her breast. The comfort, the love that flowed from her. He could hear her heart beating. Badoom, badoom, badoom, badoom. He closes his eyes and breathes her scent. He was warm, he was loved, he was happy. Now he holds her head against his shoulder. He strokes her hair, her dark, dark hair. He murmurs the song she used to sing to him: 'Black, black, black is the colour of my true love's hair'. He reaches down and takes her ear-lobe between his thumb and first finger. He rubs it gently. She sighs and he feels her body cleave to his. 'Don't worry, Mother, don't worry. I won't let anyone hurt you. I will never leave you. No one else matters to me the way you do. Ssh, ssh, don't worry.'

He made for the door, then stopped. He turned and said, 'My father didn't care. He didn't want to know. I promised her. I swore to her. I would never let her go back there. No matter what.' He opened the door. He walked through and slammed it behind him.

Vanessa was cold. She was shivering. Her teeth chattered. She couldn't control them. She wanted to be brave and strong. She wanted to fight back. But there was no fight left in her. Her head ached and one eye was swollen and half closed. Helena rowed the boat smoothly across the lake's dark surface. The dog sat beside her. His paw rested on Helena's thigh. Helena was singing. Vanessa knew the song. They had learned it one year in school. The choir had sung it at the end-of-term concert.

> *Black, black, black is the colour of my true love's hair,*
> *Her lips are like some roses fair,*
> *She has the sweetest smile, the gentlest hands,*
> *And I love the ground whereon she stands.*

Helena's voice was loud. She screamed out the words.

> *'I love my love and well she knows*
> *I love the ground whereon she goes,*
> *I wish the day soon would come*
> *When she and I will be as one.*

'Sing it, little bird, sing with me.' She twisted her hands through Vanessa's hair.

The hunter moves quickly and quietly through the trees. He is conscious of the obstacles he will meet. Dry sticks that might break with a loud snap. Uneven ground upon which he might stumble or fall. Low-hanging branches that might snag his hair or clothes. He sees everything. He stays upwind so his quarry will not smell him. He keeps his head and body low so he will not be betrayed by his silhouette against the skyline. He stops. He listens. He looks. He sees his prey. He calculates the distance. He slips a magazine into the barrel of the rifle. He pulls back the bolt. The first bullet slides into the chamber. He lifts the rifle to his shoulder. He closes one eye. He lines up the target in his sights. He squeezes the trigger. The bullet travels at three thousand feet per second. Three times the speed of sound. As it breaks the sound barrier the sonic boom crashes through the air. It ricochets from rock wall to rock wall. The target drops. He pulls back the bolt. The spent bullet spins from the chamber and the second slips into its place. He fires again. Again the sound crashes across the lake. The second target drops. He pulls back the bolt. The spent bullet spins out, the third bullet takes its place. He puts down the gun. He wipes his hands on his shirt. They are sweat-covered, slippery. He picks up the gun again.

Vanessa opened her mouth. But no words would come. And then, and then. A noise so loud she thought her ear-drums would burst. A crash that rolled around the lake. From rock face to rock face, from the trees across the water. And Helena dropped, slumped, the oars slipping from her hands. Her body collapsed in the boat. Almost immediately before Vanessa could draw another breath, another crash, as if the world was ending. And the dog's body exploded. A fine spatter of blood coated her face. And she opened her mouth again and this time there was a voice. A scream that tore from her.

'Help me, help me, help me! Please, help me!'

McLoughlin heard the sound too. The crack, then the echo. And almost immediately, the second shot. A deer hunter, he thought. Two shots in three seconds. He waited for the third. Three bullets in the magazine. There would be three shots.

Dominic looked through his sights. The boat was drifting. The oars hung uselessly in their rowlocks. The girl was screaming. He couldn't see Helena or the dog. And now he could see nothing more. Tears filled his eyes. They blotted everything out. The lake, the boat, the girl, the dog, his mother. He picked up the gun. It would end now. All of it. He jammed the gun beneath his chin. For the third time he pulled the trigger.

THIRTY

Stay near to me and I'll stay near to you.

McLoughlin couldn't get the words out of his head. They kept on bouncing around in his memory. *Near to me, near to you, near to me, near to you.* He couldn't think at first where he had heard them. Then he remembered. It was Marina's favourite poem. Read at her funeral. McLoughlin sat at the computer, did a search, found it. He printed it off, read it out loud a couple of times, folded the page and slipped it into his pocket. Then he put on his jacket, picked up his car keys, and walked out into the evening sunshine.

McLoughlin had brought wine and flowers. He had parked his car outside the house. He waited. The minutes passed. He replayed the phone conversation in his head.

'Michael, hi, it's Margaret. How are you? How's your hand? I hope it's OK.'

He hadn't known what to say. He had tried to speak but he couldn't find the words.

'I want to see you. There's something I have to tell you. Do you think you could come and see me?'

He cleared his throat. 'Sure, of course. When?'

She had asked him to come in the evening. He had put down the phone. Then picked it up again. Pressed the button to call her. Then disconnected. Quickly. He didn't know what he would say.

He sat in the car and waited. It was still warm, although he could see it was raining out at sea. Smears of dark grey hung low on the horizon. And above him a thundercloud pushed its ice-cream peaks into the dark blue sky.

He watched the clock on the dashboard. She had asked him to come at eight o'clock. It was five to now. He was tired and his hand ached. The doctor in A and E had stitched it. Given him a shot of antibiotics. Written a prescription for painkillers. Asked him if he'd like some sleeping pills. McLoughlin had shaken his head.

'Well,' the doctor rested a hand on his shoulder, 'if you're sure. I know you had a pretty nasty experience. If you need help don't hang about.'

A pretty nasty experience. That was one way of putting it.

He got out of the car. He opened the boot. He picked up the two bottles of wine wrapped in tissue paper, and the bunch of flowers. More delphiniums. He felt like a kid on a first date. Now he stood with the bouquet in his hand. He pushed open the gate. It squeaked loudly. He walked up the path and knocked on the front door. The catch had slipped and it swung open at his touch. He stepped into the hall. He went down the stairs into the kitchen. Margaret was sitting in the garden. She was reading a newspaper. He stood silently, holding his wine and his flowers, and he watched her. She looked different. Her hair was short and grey. But when she lifted her head and smiled the difference disappeared. *Near to me, near to you, near to me, near to you.*

He sat beside her on one of the old deckchairs. She

poured him a glass of wine. 'New Zealand?' He bent his head to smell it.

'Yes, it's from Hawke's Bay in the North Island. One of the best wine-growing areas. I'm amazed how much New Zealand wine you can buy here.'

'It's very popular. Of course, it's easy to drink.' This was awful. Worse than he had imagined. He wished he hadn't come.

She put her glass on the table. 'Michael,' she said.

'Yes?'

'As I said on the phone, there's something I have to tell you.'

He wanted to scrutinize her face. Relearn the topography of her features. Memorize for future reference the fine lines between her eyebrows and around her mouth. The slight slackness of skin beneath her chin and over her collar-bone. The web of small wrinkles on the backs of her hands. He wanted to lean close and soak in the scent from her body. He picked up his glass. 'What about?'

There was silence. Then she said, 'About Jimmy Fitzsimons. About how he died.'

It was hard to believe. After so many years she was sitting beside him in the evening sunshine.

'You see . . . You see, what happened was, I couldn't leave it like that. Justice had to be done and seen to be done. So . . .'

What was the best way to punish him? I had to make him suffer. The punishment had to fit the crime. Jimmy killed Mary. He tortured her. He humiliated her. He kept her prisoner. Then he killed her. So that was the first imperative. I wanted him to die where Mary died. It wasn't so difficult to get him to the cottage because he wanted me. And when we get out of the car and even though it's dark I can see that he is smiling. He unlocks the door to the house and he stands back for me to walk through. Such a polite gesture. Standing back to let the lady enter. And I have help to knock him unconscious.

'. . . I wasn't alone. Someone helped me. The man who was Mary's father.'

'It's OK,' McLoughlin said. 'You don't need to . . .'

'But I do, I do. I want you to know. I've thought about you a lot over the years.'

Patrick helps me with everything. He even helped me with the trial. I wanted Jimmy to get off. Because the only punishment for him was death. Prison wouldn't have been enough. He wouldn't have paid for what he did. So Patrick helped me. And then he helps me again. Knocks Jimmy out and drags him into the shed where Mary died. The bloodstains are still visible on the wall. The marks of her suffering. I chain Jimmy to the ring set into the concrete, the way he chained my daughter. Then I wait for him to regain consciousness. Patrick finds the photographs he had taken of her. I want him to die looking at them. I want him to know that his suffering has a purpose.

'Yes, the photographs.' McLoughlin could see them. The images made his stomach convulse.

*

But he misjudges me. He thinks that I will let him go. That I am a kind, civilized person. A good person. That I just want to frighten him. But he's got it wrong. I strap the tape across his mouth, and around the back of his head, around and around until only his pale blue eyes are visible. And then I tell him how he is going to die. First will come severe dehydration. Extreme thirst, dry mouth, thick saliva. He will become dizzy and faint. He will have cramps in his arms and legs as sodium and potassium concentrations in his body increase and fluids decrease. He will want to cry but he will have no tears. His stomach will be racked with pain. He will be nauseous and he will dry-heave as his stomach and intestines dry out. His lips will crack and his tongue will swell. His hands and feet will become cold as the remaining fluids in the circulatory system are shunted to the vital organs in an attempt to keep him alive. He will stop urinating and suffer severe headaches as his brain shrinks. He will become anxious, then lethargic. His kidneys will cease functioning. Toxaemia will build up in his system. He will have hallucinations and seizures as his body chemistry becomes imbalanced. Eventually he will go into a coma. His blood pressure will become almost undetectable as major arrhythmia stops his heart.

'I told him all this. Then I left him. Patrick hammered a piece of board across the window. The last sound he heard.'

'Not quite. Not quite the last.' McLoughlin stared at her. 'Not the last at all.'

Her face was suddenly very pale. Even her lips were bloodless. 'What do you mean? What are you saying?'

He didn't reply.

'Michael, please, tell me what you mean.' A tremor ran through her body. She made as if to stand, but he put out his hand and pushed her back into her seat.

'I'm saying that I saw Fitzsimons after you left. I watched you and Patrick Holland leave. Then I broke into the shed. Fitzsimons misjudged me too. He thought I was going to save him. But I didn't. I did, however, save you. I cleaned your fingerprints off the tape. And I, unlike you, couldn't bear to leave those photographs of Mary in Fitzsimons's tomb. So I picked them up and took them home. I've kept them ever since. They're in a safe place. So you see, Margaret, you don't need to explain anything to me. I know already what you did.' He took her hand. 'I've thought of you every day. I've dreamed about you. I've talked to you. There's a poem I came across recently. Its first lines are "Stay near to me and I'll stay near to you, As near as you are dear to me will do." That's how I feel about you, Margaret. I have been near to you for the last ten years. As near to you as I am now.' He lifted her hand and kissed it. Then he held it close to his cheek. 'The one thing I don't understand,' he said, 'is why you are here. It's not safe, you know. It wouldn't take much to put you at the scene that night.'

She opened her hand against his cheek and stroked it. 'That doesn't worry me any longer. At the time I thought I did the right thing. All I wanted was revenge, punishment, to destroy him as he destroyed Mary. But it didn't stop there. I have been destroyed by it too. Every time I eat I think of how he died. Every time I drink I think of how he died. Every time I stretch out at night to sleep I think of the cold of that concrete floor. I know what he suffered.'

She stopped. The air was perfumed with jasmine. She thought of the Latin. *Per fumare.* By means of smoke, incense, to take away the smell of the dead.

'It was my decision to kill Jimmy Fitzsimons. Mine and mine alone. I don't want anyone else to suffer. I had to wait until it was safe for Patrick. He's dead now. None of this can touch him. But can it touch you? I don't want you to be damaged by what I did. It wasn't your crime. It was mine.' She slid her hand down his face, down his chest, on to his thigh. Then she reached for the bottle of wine. She filled his glass. She filled hers. She lifted it to her mouth. She drank. He watched her throat. He wanted to kiss it. 'I've made a decision, Michael. It's taken me a long time. I've been putting it off for years. Sometimes when I was feeling brave I'd think I could do it. Then the bravery would slip away and I'd turn my back on it. But I can't any longer. I can't go on hiding. In Australia, here, anywhere. I want to be free of Jimmy Fitzsimons. I'm trapped by him. It's as if I, too, rotted away in that house near Blessington. It's as if I, too, was stretched on the rack of his suffering.'

He opened his mouth to speak, but no words came. He took her wrist. He could feel her pulse beating against his fingers.

'Don't.' His voice came out as a whisper. 'Please don't.'

'I want to ask you if you'll come with me. I'm going to hand myself in to the police. I'm going to plead guilty to murder. I will accept the sentence of the court. I will accept whatever form of justice is administered. And that will be that.'

'No!' he shouted. 'No!' He put his arms around her. 'Don't do this. Not now. You've no idea what prison's like. It'll destroy you. It's not some kind of a holiday camp, no matter what people say. Look, Margaret,' he grasped her shoulders, 'go back to Australia. No one knows you're here. Leave tomorrow. I'll come with you.' He could see it. The two of them. Sitting together in the evening. Talking about their day. He could get some kind of job. Security, maybe.

Anyway, he'd have his pension. They'd be fine. It would be a new start for both of them. They could leave all this behind. All the darkness, the sadness, the misery. 'It's over. It was a long time ago.' His voice was pleading. Begging.

'But it isn't over, Michael. Not for me. My life is meaningless like this.' She put her hands on his shoulders and pushed at him. 'I ran away years ago when I was pregnant with Mary. It was a mistake. I should have stayed and faced the consequences.' She caught his face between her hands. 'And I know what prisons are like. I worked in them for years. And believe me when I tell you life in prison is a cake walk in comparison to my life now. I'm doing the right thing. Will you come with me?'

He couldn't see her now. Tears smeared his sight. He tried to speak but the words caught in his throat. He wanted to hold on to the dream of their shared future. A little house in a garden filled with lush greenery. A beach stretching towards the horizon. Gleaming white sand, sea of a blue that denied description. And warmth, not from the sun that burned above them but from their closeness, their intimacy, their friendship. He couldn't bear to think she would take that away.

'Please, Michael. I need you. There's no one else. I have no one else. Please. Do this for me.' She put her face against his. Then she held him tightly as he sobbed.

They sat together in the garden. The light faded. They lay back in the old deckchairs. No words passed between them. He took her hand. I saw you, he thought. I saw you that night. I have never stopped seeing you. Ever since then I have seen you every day, every night. He stared up at the stars. He listened to the sound of her breath. Soon she was asleep. Her head lolled to one side. He took off his jacket and laid it over her. He covered her hand with his. Then he, too, slept.